NO MORE EXPECTATIONS

Also by Cathy Jo

Transitions: short stories for a rainy day

NO MORE EXPECTATIONS

A NOVEL

BY

CATHY JO

Twisted Word Publishing
http://www.twistedwordpublishing.com

Published by Twisted Word Publishing

P. O. Box 46165
Bedford, Ohio 44146
http://www.twistedwordpublishing.com

Cover design by Drummond Design.

http://www.drummondesign.com.

Twisted Word logo design by Kevin Drummond.

Cover photo (forward-facing woman) and back cover (food images) © Shutterstock.

ISBN 978-0-9834259-2-2

First Trade Paperback Printing September 2012

Printed in the United States of America

DEDICATION

This book is dedicated to the memories of:

my mother, Betty Graves (8/30/1927 – 10/2/1978)

and my sister, Patricia Jackson (7/27/1954 – 8/27/1999)

DEDICATION

ACKNOWLEDGEMENTS

Thank you, foremost, to all my family and friends who were supportive of me during the writing of this book.

To my editor, Kelly Ferjutz, a hearty thank you.

Thank you to the Page Turners Writing Group.

To my coworkers, who cheered me on and lifted me with praise that carried me to the finish line, words can't fully express the gratitude I feel in my heart for you all!

To my front cover models: Wayne Graves, Mike Reynolds, Steve Atkinson, Damien Carr, and Rashonda Patterson, I am forever grateful!

As always, I must thank the staffs of the participating KnowItNow library systems in Ohio, especially the Cleveland Public and Cuyahoga County Public Library systems. Through this invaluable resource, I was able to find answers to a few complex questions that kept me up way past my bedtime.

To Charles Newton, Human Resources Professional, thank you for your suggestions and clarifications regarding all things HR.

Jeanette McMillan-James, R.N., Creator of Readers R Us (RRU) on Facebook, thank you for your valuable assistance with medical details.

For help with judicial and criminal information, a very special thank you to three fine, upstanding women, mothers, and wives that I'm proud to have crossed paths with—Anita Laster Mays, Judge, Cleveland Municipal Court; Linda Sealey, Sergeant, Cleveland Police Department; and Tracy Martin-Peebles, Attorney. Y'all rock! Any inaccuracies or inconsistencies are the fault of the author.

Finally, thank you to all two of my readers (just kidding) who demanded—yes, demanded—to know what became of Brianya Johnson from the short story, *Expectations*. Well, here you have it!

PROLOGUE

*B*RIANYA LAY FLAT *on her back, her breath coming in spurts as she forced her mind to focus.* How did she get here? *she wondered through a haze. She was in full panic mode. If only she could pull herself up. She'd fallen hard when the man backhanded her. She must have broken two or three ribs when she crashed to the floor. Her lip felt at least twice its normal size and she tasted blood. She ran her tongue around the inside of her mouth, over her teeth, and felt an opening where there used to be a tooth. She couldn't worry about that now; she had to get to her telephone, call someone. But the man had pulled the phone cord out of the wall and she didn't know what he'd done with her cell phone.*

Brianya's life seemed to have spiraled out of control. She'd had no idea what she had gotten into when she agreed to go out with this man whom she'd seen as an ally, a kindred spirit in pain and failed relationships. Crawling to the bathroom, she leaned her back against the wall and put her head into her hands, then scooted to the claw-footed tub and braced herself against it. She tried to get a solid hold on the cold porcelain to pull herself up, but just as she was about to steady herself, a blow to the back of her head sent a jarring pain through her entire body, reverberating to the soles of her feet. She'd thought she was alone, had heard the front door slam shut when the man walked out. Or had it been some other door?

Just as she was losing consciousness, Brianya felt something cold and hard, like steel pressing against her neck, and smelled the faint odor of sulfur in the air. She heard what sounded like the hammer of a gun as it was being cocked. So this is how it would all end, in the bathroom of her new home in Shaker Heights, her life only half-lived. Brianya fought unsuccessfully to stave off the blackness that was coming in ripples, and felt the man lift the gun from its resting place on her neck. Her eyelids fluttered. Her heart quickened in anticipation of the reprieve she'd been granted. She was going to live after all. She felt a sliver of joy.

Brianya heard what sounded like footsteps coming from the front of the house. Relief washed over her as she realized the man had spared her life. She didn't dare turn around, fearing his departure might be just a hallucination. As she knelt, frozen in position, Brianya heard a movement behind her and her heart felt as if it had exploded in her chest.

There was a loud boom, and then blackness slowly overtook her as she stared, uncomprehendingly, at the trail of blood snaking its way across the mosaic tile.

CHAPTER ONE

THIRTY MONTHS, SIXTY-FIVE days, and twelve hours ago, when Brianya Johnson walked out the door of the Lakefront condominium she'd shared with Darnell Jones, she was determined to turn her life around and take charge of herself.

The first thing she did was find a mental health professional who specialized in counseling people with eating disorders to try to get to the root of her weight problem. To Brianya's surprise, she learned she was an emotional eater. Back then, if anyone had asked her why she ate, she would have said it was because she liked the way food tasted or out of boredom. But an emotional eater? No way.

Armed with this new-found knowledge, Brianya enlisted the help of her trainer-friend, Lonnie Parker, to help whip her body into the shape she knew was hiding under all those layers of emotional eating. Right after that, she joined Weight Watchers, one more time, and got busy. The physical work was tough: the gradual buildup to an eight-mile walk every day and working out five times a week at the gym. All this effort was accompanied by buckets of shed tears, and long talks with God. Now here she stood, two and a half years later, 206 pounds lighter, the better for it. She had won half the battle; keeping the weight off was the other half.

If Brianya hoped to accomplish the myriad tasks on her to do list today, she needed to get a move on. First, she had to bring some sort of order to the basement of her newly purchased home. Brianya still couldn't believe that she had bought a house in Shaker Heights, the place where she'd dreamed of living since she was eleven. One hundred eighty-four days ago, money in hand and a longing to call something her own, Brianya had made her girlhood dream a reality. When visiting her grandparents, she and her grandfather would often walk the tree-lined streets of Shaker, making up stories about the people who lived in the houses. Maybe someday, a kid would peek through her windows and make up stories about her, Brianya mused as she stood in the middle of the room, feeling overwhelmed. There were still a few minor things she wanted to change to make her four-bedroom, two and a half-bath, brick Tudor feel more like home, but for now everything was good.

Feeling like a fish out of water, Brianya took in the contents of the basement—old kitchen chairs and table, washing machine and dryer, lavatory, sink, vintage pool table, plastic totes filled with clothes and other items needing sorting—and wondered where to begin. She nudged one of the totes over to the table with her foot and began emptying it. In the middle of sorting, Brianya stopped and stared at the mirror with open admiration of the 147-pound woman whose reflection resembled that of her own. Five weeks into this current frame and already Brianya was wearing her new body like an old pair of comfortable leather shoes. She turned sideways, gawking with satisfaction at how well proportioned she was—38C bust, 37-inch hips, and a 28 ½-inch waist. To her joy, this hourglass figure had surpassed even her expectations for her five foot six, medium-build frame.

Brianya ran her hands up, down, and across her new curves. "Amazing," she said, working her way up to a chant as she repeated the word. "I can't believe this is me. Me, me, me! Thank you, God, for walking along side me on this journey and for picking me up all those times that I fell and wanted to stay down. And please, Lord, let the rumors stop; this is your work, mine and yours. A-a-a-a-men!" This time the tears that flowed weren't out of frustration or self-pity. No, these tears laughed in the faces of the naysayers, those who sought to "encourage" her by warning her not to get discouraged when she found that she could "only take off, at best, sixty or seventy pounds, because, let's face it, fatness is a genetic trait." Yes, these tears shut the mouths of whoever had heightened the rumor and hurried it along that Brianya was sick and that's why she had lost so much weight.

"Bulimia, I hear it is," baldheaded Amber had said, looking like a joke gone bad.

"No, girl, I think she has cancer. That's why she cut all her hair off; she didn't want nobody to figure it out," Evelyn, I-ain't-had-a-man-since-the-eighties, had chimed in.

"Humph! If you ask me," said Sheila—and everybody knew not to ask her anything, because she didn't know when to shut up—"I think it's because of that man she was fooling around with a few years back. Y'all know she didn't have no business being with somebody as fine as that! That relationship was doomed from the jump. Now she's popping anti-depressants like they're candy. That's why she ain't been eating."

Raucous laughter coupled with the sound of open palms bumping against one another filled the ladies' room as Brianya turned the lock on the stall door, the one furthest from the entrance, where, apparently, the women had forgotten to look, and sashayed out. Blatant ignorance didn't deserve a dignified response and Brianya didn't offer one, just smiled at the trio standing there, slack-jawed, eyes bugged out, silent, cowards that they were. They hurried out so quickly that one of them almost knocked over the elderly woman entering the restroom, when they pushed past her, in a hurry to escape.

"Brianya, honey, if I didn't know that was you preening in that mirror, I'd have thought you were someone else. You looking so good these days!" said the small, robust woman, a shock of white hair happily parading at her temples. She smiled as she squeezed Brianya's arm before ducking into a stall.

Brianya giggled girlishly, dipped her finger under the spigot to catch the small trickle flowing from the faucet, smoothed down the edges of her hairline, and said, "Thank you, Mrs. Mitchell. How are you feeling this morning?"

"Oh fair to middlin', baby. Arthur's been acting up again, won't let me do but so much today. I declare, if it wasn't for him pressing in on me, I wouldn't know the feel of a man's touch." The gurgling sound of the flushing toilet drowned out most of the

3

woman's cackle, tickled, apparently, by her own joke. Brianya smiled, and noted that this was the third time she'd heard Mrs. Mitchell make that joke about her arthritis in as many days, and wondered if the woman was all right. Since her husband's passing, eight months ago, the elderly woman seemed to be losing pieces of reality in small but discernible increments.

"Did I tell you that my niece is thinking about having the same surgery you had?" Mrs. Mitchell said as she fell in step as they approached Brianya's office.

Here we go with the rumors again, Brianya thought, but said, "What surgery would that be, Mrs. Mitchell?" in feigned ignorance, as if she didn't already know.

"You know, honey, that stomach surgery. The one they do up there in . . ." Mrs. Mitchell scrunched up her face, her lower lip jutting forward, "California, I think it is."

Gastric bypass surgery; the Fobi pouch. Brianya had heard of it. Had heard of similar surgeries being done at St. Vincent Charity and University Hospitals, too, even Cleveland Clinic. Had even looked into it herself, but decided to pass. Who wanted to walk around with a stomach the size of an adult thumb, popping vitamins and iron pills, chewing Tums, and eating teeny tiny bits of food for the rest of their life? Not Brianya, that's for sure. As far as she was concerned, that surgery was a drastic measure, a last resort and an easy out. Brianya wasn't ready to throw the towel in on her efforts just yet.

Before this last attempt, she'd only tried Optifast, Medifast, the Atkins diet, the Grapefruit diet, the Scarsdale diet, the Cleveland Clinic diet, Physician's Weight Loss, Nutri Systems, Jenny Craig, Weight Watchers (seven times), Overeaters Anonymous, TOPS, Dexatrim, black market diet pills, and a slew of fad diets too numerous to recount. Yet something, some niggling hope ensconced in that secret compartment way in the back of her mind, the one she unwittingly kept locked away, her if-all-else-fails last-ditch effort, came bursting forth at just the right moment, grabbed onto her willpower and doggedly pushed her until she was knee-deep in curiosity: How would she look two sizes smaller? Three? Five? More sweat, more tears, more cravings denied, put off until she felt she could handle eating one piece of chicken, or one helping of spaghetti, or four cookies in a sitting, then three, then two, not one though. She never ate just one; why bother?

The outrage Brianya felt every time someone suggested that she'd had gastric bypass surgery, discounting all the hard work and effort she'd put into her transformation—was still putting in—came to the fore and before she knew it, the words were out of her mouth, giving no thought to Mrs. Mitchell's feelings. "Why would I want to have my stomach stapled to the size of an adult thumb, ruining my life? You think I want to watch my hair fall out in clumps, because that's what I heard happens after you have that surgery. I have no desire to walk around feeling like a freak for the rest of my life, sucking down calcium tablets, popping iron pills, and getting shot up with vitamin B12, thank you very much!"

The crestfallen expression on the older woman's face and the wetness dotting her eyes told Brianya that she had gone too far. "I'm so sorry, Mrs. Mitchell, I really am. My comments weren't directed at you. It's just that I know I've worked my butt off, literally, to get rid of this weight and it ticks me off to hear people putting it all down to surgery or some sickness, or whatever. I apologize for hurting your feelings. Please, forgive me."

Mrs. Mitchell smiled. "I understand, baby. I've heard the rumors, too. I'll forgive you if you can forgive an old lady for getting caught up in the rumor mill?" she said, her eyes downcast.

"Sure, Sweetie. Anything for my favorite person," Brianya had said, and smiled real pretty for her audience of one.

Brianya thought back to when she began her dietary makeover. She didn't think her new eating habits would ever become a routine part of her life, but eventually they did. Some days she wanted to throw her hands up and say forget it, but she couldn't—wouldn't—allow herself to be defeated. A chubby child

5

who grew up to be a fat adult, Brianya had always known that someday she'd make the time to get the weight off.

Small incidents had gradually grown into major ones, and she'd found herself frustrated by the lack of common decency shown women of substantial size, as she liked to think of herself back then. Not one to abide other people's ignorance, and her health rapidly deteriorating (osteoarthritis in her left knee, chronic shortness of breath, 307 cholesterol, pre-diabetes, and hypertension), Brianya decided that Darnell's departure—and a thoughtless comment made by a doctor, who thought Brianya was out of earshot—was as a good a starting point as any.

Although she was comfortable with her new body in many ways, getting used to it in other ways was a huge adjustment that Brianya was still undergoing. Not having to turn sideways as she walked through doors, or embed herself into desks and file cabinets when someone walked past her in the office, or allow for extra prep time in the morning because she moved at a snail's pace—all these felt good. The biggest adjustment had been in how she saw herself mentally. She no longer thought of herself as a woman of substantial size. Neither did she see herself as an attraction at a circus show anymore. And no one would ever call her "Fat Brianya," or "The large woman," or "The big woman with the pretty face."

A pretty face, indeed. Copper-penny brown her complexion, the backdrop to an artist's conception of paradise: cocoa-colored large, inquiring eyes that looked down the bridge of a Native American nose—courtesy of her mother's side of the family—its nostrils small and delicate. Her lips, full and perky were the lips of a woman born to kiss, to be kissed. And high cheekbones gave the impression of a perpetual smile.

Of all the monikers strangers had bestowed upon her, "The big woman with the pretty face" was, back then, the most accurate. Since her transformation, Brianya had modified that moniker to "The pretty woman with the hot body!" One last, long, gloating look in the floor-to-ceiling mirrors in the recreation room of her finished basement was all the affirmation she needed to rejoice. "Hot body! Hot body," Brianya chanted as she two-stepped around the basement.

Brianya's weight wasn't the only thing that had changed. Six months ago, she'd gotten a well-earned promotion to Director of Human Resources at Mellow Beans Coffee Corporation, located in downtown Cleveland, and she was now busy getting acquainted with this new position and its responsibilities. Brianya smiled reflectively, proud of what she'd managed to accomplish before the age of forty.

Ever since she had interned at M.B.C.C., while a freshman in college—so many years ago—she felt that her former boss was grooming her to step into his shoes, not just to walk in them, but to run. Moving in new directions, M.B.C.C. had expanded its profit margin to include more than just the U.S. markets. They were also venturing into new territory, partnering with other industries. At last, so many years after she had stepped off the stage at the Cleveland State University Wolstein Center with an MBA in Labor Relations/Human Resources, her former boss, Mr. Styles, had vacated his position, passing her the torch, so to speak. She accepted the promotion by dropping her oars in the water and rowing like it was nobody's business. Mellow Beans Coffee Corporation was heading upstream and Brianya was in it for the long haul.

Since the new job kept her busy, there was no room for a personal life, much less relationships. With contract negotiations and organizational restructuring coming up, she'd have even less time for herself—an inconvenience Brianya was willing to allow.

Brianya packed the last of the sizes thirty-two and thirty-four dresses in a cardboard box. She'd take them with her today when she went to Love's House, an undisclosed safe haven for women and children in transit from domestic violence situations, where she volunteered two Saturdays and two Mondays out of the month. On a certain level, Brianya found it satisfying to be helping women–families–put their lives back in order. But the children—their small, frightened faces confused—were difficult to watch sometimes. Of all the victims, they suffered the most. Thinking of their jaded innocence brought a lump to Brianya's throat, making her wish she could give them happier childhoods.

Her childhood had been a happy one. Complete with one brother, ten years her senior; one sister, four years her junior; and a mother and father who loved each other. That's why she couldn't imagine the horror those shelter children experienced, exposed as they were to that sort of violence, watching their mothers being physically struck. The thought made her cringe.

Sometimes the women were so mentally drained that by the time they reached the shelter, it took weeks before they would open up and share their heart's pain. Brianya had noticed that a common thread of shame ran throughout all the women's stories. They were ashamed to have let the abuse go on for so long. Ashamed that they had allowed themselves to get into this type of situation in the first place. Ashamed that their friends and family would think less of them if the truth ever came out. The educated women often voiced the opinion that, prior to their becoming victims, they thought of domestic violence as a problem that affected only the poor and the uneducated. Experience had taught them how wrong their views were. Their shame tended to run deeper than most.

Shame was something Brianya understood. Darnell had made her feel ashamed, humiliated even.

Brianya selected an orange and black rayon dress from the top of the pile and held it up to her. Hand-sewn sequins bordered the neckline. It was the only item that had survived the relationship because it had been at the cleaners for repair. This was one of Darnell's favorite dresses. The night Brianya wore it, they were on their way to a fundraiser dinner for pediatric leukemia. Her slender hand caressed the cool fabric as the memory threatened to flood her mind. She swatted it away and tried to concentrate on what she was doing.

Even though their relationship was over, the memory of that night was still too much to bear. She couldn't stand thinking of the woman she was then. So vulnerable. So needy. Desperate. Ready to allow herself to be denigrated, and for what? A circular piece of metal with a clump of carbon slapped on top, and as worthless as a three-dollar bill. Everything associated with the ring would have cost Brianya a little piece of her self-worth, which would, in effect, render the ring valueless. Once upon a time, she would have hated Darnell for the way he treated her; now, however, she felt only . . . What did she feel? Brianya searched her thoughts and came up empty. She felt absolutely nothing for Darnell.

She fingered the small, barely-noticeable neatly-repaired tear at the neckline, where Darnell had, like a madman, almost ripped the dress from her body, and sighed. In spite of all that had happened between them, no man had made her feel as alive and as desirable as Darnell had; not before him, and not since. When he left, he'd taken with him a little piece of her dignity and because of that, Brianya promised herself that the next man to warm her heart and her bed would be her husband.

Wiping sweat from her brow, Brianya folded the dress and placed it back into the pile with the other clothes. She closed the boxes and fastened them with tape, her long fingers imprisoning memories along with clothes. Good riddance to old rubbish!

Climbing the stairs to the garage, Brianya wrestled the boxes into the back of her gold Chrysler 300. Just as she was about to head back into the house, she heard footsteps approaching her front door. She waited and listened to see what the visitor would do, but she heard nothing. The doorbell remained un-rung, and there was no sound of knuckles rapping on the screen door. It was probably just the mail person. They were always cutting across the grass to the next house.

Brianya headed back downstairs to finish her chores. A few minutes later, she heard the faint sound of knocking. When she

No More Expectations

went upstairs and opened the door, she couldn't believe who was standing on the other side of it.

CHAPTER TWO

THE LAST PERSON Brianya expected to see standing on the other side of her door was Monty Belvoir. Of all Darnell's friends back then, Monty was her least favorite. He was loud-mouthed, confrontational, and wired. Now here he was standing on the other side of her door, his eyes an indescribable color, boring into her, looking doughy-eyed and desperate. For the last five weeks, Monty had called Brianya at work, trying to persuade her that he was worth a shot. She figured it was just a matter of time before he showed up on her doorstep. The Internet being what it was had made it almost impossible for anyone to have total privacy anymore. If you knew how to search, there was no piece of information that was unobtainable. Honestly, she didn't think Monty was that savvy. Yet, there he was.

Brianya folded her arms across her chest and scowled. "What do you want, Monty?"

"We both know what it feels like to have love unreciprocated," Monty said, looking intently at Brianya, like he was trying to telegraph a positive response. "We could be good company for each other. Let me prove it to you."

Brianya rolled her eyes in contempt at the ignorance he displayed. "My answer is the same now as it was the last *five* times you had the gall to ask me out on a date." she said as she closed the door in Monty's face.

"You need to stop punishing me for what Darnell did to you." His words were barely audible through four inches of solid wood.

What Darnell did. That statement, as simple as it sounded, was anything but that. His actions had left her feeling broken, almost unsalvageable. But when it came right down to it, if she was being totally honest about the whole ugly mess, what Darnell *did* was do her a favor. Had it not been for his underhandedness, Brianya would still be 353 pounds, unhappy, and willing to settle for any man willing to send a smile in her direction. It had broken her heart and almost her spirit that Darnell could so easily deceive her.

She had wanted the white picket fence, the Ozzie and Harriet happy-ending with Darnell, but he was incapable of giving her that. When she came to terms with that admission, Brianya had painstakingly moved on. Just like Monty was doing now. She could see his back through the blinds as he retreated to his car.

Brianya had to hand it to Monty; he had gall. Too bad it was wasted on her. *Oh well*, she thought, putting the chain back across the door. Gall or no gall, Monty was a part of a past that she never wanted to revisit. The next time he came around—and he would come around again, of this she was sure—Brianya would have something waiting for him: her brother, Andre.

In less than three hours, Brianya was due at an afternoon luncheon to help raise money for AIDS research. Before getting on the road, she made a quick call to her brother to fill him in on the Monty situation.

"You ain't got to worry about that fool, li'l sis. He step to you again, you 9-1-1 me."

Growing up, Andre had established his place in his sisters' lives as their protector. A role Brianya had hated. Her brother's reputation of having gang ties had cost her many dating opportunities, although he wasn't in a gang. When Andre was ten years old, the Black Panthers, a group of community-conscious young men, who were doing charitable works in Black communities, had dubbed him a 'baby Panther.' To this day, his reputation preceded him.

Andre started to protest and Brianya cut him off. "Look, I don't want you calling up any of your hoodlum 'friends' and going all combat on Monty. I just want *you* to check him. Do you hear me, Andre?"

"Yeah, sure. I hear you, li'l sis," he said noncommittally.

Realizing there was no use arguing the matter with Andre, who had no intention of taking orders from someone 10 years his junior, Brianya said her good-bye and headed out the door.

She hadn't been on the road thirty seconds when the familiar ring tone of *Single Ladies (Put a ring on it)* startled her. A quick glance at the display screen told her it was her best friend, Dreama Buchanan. Brianya let her finger hover over the ON button of her Bluetooth headset before accepting the call. With Dreama, there was always drama. That's why she had given her the nick name Drama-Dreama within two months of meeting her. "What's up, Drama?"

Dreama made a smacking noise with her lips. "Whatever! What you fixin' to do?"

"I'm on my way to the shelter to drop off some clothes. Then I've got to pick up some pantyhose on my way back home, because in less than three hours I need to be at the Crowne Plaza hotel for an AIDS fundraiser." Brianya let out a huge breath.

"Oh. Well, I need you down at the shop. One of my stylists quit on me and left a bunch of mad clients. I got my nail tech, Trina, filling in as a stylist. *Thank God*, she has a license to do hair. I need you to come fill in for Trina. Girl, this place is wall-to-ceiling with folks wanting to look cute for Labor Day."

"Dreama, I don't have time. Besides you know I'm not a licensed nail tech. Call Cin, she's licensed. Her lazy behind isn't doing anything today." Cinthia, Brianya's younger sister worked off and on at nail shops when she got bored or needed pocket change, or when their parents made a big fuss about her mooching off them.

"So, you heard about Darnell, right?" Dreama asked as an afterthought.

The question took Brianya by surprise. "Heard what?"

"You didn't know?" Dreama paused. "Hmmm . . . I don't know if I should be the one to tell you."

"Fine. Don't tell me. I don't care anyway."

"Okay, then. I'll talk to you later," Dreama said on a sigh as deep as the ocean. Brianya could imagine her making a show of pressing the "end" button on her telephone.

Brianya put on her left turn signal and waited a beat. "So, you're really not going to tell me?"

"I knew you couldn't resist! Girl, him and that *woman* he left you for broke up and he's moving back to Cleveland to ink a deal with some guys in a nightclub venture. He'll be back next month!"

Brianya's heart skipped a beat. She hadn't seen Darnell in almost three years. Although she had warned him not to try to contact her, he had ignored her and called a few days after their breakup. She had been working on a workers' comp claim at her desk, when the phone rang at five minutes to five on a Friday afternoon.

"Hey," said the familiar voice on the other end of the telephone.

Brianya froze. Why was he calling her when she'd specifically told him not to? He was probably regretting the way he treated her and ready to come crawling back, sorry that he had taken advantage of her, missing the good thing they had. "Hey," Brianya had said in response.

"I hate to bother you at work on a Friday evening. I know you're trying to get out of there and get your party on."

He had never known her to be a party person. This was no doubt some lame attempt to feel her out. Either that or he was probably nervous and this was his attempt at breaking the ice.

"Something like that."

Darnell cleared his throat. "I was sitting here wondering—" A female voice interrupted him. From the muffled sound of his voice, Brianya could tell that Darnell was covering the mouthpiece with his hand. "I'm about to ask her that now," she heard him say to the woman. To Brianya he said, "I was wondering if you had seen a tan box with some bank papers in them when you were clearing out my condo?"

Disgusted, Brianya had slammed down the phone.

Dreama's inquiring voice brought Brianya back to the conversation and the present. "Bri, did you hear me, girl? I said the baby ain't his."

"You said what?!" Brianya almost choked on her own saliva. Several drivers began honking for her to make the left turn. "Humph! That's what he gets!" She swung the car into the parking lot of Love's House, turned off the engine, and began unloading the boxes.

"You think he'll try to hook up with you again?" Dreama asked and laughed, knowing Brianya's response.

"Bye!" came the predictable reply, and Brianya ended the call. Dreama knew better than to ask that question. It was a good thing that Brianya had already arrived at her destination. The last time Dreama had joked about the possibility of she and Darnell getting back together, Brianya had almost rear-ended a Hummer she was trailing on I-480 East.

One errand down and one to go, Brianya was in and out of TJ Maxx in record time. Arriving home, she had just under an hour and forty minutes to shower, do something to her hair, decide which one of the two ensembles she'd laid out earlier to wear, and get to the event on time. She hated being late.

Brianya was slipping her feet into her sandals when the doorbell rang. She grunted as she looked out the side window.

"Make it quick," Brianya said, swinging the door wide open. "I'm almost late."

Andre eyed his sister and appraised her wardrobe. His disapproval showed in his tone. "That neckline is a little low, sis."

"What are you, my father? Did you come here to critique my clothes, or did you want something?" Brianya snatched her purse and car keys off the table and headed for the garage.

Andre stood in the living room, looking stoic. "I need to store my car in your garage for a few days."

"Again?" Brianya protested. "Why don't you just pay off the car? You know you've got the money."

"Get out of my pockets, li'l sis," Andre said, turning his pockets inside out. "So, you gonna let me do this thing or not?"

"Whatever!" Brianya tossed Andre the extra garage door opener from her keychain. "Lock up when you leave and make sure the garage door is closed this time."

***

Brianya flitted through the crowd hob-nobbing with executives and chatting up their wives, making sure wine glasses never went below half-full. It was a proven fact that the only time the wealthy were more charitable than the poor was when they were three sheets to the wind. Brianya planned to capitalize on that tonight. Every year, Mellow Beans held an AIDS fundraiser, and each year they topped the previous years' donations. Tonight they were going for a quarter of a million dollars. By last count, they were just shy of $100,000 from goal.

Ralph Calhoun, a major shareholder in the MacDonald Investments firm, three floors above MBCC, caught Brianya's eye and beckoned her to him. "Might I trouble you, beautiful lady, to bring me a glass of the *good* drink?"

The *good* drink, reserved for the more generous donor, was a costly French wine, not to be given out willy-nilly. It was obvious from the way he slurred his r's plus the balancing act he was doing with his glass as he proffered it to Brianya, that Ralph Calhoun had already had too much to drink. Brianya took the glass from his outstretched hand and offered to bring him a cup of coffee instead.

"No, my dear, that simply will not do. I just pledged fifty thousand dollars on behalf of my firm and I aim to have my reciprocity. I can have it by way of the bottle, or by way of you accompanying me up to my suite and showing me how grateful

Mellow Beans is for my generosity." The glassy-eyed leer that followed his lewd and ridiculous suggestion caused Brianya to bristle.

"Let me tell you something, you dru—." Brianya caught herself. Too much money was at stake and she didn't want to be the reason Mellow Beans didn't reach their target. Rumor had it that if they made goal, year-end bonuses would be hefty. So, like any good team player, Brianya checked herself. But before marching off to get Mr. Calhoun a glass of the "good drink," she leaned in close, his ear only inches away. "Our firms have enjoyed a casual and very profitable working relationship until now, Mr. Calhoun. But, please, make no mistake, if you ever speak to me in the manner that you just did, MacDonald Investments will find itself several hundred clients lighter."

On her way back from giving Mr. Calhoun his drink, a familiar voice greeted Brianya. She turned and stared into the face of a man she never thought she'd have to lay eyes upon ever again. Marlon Taylor, the sweet-talking swindler, had once worked for Mellow Beans and was suspended for misuse of company resources and attempting to pass along confidential, proprietary information to a woman on Facebook. The only thing that saved him from prosecution was the IT tech's inability to find concrete evidence that he'd actually committed a crime.

Blaming Brianya for his three-week, no-pay suspension, Marlon threatened to sue MBCC and hold Brianya personally and professionally responsible. He had done neither. Instead, while on suspension, he mistakenly posted a message as his status update that should have been private, disparaging as it did MBCC and several high-level executives. Clearly a violation of company policy and a firing offense, Brianya was left with no choice but to report it.

"Well, well, look at you!" Marlon's greeting dripped sarcasm. "If I weren't beholding you with my own eyes, I wouldn't have believed the rumors." Marlon gave Brianya a head-to-toe once-over. "A big improvement from the way you used to look." He straightened his tie, a gesture meant to appear nonchalant, but Brianya could almost see the wheels of Marlon's pea-sized brain turning with malicious intent. "Oh, I hear congratulations are in order." He proffered his hand. "I guess all that bootlicking finally paid off. I always did say you did your best work on your knees."

Brianya's mouth flew open, and she noisily sucked air into her lungs. Considering the occasion, she thought about letting the comment pass. They were only words, untrue as they were. *Not every comment deserves a response. Besides, he's only trying to get a rise out of you. If you take the bait, he wins.* She moved in close to Marlon so that only he could hear her. For the second time that afternoon, Brianya found herself closer to a strange man than she cared to be. "You're a small minded, inconsequential man-boy, who *has* nothing, *is* nothing, and never will *be* anything. That you're even allowed to breathe the same air I breathe is one of life's greatest tragedies." She stepped back and gave Marlon a challenging look.

From the look of astonishment on his face, it was clear that Marlon thought he was dealing with the old push-over, gullible Brianya. "I see you finally learned to speak up for yourself."

Brianya eyed Marlon's outdated hairstyle and shook her head. "You do know, don't you, that the high-top fade went out in the nineties? Oh, but on your wages, I guess you have to work with what you get. Speaking of which, how's public assistance treating you?"

"About as well as your ex treated you when he played you." Marlon's eyes sparkled with mischief. "Speaking of your ex—my frat brother—I guess you might have heard by now that we're about to hook up this sweet little hotspot on Emery Rd."

"Oh, yeah? That sounds like a good venture for two losers!" Brianya turned to walk away.

"But wait—there's more!"

Brianya turned around to see a smirk of satisfaction playing at the corners of Marlon's mouth.

"You know how Mellow Beans is always looking for new ventures to help expand their profit margin? Well take a good look, 'cause you'll be seeing a lot more of me. I'm part of that new pilot program."

Brianya weighed Marlon's words. He had to be joking; he was messing with her, trying to provoke her further. She fixed him with a smirk of her own that was worthy of an Oscar and stormed off.

Brianya's nostrils grew wide and her hands became fists at her sides as she moved swiftly through the crowd, trying to find the one person who could shed some light on what Marlon, obviously on drugs, was talking about. She spotted her secretary, Debbie Ashton, tucked behind a 9-foot ficus-tree cozied up with an eager looking man from purchasing, his hand gripping her buttocks.

Marching up to Debbie, eyes narrowed to slits and brows knitted together, Brianya grabbed her by the arm, almost dragging her to a quiet corner. The bewildered expression on the woman's face was no deterrent for an angry Brianya. "Why am I just now hearing about an arrangement Mellow Beans made with Marlon—The Snake—Taylor to be a part of the new pilot program?" Brianya hissed in Debbie's ear. She was seconds away from firing the woman. The pilot program was designed to give ex-employees, who left the company on good terms, an opportunity to work part-time for MBCC, while at the same time signing on as franchisees. Just as Debbie was about to answer, Brianya heard the familiar voice of a long-time friend, whom she hadn't seen in years, and turned toward the voice.

Taking advantage of the distraction, Debbie shook herself free. "I don't know anything about a deal with Marlon Taylor." She rubbed her arm and examined it for bruises. "If there is an agreement, it's hush-hush. I never saw any paperwork for you."

"Hmmm... Well... I'll deal with you on Tuesday!" For now, Brianya let Debbie off with a warning, deciding not to fire her on the spot. She turned fully to investigate the source of the familiar sounding voice and nearly stumbled backward at the sight of the woman.

"Cashmere!" Brianya straightened up and pulled herself together. "I thought that was your voice I heard!"

Cashmere stared at Brianya as though she'd never seen her before. "Excuse me, but do I know . . . ?" The words trailed off as she realized who was standing in front of her. "What the . . . Bri? I can't believe my eyes! I heard you had dropped a couple of pounds, but girl! You look great!"

The women excitedly greeted each other then embraced.

"Thank you," Brianya said, blushing. "You're not looking too shabby yourself, Cash!" Brianya openly admired Cashmere's attire, from the teardrop diamond earrings to the designer suit that looked tailor-made, to the red-bottom 5-inch designer pumps. "It's been too long since I've seen you, Cash. What are you doing here?"

Cashmere Masters was one of Brianya's oldest friends. They'd met in elementary school, in the fourth grade, when Cashmere had spit on Eddie Edmonds for pulling her ponytails repeatedly.

"I'm here both personally and professionally. I'm representing the Myers and Hart Graphics Design Studio. And you know that AIDS research is something I'm passionate about."

"Oh, that's right!" Brianya said, remembering that Cashmere's ex-fiancé was HIV-positive. She reached out and gave Cashmere's arm a gentle squeeze. "Is everything okay with you?"

Tears pooled in the corners of Cashmere's eyes. "I'm still standing," she said and smiled weakly.

"Yes, you are!" Before Brianya could say more, she heard the voice of the MC announcing her name. "I hate to cut our conversation short, Cash, but that's my cue. Look," she said fishing a card out of her purse, "call me so that we can talk. It's been too long and we've got a lot of catching up to do." Brianya handed Cashmere her business card, gave her a warm hug and a peck on the cheek, and made her promise to call.

"I will," Cashmere said, tucking the card away.

For someone living with a deadly disease, Cashmere was holding up well. True, you couldn't tell just by looking if a person had HIV. So why, Brianya wondered, had it surprised her to see Cashmere looking so vibrant and refreshed? She was the picture of good health. She looked happy, at peace even, Brianya thought as she made her way to the front of the crowd.

CHAPTER THREE

BRIANYA RAISED THE garage door and got the shock of the morning. Monty's six-foot-six-inch baller's body blocked the driver's side door of her car. Having no room in the garage because of hiding Andre's car, Brianya had to park in the driveway last night.

"Hear me out, before you cuss me out, alright?" Monty said, seeing the battle-ready expression on Brianya's face.

"What do you have to say to me that's so important that you're willing to risk getting cut?" Brianya said, her voice calm, as she eased the 4-inch folded knife out of her handbag.

Eyeing the knife, Monty backed away from the car door and threw his hands up in surrender. "Look, all I want to say is, I was never involved in what went down with you and D. I was on the road most of the time playing ball. Plus, I had my own stuff between me and my girl that I was dealing with."

"Why do you keep rehashing the past? It doesn't matter to me whether you knew or didn't know. Bottom line is, I'm not interested. Okay?" Brianya folded the knife and put it back into her purse. She wouldn't need it this morning. Thank goodness. If anything, Monty was more annoying than harmful.

"Just give me a chance. Let me buy you a drink after work today, alright? As acquaintances, that's all."

It seemed to Brianya that Monty was coming close to begging. She shook her head and rolled her eyes. *Pathetic!*

"Let me ask you this," Brianya said, opening the car door and placing her things in the passenger seat. "Where were you when I was 353 pounds?" Ever since she had lost over 200 pounds, men from the past had been sniffing around her like a dog after a piece of meat. Whenever Brianya put that question to them, they never had an answer worth listening to. She didn't wait for Monty to fix his lips to tell his lie. She started the car, rolled the windows down to let in the cool morning air, and pulled out of her driveway. Brianya drove a few feet then slowed. She leaned out the window and glanced back at Monty, who stood glued to the spot, and shook her head. As she drove away, her hand on the volume knob of the radio, inching up the sound, she could've sworn she heard Monty shout, "I was in a relationship!"

***

Brianya tried to push Monty's words out of her mind. His answer shouldn't have made a difference. Yet here she was 45 minutes later still thinking about those words: *"I was in a relationship."* It was a moot point, because the fact remained that he was not someone with whom she'd want a relationship. He was too much—too wired, too loud, and too confrontational. Wired and loud she could deal with. Confrontational, she couldn't. Brianya didn't like confrontations any more than the next person, but she also didn't go actively looking for them the way, it seemed, Monty did. In fact, one of the reasons why Darnell hadn't often included him in his weekly sports marathons was because whenever Monty was around trouble was sure to follow.

Brianya pulled into her parking space in the North Coast parking garage and shut off the engine. She took a few moments to gather herself before she started the short walk to her office. Every morning, she took time to cleanse her mind of the negative energy produced by driving the freeways. She found that her day went much better when she dumped the mental garbage first. A tap on the window startled her.

Celine Connors, the Administrative Secretary from the law firm two floors above, beckoned Brianya to roll down the window. For six years, the two women had seen each other in passing but only within the last three years had they formally met and grown very close. Celine had battled breast cancer and beat it three years ago. She had confided that to Brianya the first day they met, which may have seemed strange if Brianya hadn't confided her ugly breakup with Darnell. It turned out that Celine and the woman that Darnell had gotten pregnant were cousins.

Brianya fixated on the gold chain necklace draped around Celine's neck; it was the same necklace she'd worn when they first met.

"That's funny," Celine had said then as she sized up Brianya and appraised her appearance. "I would never have taken you for a nail biter." Brianya had narrowed her eyes in suspicion. "Hi, I'm Celine Connors. I work two floors above you." Celine proffered her hand for Brianya to shake.

Brianya immediately noticed the woman's own nails, how brilliantly they shone with what looked like several coats of clear polish, the nail beds and cuticles perfectly formed, the tips the shape of a half moon. Embarrassed, Brianya slowly removed the fingers of her left hand from her mouth and wiped at her lips. "Bad habit," she admitted. Giving Celine a small smile, Brianya shook the outstretched hand.

"Hmmm . . . Well, whoever or whatever it is that has you gnawing on your nails like lunch must be important. One more bite and you would've drawn blood." They laughed easily and Brianya found herself drawn to Celine's friendly nature.

Three hours later, they were sitting in Panera Bread drinking tea and coffee as Brianya spilled her guts to Celine about her breakup with Darnell.

"Did you say Tricia Yancy?" Celine had asked when Brianya finally came up for air.

"Yeah, you know her?"

"Yep! She's my cousin. More like distant cousin, really. . . ."

Celine's persistent rapping on the car window brought Brianya back to the present, and she looked up in surprise. "Morning, supermodel!" Celine joked.

Brianya hurried out of the car.

"Girl, if I didn't know you back in the day, I would swear that you were born with this body!"

Brianya tapped Celine playfully on the arm and giggled. She did a mock runway sashay and looked up, too late, to see Ed Hollister from MacDonald Investments watching her.

Brianya made a face at Celine and got serious. "Goodness, I'm so embarrassed!" she whispered.

"Don't be. He's been watching you for the last 3 months! You hadn't noticed?"

"No! Isn't he married?"

"Divorced. Nine months ago."

"Too fresh!" Brianya thought a moment, and then reconsidered Ed Hollister's status. "Any kids?" She was going for nonchalant but didn't quite make it.

Celine raised an eyebrow at Brianya and half smiled. "None that I know of. If you're interested, I can set it up. Just say the word!"

"Really?" she asked, more excited than she cared to let on. Did she want to go down that road again? Dating in the new millennium had given new meaning to the phrase 'friends with benefits.' Okay, so she wasn't in her twenties anymore and the nineties were long gone, but honestly, why bother? The outcome was too predictable. But . . . on the other hand . . . "Nope! Not interested!" Brianya declared with finality.

They arrived at the elevator and Brianya tapped the up button.

Celine chuckled. "Okay, but you shouldn't sleep on that, Brianya. I hear he's a good catch."

"Oh? Then why aren't you all over that?" When Celine didn't respond, Brianya realized why. How could she be so insensitive? She'd forgotten that Celine hadn't gotten over the fact that her ex had left her midway through her chemo treatments. Her self-esteem, like Brianya's, had taken a major blow and, like Brianya, she'd sworn off relationships and sex.

"You know what, Celine? It's about time we ended this moratorium on relationships. Starting today, I'm officially back on the market! You in?" Brianya raised her hand for a high-five, but Celine didn't respond. "Don't leave me hanging, girl."

An apprehensive smile danced its way across Celine's chubby face. She raised her hand slowly and touched palms with Brianya. "I'm not saying I'm all the way in, but I'm definitely willing to consider it. As a matter of fact, there's someone who's been trying to get with me for a few months."

The elevator doors opened and the two women stepped in.

"Well, that's a start. You definitely need to follow through with that. Anyway, I'm ready to take back the power I've given Darnell over my life for the past 3 years. I'm calling the shots now, on my own terms." Brianya hefted her satchel onto her shoulder and peered appraisingly at Celine. "You know what, I changed my mind. Go ahead and set something up for me and that fine specimen, Ed Hollister!"

"What? Are you sure, Bri? 'Cause I'll do it as soon as I get to my desk."

Brianya thought briefly. "No time like the present. Work it out, girl!" she said and stepped out of the elevator.

"Hey, Bri!" Celine called as the elevator doors began to close. "You wanna do lunch today? I need to run something by you."

"Sure!" Brianya threw over her shoulder. "Twelve-thirty." For a brief moment, as she walked through the door to her office, Brianya wondered what Celine wanted to run by her then dismissed the thought. She'd find out soon enough.

"Good morning, Debbie," Brianya said, giving Debbie a stern look.

"Good morning, Ms. Johnson," Debbie returned icily.

Brianya knew that tone. Debbie's attitude was salty because of the way Brianya had approached her Saturday at the fundraiser. The only time her secretary called her Ms. Johnson was when she was upset with her. Brianya wasn't about to apologize, even though she knew that she should. Although she was Debbie's boss, she had no right to treat her as she had. If Debbie wasn't a screw-up to begin with, maybe she wouldn't have accused her of not doing her job in the first place.

Are you acting high and mighty, Brianya Denise Johnson? Brianya heard her mother's voice in her head. Alice Johnson had drilled into her children that God hated it when people acted high and mighty, and that you should never lord your position or station in life over anyone, especially those in your charge. Brianya knew those were words of wisdom to live by, even if for once she wanted to ignore her mother's sage words and do what she wanted to do. But she couldn't do it.

"Debbie," Brianya said, backtracking to Debbie's desk. "I want to apologize for my behavior on Saturday. I shouldn't have accused you of not doing your job, and I *definitely* should not have put my hands on you. I'm sorry."

Debbie beamed and jumped up and gave Brianya a big hug.

Although Debbie was known for her unexpected displays of affection, Brianya had not expected this. She smiled. "So I guess this means you forgive me?" Brianya said as she disentangled herself from the woman's embrace.

"Oh yes! I can't stay mad at you, Brianya. And I don't want you to be mad at me, either. You're one of the coolest bosses I've ever had!" Debbie extracted an envelope from her desk and handed it to Brianya. "This was on my desk when I got in this morning."

Brianya took the envelope and began opening it.

"No! Please, for my sake, wait until you've had your coffee before you look inside," Debbie said and chuckled.

"That bad, huh?" Brianya entered her office and tossed her satchel in the chair in the corner, placed her purse in a bottom drawer of her desk and locked it. She glanced at the LED display on her office phone and saw that she had 19 new messages. What was so urgent that the person needed to call her nineteen times, if, in fact, they were all from the same person? Her friends and family had her cell number, so that ruled them out. Could have been wrong numbers.

Brianya scrolled the display screen and noticed that all but five of the calls were from the same 804 area code. The other calls were local. One was from a firm she recognized, MacDonald Investments; it had come in on Saturday night. Brianya decided to listen to it first, since it was likely to be about business. She hoped it wasn't Mr. Calhoun rescinding his pledge. She put the phone's speaker on low and dialed her voicemail, then skipped through until she got to message number 18.

Hello, Miss Johnson, this is Ed Hollister from MacDonald Investments. I'm not sure if you check your messages over the weekend, but I wanted to leave this anyway. Forgive my cowardice for not telling you this in person, but I wanted you to know that you looked absolutely stunning today! I also wanted to tell you that I admired the way you handled Mr. Calhoun. He can be a bit recalcitrant. Congratulations to you and your company for reaching your goal. You did a wonderful job of pumping up the crowd and motivating us to dig deep in our pockets when you sang God Bless the Child. By the way, I'm glad to know that we have something in common: I can't carry a tune either! Have a great weekend.

Brianya let out a huge gust of air. She hadn't realized that she'd been holding her breath. Where had he been that he'd overheard the exchange between her and Mr. Calhoun? She'd seen him only once and that was when she was on the stage butchering the famous song by Billie Holliday and Arthur Herzog, Jr. Brianya smiled to herself as a tingle of excitement ran up her spine.

She skipped to the beginning of her messages and listened to them in order. Her heartbeat quickened when she heard the voice of the first caller.

Hi, Anya. I know it's been a minute since I last seen you or talked to you. We didn't part on good terms, and I take full responsibility for that. I miss you, baby. I'm heading your way in a few weeks and I wanna see you. Hit me at 804-555-3433.

Brianya put her fist in her mouth and screamed.

Debbie came running to the door of her office. "Brianya, are you okay? You sounded like you were in pain."

"I'm fine, Debbie; no need to worry," she said, downplaying her reaction. "On your way out, shut the door, please?" Brianya didn't want to take any chances of Debbie overhearing her voicemails. Discretion wasn't one of her strong suits.

"Sure," Debbie said, looking puzzled and a little put-off. She closed the door behind her and Brianya continued listening to her messages.

They were all, basically, the same: Darnell pleading with her to call him so they could get together when he came to Cleveland. He must have lost his mind up there in Richmond, Virginia if he thought for one second that she would ever sit down and break bread with him again. Brianya deleted the first fifteen messages and the one after that when she heard the computerized voice of a telemarketer.

Ms. Johnson, this is Susanne Hastings from Rowdy Entertainment, the next caller announced. *I'm calling on behalf of Mr. Marlon Taylor, regarding the franchise disclosure document and the contract that Mellow Beans sent over two weeks ago. Mr. Taylor has circled areas of the FDD and the contract that he has issues with. I've messengered the documents over to you personally, via Mr. Taylor's instructions. Upon receipt of the documents, please call our offices at 216-555-4683.*

Brianya wrote the information on her calendar. Why had Marlon gotten the FDD and the contract at the same time and why was he sending her the documents? Any issues he had should go directly to the legal department or Hamfred Larson. Brianya had nothing to do with his deal, other than writing up the job description and salary recommendation. Clearly, Marlon was messing with her. She slammed the pen down on her desk and listened to the last message. It was from Cashmere, saying she had lost Brianya's cell number and could they get together on the following Saturday to catch up? She had so much to share with her old friend. They hadn't really talked since Cashmere had moved back to Cleveland six years ago. Cashmere had rebuffed every attempt Brianya had made to reach out to her. *What a way to live,* Brianya thought, *in the shadows, always afraid that someone might discover your secret. It was embarrassing and humiliating.*

Although she would've liked to ruminate on her friend's predicament, she had a more pressing matter at hand. Brianya picked up her handset and called the woman at Rowdy Entertainment to discuss the documents she'd sent.

When the conversation ended, Brianya screamed and threw the phone across the room. She never should have called. She should have just forwarded the papers to the legal department.

Debbie rushed into Brianya's office in a panic. "What happened, Brianya?" She eyed the broken pieces of the telephone, lying in a heap in the corner of the room, and retreated to the doorway. The wild expression on Brianya's face clearly alarmed Debbie. "I'll be at my desk, if you need me," she mumbled and made a quick exit, closing the door behind her. She had never seen her boss in such an anxious state and it was clear by her behavior that she didn't quite know what to make of it, or how to handle it.

Brianya's blazing eyes darted from one end of the room to the other. She felt trapped. She needed to get some air or she would pass out. How could Hamfred Larson be so foolish? Didn't he care anything about MBCC's legacy? After all the care that Mr. Styles, Brianya's predecessor, had taken to make sure that MBCC didn't receive negative press for what Marlon Taylor had done, that good deed would come back to bite the company in the behind.

Marlon must have used the CEO's proclivity for dressing in women's lingerie to weasel his way into the pilot program. How he could have known about Hamfred, Brianya had no idea. The only reason *she* knew was because Debbie and Mr. Larson's secretary were friends. The secretary had walked in on her boss while he was trying on a bustier in his office one Saturday. She'd told Debbie, who told Brianya, and, apparently, someone had told Marlon. Whatever the case, Marlon used what he knew to get

Hamfred to reduce the employment obligation to only two years instead of five. And on top of that, the original pilot program agreement stated that employees in the program would answer to the HR Assistant. Marlon, however, would answer directly to Brianya, the HR Director. Brianya thought she had seen the last of that loser the day security had frog-marched him right out of the revolving doors. Not only was he back, but she would have to deal more directly with him now; more than she did when he was a full-time employee. *Hamfred Larson and his twisted perversions!* Brianya wanted to wring his neck.

Unable to contain herself, Brianya called Celine to let off steam and to make sure they were still on for lunch.

***

"I can't believe I have to deal with that snake again!" Brianya said, sitting across from Celine in the Galleria. She crammed a forkful of arugula salad into her mouth, barely chewed, and gulped down half a bottle of water.

"Take it easy, Bri. You look like you're about to stroke-out." Celine had been listening to the same diatribe for the last 38 minutes—first on the telephone and now as they ate lunch. She had news of her own to share with Brianya, but she couldn't get a word in edgewise. It was just as well, because given the state that Brianya was in, her news probably wouldn't go over well.

"Is it even legal what Hamfred is doing? Given the price we're charging Marlon for the initial investment, we're practically giving the business away! He's an ex-vet, so he gets to use that VetFran Initiative. But get this, he's paying way less than ten percent!" Brianya tore off a huge chunk of sour dough bread and slathered it with cream cheese. At this point, Brianya didn't care that she was divulging confidential information. All she could think about was venting. She knew Celine could be trusted. Besides, Celine had divulged plenty of confidential information herself.

Celine watched as Brianya tore another chunk of bread and shook her head. "You're racing your way back up the scale. Keep eating like that and you'll be back at 353 pounds in no time." She laughed, but Brianya didn't think it was funny.

"I can't help it! I'm upset!"

"Well," Celine began with caution. "I hate to tell you this, because it might upset you even more. But you know when you said that we should end the moratorium on relationships?"

Brianya nodded.

"Well, I was sorta kicking around the idea of going out with this person who's been hounding me for almost five months." Celine looked sheepishly at Brianya.

"Why would that upset me?" Brianya asked, confused.

"Well . . . it's someone you don't really care for."

Brianya looked even more confused. Besides Ed Hollister, the only men they both knew were Hamfred Larson, the CEO at Mellow Beans; Ricardo Juarez in maintenance, and Brianya's ex, Darnell. Hamfred and Ricardo were married. She knew Celine couldn't be talking about Darnell. Celine was a friend—Brianya thought—and she couldn't imagine her doing something as underhanded as going out with her ex. Even though their relationship was long over, there was still the fact that Darnell used to date Celine's cousin. Was Celine really that type of woman?

Celine read the intense expression on Brianya's face and figured out what she was thinking. "Don't even think it, Bri! I would never go there! Darnell is your ex and my cousin's ex, and he's too much like *my* ex for me to ever even *consider* going out with him!"

"Who, then?" Brianya asked, relieved.

"Marlon Taylor."

"What?" Brianya shouted, slapping her hand loudly on the table. "I know you didn't just say what I think you said! 'Cause what I *think* you said is, you lost your ever-loving mind and you're consider going out with that low-life-sneak-thief-snake-in-the-grass, Marlon. Is that what I heard you say?"

The other diners turned around to stare at Brianya and Celine.

"Calm down, Brianya, and tell me what you *really* think," Celine said, sarcastically. "I said I was only kicking around the idea."

"Well, kick that idea right out of your head. You're better than that, Cee Cee," Brianya said, reverting to the nickname she'd given Celine right after she'd undergone her first round of chemo, in an effort to make her feel better. Celine had told Brianya that she had never had a nickname because her mother thought her name was too beautiful to bastardize.

"Let's talk about something else," Celine said, looking disappointed.

As they made their way back to the North Coast building, Brianya calmed down enough to fill Celine in on the call from Ed Hollister.

CHAPTER FOUR

A COUPLE OF WEEKS had passed, and Brianya had yet to return Ed's phone call; she wasn't sure if she was really ready for the dating scene again. For all her big talk to Celine, it terrified Brianya to open herself up to possible mistreatment at the hands of someone she cared about. Not that she cared about Ed Hollister; she didn't even know him. But who knew where things would go? She could play it safe and just date for kicks and giggles, but she wasn't that type of person; and Ed didn't seem that way, either. Brianya wanted a relationship with promise. The casual scene had never been her bag.

"It would make things much easier if I could be like those people who know how to have a good time without getting bogged down in details and labels," Brianya said to Cashmere, over a plate of "spaghetti."

They were at Brianya's house enjoying a meal of spaghetti made with spaghetti squash, homemade spaghetti sauce with mushrooms, onions, garlic, basil, bell peppers, and fake ground turkey made from soy products, and gluten free garlic bread. "I know what you mean," Cashmere said, taking a healthy swig from the glass of wine Brianya had just handed her. "Thank goodness, I never have to worry about that aspect of dating."

Brianya had invited Cashmere over for Sunday dinner so they could play catch up. Although years had separated them, it was as if they had never lost touch. Very few friendships could sustain such a long absence, but in their case, the absence seemed to have fortified their friendship. It was good to be back in the company of an old, familiar friend. "What do you mean? Don't tell me you went and joined a convent." Brianya laughed at her own joke.

"Nah, nothing like that. When Ray died, I promised God that if he let me live HIV positive that I would live celibate for the rest of my life," Cashmere stated matter-of-factly.

Brianya was speechless at her friend's words. She had wanted to ask Cashmere about her status, but couldn't bring herself to ask; it felt so intrusive. Now that Cashmere had verified what Brianya had feared, she absolutely, positively, did not know what to say. Her eyes clouded with tears and she wiped them away with the backs of her hands.

"Oh, no, Bri!" Cashmere said vehemently. "Don't cry for me! God's got me in his care."

Brianya stared at the beautiful woman sitting across from her: the perfectly symmetrical face, with the small button nose, almond-shaped eyes, and the perky little lips. It pained her that some deserving man would never be able to enjoy such unadulterated beauty. It wasn't fair! This time she didn't stop the tears that flowed.

"Come on, Bri. This is supposed to be a joyous occasion—two friends getting back together after years of being apart. Hey, let's drink to old friendships." Cashmere raised her glass and waited for Brianya to do the same. "To two of the hottest women Cleveland has ever seen!" Cashmere said.

Brianya wiped at her eyes and half-heartedly raised her glass. "I'll drink to that!" she said, manufacturing a cheeriness she didn't feel.

The hours passed with Brianya filling Cashmere in on her breakup with Darnell and her weight loss journey, and her decision to remain celibate as well.

"So what about this Ed Hollister? He sounds like someone with his head on straight." They were sitting on the deck out back listening to music.

"I don't know if I want to get involved with a man who's been married before. I don't like the idea of being compared to the ex-wife. You probably think I'm being naïve, and maybe I am."

"Yeah, a little. Really, where are you gonna find a man in this day and age who hasn't had at least one wife? That's unrealistic, in my opinion. I mean, I know men like that do exist, but they usually live in their parent's basement and play on PlayStation 3 all day. Or they're behind bars, and in that case you wouldn't want them anyway. Know what I mean?" Cashmere said.

Brianya did know; she nodded in agreement.

The opinion was that a prison record carried with it two stigmas: one, you spent your time being someone's boyfriend, or someone was your boyfriend; two, you were un-rehabilitateable. Whether there was truth to the first opinion, Brianya was unwilling to find out, so she automatically refused to date any man she knew had been in jail, which narrowed her prospects considerably. Especially since she would never consider dating outside her race. Not that she had anything against other races; she just happened to be one of the few Black women left who *loved and dated* Black men exclusively.

"Realistic or not, that's what I'm holding out for."

"So, then, what about Monty? I think he's the real deal." Cashmere didn't know Monty personally, only what Brianya had told her; and what she had seen of him on the basketball court during his stint in the NBA.

"Real or not, I couldn't deal with him being confrontational. You know me, I'm a peaceful person."

"Well, then, that only leaves Darnell," Cashmere said and grinned toothily.

Brianya shook her head and turned up the volume on the iPod as Charlie Wilson belted out his latest song. They sang along and pantomimed the words they didn't know.

"Oh, I forgot to mention that my dad's playing matchmaker now. He set me up on a date with someone from his work. He's much older than I am but I said yes just to humor my dad, but then the guy was a no-show. He called later that day to apologize, saying he had a family emergency and wanted to reschedule. In all honestly, Cash, I'm not feeling this date."

"Go. Have a good time. And leave it at that. It's just a meal, not a marriage proposal. You really do need to loosen up, girl. You'll run a man off even before he can get to know you good."

CHAPTER FIVE

A FEW DAYS LATER, climbing the stairs to her parents' home, Brianya was thinking about Cashmere's words. She would take her friend's advice and loosen up, learn to go with the flow.

Cinthia answered Brianya's knock and immediately started in on the goings-on in the Johnson household. Before Brianya could tell her that she didn't give a rat's patootie about ham hocks and salt pork versus smoked turkey in greens and green beans, the telephone rang.

Brianya headed for the living room, where her mother spent her evenings watching the evening news and Jeopardy. Before greeting her, Brianya stood and watched Alice Johnson as she answered correctly almost all the questions Alex Trebec put to the contestants. Alice, who had never had to work a day in her life, was an avid reader, read everything she could get her hands on. In that respect, Brianya was nothing like her mother. She hated reading, except for the occasional mystery novel, and only did it if it was required. It was ironic that she should choose a profession that required tons of reading.

"Bri!" shouted Cinthia, loud enough to wake the dead. "Come get the phone!"

A phone call for her? No one knew she was at her parents' house. "Who is it?" she asked as she crossed the threshold into the kitchen.

Cinthia didn't answer, just thrust the phone at Brianya.

Hearing the voice on the other end, Brianya cursed under her breath. She covered the mouthpiece of the telephone with her hand, glared at her sister, and mouthed a reproachful, "Why did you give me this phone, girl?"

Cinthia waved her hand dismissively at Brianya. "I'm not your secretary. He asked for you. I gave you the phone. End of story."

Smart mouthed brat!

Darnell was steadily talking and Brianya was half-listening. "Um-hmm . . . Um-hmm . . . Yes, I'm listening. I heard every word you said," Brianya said in an exasperated tone.

"Well, at least you didn't hang up on me this time."

"How did you know I was here, Darnell?"

"I didn't. Since you won't give me your home number, I took a chance that you might be at your parents' house. I know how close you are to your family."

"Don't call me here again! My parents don't need the aggravation."

"Your father didn't seem aggravated when I called the other day."

"Well, I am. So don't call here again. Save your long distance money to call your own family."

"I'm not calling you from Richmond; I'm back in Cleveland," Brianya sucked her tongue. "Don't be like that, Bri. I'm serious about you going out to dinner with me next Saturday," Darnell said seductively.

Darnell had been blowing up her work phone leaving messages about taking her to dinner. Brianya had ignored them all, and he still didn't take the hint. It was just like Darnell to be so full of himself, thinking that with a little persuasion and sweet talk, Brianya would let him back into her life. Despite her protestations, Darnell's liquid voice was moving her in a direction that she did not want to go. Quickly, she snapped out of it.

"Did you hear me, Bri?" Darnell asked anxiously.

"I heard you," she snapped. "Now you hear me. I was finished with you almost three years ago. So there's no reason for us to see each other; no need to talk to each other, and definitely no reason to ever go out together. Good-bye, Darnell. Have a nice life!"

"Wait, Bri! Don't hang up."

Brianya was two seconds away from a dial tone. "What is it?"

"I love you," he said softly.

Humph! she thought, nonplused. One of the most overused and most deceptive words in the English language, love. L is for the lies you'll tell me; O is for your obnoxious behavior; V is for the vicious things you'll do to me; E is for the evil intent that colors your actions. "You know something, Darnell?" Brianya said as if a truth had dawned "I believe you do love me." That said, Darnell's two seconds were up. The receiver made a clicking sound when she placed it in its cradle.

"Cin!" Brianya shouted as she headed toward the family room.

"Brianya Denise, stop all that yelling before you wake up your daddy!"

"I'm sorry, Ma. Where's Cin?" Brianya joined her mother in the family room.

"What are you two fighting about now?"

Alice Johnson had raised her two girls to get along. And for the life of her, she couldn't figure out how they could be so opposite. Whenever Brianya and Cinthia were in the same room, there was bound to be a tussle of wills. Brianya was more like her mother—laid back, quiet. While Cinthia, hotheaded and stubborn, was like her father. A tidbit of information her mother never let go unnoticed when Brianya acted less than ladylike. Brianya was positive that her mother would remind her, once again, of how unladylike she was behaving.

"She did something I didn't appreciate."

"She's just mad because Darnell tracked her down," Cinthia said, rounding the corner and flopping onto the recliner.

"That's the second time he's called looking for you, Bri. What does that boy want now?" Alice was none too pleased when Darnell had mistreated Brianya the first time. And she was not happy about him calling her home, leaving messages for her daughter.

"He wants to get back with Bri now that she lost all that weight," Cinthia chimed in as she assessed Brianya's backside. "You ain't got that big ole butt no more!" she said laughing. "Hey Bri, remember that song about the big ole butt? "Brianya got a big ole butt, oh yeah! . . ." Cinthia sang, snapping her fingers to a tune in her head.

Brianya stood up and pulled her sweater over her behind, showing off her new shapely rump. "Look at me now, sister. Your behind is bigger than mine."

"Brianya Denise! You ought to be ashamed of yourself." Her mother enunciated every syllable as she swatted at Brianya with the TV guide. "Carrying on like a heathen! Why don't you act like a lady?"

Brianya fell backward into her chair, laughing hysterically. "Sorry, Ma, I couldn't help myself!"

"You better be glad Mommy is sitting right there," Cinthia said. At thirty-three, Cinthia still called their mother Mommy. For that, Brianya wanted to twist Cinthia's lips the way their grandmother used to do when they were younger and got to sassing off at the mouth. Cinthia's child-like ways sometimes infuriated Brianya. She wished her sister would grow up and become more responsible.

"Why, what would you do if she wasn't here, cuss me out? With your gutter-mouth self."

"Look who's talking. You cuss more than any church-going person I know, Cin."

"Well, at least I go to church."

"Isn't that the truth," Alice said, looking slyly at Brianya out of the corner of her eye. Alice felt that if her daughter would only come back to church on a regular basis, Brianya could find a good, decent man and that would reduce a mother's worry, at least somewhat.

"I don't know what for. It's not like it's doing you any good."

Alice cut in, seeing where the conversation was heading. "Brianya, remember you promised your daddy and me that you'd come to church this Sunday. I told Reverend you'd be there. He said he'd be sure to have the choir sing Amazing Grace for you."

"Really?" Brianya asked excitedly. Amazing Grace was her favorite song. Ever since she was tall enough to reach the keys on the piano, Jesse Greene, the choir director, would let her pluck away as Sister Anderson belted out Amazing Grace, beautifully, like a songbird, during choir rehearsal.

"Sure. Reverend's been trying to get Sister Anderson to sing that song for months. Sister said she would only do it for special occasions. When I told her you were coming, that's all the encouragement she needed.

For the last year and a half, Brianya had been promising her mother she'd visit Temple church, the church that she was reared in, but something always came up. She couldn't keep putting it off. "I'll be there, Ma. What time are services?"

"Same as always."

That meant all day. Sun-up to sun-down.

Above their heads, Brianya could hear her father puttering around. She checked her watch; it read 9:30.

"Daddy working tonight?" Brianya asked.

"You know your daddy," Cinthia said, imitating her mother's airy voice and sucking her tongue.

Alice gave her a warning look, but smiled nonetheless.

Brianya knew her father. Roger Johnson was the hardest working man she knew. She couldn't remember a time when he didn't have more than one job. Working kept his mind fresh, kept him young, he'd said. There must be some truth in that, because her father could easily pass for fifty, fifty-five at the most; though in reality he was sixty-five. In two years he'd be retiring from his supervisory job at the main Post Office.

"He's filling in for George, supervising the cleaning crew for the Med Centers. I don't mind him going to the centers in the

Heights, but tonight he's got to drive all the way out there to Stow. No telling how the weather will hold up. They say it's supposed to thunderstorm tonight. Alice worried her face into a frown and sighed. "I try to get your daddy to sit down, don't work so much, but he doesn't pay me any attention."

Brianya sat beside her mother on the couch, patted her hand, kissed her on the cheek, and hugged her. "Try not to worry too much, Ma. You know how Daddy has to think something is his idea before he'll listen to reason." She stood up to leave, smoothing down her skirt. "It's getting late. I'd better go say hi then head on out."

Brianya's relationship with her mother was more like sisters than mother and daughter, but her relationship with her father was at times strained. They'd gone through some rough spots in her teen years and it had left things between them just a tad bit tarnished. On the whole, though, they were good together, and their conversations flowed easily.

"I'm coming up, Daddy," Brianya called up the stairs, in case her father wasn't fully clothed. Announcing her entrance was a habit she had acquired after accidentally walking in on her father and seeing him standing, stark naked, in the middle of his bedroom, when she was five.

"Come on up; I'm decent."

"How you feeling?" Brianya said, approaching her parents' bedroom.

"I feel good," Roger said, then peered at Brianya and smiled broadly. "You look good, Daughter. Can't hardly recognize you anymore, you got so small. No wonder that young man's been calling over here looking for you." He sat down to put on his socks, and Brianya joined him at the foot of the bed.

"I hope he wasn't pestering you, Daddy. I didn't think he would call here."

"No, he wasn't pestering me. That's your mama with the attitude." He looked at Brianya questioningly. "You going out with him again?"

"After the way he did me? I don't think so!"

Roger got up and strolled to the bathroom and Brianya followed, sliding past him to sit on the edge of the tub. He took out a jar of hair pomade and slapped a generous portion of the clear gook in the palms of his hands, massaged it through his hair, then wet a boar's hair brush and scooted it through.

"Daughter," Roger said between strokes, "you'll have to put that behind you."

Brianya's expression turned to stone. She couldn't believe her father was actually taking up for Darnell. "Daddy! I'm surprised at you."

"What? You think you the first woman to get dumped by a man just because you're fat? . . . Uh, pardon me," Roger said, clearing his throat and beaming, then said in his best imitation infomercial voice, "*used to be* fat."

Brianya didn't want to, but she laughed; she could never keep a straight face when her father clowned. Now serious, she said, "No, but he could have chosen a better way to tell me."

"Maybe he should have sent you one of those singing telegrams or something." Roger chuckled, but when he saw the anger flash in Brianya's eyes, he got serious. "Look, Daughter, it's been three years almost. Let it go. Look at the positives: you got your health; you took off a few pounds; and you have a good job, even got a promotion. From what he told me, he's doing good for himself, too. Says he wants you back because he realized he made a mistake. Give the man a break, Daughter. It's not like he cheated on you." Roger put down the brush. "He didn't cheat on you, did he?" he asked, checking to make sure he had his facts straight.

Brianya sighed wearily and lied. She knew what her father was capable of if he thought for one minute that a man had disrespected one of his daughters in that way. Brianya had witnessed her father beating Cinthia's ex with a razor strap after Cinthia had told him that the guy had cheated on her several times. "No, Daddy, he didn't cheat. Not that I know of, anyway." Brianya didn't like lying to her father, but the alternative was worse. Frankly, she was surprised that her father hadn't heard about Darnell and the other woman. But then again, they didn't exactly run in the same circles. On the other hand, everybody knew that Temple church was the hotbed of gossip, what with Selena Ford going there. The girl couldn't keep a secret if you paid her.

"Well, there you go," Roger said.

"I just can't believe you talked to that man. Like everything is all good."

Roger smiled at his daughter's incredulity. "It is for me. I got no problem with the young man." He spread shaving cream across his caramel-colored face, turned on the faucet, found a comfortable temperature, and held his razor under the cascade. "A man don't come back after almost three years just because he misses you. He got to have a better reason than that."

Brianya didn't want to admit it, but her father was making sense. Even still, she thought, sense or no sense, humiliation always remembers its enforcer. "When somebody tramples on your self-esteem, Daddy, you don't go back for a second helping."

Roger patted his face with the fluffy sea-green towel. "He made a mistake. Mistakes happen, Daughter. The man was running scared. He grabbed whatever excuse he could find. *Which*," he said, pushing the word out abruptly, "happened to be your weight, *which*, unfortunately, hurt you. He may not have been all that comfortable with a large woman, but I'll bet you one thing: your weight wasn't the issue. That fella needed to get away to sort out his thoughts, and the excuse he gave you was the easiest way out." Roger stroked the left side of his face with the razor then turned his face sideways to admire his handiwork. "Stuck around for eight months, didn't he?" he said, bringing the

45

razor once again to his face. "You don't stay that long and stay faithful if you don't like the way your woman looks."

Brianya folded her arms across her chest, clearly not appreciating her father acting as Darnell's ambassador, and spat out, "Mistake or no mistake—*which*," she said, mimicking her father, "I'm not buying—the facts remain: I'm through with him, and I wish he'd stay out of my life."

Roger sloshed water around in the face bowl, rinsing the tiny hairs down the drain. He wet the sponge and wiped around the outside of the drain. He dried his hands and jangled the keys in his pocket. Glancing in Brianya's direction, he saw the familiar wide-nostril expression of annoyance, and raised his eyebrows questioningly. Then he turned and shuffled out the door, ambled down the stairs, telling Brianya to get the light on her way out. "Seems to me," Roger said, when they reached the first floor, "that you hell-bent on getting revenge." He opened the closet door and retrieved his jacket. When Brianya didn't reply, Roger knew he was right. Otherwise, her tongue and teeth would have been on a collision course, tripping all over her words. He shook his head, let out an exasperated sigh, said, "Like your granddaddy used to tell me, 'the only way to skin a cat is to kill it with kindness.'"

Good ol' granddaddy Johnson, with his quirky sayings, sure was right on the money with that one, Brianya mused, kissing and hugging her father goodnight. "Love you, Daddy."

"Me too, Daughter. Oh!" Roger said, the beginning of an afterthought, but before he could finish, Brianya cut him off.

"Don't forget that I'm going to church this Sunday, right? I know, Mama already reminded me."

"That's not what I was going to say. I was going to tell you that E.J.'s been asking about you." Roger pulled his brown skullcap down over his wave cap.

Endo Jamison, late forties and average looking, was a mail carrier out of the main post office, where her father worked. Four months ago, when she'd stopped in to take her father to lunch, Endo had walked out to the lobby with Roger, got a glimpse of Brianya's hippy strut and from that day on kept sending messages through Roger, who always made sure to relay them to Brianya.

"I'm not thinking about Endo, Daddy, with his no-show self. Did he tell you that he stood me up last weekend?"

"He didn't tell me that," Roger said, creasing his forehead. "Just said he was supposed to take you out, but he had family trouble. When he called to tell you about it, he said you wouldn't talk to him."

"That's because I didn't want to hear any excuses," Brianya said, rolling her eyes upward.

Roger shook his head slowly. "You keep on with that attitude, Daughter, and you'll be alone for a long time."

"What's wrong with being alone?" she asked, knowing what her father's response would be. Roger was a firm believer that men and women were put on this Earth to marry and procreate, and any woman—because he was much harder on women—who was single past the age of thirty was defective in one way or another.

"Sometimes a lemon can use a little sugar, Daughter."

"Mama!" Brianya bellowed. She knew where her father was going with this conversation and it was time for modern thinking women to, once again, set primitive thinkers straight. Though Alice was sixty-four, she was one of the most forward thinking women of her generation that Brianya knew.

Alice joined her daughter and husband at the door.

"Will you tell your husband that this is a new millennium and that women's lives don't center around snagging a man so that they won't be *alone* later in life."

Alice gave an exaggerated look of shock and said, "Humph! I don't know what you're talking about, girlfriend. That's the only reason I married your daddy."

Brianya sighed and laughed along with her mother.

47

Roger threw his hands up, pecked his wife on the cheek, and headed out the door. "That's what's wrong with you women." Roger opened the door of his beat-up Ford Escort. "Always hollerin' about how you don't need a man. But the minute something breaks down, you all can't get to us quick enough."

Alice mashed the button to the garage door and Brianya watched as it rolled up, thinking how well matched her parents were. *When and if I do find someone, we'll go together like fried bologna and mustard.* At the thought of food, Brianya's stomach gurgled.

"Is there any more meatloaf left, Ma? I'm hungry," Brianya said turning around and heading toward the kitchen.

"Cinthia put it in the fridge. Go on and help yourself to some. I'm going up to bed. Lock up when you leave."

"Where is Cin?"

Alice yawned. "Fred came and they went somewhere; I don't know. Don't forget to put the deadbolt on," Alice said, climbing the stairs.

Brianya glanced up at the clock on the wall; it read 10:20. *Must be nice to have someone to spend time with*, she thought, reaching inside the refrigerator and taking out the leftovers. Even though Cinthia's relationships tended not to last too long or go very deep, it was still nice to be the center of someone's world for a minute.

Brianya put the food on the stove. After cutting a small slice of meatloaf, she put it on a plate, adding a small serving of mashed potatoes, covering them with a tiny bit of onion gravy, then put the plate in the microwave. The timer dinged and she glanced up at the wall-clock again. Ten thirty on a Friday night. Why was she sitting at her parents' kitchen table, getting ready to stuff her face, when she should be out with some interesting somebody, talking weather, portfolios, the state of the world, or whatever, and the possibility of a second date? I'll have to do something about that, she thought.

CHAPTER SIX

B RIANYA PULLED A piece of paper from her purse and dialed the number written on it. He answered on the third ring, just as she was about to hang up. "Hi, Endo. This is Brianya." So he was home on a Saturday night too, Brianya thought, and wondered if his weekend solitude was by choice or by circumstance.

"Oh, you're talking to me now?" Endo sounded perturbed.

His baritone voice caused a pleasant shudder to shimmy through Brianya. She ignored his statement. "I got the messages you've been sending through my dad. And I want to apologize for my bad behavior," she said shyly.

"Yeah. I thought that was rude, the way you treated me. But I forgive you." Brianya could hear the smile in his voice. "So, tell me, to what do I owe this surprise phone call?"

"Chalk it up to progressive maturity."

"Ooo-kay," Endo said. "So, does this phone call mean that you're willing to give me another chance?"

"Maybe," Brianya teased.

"Well, *maybe* I can take you to dinner tomorrow night?"

She thought for a minute, said, "I haven't been skating in a long time. Would you mind if we did that, instead?"

"I'm game. It's been a while for me, too."

After a few minutes more of chatting and finalizing the plans, they said good-bye.

Brianya nibbled a corner of the meatloaf and tasted a little of the mashed potatoes. It was so good, she wanted to dive right in, but instead she used self-control. When she finished, she washed the dishes, dried them, and put them away.

Driving up Wade Park, heading home, Brianya's thoughts were on Endo, and she found herself actually getting excited about their upcoming date.

***

"No, Endo. Don't let me go. I can't stop!" Brianya went swirling around in a circle at a dizzying speed, her arms flailing every which way. She couldn't get control of the rented skates; it felt like one of the wheels had come loose. As she spun out of control, a woman with her head bowed, lost in the rhythm of the song *Rappers Delight*, headed her way. "Watch out!"Brianya screamed, but the dancing woman didn't hear her. Next thing Brianya knew, she was flat on her behind, scooting past several snickering skaters before finally coming to a complete stop in the middle of the rink.

Endo rushed over and held out a hand to help her up. "Ooo, dang! I'm sorry, Brianya. I know that must've hurt." He scrunched up his face, trying not to laugh.

"Ya think? I told you not to let go," she said angrily.

"The way you kept bouncing around, I thought you had the groove."

"I was bouncing around because I was trying to un-stick the wheel." Brianya got to her feet, brushed the dirt off her jeans. She turned around to check the location of the woman, and saw her victim charging toward her, like an angry bull flinging cuss words left and right.

"Come on now, there's no need for all that kind of language," Endo said jumping between the two women. "It was my fault, Miss," he apologized, not giving Brianya a chance for a comeback reply. "It's been a long time since she's skated; I let her go too soon."

The woman looked Endo up and down, and snarled at Brianya. "You better be glad didn't nothing get broke," she said in a tone that, Brianya assumed, was supposed to scare her.

"Or what?" Brianya said, jumping from behind Endo and falling flat on her behind, again. She wriggled on the floor in pain, embarrassed that the woman now walking away, laughing hysterically, had witnessed her making a fool of herself for the second time.

Endo was almost suffocating, trying not to laugh.

Brianya was furious.

"Help me get these skates off, Endo!" she demanded. "And take me home!"

Neither of them said a word as they drove away from the skating rink.

Brianya could see Endo sneak a peek at her out of the corner of his eye, every two blocks or so. He was probably scared that if he opened his mouth, Brianya would shut it for him real quick. Endo was a goofball. That's why she hadn't been in any hurry to respond to any of the messages he'd sent through her father. He didn't wear pocket protectors or anything like that, but everything about him screamed NERD. Except his voice. Brianya loved Endo's sexy voice. Too bad they came as a package. She could fall asleep listening to that voice every night, the sing-song, poetic way he spoke Brianya's name. The way he spoke it now.

"Brianya, I'm sorry for the way things turned out tonight. Next time maybe we can do something a little less challenging, like, say, skydiving."

Brianya shot Endo an I-know-you-must-be-joking look and he burst out laughing. So did she. A second date with Endo was definitely not on her to-do list. But . . . she could be persuaded. Maybe.

"Seriously, Brianya, I'd like to take you to see *The Taming of the Shrew*. Make it up to you."

"That's one of my favorite plays!" Brianya exclaimed. How did you know that?"

"Your dad told me," Endo said, a big grin of satisfaction plastered across his face.

Aww . . . How sweet is that? Hmmm . . . He's not a bad looking guy, cute actually. I love those long, thick, curly eyelashes. Back up! I am not going out with this goofball again! Lighten up, girl. Stop being so judgmental, Brianya. Give the guy a chance. How bad could a theater date with him be? "Okay, Endo," Brianya said, willing to take a chance. "I'll go."

"Oh, goody!"

Goody? Who says that?

"The play is in two weeks. You should dress casual but somewhat dressy. You don't have to get all dressed—"

Brianya touched Endo's arm, smiled sweetly, and said reproachfully, "Endo, I've been to the theater before. I think I know how to dress."

"Oh. Right. Sorry. It's just that I'm so glad you said yes. I bought the tickets some time ago and I was going to call you, but you beat me to it."

So that sneaky father of hers knew exactly what he was doing when he played up Darnell, acting like he thought Darnell was the best thing walking, knowing she would disagree. Then telling her what Endo had said.

Endo turned too wide into Brianya's drive and bumped the rock at the edge of the driveway.

Brianya shook her head and looked at the digital clock on the radio, 8:15 on a Saturday night, the day before church day. Good thing it was still early; she'd need time to recuperate from the fall, before sitting on a hard church pew all day. "Well, Endo, in spite of my sore behind, I had fun tonight," Brianya said as she put her hand on the door handle.

Endo bounced out of the car and landed in front of Brianya's door in lightning speed. "Here, let me get that for you," he said, yanking the door open and holding out his arm for her to latch onto.

"You didn't have to do that, Endo, really, I'm okay."

"No problem." He helped her out of the car and up the stairs, as if she were an old woman. "Give me your keys; I'll get the door for you."

Oh no! Brianya thought, in a state of panic. He's gonna want to come in and chit chat. She'd had enough of Endo and his sugary sweetness for one night. "Uh . . . if you don't mind, I'm really tired and I'd like to just sit in a nice warm tub and soak my . . . you know . . .," she said, pointing to her behind.

"Sure, sure. I understand. Next time, huh?" He released her arm and backed down the stairs.

"Yeah, next time." Endo watched Brianya as she fumbled inside her purse for her keys. *I don't know what he's standing there for; I wish he would leave.* "I found them," she said, holding the keys up for Endo to see, so that he could go on about his business.

"Um, Brianya," Endo said, then cleared his throat nervously. "The play is two weeks away. Be okay if I call you in the meantime?" he asked bashfully.

"I don't see why not." Brianya smiled then stepped inside the house. "Bye, Endo. Take care."

"Okay now. I'll call you."

Brianya switched on the hall light. "What a day!" she shouted, safely on the other side of the door. There was a time, way in the distant past, when she would have given a chivalrous man like Endo top billing. But thanks, or no thanks, to Darnell she'd learned her lesson. Men, especially the ones with hidden agendas, always represented themselves as gentlemen. Then, somewhere down the line, the routine changed, and out went the pretenses and in came the real person. *No thanks!* Brianya neither wanted nor needed a pretender. She switched off the hall light and was on her way up to soak her aching rear, when the doorbell chimed.

CHAPTER SEVEN

B RIANYA OPENED THe door, prepared to ask Endo what part of "I'd like to soak my sore behind," didn't he understand. Only it wasn't Endo.

"You have got to be kidding me! What part of 'I'm not interested' did you not comprehend?"

"And good evening to you too, Brianya," Monty said sarcastically.

Brianya moved to shut the door, but Monty slid his foot between the door and the frame and held it open with his hand. "Just let me talk to you, Brianya," he pleaded. "That's all I want to do. I promise. I won't come in unless you invite me, but I just want to talk to you. You can call your brother or your father, or whoever, to make sure I stay in line, but I promise, I just want to talk to you."

He had that wounded look in his eyes again—those beautiful sparkling eyes that defied a color definition—and Brianya found it hard to resist him this time. "If I let you in to talk, will you leave me alone after this?"

"If you don't like what I say, then I'll never bother you again. I promise!"

"Move your foot," Brianya commanded him. "And take your hand off the door." Monty did as he was told and Brianya closed the door while she retrieved her phone from her purse. She texted Andre that she was having a conversation with Monty and if she didn't text him again from her phone in thirty minutes then he needed to get over there like yesterday. Then she locked her phone with her security code and sat it in the charging base on the hall table.

Brianya waited for the familiar chime to alert her of a new text message. Seconds later, she heard it and looked at the display to verify that it was Andre confirming he had received her message. She let Monty in.

"Can I get you something to drink?" Brianya asked, motioning Monty to the living room.

Monty sat on the first chair he saw and looked around. "Nah, I'm good," he said, his gaze falling on the 72-inch plasma TV. "You do some serious TV watching in here! Ever watch sports on that thing?"

"Only basketball."

Monty's eyes grew wide, and Brianya thought she would fall out, overwhelmed by their beauty. She knew what he was thinking. "Yeah, I saw you play a few times. You play a decent game, but you're a little weak on the defense." When Monty looked upset, Brianya countered with, "I'm just saying! In your last season, with the NBA, in that game against the Lakers, Kobe was wide open. All you had to do was post up and block him from the left. Everybody knows when he does that spin move, which way he's gonna turn. But instead of moving left, you moved right."

"Yeah, I could've done that, but then I woulda got a shooting foul and he woulda went to the free throw line and scored anyway."

"You don't know that he would've scored. The free throw is a crapshoot. So what that he's like 80 percent most of the time, there's still that 20 percent that he doesn't make."

"Oh, so what, you're a basketball coach now? How do you know so much about it anyway?" Monty said and laughed.

Brianya noted how hearty and genuine his laughter was. She liked that he didn't appear bothered by her criticism of his ball handling. "Oh, I know about some b-ball. I've been following that sport ever since I was old enough to bounce a basketball."

"Yeah? Hmmm . . . If my knee wasn't all torn up, I'd take you for a spin on the court."

Brianya assessed Monty and got up from the leather sofa. "I don't know about you, but I could use something to drink."

"What you got?"

"Orange, apple, cranberry, and grape juice; diet Pepsi, and homemade lemonade. Or would you prefer something harder."

"Let me see what kind of culinary skills you got. I'll take a glass of lemonade." Monty watched as Brianya limped toward the kitchen. "What's up with the limp?"

"Skating accident!"Brianya said over her shoulder. As she poured their drinks in the kitchen, she thought about the last time she had been in the company of Monty. It was two weeks before Darnell had broken up with her. He was one of the friends who had gotten too drunk to drive home so he'd spent the night at their condo. That next morning, Brianya lay in bed, hating to get up, disgusted that Darnell's friends had turned her place into a pigsty. After she had showered and gotten dressed, she was about to go out into the living room, when she overheard a conversation between Darnell and Monty.

"You need to handle your business, D!" Monty had whispered. "It ain't right what you doin'!"

"Oh, I'm gon' handle mine," Darnell had said. "You can believe that!"

Brianya had no idea what the conversation had been about, and she didn't know why all these years later, she would be thinking about it. She couldn't help wondering if the conversation had been about Darnell and the other woman. Thinking about it now, she remembered how upset Monty had sounded. As if he took what Darnell was doing personally. She wondered if he would tell her the truth if she asked him about it.

Brianya limped into the living room carrying a serving tray of hummus and pita chips with two ice-cold lemonades. Monty jumped up to help her. He took the tray and sat it down on the table.

"Wow, you didn't have to do this," he said appreciatively. "What is this anyway?" He was pointing to the hummus.

"That's hummus and these are pita chips. Ever had them before?"

"Pita chips, yes. Hummus, no." He made a face and stared at the bowl. "Looks like paste."

"Try it."

Monty reached for a pita chip and dipped it into the pasty concoction. "Not bad. I could get used to this."

"It's a little high in fat and sodium—if you use the full amount of salt. Otherwise, it's very nutritious." In an effort to eat healthier, Brianya watched her sodium and fat intake. And she made sure that eighty to ninety percent of the meals she ate were prepared at home.

"Did you make this or is it store bought?"

"Made it myself, with my own two hands! It's made from chickpeas, lemon juice, tahini, sea salt, garlic, and olive oil."

"I see," Monty said, reaching for another pita chip and scooping out a chunk of the hummus.

"Enough talk about food and sports," Brianya said. "Why were you persistent about talking to me?"

"Whoa. You just come right out with it, huh? I like that." Monty swallowed hard and Brianya could hear it from where she sat. "Well," he said taking a huge gulp of his lemonade. "You know, I didn't wanna disrespect what you and D had back in the day, or what me and my girl had, so I just kept my feelings to myself. But I always did think you were a classy lady. Too good for Darnell, to tell you the truth."

Brianya listened with interest and decided to ask about the conversation she'd overheard. "That morning that you and a couple of other friends stayed at our condo, I heard you and

Darnell having a conversation in the living room. You told him that he needed to handle his business. What was that all about?"

Monty looked confused. Brianya read in his facial expression that he remembered the conversation too. "Oh, that," he said, apparently unsure if he wanted to go down that road.

"Not that it matters," Brianya said, trying to fluff off her question, a little embarrassed that she had asked it in the first place.

"Naw, naw, it's not that," Monty reassured. "It just seems to me like this thing with Darnell is still raw with you and I don't want to pull out old skeletons."

"I'm totally over Darnell, but you're right, let's not pull out old skeletons. Just forget I asked. It's in the past, and what's in the past should stay there." Brianya checked her watch. It was one minute before the time she needed to text Andre to let him know that everything was cool. She excused herself and went to the retrieve her phone from the charging station to text Andre. When the familiar message chime sounded, Brianya locked the phone and let it finish charging. She turned to walk back to the sofa and almost jumped out of her skin when she saw Monty standing behind her.

"Excuse me. I didn't mean to startle you. May I use your bathroom?"

Brianya pointed him toward the half-bath off the kitchen and composed herself. She could add space-invader to the list of things that Monty was. With the strikes adding up, there was no way Brianya could see past them to give him a fair shot. Besides, she didn't like all the attention that he was showering upon her, as if she was someone special. She was just Brianya.

"You know, I think you deserve to know the truth, Brianya," Monty said re-entering the living room and sitting down. "I did know about D and that other woman. But I had just heard about it that night. I told him that if he didn't come clean to you then I would. He said that if I did, he would tell my girl that I was sweet on you. Since I was going through some things in my own relationship, I backed off. Then I thought about it again that morning and decided that I would take the risk. So I let him know again, that morning, that I thought what he was doing to you was foul and that he needed to correct the situation. And that's what you overheard."

Monty's eyes were full of regret as he told Brianya the facts. She stared at him, unable to find the words to convey her thoughts and felt a new humiliation wash over her, as if the years had done nothing to dull her pain.

Finding her voice, Brianya said, "So Darnell knew how you felt about me, and that didn't bother him?"

Monty looked away, unwilling to answer.

The room grew still and quiet.

"Look, it's in the past, right?" Monty said, breaking the silence. "You've moved on. Don't give him back that control, Brianya. He doesn't deserve it."

Monty fidgeted in his chair and Brianya could tell that he was resisting the urge to comfort her physically, although she really could use a hug.

"So you know my story," Brianya said, rallying back. "The other day on my doorstep, you said we both know what it feels like to have love unreciprocated. What's your sob story?"

Monty told her about the women who wanted to get close to him just because he was in the NBA, which, he acknowledged, was no big deal. It came with the territory. But the one he thought would be Mrs. Belvoir for sure, had crushed him almost to the point of no return. He looked uncomfortable by the admission. "I was so sprung that I gave her access to all but one of my money accounts. Got her credit cards in her name, paid for her to get her MBA. Even bought her a new car."

"No?!"

"Yeah, I did. I wasn't making nearly as much bank as the other ball players. I just knew how to invest what I had wisely. She almost cleaned me out. If it wasn't for my accountant getting suspicious about a lot of small, consistent withdrawals, I would be asking you if you wanted to supersize that order at Mickey D's."

"That's deep!"

"Yeah, but you know what really blew my mind?"

Brianya didn't have a clue.

"All the while I was head-trippin', I kept thinking about you and how real you are, and down to earth. And how I shoulda let D tell my girl about how I felt about you. And wondering if I had lost my shot at you. Then I heard you had lost all that weight and I gotta admit I was a little worried."

"Oh, you had heard the rumors, too?"

"Rumors? Nah, I hadn't heard any rumors. I was worried that losing the weight might have changed you."

Brianya was having trouble taking this all in. How could she have been this wrong about someone? He clearly was not the Monty that she had known. Time had mellowed him and experience had matured him. She didn't know what to make of his statements.

Intrigued, she said, "Changed me how?"

"Changed you like maybe you wouldn't be that same sweet, loving person that I knew."

"Oh . . . I see," she said, her mouth turned downward. "So, have I changed?"

"Well, let me put it like this: You're in hiding, but I know you're in there.

"What does that mean?" she said, attitude at the ready.

"Pulling knives, threatening to do bodily harm. That sort of stuff. I remember you as all sweetness. That's all I meant."

"Hmmm . . . You're right I'm still in here, but I'm older and a whole lot wiser. And I'm not gonna just give my goodness away to the first joker that comes my way saying all the right words. It's a new day and I got a new playbook. If you can't play by rules, then you don't play at all."

"I like the way that sounds," Monty said, assessing Brianya's curves. "So what are your rules?"

"One in particular: You don't get the candy until you buy the store."

CHAPTER EIGHT

THE ELEVATOR DOORS opened and Brianya stepped in. She was feeling ill-at-ease about sitting in on the meeting with Marlon Taylor. She had insisted that is wasn't necessary for her to be there, but Hamfred Larson the CEO had insisted that all parties involved in the pilot program be present. Brianya was lost in thought when the elevator doors, which had barely closed, were forced open again. In walked Ed Hollister, a beautiful sight to behold.

"Morning, Ms. Johnson," Ed said and before Brianya could reply Celine and Marlon joined them, holding hands.

Despite her personal opinions, Brianya spoke to the couple and remained professional on the ride up to the fifth floor. Against Brianya's protestations, Celine had decided to give Marlon a chance and let the chips fall wherever. She couldn't hide behind a bad relationship forever, she'd said.

"But you know his reputation," Brianya had warned. "He hasn't changed. If anything he's gotten more cocky."

"How do you know that?" Celine had asked defensively. "You said you haven't seen or heard anything about him until the day of the fundraiser."

How could Brianya explain that it was something she felt deep inside that made her sure that Marlon hadn't changed without sounding like a cuckoo? "I told you what he said to me that day." Her words had sounded weak. "Someone who's changed wouldn't have said the things he said to me."

Celine had agreed, but told Brianya that they had two different situations and that what went on between the two of them was their problem, not hers. "I know you don't want to see me get hurt, Bri, and I respect and appreciate that. But life is too short to live it on the sidelines. I'm ready to stake my claim and take my chances. I'd like to know that you're there for me if I need you."

Brianya hadn't wanted to say, "Yeah. Sure," but she did, ever reluctant, and Celine knew it. Now almost three weeks later they were acting like lovesick teenagers. Brianya felt sick to her stomach.

"I'll see you for lunch," Brianya told Celine, stepping out of the elevator.

"Not today, sorry. Marlon's taking me to lunch."

Without turning around, Brianya acknowledged the comment with a wave of her hand.

It was only eight o'clock and Brianya's meeting wasn't until nine. She'd use the extra time to go over the job description for the thousandth time, making sure that she covered all the bases, especially since Marlon was the person who would initially start the program.

"Excuse me, Ms. Johnson," a voice from behind her said. "I'm free for lunch today."

Brianya turned abruptly at the sound of the familiar voice. She hadn't noticed Ed exit the elevator with her.

"You never returned my phone call." Ed was apologetic; though what he had to apologize for Brianya didn't know.

"You're right. I didn't."

Ed waited for more, but Brianya said nothing. "So——?"

When Brianya still didn't elaborate, Ed started to walk away. "Look, Brianya," he said turning back. "I think you're a fascinating and beautiful woman, who got the raw end of the deal a few years back. I can't speak for all men, but I can certainly speak for myself: I would never have treated you that way, and I apologize for all the knuckleheads out there who're like your ex. But that's in the past. As for the present, I want to get to know you, spend time with you. I'm not into playing games; I'm too old for that. And even when I was a younger man, I didn't go in for that sort of thing. I think people should say what they mean. If you think I'm someone you can stand to be around and you want to get to know me better, too, then what's the harm in getting a bite to eat?"

"Wow. What can I say to that?" Actually, there was something she could say, but she hesitated to put the question to him. Deciding that there was no time like the present, she laid it all out on the table. "Let me ask you this, Ed: Where were you when I was 353 pounds? I can't recall one time that you showed any interest in me before I lost the weight. Now, all of a sudden I'm fascinating and beautiful and you feel the need to apologize to me for the behavior of someone that you don't even know."

Ed gave a look of surprise, but otherwise seemed to take the comment in stride. "You want the truth?" he asked as though it was a challenge.

"I'm a big girl—no pun intended," Brianya said smiling.

"First, I was married. Second, I don't date fat women."

"Excuse me?!"

"I'm not trying to be insulting or anything like that. But the fact is, I take care of my body and my health. That's the kind of woman that appeals to me. Don't get me wrong, you're just as beautiful now as you were at whatever weight you were, but now that your health and your weight are a priority to you, I'm physically attracted to you. I know you work out, because I've seen you at the gym, and I assume you're eating better because exercise alone can't give you the sort of glow you've been sporting over the last year."

Brianya's cheeks grew hot but she managed to maintain her cool. She wanted to blast Ed for his comment about not dating fat women, but what argument could she make? His comment assumed that *all* heavy-set women were unhealthy and didn't work out, which Brianya knew to be untrue. Even at her old weight, she was more active and limber than some women half her size. True, her choice of food could have used an overhaul. *Humph,* Brianya thought. *Let's face it, if I was active* and *making all the right food choices, I never would have ballooned up to 353 pounds in the first place.* She had to respect the fact that not to date fat women was Ed's right and his preference, just as it was her preference not to date men who had been in prison. Even still, the comment rubbed her raw.

Ed was right in one respect: Brianya's improved complexion was a direct result of her making better food choices. She ate meat only once a week, very little, if any, dairy, and she'd increased her Omega-3 intake. He had really been paying attention. A little too much attention, maybe. And that comment about the gym concerned her.

"When have you seen me at the gym?"

"I go there sometimes on Sunday mornings if I didn't get a chance to go on Saturday. As a matter of fact, I saw you there a few Sundays back, the weekend of your company's fundraiser."

"Hmmm . . ."

They stood in the hallway outside Brianya's office talking for another fifteen minutes and in the end Brianya ended up saying yes to a lunch date.

With only fifteen minutes before the meeting, Brianya decided to use the time to meditate and cleanse her mind of the negative thoughts that had crept in as a result of the upcoming proceedings.

Eleven people sat around the rectangular table in the conference room, hammering out the details of Marlon Taylor's Former Employee Franchise Pilot Program contract and putting the final touches on a deal that Brianya felt uneasy about. She wanted to strangle Hamfred Larson, shake some sense into the man. But, short of losing her mind, there was no way to explain that type of behavior. So she bit her tongue, checked her anger, wishing this fiasco was over and she could get back to productive work. Brianya caught a glimpse of Marlon's expression just before he signed the contract and she could swear that she saw him sneer at her. She was instantly on alert and made a mental note to make certain that every I was dotted, every T crossed whenever he submitted paperwork.

The meeting went longer than Brianya had expected. It was five after twelve and she had just enough time to rush back to her office, use the restroom, and grab her purse.

"Mr. Hollister called from MacDonald investments," Debbie announced as Brianya rushed past her desk. "He said he's running about 20 minutes behind and if you didn't want to wait to call him to reschedule; otherwise, he'll meet you at the restaurant." Debbie gave Brianya a questioning look and appeared to debate fishing for information. "I know this is none of my business, Brianya, but I'm glad you're finally going out with Mr. Hollister."

"And why is that?"

"Well, because he's older. I think women who got it going on and who make top salary need a man who's mature enough to handle that."

"Four years isn't that much of an age difference, Debbie." Maybe her secretary was right. Maybe those four years could make a difference.

"Well, yeah. But he's also in your league." Debbie pulled out a nail file and began filing her nails, a nervous habit of hers whenever she spoke candidly to her boss.

"Well, it's just a lunch. So don't go getting your hopes up," Brianya said, heading for her office.

"Um hmm," Debbie said, smiling conspiratorially. "It's gotta start somewhere."

Brianya hadn't been in her office five minutes before Debbie knocked on her door and stuck her head in. "I forgot to tell you that Darnell Jones stopped by while you were in your meeting. He said you guys went way back and that he was on his way to a meeting on the 12th floor and just dropped by to say hello."

"What time was that?"

"Around ten. Hey, maybe he's almost done and he'll come back before you leave for lunch," Debbie said innocently, obviously unaware of who Darnell was.

Brianya ignored the comment. "The next time he comes, call security."

"Now why would she do that?" said a voice from behind Debbie. Debbie, looking startled, let out a scream. "Sorry, I didn't mean to scare you," the man said.

Debbie looked embarrassed and scampered back to her desk.

Brianya would know that voice anywhere. When Darnell stepped out of the shadows and into Brianya's office, the look on his face was priceless. He opened his mouth to speak but no words came out. The saying about living well being the best revenge crossed Brianya's mind and she felt the full weight of its meaning as she savored Darnell's shocked expression. Darnell, on the other hand, except for not being bald anymore, hadn't changed at all.

Her voice shook when she spoke and a flood of emotion came rushing to the fore as she tried to maintain her composure. "Evidently, I didn't make myself clear the last time we spoke when I told you to stay out of my life."

"Wow!" he said, ignoring Brianya's flippant remark.

"Get out before I call security." She reached for the telephone.

"Wow!" Darnell said again. He assessed Brianya from head to toe. "Bri, baby, *you look good!*"

Brianya picked up the telephone and dialed the first three digits of the security office.

"Okay, okay, okay, Bri." Darnell moved to the desk and pressed the button before she could dial the last digit. Brianya snatched her hand away but not before Darnell's fingers lightly brushed the back of her hand. "I don't know what I was expecting but obviously it wasn't this. I mean, I heard in the wind how you had dropped a couple of pounds, but. . . . Umph, umph, umph! *Girl*, you look good!"

Brianya heard the words but they didn't fully register because her mind was still processing the touch. It was strange how something as inconsequential as a whisper of a touch could have such a huge impact. She rubbed her hand down the side of her skirt and tried to mask her feelings in a nonchalant expression that she wasn't totally committed to.

"I hope you haven't eaten yet because I want to take you to lunch."

"Again, apparently I didn't make myself clear enough the last time you called."

"No, you were clear. But I'm not taking no for an answer." He let out a breath. "I know that what I did devastated you. I was wrong, no two ways about it. All I can say is that I was a different person back then. My head wasn't on straight. I took our relationship for granted; I took you for granted. I can understand if you're not feeling me right now, Bri. But I want to make it up to you. I want to show you that I'm a changed man. You know, I got some real promising things in the works and I want you to be a part of that." Darnell moved to where Brianya stood on the other side of the desk. "I owe you that, Bri, for being there for me when nobody else was." He stroked the side of her face with the back of his hand. "I love you, Anya. Always have. Always will. Please accept my apology," Darnell begged.

Brianya stepped back, out of Darnell's reach and leveled a look of incredulity at him. "Are you serious? Really? Look, I don't have time for you or your pitiful apology, which, by the way, was unnecessary. I'm so over you, like yesterday. Take your tired behind out of my office and out of my life and leave me and my family alone. Or the next person I call won't be security!"

CHAPTER NINE

SITTING ACROSS FROM Ed at the Au Grill Restaurant inside the Holiday Inn hotel on Lakeside, Brianya tried hard to concentrate on Ed's words, but the confrontation with Darnell had shaken her.

"You seem distracted, Brianya," Ed said, spearing a chunk of chicken with his fork. "Everything okay?"

"Yep." She took a swig of unsweetened ice tea. "I had an unexpected visitor after my meeting today, that's all." Brianya felt she owed Ed an explanation but she didn't want to get into a full-blown conversation about it.

"Well, whoever it was must have really got into your head because you've barely said two words since we got here. You could have cancelled; I would have understood."

"What, and miss out on a free meal? You must not know me," Brianya teased, feeling more in the moment.

Ed laughed and she noticed a small chip in his bottom tooth. She smiled thoughtfully at Ed and asked for the story behind the chip.

Ed looked slightly embarrassed. "A minor disagreement that's all."

Sensing that he didn't want to talk about it, Brianya pushed. "How minor?"

Ed appeared to contemplate a reply then turned the conversation back on Brianya "So, who was it that came to your office and upset you?"

Brianya laughed and sorted through her Caesar salad for a chunk of cheese. "Okay, I get it."

"Good. So, tell me, Brianya, how do you like to spend your weekends?"

"I'm sort of a homebody. But not lately. I've been volunteering at the Rape Crisis Center, manning the hotline on the Saturday mornings that I'm not volunteering at the Domestic Violence Center."

"I'm impressed! I take my hat off to you. I think what you're doing is a beautiful thing." Ed had stopped speaking and stared at Brianya. "When I was in high school, I dated a girl who had to use the services of the RCC."

Brianya noted that Ed used the acronym instead of the name. It wasn't unusual; some people found it difficult to say the word rape, particularly victims, or even those close to them. "I'm not prying," Brianya said apologetically, "but I noticed you used the acronym, RCC."

Ed's face went dark and his lips became a thin line. "Yeah."

Brianya waited for him to say more. After a full two minutes had passed, she realized that Ed wasn't going to say more. Should she be worried that this man, who was interested in her, might be a rapist? Anything was possible. He didn't look like a rapist. Although she knew better than to think that, she couldn't help it. There was no "stereotypical" look. If there were, at least she would have something, as erroneous as it might be, by which to judge. The correct course of action, she knew, would be to ask Ed. Oh sure, he'd tell her truth. Brianya imagined the conversation:

Ed, are you a rapist?

Look at me. Do I look like someone who has to resort to that *to get sex?! The friend that I mentioned called the RCC after we had* consensual *sex, claiming that I raped her. Oh, sure, her mouth was saying no, but I could tell that she wanted it by the way she always dressed. Plus, she never complained when I felt her up.*

Ed was staring at Brianya expectantly. "I'm sorry, did you say something?" She kicked herself mentally. Had she missed his explanation about the use of the acronym? She had to stop zoning out.

"It was nothing," Ed said.

Dang! Brianya thought. *I missed his explanation.* She had to find out before they left the restaurant. Brianya liked Ed; so far, he seemed like a stand-up sort of man. She was looking forward to getting to know him better. But there was no way she was going to be able to do that if she didn't find out the story behind his reluctance to say the words Rape Crisis Center. Brianya mentally dug into her bag of tricks and pulled out the sympathy card.

"I can imagine that it was difficult for your friend to make that call." Brianya let the corners of her mouth fall a bit and held Ed's gaze, hoping he'd take the bait. "I don't care how long I help man the phones; I'll never get used to the despair and fear I hear in a woman's voice when she admits to having been violated. Especially if it occurred at the hands of someone she trusted." Brianya meant every word. She just hoped it was enough to coax Ed into revealing whatever truth lay behind his resistance.

Ed fixed his gaze on the space beyond Brianya, his visage set hard as stone in a mask of revulsion. Brianya instantly regretted pushing the subject. Her voice was small and calm when she spoke, careful not to anger him any further. "I didn't mean to upset you. I'm sorry." Her heart beat a mile a minute. "If you don't mind, I'm going to head back to the office." She made to rise. "I enjoyed lunch. Thank you."

"No, no. You haven't upset me. Please, sit back down" Ed said in a rush. "I haven't thought about that young lady in a long time. I used to keep in touch, but a few years back we lost contact."

Brianya hesitated before sitting down. She may as well stay and hear Ed's answer; after all, that is why she'd asked.

Ed's features softened around the edges. "I was a typical seventeen year-old boy, always looking for the fast girls, who'd let me get to home base. I had been badgering her to go all the way and she kept turning me down. I couldn't believe it." Ed shook his head. "I mean, everybody knew she wasn't a virgin; she was on birth control according to her best friend. She had been with almost every senior in the school, and she was telling me no? Of course, my seventeen-year-old ego was not about to accept no for an answer." When Ed lifted his water glass to take a sip, Brianya noticed a slight tremble in his hand.

"So the night of homecoming, we were all sitting at the top of the bleachers and I called her out." As difficult as it was for Brianya, she remained silent and let Ed tell his story. "She was sitting next to two of my friends who said she had slept with them. So I said to her, 'Oh, so you gave it up to Jay and Isaiah, but I ask and all of a sudden you're a virgin?'" Ed let out a sigh. "It's funny how the conscience works. As soon as I said that, I regretted it. If you could have seen the look on her face."

"I can imagine," Brianya said unable to keep quiet any longer. "You really *should* have been ashamed of yourself. That was cruel and uncalled for."

Ed nodded in agreement. "Oh, you don't have to tell me. We broke up that night and every time I tried to call her to apologize, she wouldn't take my call. She even had her friends lie to me and tell me that she had tried to commit suicide and her parents were transferring her to a new school."

Now it was Brianya's turn to harden her face and shake her head. Even though all of that had happened over twenty years ago, Brianya's opinion of Ed had changed. She had known boys like him in high school. They were the type that thought that every girl should fall at their feet and worship them just because they were popular and handsome. She abhorred boys like that. They usually grew up to be men who never stopped thinking they were God's gift to the world. Brianya had heard enough. She no longer cared why Ed couldn't or wouldn't say the words Rape Crisis Center. He'd said plenty of words already, none of them worth listening to anymore. He was probably deriving some perverse pleasure in retelling the story of how he humiliated some troubled young girl into trying to take her own life. Brianya had already given Ed too much of her ear. It was time to go. First, she had to let him know what she thought of him. He was a pompous, arrogant, small, insignificant man who needed to be put in his place.

Before Brianya could open her mouth to call down fire and damnation on Ed, he said, "Finally, I said forget the telephone, and I went to her house. It was awkward at first, because I had never apologized to anyone before. And I had never seen a girl cry. She admitted that she did try to commit suicide, but not because of anything I'd done. She confessed that her stepfather had been molesting her since she was five years old. That's why she was on birth control pills. He made her get them so she wouldn't get pregnant." Ed ran his hands over his mouth.

Brianya's mouth gaped open and her eyes went wide with shock. So taken aback was she that she couldn't speak. She hadn't seen that coming.

"I couldn't talk her into going to the police, but she did agree to call the RCC hotline," Ed continued. "You know what's weird?" He didn't wait for an answer. "Till this day, I can't bring myself to say that word. It's an ugly word and an even uglier act."

"Wow!"

"We became good friends after that. Her mother didn't believe her when she told her, so she ended up going into foster care for about a year, until she turned eighteen. I used to keep up with her, but around five years ago, she moved out of the U.S. and we lost touch." Ed looked thoughtful. "So, if you ever doubt that what you're doing by answering those telephones is making a difference, just remember my friend. Because of the volunteer who was on the other end of that phone line, a young lady was able to be free of a horrible situation, and she's out there making a difference in other young people's lives by advocating for teens."

Brianya's eyes became moist and she turned her head and dabbed at them with her napkin.

"I didn't mean to get heavy on you," Ed said. "I wanted you to know that what you're doing in your volunteer work is important." Ed smiled. "Okay, now, let's lighten the mood around here."

Relieved for a change in subject, Brianya asked, "So, how do you spend your weekends?" She wasn't sure if he had mentioned it earlier.

"Well, like I said *before*," Ed said and smiled. "I'm usually working. But on those rare occasions when I'm not, I'm at my mom's house making whatever repairs she needs."

"Sorry," Brianya apologized. "I guess I wasn't paying attention the first time."

"No problem. So . . . maybe one of these Saturday's we can get together and just hang out."

"We'll see," Brianya said. "You got my number."

"Cool." Ed smiled and looked curiously at Brianya. "Now that we've got all that heavy, awkward stuff out of the way, let me ask you this: Have you fine-tuned your portfolio lately?"

They both burst out laughing because that was the McDonald Investment firm's slogan. All kidding aside, Ed said, Brianya was long overdue for a reexamination of her retirement account.

***

"Did he really say the company slogan to you?" Celine asked when Brianya filled her in on her lunch date with Ed.

"He did, but it was at the end of lunch and we needed to change the mood." Trying to do several things at once was proving impossible as Brianya tripped over the grocery bags she'd placed on the floor. On her way home from work, she'd stopped at Trader Joe's for a few items.

"So, what do you think? Is he dateable?"

"Dateable? Who says that?"

"You know what I mean," Celine said and laughed.

Brianya kicked the back door shut and started putting away groceries. "If you mean is he relationship material, then yeah, I guess so." She moved items around in the freezer to make room for the black bean burgers she'd bought. Staring absentmindedly into the freezer before closing the door, Brianya asked, "How well do you know Ed?"

"We go back about five years. Why?"

The caution in Celine's tone worried Brianya. "It's nothing, probably. But I mentioned my volunteer work with the Rape Crisis Center and he told me about someone that he used to date having to call the Center, only he used the acronym instead of the words. Then he told me the story about his friend and said that's why he couldn't say the word rape. He ever tell you that story?" For the rest of the day, Brianya had kept going back and forth on whether to believe Ed. It sounded real enough, but then some people were so adept at lying that they could make anything sound real.

Celine seemed to hesitate then answered. "I know all about that, but not through Ed. Tammy is a mutual friend. When I was looking for a keynote speaker for a friend who hosts a ladies day luncheon every year, Ed introduced me to Tammy. She spoke about her experience at the luncheon."

"Well, it's good to know that he was telling the truth and not just trying to score sympathy points. So, what do you know about his chipped tooth?"

Celine laughed. "You're on your own on that one. I asked about it and he shut completely down."

An awkward silence followed Celine's comment and Brianya knew that Celine was hesitating about talking to her about Marlon. As much as she wanted to be that supportive rah-rah girlfriend, Brianya couldn't bring herself to accept that Marlon had changed the way Celine believed he had. Leopards and ducks and all, a zebra couldn't change its stripes. In the spirit of true friendship, Brianya couldn't expect Celine to be there for her and be supportive in her dating efforts, if she wasn't willing to do the same. She swallowed her concerns and reluctantly asked how things were with Celine and Marlon.

Celine beamed. "I was hoping you would ask me about him, girl! Things couldn't be better. Bri, I know you don't believe he's changed but he has. He's really looking forward to doing business with Mellow Beans and the nightclub venture with his frat brothers. He even said he felt bad about the words y'all had at the fundraiser."

Brianya rolled her eyes. "Hmph!"

"Okay, forget it! I can't talk to you. No matter what I say about him, you gotta be all negative about it."

"You're right," Brianya said unapologetically.

"Okay then let's do this, you don't mention anything to me about the men in your life and I won't mention anything to you about Marlon. How 'bout that?" Celine said sarcastically.

"Deal!" Brianya agreed.

CHAPTER TEN

WHY SHE HAD agreed to that stupid ultimatum Brianya didn't know. Right now, she could use some sister-friend advice about tonight's date with Ed from someone who knew him. She could call Celine on the pretense that she needed her opinion about what to wear on a date without telling her who the date was with and hope that she would push for details. That way, it would be Celine who was doing the asking and not the other way around.

Brianya hit the speed dial number that would call Celine's cell and got her voicemail. She didn't leave a message. In desperation, she tried Dreama's number and got the same response. What was with everyone? It was just Wednesday night, not like a weekend when she'd half expect not to get anyone.

As a last resort, she dialed Cashmere's number. A nervous tremor wriggled inside her. Brianya didn't yet know how she felt about Cashmere's situation. Knowing that her friend's dating days were over, Brianya didn't want to draw unnecessary attention to that fact by asking her for dating advice. It seemed cruel in a way. She wouldn't bring up the subject; she'd let the conversation take its natural course and if the subject of dating came up she'd ask for Cashmere's opinion on what to do about this question mark that hung over her head concerning Ed.

Cashmere breathed a winded greeting into the telephone.

"Did I catch you at a bad time?" Brianya asked curiously.

"No. I was just finishing up my cool-down from my workout. Twenty-eight . . . twenty-nine . . . thirty."

"I'll call you later," Brianya said on a sigh. She'd struck out again.

"No, it's okay, I can talk. One . . . two . . . three."

Desperate, Brianya took what she could get. "Are you sure?"

"Nine . . . ten . . . eleven. I'm sure. Thirteen . . . fourteen . . . fifteen. What's up? Seventeen . . .eighteen . . . nineteen."

"You were on my mind so I thought I'd call to say hello and see how you're doing."

"Twenty-eight . . . twenty-nine . . . thirty. Done!" Cashmere let out a loud breath of air. On the other end of the phone, Brianya could hear the crackling sound of a plastic bottle being squeezed. "I'm good. Nothing much happening my way. Just trying to keep myself in good health. Well . . . you know. Under the circumstances. What about you, anything new?"

Brianya's eyes moistened and she swallowed to relieve some of the dryness in her mouth. "Actually, something is new. I took your advice and decided to just go with the flow." She told Cashmere about her date with Endo and how Monty had showed up that same night. And about Darnell's visit to her office and finally about her date with Ed.

"So, tonight I'm going on a second date with him—Ed, not Endo. Endo is next weekend."

"Dang, girl! You have been busy! You need to tell me your secret."

Brianya laughed nervously. "*I* don't even know what the secret is. I'm just being me." Brianya thought a second. "You know what? I never expected all of this attention. I'm not comfortable with it."

"Really? Why not; what did you expect?"

"At first, all I could think about was getting revenge for the way Darnell treated me. I wanted him to see how good I looked and to come crawling back, begging forgiveness for the way he treated me. Then as more and more of the weight started coming off, I noticed that I was feeling powerful for the first time in my life and I liked that feeling. It felt good being in control. I can't even begin to tell you how powerless I felt after the breakup—all my life really." She sighed. "The breakup was just the catalyst that got me to the point where I was finally forced to confront feelings that I never allowed to the surface. When I realized that I was gaining control by confronting my issues with food—that I even had issues—I never wanted to lose that control again. But this attention that I'm getting from men. . . . Honestly, Cash, I don't know if I can handle that." Brianya bit the inside of her lower lip. She had never shared her private concerns about the weight loss, not even with Dreama. It left her feeling exposed. It also felt wrong that she should burden someone (other than a professional) with her feelings.

"Wow, you said a mouthful. That's what I get for asking," Cashmere said jokingly and laughed. "Are you gonna be around in the next twenty minutes? I need to shower before all the hot water is gone. We'll pick up where we left off when I call you back."

Brianya's brows furrowed. "Oh. Uh, sure. No problem. Ed won't be here until 7:30."

When they hung up, Brianya scolded herself for being so insensitive. There she was going on about her dates and all the attention she was getting from men and how she couldn't deal with it and poor Cashmere's dating days were over. She made a mental note to apologize to Cashmere when she called back. Besides, Cashmere had her own problems. Why she should care about anyone else's?

Brianya jumped in the shower herself while she waited. At least she'd have that out of the way. There was more than enough time for her to get ready; it was only 6:00. Last night, she'd chosen what to wear and laid out her accessories. The only thing left to do after her shower was to freshen up her hair with a few bumps from her curling iron and reapply her make-up.

When Brianya opened the door to Ed a little before 7:30, her heart was heavy. Cashmere hadn't phoned back and Brianya felt awful for upsetting her.

"I need to check something," Brianya said to Ed after they'd greeted each other. "I'll be right back and then we can go." She grabbed her purse off the hall table and headed upstairs.

Brianya sat on the foot of the queen size bed in the guest room and breathed deeply trying not to let the tears at the base of her throat fall from her eyes. Just then, somewhere in the cavern of her purse, she heard the familiar jangle of her cell phone. She answered it just to quiet it from ringing again in case Ed could hear it and think she was doing God knew what.

"Hello," she whispered into the telephone.

"Why are you whispering?" Cashmere asked.

"Cash!" Brianya said excitedly. "You called back."

"Are you okay? I said I would call you back. I'm sorry I didn't call when I said I would. I got caught up in a conversation with one of the trainers at the gym. You know how that is. I'm just trying to be like you, girl!"

Brianya laughed, relieved. "I thought you hadn't called back because I had upset you."

"Upset me? How?"

"You know. . . ."

Dead silence hung in the air and it was seconds before Cashmere realized what Brianya meant. "Oh, that! Girl, look, my situation being what it is don't stop nothing. I have yet to get to the point where I've had to have *that* conversation. Shoot, when they find out I'm celibate that news alone usually sends them packing."

The tears long forgotten, Brianya laughed out loud then clamped her hands over her mouth. "I wish I had time to talk to you, but Ed's here," she whispered.

"No problem. Actually, I was expecting to get your voicemail and I was gonna tell you to call me when you got in, if it wasn't too late. I usually go to bed around eleven-thirty or twelve. I wanted to finish our earlier conversation."

Brianya hurried downstairs after hanging up with Cashmere. Although only six minutes had passed, it felt longer.

"Must have been an important phone call," Ed said mischievously as Brianya came down the stairs.

"Sorry. That was a friend that I'm getting reacquainted with. But that's not why I went upstairs," she explained.

Ed feigned a wounded expression. "I'm just messing with you. It's cool."

"Glad to have your permission," Brianya teased. She didn't bother to explain that the friend was female. "So, how was your day?" she asked.

"Better now that I'm in the company of a beautiful woman."

Brianya rolled her eyes and smacked her lips. "Flatterer!" she said steering Ed toward the door. "Let's go." On the way out, she dimmed the living room lights and set the alarm.

"So, this is what financial wizards are driving these days," Brianya said as she situated herself on the plush leather of Ed's Mercedes.

"What did you think I'd be driving, a station wagon?" Ed said playfully, preparing to close the passenger-side door.

"Actually, no. This is just the sort of vehicle I pictured you driving."

"Glad I didn't disappoint." Ed put the key in the ignition and turned to look at Brianya. He appeared to weigh his words before speaking. "Do you mind if I ask you a question?"

"Hmmm . . . that depends," Brianya said.

"On what?"

"On whether or not you mind if I choose not to answer."

Ed chuckled. "Well, that's always your prerogative."

"Well?" Brianya said.

"Sorry. I didn't know if that was a yes or a no." Ed looked concerned. "The other day in the elevator, I got the feeling that there's some bad blood between you and that guy who was with Celine. Am I right?" He shifted the car out of park and pulled out of the driveway.

Brianya blew a gust of air from her nostrils. She did *not* want to talk about Marlon. She now regretted that she'd been so public with her dislike for him. Brianya explained the history between she and Marlon and what had happened at the fundraiser. When she finished talking, Ed was frowning.

Ed reached over and touched Brianya's hand. "When I was around five years old, my mother made me and my brother Lazlo take Taekwondo classes. I got all the way to black belt level, which means I'm very skilled in the techniques of Taekwondo. Even though I don't keep up with my training the way I used to, I can still put a hurting on a body, if it comes to that."

"I can take care of myself!" Brianya blurted out without thinking. Not another man who thought she needed protecting. That aspect of her life was becoming comical. First her dad, then Andre, now Ed? It was both reassuring and annoying at the same time. "Look, I'm sorry, Ed, I didn't mean for it to come out like that. But I've already got two men in my life who think I'm some helpless damsel. But that's not what I need. What I need is to have someone to just hang out with and not feel like I'm this wounded little kitten who needs protecting."

Ed pulled his hand away. "I hear you, but I'm just saying. That's all."

"Yeah, I know and I appreciate it. I do. But for right now, let's just concentrate on getting to know one another."

CHAPTER ELEVEN

"YOU CAN FORGET about seeing either one of them again," Dreama said to Brianya as she worked the shampoo into lather and massaged Brianya's scalp.

Brianya had filled Dreama in on her visit from Monty and her midweek date with Ed. As usual, Dreama shot straight from the hip. Brianya relaxed and enjoyed the rhythmic way Dreama's fingers danced across her scalp. Normally, Dreama didn't shampoo her clients, but Brianya refused to let anyone but Dreama touch her hair. "I don't really care about Monty, because I don't think I could look at him and not think about my life with Darnell. But Ed, I think he can appreciate where I'm coming from."

Dreama's shop, always packed on Saturday mornings, overflowed with clients waiting to occupy the chairs of some of the hottest stylists in Cleveland. For five consecutive years, Tender Lovin' Locks had won the Curling Iron Award (CIA) and along with it, more clients than the shop could reasonably handle. Between the six stylists and four nail techs, they could barely manage the workload today. And it was a miracle that Dreama could find time to fit Brianya in for a relaxer and trim. Today was her theater date with Endo and although she wasn't really feeling him, Brianya wasn't about to be seen out on a date looking tore up.

"Believe me, girl, ain't no man trying to be with somebody who won't give up the goodies. Let me say that another way: ain't no *fine* man, trying to be with somebody who won't give up the goodies. Is he fine, girl?" Dreama applied conditioner to Brianya's hair and covered it with a plastic cap.

Some of the women at the nearby shampoo bowls threw curious glances in Brianya and Dreama's direction. One of the stylists, looked at Dreama, shook her head and rolled her eyes playfully.

Brianya gave Dreama a look that was meant to question her intelligence and the two women burst out laughing.

"Be right back. Let me check on my other client," Dreama said still laughing as she walked away.

Brianya thought about the conversation she and Ed had had while they ate dinner Wednesday night. When she had asked Ed why his marriage had failed, Brianya was taken aback by his honesty. She knew few men who would admit their personal failings and those that did usually shifted the greater amount of blame to the woman or something else that was out of their control.

"I was a knucklehead. I wasn't taking care of business, no two ways about it. My wife would tell me all the time that I needed to pay more attention to her, make her feel like a woman. But I dismissed it. Figured it was just the hormones talking, you know, 'that time of month.' I kept right on doing what I was doing—giving her money, buying her things. One day I looked up and she was serving me with divorce papers—on the grounds of extreme cruelty and gross neglect of duty." A wistful expression had crossed Ed's face. "She was right. What I had done was cruel."

"I've never been married, but I do know the feeling of failure, especially a failure that could have been prevented," Brianya admitted.

"What do you mean?" Ed asked curiously.

"Well," Brianya said, hating that she had opened this can of worms, wishing she could change the subject. "The last relationship I was in, I saw the red flags, but I ignored them. He used to make jokes about my weight and size to his friends and to my face, and I would laugh right along with them. If he was on the phone, he would hang up real quick when I walked into the room. He even stayed gone all night a couple of times. I let it all slide because I was on a mission. I wanted to be married so badly that I allowed him to disrespect me, even helped him. My second mistake, which, by the way, I will never do again, was to move in with someone I wasn't married to."

"What was your first mistake?" Ed had asked, curious.

"Giving away the prize to someone who wasn't willing to play the game."

Ed placed his fork on the table and looked contemplative. "Does that mean what I think it does?"

Brianya nodded, looking him in the eye. "It does." The ensuing quietness magnified the restaurant noises as Brianya waited for Ed's reaction.

"I admire a woman with principles," Ed had said. But to Brianya it looked as if his interest in her had fallen a notch.

"Unscrew your face, girl, and lean back so I can wash this conditioner out of your hair," Dreama said, bringing Brianya back to the present. "So are you ready for this date with Endo tonight?"

"About as ready as I'm going to be. Did I tell you that he suggested we wear the same colors?"

Dreama guffawed and splashed a small amount of water in Brianya's face. "Sorry, Bri," she said, grabbing a towel and mopping away the water. "He is definitely the one I want you to get with! I swear, Bri. That sounds like some crazy mess you would come up with."

Brianya didn't see the humor but she couldn't help laughing anyway. She had to admit that Dreama was right. She could be corny at times.

***

"So what did you think?" Endo asked, as they moved with the crowd toward the theater exit.

"Honestly, I didn't know how I would feel about the modern version; I've only seen it done in full Shakespearean costume. But

I liked it. And I thought the actor who played Petruchio was fantastic!"

"Well, I'm glad you liked it." Endo licked his lips and scratched his chin. "Look, Brianya, I'm just gonna come out and say this. I really like you. I know I'm a little older than you, but I can make you happy. I'm stable. I got a good job. I don't have any baggage. No ex-wife, no baby mama drama. None of that typical stuff that someone my age would usually have. If you give me a chance, I can show you how right we are for each other."

They stepped out of the theater onto the street and Brianya breathed in a mouthful of cool air. "Wow! You just put it all out there." Brianya jammed her hands into her coat pockets and stared at Endo. "I'm sorry, but I can't respond to that right now."

A strong gust of air blew up the back of Endo's cashmere coat, causing him to shudder involuntarily. He cupped his hands together and blew into them before rapidly rubbing them together. They walked in silence until they reached the lot where they'd parked.

"Just think about it," Endo said after starting the engine.

They rode in silence for a while.

"I don't want to hurt your feelings, Endo," Brianya finally said. "But the truth is, you're nice and sweet and I'm sure you'll make some woman very happy, but I'm just not sure that I'm that woman." What was she saying? Goofiness aside, he was just the type of man she was looking for. He had no children. No ex-wife. Had never been incarcerated. So what he was a little older. That's probably what she needed. The men her age were all about games, and most of them had tons of baggage. Okay, so Endo was the *sensible* choice, but Brianya didn't feel anything for him. No fireworks went off; butterflies didn't flitter in the pit of her stomach when she looked at him.

"I understand," Endo said. "So let me ask you this: Why do you think you're not that woman?"

That was an odd question. She hesitated before answering. "Because. . . . I just don't feel that way about you."

"Oh," Endo said, nodding. "You mean you don't get all hot and bothered when you think about me. Or you don't hear bells and whistles go off when you look at me." Endo made the statements like this wasn't the first time he'd had this conversation. "Look, none of that stuff is what lasting relationships are built on. I mean, it's all good to get you going. But in the long run, it's just superficial. Give me a chance; get to know me, then tell me if you feel the fireworks and see stars."

Brianya found herself slightly attracted to Endo's confidence. Maybe she should give him a chance. "Hmmm . . . I see you believe in the hard sale. I gotta give it to you, Endo. I admire your confidence."

"You call it a hard sale, but I call it knowing what you like and going after it." Endo turned left onto Onaway. "Take all the time you need, Brianya, because I don't plan on going anywhere. When you're ready, I'll be right here."

Brianya was speechless. Where was the goofy person from the skating rink? "You know what they say about putting all your eggs in one basket," Brianya said as she braced herself for the jolt she was sure would come when Endo ran into the rock to the left of her driveway.

As if not wanting to appear desperate, Endo amended his statement by adding "But don't take too long because a good man like myself won't stay available forever," and laughed as he expertly maneuvered his way around the rock.

"Hmmm . . ." was all Brianya said as Endo parked and shut off the engine.

Like before, Endo was out of the car at lightning speed, holding the door open for Brianya, and walking her to her front door. "I know you probably have to get up early for church tomorrow, so I'll say good night."

Although his mouth spoke the words, his expression was hopeful that she'd invite him in. To Brianya's surprise, she asked Endo if he wanted to come in for coffee and dessert since they'd skipped dessert at the restaurant. "I brought home a ton of paperwork so I won't be going to church tomorrow. My parents aren't too happy about that, but I'll make it up to them."

"Well, in that case, sure I'd love to come in."

As they sat at the kitchen table drinking coffee and eating homemade pumpkin bread, Brianya couldn't help noticing how often Endo glanced at his watch. "Am I keeping you from something?" she asked.

Endo covered the watch with his hand and looked embarrassed. "Oh, sorry. Will you excuse me for a second? I need to make a phone call."

Well I'll be! Mr. Nerd is a player. Didn't see that coming! Brianya thought as she watched Endo go into the living room where he could talk privately.

"I'm sorry about that," Endo said re-entering the kitchen and sitting down at the table. "I call my dad every night at this time and check in on him. I feel better knowing that he's okay."

"Really? Oh." Brianya felt foolish. "I won't even tell you what I was thinking," she said and laughed.

"Yeah, well, you know I keep a harem of women and I gotta keep 'em in check," Endo said straight-faced.

Brianya looked at him quizzically, not sure if he was totally joking. *Quit being stupid, girl! You know this man does not have a harem of women!*

"If I'm reading your expression correctly, I'd say you think I'm serious."

"Let me put it like this: I don't put anything past anyone."

Endo reached across the table and placed his hand on top of Brianya's and she flashed back to that awful day at the condo with Darnell. She abruptly pulled her hand away, got up, and began clearing the table.

"Did I do something wrong?" Endo asked confused.

"Uh, no. Just thought I'd move these dirty dishes out of the way." She was starting to think that inviting Endo in wasn't such a good idea. That this whole getting-to-know-you thing wasn't such a good idea. Clearly, she wasn't ready. It had been almost three years. She felt nothing for Darnell. Yet, why did he still have this hold on her? She couldn't really move forward until she found the answer to that question.

"Brianya, it's obvious that I've upset you. Look, I'm sorry for whatever it was," Endo said getting up from his chair. "I'll take off now. Thanks for the coffee and dessert."

What was she doing? She was giving Darnell back the power to run her life, just like Monty had said. Well Monty was right about one thing: Darnell did not deserve it. Endo was a nice guy, sweet even. Why should she cheat herself out of the chance to get to know him? She'd just have to find a way to deal with the old feelings that resurfaced and move on.

"You don't have to leave, Endo. Really, you didn't do anything wrong. It's just something that I'll have to work out. That's all." Brianya unwrapped the rest of the pumpkin bread and put it on the table along with two plates. "Help yourself," she said, setting two more coffee cups on the table and pouring.

Endo looked relieved. "Thanks." He reclaimed his seat at the table. "Honestly, I really didn't want to leave. You and I can talk anytime, but not having any more of this bread, now that would be a shame!"

They burst out laughing.

"So, Brianya," Endo said becoming serious. "Tell me two things about yourself that you're most proud of."

"Two things, huh?" Brianya leaned back in her chair and folded her arms. "Well, I'm proud that I've lost a ton of weight. That's what I'm proudest of. And I'm proud that I know how to choose my friends wisely. I know that sounds strange, but have you seen what passes for friendship nowadays? What about you, Endo Jamison?"

Endo's eyes grew big at the mention of weight loss. "Wait a minute. Hold up. I want to hear about the weight thing. I mean, I know you should never ask a woman how much she weighs, but can I ask you how much you lost?"

"I don't have a problem telling you. I used to weigh 353 pounds and I lost 206. You do the math."

"Don't take this the wrong way, but you were really up there!"

"You're right. It was hard work getting to where I am now, and so worth it. I'm surprised my father didn't mention my weight loss to you."

"He didn't say anything." Endo paused. "I'm sitting here looking at you, and if I you hadn't just told me that, I would think that this is how you always looked." Endo was looking at Brianya in amazement. "Two hundred and six pounds? You don't have any of that hanging skin that some people have when they lose massive amounts of weight. You really look great!" Endo couldn't take his eyes off Brianya's body.

Starting to feel a little uncomfortable with all the praise, Brianya thanked Endo for the compliments and put the focus on him. "Now that you know my two proudest accomplishments, tell me yours?" She unfolded her arms and crossed her legs. She poured herself another cup of coffee and waited for his response.

"Okay. I hope you don't think this sounds mushy or anything. But I'm proud that I'm loyal to the people I care about. And that as of last month, I no longer have a mortgage."

"Congratulations, that's impressive. Someday, I'll be able to say the same. What's your secret?"

"No secret. All I did was take all the extra money I got— raises, tax returns, bonuses, etc.—and pay them on the principal. You have to be disciplined. If you want something bad enough, you'll do whatever it takes to get it." Endo looked Brianya in the eye on that last statement.

"That's good advice about using your extra monies to pay down the principal. And what you said about loyalty, that's good to hear, too. We live in a world where the concept of loyalty seems to be a bad thing. I'm glad to hear that it's important to you."

"Yep. It's right up there with breathing. If I call you my friend then you can bet on my loyalty."

Brianya pursed her lips and nodded, visibly impressed by Endo's depth. He was turning out to be full of surprises. "That's really deep."

"Your father told me that you recently got promoted to HR director. Congratulations."

"I don't know if it was a blessing or a curse." She laughed. "Help yourself to more coffee and bread," she added. "I like what the promotion represents and I enjoy the work—most of it. But we're restructuring some of our departments and shifting people around and it's proving to be a challenge that, honestly, I don't feel I'm up to. Some of these people have been working for the company since before I was born. Some of them want to retire, but they can't afford to. When the financial institutions burped in '08 a lot of them lost huge amounts of money, myself included. Well, not a huge amount," she amended, "but significant. At the same time, because of age and illnesses that come along with it, our health premiums are through the roof. Not to mention that they're at the top of the pay scale." Brianya sighed and put her head in her hands. "I just don't think I have the heart to do what needs to be done."

Endo assessed Brianya. "Two things," he said, holding up two fingers. "One, put yourself in the other person's shoes. Two, ask yourself, 'Can I live with the decision I make?'"

Brianya smiled at Endo's naiveté. "You're a good-hearted person, Endo Jamison. I think that's what I appreciate most about you. But you don't have a clue when it comes to Corporate America. The bottom line is that businesses are in business to make money. And while it would be ideal for me to keep things at status quo, it's not reasonable or practical. It's tough out there, I know. But in order for MBCC to stay profitable and stay in the black, tough decisions have to be made and unfortunately, I'm the one who has to make the recommendations. That's the paperwork I'll be doing tomorrow."

"You're wrong there, young lady," Endo said somberly. "I know all too well about Corporate America. I was a victim of the great downsizing movement back in the 90's. I did the whole suit and tie thing for 8 years. I was a scout for a toy manufacturing company in PA. I was making money, hand over fist for that company. In just two years, I had worked my way up the ladder from mailroom clerk to scout. Had an office and everything—expense account, company car. Three years into the job I bought a house, proposed to my girlfriend; she accepted. Life was good! Then the financial bubble burst and I got caught in the middle. Last hired, first fired. There I was, the lowest one on the totem pole; a single man, a brand new mortgage and no way to pay the bills. In three years, I brought in more business than the other four scouts combined. I wasn't making half the salary they made, but somehow the company thought it made more sense to let me go." The room grew quiet.

Brianya let Endo's words sink in.

"So, I might seem clueless, but I can promise you I'm anything but that. I'm speaking from experience."

Brianya cleared her throat. She didn't need to ask about the girlfriend. Endo had said he'd never been married. But she asked anyway.

"She hung in until the severance pay ran out, then she split. I can't much blame her. She wanted a family, a husband who could take care of her and I wasn't in any position to give her either."

Brianya's expression clouded over as she thought about what Endo had said about being loyal to the people he cared about.

Endo looked at the clock on the microwave. It read 11:45. "Well, I'd better be pushing on," He said rising from his chair and gathering the dishes from the table, putting them in the sink.

At the mention of the time, Brianya's eyelids grew heavy. She hadn't felt sleepy talking to Endo; she'd felt attentive and alert. But now, suddenly, she could hardly keep her eyes open. She walked him to the front door and watched as he grabbed his coat from the back of the sofa and shrugged into it. The camel colored coat looked good against his dark complexion, making his face shine radiantly. His skin looked smooth, not a blemish anywhere. Although he was much older than she was, he could easily pass for someone much younger.

"Brianya, I want to thank you for a beautiful evening. I hope we can do this again, soon."

"I'm the one who should be thanking you. The play was wonderful, dinner was fantastic, and the conversation was enlightening. I enjoyed your company." She offered Endo her hand to shake. He gave her a two-handed shake and asked if he could call her sometime.

"You got my number. Don't be a stranger."

CHAPTER TWELVE

Endo wasted no time in calling Brianya to make plans for the following Saturday. Unfortunately, for him, she already had plans. Monty had finally convinced Brianya to take a chance on him and this Saturday he was taking her to dinner and a movie. Although Monty should be the last person who made Brianya feel nervous, he did. And she didn't know if it was pre-date jitters or something more profound.

Brianya wiggled out of her shoes and stretched her toes. Only two hours left to her workday. Soon she'd be home sipping on Moscato and listening to her new John Legend CD. She checked the clock on her desk—nine minutes before the unpleasant task of sitting in on a disciplinary hearing of a long-time employee who'd been written up for excessive unexcused absences. This part of the job is what she found most taxing.

On the way back from the meeting, Brianya heard the familiar jangle of her cell phone. She fished in her purse and retrieved the phone just before it went to voicemail.

"I didn't catch you at a bad time did I, Anya?"

Brianya's heart skipped a beat at the use of the shortened form of her name that only Darnell used. "What do you want?" she said in an exasperated tone, while screwing up her face.

"You."

Not bothering to say goodbye, Brianya switched off the phone and tossed it in her purse. On second thought, she retrieved the phone, scrolled to calls received and saved the number and added Darnell's name so next time she'd know not to answer.

Brianya was about to remark to Debbie that it was almost quitting time, when she noticed that Debbie wasn't at her desk. Probably making her last minute restroom stop. As she rounded the corner to her office, she stopped dead in her tracks. *Not again*, Brianya thought and moaned. Sitting in the chair opposite her desk, as if he owned the place, Darnell looked too comfortable.

Brianya eyed him suspiciously and tossed her purse on her desk.

"What? No hello?" Darnell asked. "I figured since you so rudely hung up on me, the least you could do is say hello?"

Brianya took in Darnell's appearance and something about the way he was dressed told her that he had planned this visit. Darnell had never been a suit and tie kind of person and he certainly wouldn't put one on unless he intended to drop by unannounced. Something was definitely up. "What's with the get up?" she asked.

"What get up? This is how I roll now. Had a meeting with my lawyer about the deal I'm getting ready to ink. Thought I'd stop by to see what you were gettin' into tonight." Darnell brushed the knees of his trousers and leaned back in his chair.

Brianya laughed and shook her head scornfully. "I don't get it. What is up with you men? What, all of a sudden, y'all don't know what the word no means? I told you the last—"

"Hold up! What do you mean, us men? Somebody sweatin' you after you told them no?"

Brianya hung her head in exasperation.

"No, Anya, I'm for real. Somebody tryin' to get at you? Let me know."

"Seriously?" she asked, shaking her head in disbelief. After the way he'd left things with her three years ago, now he wanted to play the role of Mr. Protector? "You know what, Darnell? I'ma need you to get out of my office right now. 'Cause you about to take me someplace I do not want to go!" Without warning, Brianya picked up the phone and dialed the number to security. "This is Ms. Johnson. I need an escort in the HR department of MBCC."

"That's wassup, huh?"

"Yep! That's what's up."

***

"Now see, that's what I'm talkin' about! When respect ain't given, you got to take it, girl!" Dreama said into the phone, when Brianya told her what had happened at work.

"You should've seen the pitiful look on his face when security escorted him out of my office. If he was smart, he would've left before they got there. But he had to stick around trying to talk me into getting back with him." If security had gotten there a minute later, Brianya would be telling a different story. Darnell always knew the right words to say to get his way with her and today he had come dangerously close to accomplishing his goal. She had to admit that he was making inroads into her resolve. If he kept this up, she might have to go back on her word.

"You know that ain't the last of him, don't you? See that right there, that's just gon' make him chase you even harder." Dreama made smacking noises into the phone. She was eating, as usual. "You need to tell Andre and let him deal with Darnell."

"No, what I need to do is get a restraining order. I can see this has the potential to get real ugly."

"Do what you gotta do, Bri. But do it quick, 'cause he ain't givin' up," Dreama warned.

The warning sounded ominous. Brianya knew Dreama was right. When Darnell wanted something, he went at it hard until he got it. It was like that when they first met. He'd interrupted a conversation she was having with a man at the bar, while they'd waited for an available table. He'd even threatened the man with physical violence. Back then, Brianya hadn't seen it as a potential problem; she'd thought nothing of it. In light of Darnell's recent behavior and their past, Brianya wasn't willing to take any chances.

"I'm going to the courthouse before I go to work tomorrow and get that taken care of."

"You do that. In the meantime, I'm gonna get Curtis's cousin's phone number. You met her; she's a policewoman for the Shaker police department."

"The tall, cute, young girl, with the pretty long hair?"

"Yep, that's the one. She can probably drive by on her rounds when she's working nights. Keep an eye out. She might even have some friends in the Cleveland Police department who work the district where you work. Maybe they can look out for you too, make sure he don't try to retaliate when you get that restraining order."

Dreama was a year younger than Brianya, but she always had Brianya's back, was always looking out for her friend. She was more like the older sister that Brianya never had. Brianya always hoped that someday Dreama and Andre would get together, but with Curtis in the picture, it looked like that wish would have to remain unfulfilled.

"Thanks, Drama," Brianya teased and waited for the backlash.

"You might think I'm overreacting, but you should know better than anyone how things can go sideways, volunteering at the Domestic Violence Center." Dreama let out long sigh.

"Yeah, I know. Anyway, I don't believe things will get that out of hand, but at any rate, it's better to be safe than sorry. Thanks for looking out for me, Dreama. I really appreciate it."

"Oh, I'm not doing this for you. I'm looking out for myself. If anything happens to you, who am I gonna mooch off of when I can't pay my bills?" They both laughed. "Hey, I gotta go. Curtis just pulled up. We're going to Smitty's for a couple of hours. You wanna hang?"

Smitty's was a hole-in-the-wall bar and grill on the lower east side, where Brianya and Dreama used to hang out in their younger days. Brianya hadn't been to the place in years and she had no desire to go there tonight. "No, I'm gonna pass. You and Curtis go and have a good time."

After they hung up, Brianya grabbed her coat out of the hall closet and snatched up her purse and headed for the garage. Her original plans to kick back and drink Moscato and listen to music were tossed aside when she decided she needed to take a ride, get her thoughts in order.

She found herself in the parking lot of the Mind Your Body 24/7 Fitness Center, the gym where she'd normally be on a Wednesday after work. This was the perfect place for her to work off some steam and clear her head at the same time. Brianya grabbed her gym bag and gym shoes out of the trunk of her car and headed inside.

She tried to sneak in unnoticed by Lonnie but he spotted her as soon as she walked in and threw a hello wave in her direction. Approaching her with a stern look, he furrowed his brows. "Get dressed. Be out in five minutes. No excuses!"

Brianya knew that tone. That was Lonnie's I-mean-business tone. She had heard it enough over the past two and a half years whenever she tried to beg off or excuse her way out of working out. She hadn't been to the gym in two weeks and she was pretty sure that today she'd pay for it in blood, sweat, and tears. It was just her dumb misfortune that she caught Lonnie between clients.

An hour later, Brianya wanted to fall out from exhaustion after an intense 30-minute run on the treadmill and another 20-minute speed circuit workout, with five minutes of stretching on the front and back ends, but instead she went to the locker room and took a shower, letting the cool water revitalize her.

"So, what's this I hear about you getting back with D?" Lonnie asked, when Brianya emerged from the women's locker room.

"Who told you that lie?" Brianya asked, surprised.

"I got my sources."

"Yeah, well you need to tell your *sources* that they shouldn't go around spreading lies!"

"What? You sayin' it ain't true?" Lonnie picked up several dumbbells from the floor and dropped them onto the rack.

"That's exactly what I'm saying! As a matter of fact, I'm going to the courthouse tomorrow morning to file for an Order of Protection because he's been stalking me since he got back." Brianya's face grew flush at the mention of her plan. "Look, Lonnie," Brianya said more calmly. "You know Darnell better than I do. Do you think I'm overreacting or should I be worried?"

Lonnie spotted his next client on the way over and quickly gave Brianya a three-syllable answer. "Be worried."

Brianya spotted Lonnie's client at the same time he did and she did a double take. Ed Hollister, dressed in loose fitting sweat pants and a hoodie, smiled at Brianya as he approached.

"Brianya! How are you? It's been a minute since I've seen you." Ed unzipped his hoodie, took it off, and laid it across the flat bench. Then he stepped out of his jogging pants, revealing form fitting workout gear.

Oh, dear Lord in Heaven! Brianya thought as Ed disrobed. Ed obviously took great care of his body. The suits he wore, expensive and obviously tailor-made, didn't quite tell the whole story. It was all Brianya could do to hold her composure and keep her tongue inside her mouth. A strange feeling came over her and she instantly felt self-conscious. Why was a man with a body as beautiful as his and an intelligence that was equally as impressive interested in her? So, she'd lost 206 pounds. Her body was nothing compared to his. Suddenly the reality of her situation hit her and all Brianya wanted to do was drive to the nearest Pizza Hut and order the biggest meat lover's pizza she could find and dive right in.

"I've been so busy that I haven't had time to do much besides go home and drop into bed." It wasn't entirely a lie.

"Work keeping you that busy. That's good to know, because I was starting to think you were avoiding me," Ed said jokingly.

The puzzled look on Brianya's face and Brianya's lack of laughter shut Ed down. "I don't know what you're talking about," she said, genuinely confused.

"I left a voicemail on your cell two days ago, and when I didn't hear from you about going out tonight, I thought you'd lost interest."

Lonnie watched, with an amused look on his face, as Ed moved in closer to Brianya. "I like you, Miss Johnson. I thought that was obvious on our last date."

He touched Brianya's forearm and heat went through her. It wasn't obvious to Brianya that Ed liked her; after she'd told him about her celibacy, she thought *he'd* lost interest. Ed wasn't an easy person to read, she was learning. Clearly, he said what he meant and meant what he said. "I didn't get the message," Brianya said, a small smile of relief playing at the corners of her mouth.

"I'll be finished here in about an hour. Can we meet at the Starbuck's next to Corky and Lenny's on Chagrin around 9:00?"

Brianya glanced at the clock on the wall. It read, 7:50. "Okay," she said, pleased that she had been wrong about Ed's feelings.

In the parking lot, Lonnie caught up with Brianya. "So I guess what I heard was a lie then," Lonnie said, pressing the issue about Darnell.

"Guess so." Brianya paused. "Who told you that, anyway?"

"Actually, it was Darnell. He made it seem like y'all were ready to go out and put a down payment on some rings and a house."

"What? And you believed that?" She couldn't keep the disappointment from seeping out. "You know me, Lonnie. How could you even think that was true? You of all people know how messed up my head was after the breakup. I don't even know what to say to you right now. I mean even if you thought I was about to go that route again, I would hope that you would try to talk sense into me." There had been days when Brianya could hardly lift a two-pound dumbbell because she was so emotionally drained, trying to bring order to her chaotic life, and Lonnie was there pushing and encouraging her to think about the big picture. Telling her to leave it on the gym floor, to never look back. Had even jokingly told her that if she ever even thought about getting back with Darnell, he'd work her so hard, she'd regret the day she ever asked him to train her. So how could he stand there telling her that Darnell told him they were getting back together and he'd done nothing to stop her? Brianya got into her car and started the engine.

"You're right, Bri. I should've come to you. I apologize." Lonnie's guilt-stricken expression did nothing to assuage Brianya's hurt feelings. "Now that I know the real, I'm telling you, you need to watch your back. D is determined to get you back. And he ain't stopping at nothing. If you're thinking about hookin' up with my client, Ed, then I would keep this situation with D on the low. Especially since you say he's stalking you."

"Yeah," Brianya said and sped off without saying goodbye.

***

Brianya watched the cars pull in and out the parking lot as she waited for Ed to return with their food and drinks.

"You're sure you won't have more than Chai tea?" Ed asked, putting their drinks and his protein plate on the table. "You should eat protein after a workout."

"I know. I had a protein bar about an hour ago." Brianya was happy to be out with Ed, but ever since Dreama's and Lonnie's warnings about Darnell, she couldn't shake the feeling that something bad was about to happen. She debated whether she should mention anything to Ed and decided to take Lonnie's advice.

"You know, Brianya," Ed said, taking a sip from his cup. "I meant what I said the other night about admiring a woman with principles. I think it takes a lot of discipline to do what you're doing."

"It's not so difficult if you don't put yourself in situations where you're forced to choose."

"Hmmm . . . So tell me, how does a woman as pretty as yourself go about doing that?"

"Simple," Brianya said and plucked a piece of cheese from Ed's plate. "I don't date."

Ed raised an eyebrow. "Ever?"

"Not since my ex," Brianya admitted.

"Really?" Ed asked, as if he found that hard to believe.

"Yep. After I got over that fiasco, I promised myself that I was going to do things differently. What I had been doing up to that point wasn't working, so I decided that it couldn't hurt doing things the right way."

"What is the *right* way?"

"Well." Brianya hesitated. She had thought her metaphor about not giving away the prize to someone who wasn't willing to play the game was clear the other night when she told him. Apparently it wasn't. If she spelled it out for him and told him that the right way for her was after "I do" it might scare him off. On the other hand, if she didn't tell him, she could be giving him false hope. She took a deep breath. "It means that the next man I have sex with will be my husband."

Ed swallowed hard and looked down at the table. "That's . . . I mean . . . Wow!" He twisted in his seat. "Your husband, huh? That's a tall order."

Brianya smiled, enjoying Ed's discomfort. "It is and I'm worth the wait."

"I don't doubt that you are." Ed regained some of his composure. "I can honestly say that I've never met a woman that I was interested in who's celibate."

"And I can honestly say that I've never been celibate before." They burst out laughing.

"Has anyone ever told you that you have beautiful teeth?" Ed asked.

"Someone just did. Thank you."

"You know, you're kinda smooth-talking for a celibate woman."

Brianya chuckled and took a swig of her chai tea.

They talked some more and Ed told Brianya that he used to be a volunteer firefighter in the small town of Cadiz, Ohio, where he grew up. After he graduated from high school, he was unsure of what he wanted to do with his life. His best friend, who was given 700 hours of community service at the fire house for a crime he committed, talked him into volunteering. Not much ever happened in his hometown so the firemen spent most of their days hanging around the fire station working out, debating the stock market, and waiting for the next big fire or rescue mission. That's when Ed became interested in bodybuilding and finances. When his friend's sentence was up, Ed decided to go to college to get a degree in finance.

As Ed talked, Brianya discreetly took in his features. His caramel-colored skin, like her father's, was almost flawless, except for a small dark spot along his jaw line; it looked like it could be a birthmark. His brown eyes lit up like a three-year-olds, when he talked about riding on the fire truck. His hair had a slight curl to it and Brianya wondered if it was natural or chemically enhanced. When his fingers brushed hers, as they both reached for a piece of cheese at the same time, she noticed that his nails looked professionally manicured. In his line of work, appearance meant a lot and she wouldn't hold it against him. Brianya guessed his weight to be somewhere between 180 and 200 pounds, and his height between 5 ft 10 inches and 6 feet. He looked to be around her brother's height. Outwardly, everything about him was perfect. Still, she wondered why he was interested in her when there was a world of beautiful women out there, man of whom would jump at the chance to be with him. Women that he wouldn't have to wed to bed.

"So I moved to Cleveland and the rest, as the saying goes, is history. What about you, Miss Johnson? Did you choose your destiny or was it chosen for you?"

"I chose." Brianya finished chewing the cheese then washed it down with another swig of tea. "There's not much to tell. I had an uncle—my dad's brother—who was chronically unemployed; not because he was unemployable. Nobody would hire him, he said, because he was black. I was only seven or eight so to my young mind that was a huge injustice. I remember saying to my dad at dinner one night that when I grew up I was going to make sure that all the black people in the world had jobs. My dad asked me how I was going to do that. Of course, I had no idea. So my brother, who had just graduated from high school and was full of himself, says 'dummy, you gotta graduate at the top of your class and you gotta go to college and graduate at the top of *that* class 'cause if you plan on hiring *all* the black people then you can't be a dummy yourself!' And the rest, like you said, is history."

The clerk behind the counter told them that it was ten minutes past closing time. They finished eating and Ed apologized to the clerk.

"Can I ask you something, Ed?" Brianya said as they walked toward her car.

"That depends."

Brianya looked amused. "On what?"

"On whether or not you mind if I choose not to answer."

Brianya laughed, remembering that's exactly what she had said to him the other night.

"Seriously, I don't mind."

Without further preamble she blurted out, "Why me?"

"What do you mean?"

"I mean, you're a good looking man. You're educated and smart. You've got a good job. Got all your hair and your own teeth." Ed burst out laughing. "You don't live in your parents' basement. And you could have any beautiful non-celibate woman out here. So, why me?" Brianya's heart beat fast. She didn't mean to be so forward, but the question was out in the universe now.

Ed appeared to choose his words carefully. "Funny you should ask that, because as we were sitting in the coffee shop and I was telling you about my career choice, I asked myself the same thing.

It's weird how you can be talking about one thing and thinking about another," he said offhandedly.

To the long list of perfect qualities, Brianya added 'intellectually stimulating.' They could have a completely separate conversation on that subject alone, since she had minored in psychology.

"Here's what I came up with," Ed continued, "the heart wants what the heart wants. Simple as that. I know that's oversimplifying the answer, but that's it in a nutshell."

They reached Brianya's car. She asked, "Can you be more precise?"

"You're not cutting me any slack are you? All right, Miss Johnson, here it is, *precisely*. When I see you as you are today and I remember you as you were a few years back, I'm in awe of you. Back then, you were a woman who obviously had some issues with food but you still carried yourself with dignity. You always had yourself together; your appearance was impeccable. I'd heard the rumors about how your boyfriend treated you; he made jokes to your face about your weight, that he got some woman pregnant, and he left you for her." As Ed talked, his eyes never left Brianya's.

Brianya looked away, old hurts resurfacing.

Ed reached up and turned Brianya's face back toward him before he continued talking. "When I saw the weight start to come off, and I heard the rumors about why and how you were losing it, I knew that none of it was true. A body like yours doesn't happen over night; that's something that you had to work at. I was proud of you and I silently rooted for you. As more and more of the weight came off, I noticed how much more confident your stride was when you walked to the elevator every morning. Most women who had been through what you had would've given up and given in. But not you. You fought back and you won. I don't know if you knew how long and hard that road was gonna be, but you stuck it out."

Brianya smiled a little, thinking about all the times she wanted to give up and how Lonnie wouldn't let her. At the thought of Lonnie, her expression changed.

Ed looked at her puzzled, misreading her expression. "I'm serious, Brianya. Everything I've said to you is true. When my wife served me with divorce papers and I knew my marriage was over, I made up my mind that when everything was final, I would approach you. I knew that I wanted a woman like you—a woman with fortitude and determination—in my life." The words had come out rapid-fire, as if he didn't get it all out in 30 seconds or less a timer would go off and Brianya wouldn't believe another word. "Then you tell me that you're celibate and that ratchets up the respect meter for you a few more notches and it makes you that much more desirable. Now, I'm getting to know your mind and I like what I'm learning. So if you tell me you're saving yourself for your husband, I can't do anything except respect that. It makes me want to get to know even more about you."

"Wow! Ask and you shall receive," Brianya said, quoting a familiar scripture. "Thank you for your praise and that beautiful compliment, Ed."

Ed smiled in reply. He took Brianya's hands in his and moved in close. "I've wanted to do this all night. May I kiss you?"

Brianya stepped back, shook her head. "No," she whispered.

"I understand," Ed's tone was flat. "How about a hug, then?"

"I think I can handle that." Her nervousness showed in the quavers in her voice. The embrace was light, but Ed's arms felt like a fortress. Brianya had thought the hug would be safer than a kiss, but she was wrong. She quickly pulled herself from Ed's embrace and mashed the unlock button on her key fob.

"Can we get together for lunch next week?" Ed asked, as Brianya got into her car.

"Sounds doable. Just let me know when." She fastened her seatbelt and looked shyly at Ed. "Thanks for the tea and cheese."

Ed nodded. "Drive safely."

Brianya watched through the rearview mirror as Ed watched her drive out of sight, and then let out a huge sigh. *Oh my goodness! What just happened?*

CHAPTER THIRTEEN

"YOU DID WHAT?" Celine asked, when Brianya told her about her coffee date with Ed. "What's the harm in kissing him, Brianya?"

Brianya was so stunned by the evening's turn of events that she had to call Celine, despite it being nearly 11:00 when she got home.

"Nothing. It just wasn't the right time. Besides, our emotions were too high. One thing could have lead to another; and you already know that I'm not going down that road again." Brianya pulled her earring off and shuffled the phone to her other ear. She dropped the earrings into the jewelry box, removed the rest of her jewelry. "I still can't believe he said all those nice things about me."

"Why not?"

That was a good question. Why did she find it hard to believe? She mulled the question over, but her mind remained blank. There was nothing she could do about the attention, so she'd just better get used to men noticing her and even complimenting her. Maybe it wasn't the compliments she was finding hard to believe; it was the sincerity. Before, compliments always came with strings attached. Now Brianya didn't know what to make of them.

"When I figure it out, I'll let you know," she answered.

"Oh, before I forget. Are you going to the grand opening of Marlon's club? I know you don't care for him, but I really wish you would give him a chance. You're one of my closest friends, Brianya, and I want to be able to share this part of my life with you.

At the mention of Marlon's name, a pounding started at Brianya's temples. "I wouldn't set foot in that club! And in case you forgot, his partner is my ex."

Celine let out a sigh. "Yeah, about that. Look, it's been almost three years and you're still holding on to all that hurt. You need to let it go, Bri. You're only hurting yourself."

"I have let it go!" Brianya snapped. "As a matter of fact, I was doing fine until your snake of a boyfriend decided he wanted to open a club with him!"

"Right. Marlon spends all of his time scheming against you, because we all know that it's the Brianya show all day every day!"

And there it was. The truth was finally out. Brianya had wondered when the claws would show. For all of Celine's "support", there was an undercurrent brewing at the surface. As the pounds melted away and the attention increased, Celine's comments had begun to lean toward catty. Brianya would let them pass, fluffing it off to Celine having a bad day. Not today, though.

"What is your problem, Celine?"

"I don't have a problem!" Celine shot back. "I'm just sick of you making everything about you. I think your weight loss went to your head. You know something. I liked you better when you were fat. Now that you lost all that weight and got all these men trying to get at you, you think everybody should bow down to you."

Brianya's mouth hung open and she instantly felt foolish. She looked at the telephone as if it had bitten her. What Celine had said couldn't be farther from the truth. But if she—someone who supposedly knew her—felt that way what did that say about the vibe she was giving off toward those who didn't know her that well? "I had no idea you felt that way, Celine," Brianya said in a choked whisper.

"It's not just me," Celine admitted. "People have commented to me about how stuck up you seem now. Three years ago you never would have dated three different men at the same time." Celine plowed on, not bothering to take a breath. "And when did you become prudish? Celibate is one thing, but a kiss. What's the big deal about that? What, are you scared you'll catch the cooties? No, wait, I know: you're scared you might get pregnant, right?" Celine mocked. "Seriously! You need to lighten up. In case you forgot, this is the twenty-first century. Nobody waits until they're married anymore."

Three years ago when Celine was taking chemo treatments for her breast cancer, she confided to Brianya that the worst part of chemo was that it caused a lack of a sex drive. That, coupled with the fact that her fiancé couldn't deal with her altered physical appearance, was what made Celine swear off relationships and join Brianya on her journey of self-awareness and celibacy. Now that she had a clean bill of health and was in a relationship, Celine apparently didn't share Brianya's views any more.

"I see what's going on," Brianya said, sure that she had surmised the situation correctly. "Nothing's wrong with my attitude! And for your information, I'm not *dating* anyone. I'm getting to know three different men and then, if I decide I want to date any one of them, I will!" Brianya checked her attitude. She didn't like speaking out of anger, but Celine had overstepped and needed to be set straight. "Just because you sold yourself out and let Marlon get in your pants and now you're feeling—what? Let down? Guilty? You wanna try to drag me down with you. Sorry, *friend*, that's one guilt trip you're taking by yourself."

Celine let the words hang in the air and Brianya knew she had gotten it right.

"You tell yourself whatever you need to in order to justify what you're doing," Celine said and abruptly hung up the telephone.

Brianya stared at the silent phone in her hand. With shaky fingers, she mashed the off button. She headed toward the kitchen, in search of something to calm her nerves. She rummaged through the cupboards and came up empty. Since she had limited her use of sugar, she never bought the stuff anymore. There wasn't enough of the sweetener that she replaced it with to make the butter cookies she craved, which, when she considered it, was irrelevant anyway since she had replaced real butter with Smart Balance.

The contents of the refrigerator was only a fraction more promising. She grabbed a nearly empty package of cheddar cheese out of the dairy bin and looked at the expiration date. Two months past fresh. She opened the package and inspected the contents—green fuzz. Sighing, she tossed the cheese into the trash. Brianya screwed up her mouth, trying to remember the last time she'd been shopping. Now that she was back on the market, something other than food occupied her thoughts.

Brianya grabbed her coat and purse from the hall closet and switched off the lights. The fresh air would do her good; help clear her head and calm her nerves.

She pulled into the parking lot of Giant Eagle, cut the car off and sat before going into the store. She closed her eyes and meditated, repeating the mantra she'd embraced in her therapy sessions with Dr. Tobias about her need to reach for food in stressful situations: *Food is not my friend. I'll feel better if I eat better.*

As she walked the aisles of the store, Brianya kept repeating the familiar phrase to herself. By the time she reached the register, she was proud of herself for passing up the jumbo bag of Lays Garden Tomato & Basil potato chips and Cap'n Crunch cereal.

"Bri! Girl, what are you doing at the grocery store at twelve o'clock at night?"

Brianya turned to see an impeccably dressed Cashmere standing behind her with her hands on her hips.

"Hey, Cash! I'm just doing a little late night shopping, trying to burn off some negative energy. What are you doing here?"

"I worked late. I had to finish up a project for a client. She leveled a reproachful look at Brianya. "You're gonna have to burn a lot of energy to work off that strawberry cheese cake!"

"Don't look at me that way, Cash. I'm entitled to treat myself every now and then. Besides, it's not like I'm going to eat the whole thing in one sitting." Okay, so she had passed up the chips and cereal, but Sara Lee strawberry cheesecake was her absolute favorite! She hadn't had any in over two years. She wasn't using it as a crutch—really. She simply had a taste for it and while she was here anyway, why not pick one up?

"I'll make a deal with you," Cashmere said, rummaging through her purse. "I'll come over tomorrow, or later today," she corrected, eyeing her watch, "after you get off work and we'll open the box together. We'll cut it in half; you take one half, I'll take the other." Cashmere pulled out her wallet, took out a five-dollar bill and offered it to Brianya.

Brianya hesitated. "Okay, deal!" she finally said as she took the money from Cashmere. Now, if she could just make it through the night.

***

"Mmm . . ." Brianya moaned. "I missed you!"

Cashmere shot her a curious glance. "Do I need to get the two of you a room?"

They laughed.

They were sitting at Brianya's kitchen table enjoying fat slices of cheesecake.

With each bite, Brianya licked the back of her fork, making sure she cleaned the utensil of every morsel of pie. The rich creaminess of the cheesecake topped with succulent strawberries that had equal amounts of sweet and tart tasted heavenly on her palate. How she had survived two years without this guilty pleasure was a mystery to her.

"So what had you all stressed out that you had to make a midnight run to the grocery store?"

Brianya frowned at the fork in her hand then placed it on the table. She told Cashmere about everything that had happened the night before.

"Girl, you had all of that going on? No wonder you were ready to down a whole cheesecake!"

Brianya chuckled and then looked pensively at Cashmere. "You've known me practically my whole life, Cash. Even though there were some years that we sort of lost touch, basically we've been in each other's lives practically forever. Do you think I'm stuck up?"

Brianya's question caught Cashmere mid-chew and she nearly choked on her cheesecake. "Stuck up? You?" she said, sputtering the words. "Girl, please! Don't let what that *person* said cause you to doubt who you are. You are *not* stuck up! Leaning forward in her chair, Cashmere rested her elbows on the table and held her face in her hands. "Sounds to me like she's just jealous because you've lost all of that weight and got the men chasing you. To tell the truth, I'm a little jealous myself."

Cashmere's comment about Celine had sparked a memory of what had happened on the elevator this morning.

Finding it difficult to fall asleep after her conversation with Celine and her jaunt to the grocery store, Brianya spent the better part of the night tossing and turning, wondering why Celine had said what she had. When she saw her this morning in the parking garage, Brianya expected that Celine would offer an explanation and they would patch things up and move on. But that didn't happen. Celine had barely said two words to her on the ride up in the elevator; the icy silence between them was enough to freeze Lake Erie. And when Brianya exited the elevator and told her to have a good day, Celine looked her up and down, grunted a response, and repeatedly mashed the elevator button.

When Brianya didn't answer, Cashmere waved her hand in front of Brianya's face. "Hello! Is this thing on?" she said talking into her fist, pretending it was a microphone.

"Sorry, my mind was somewhere else." While she was thinking about the elevator incident, she'd also been debating whether to eat the last slice of cheesecake. Brianya eyed the pie and thought about how much time she'd have to spend working off the calories. *Whatever! This is one butt whuppin' I'm just gonna have to take!* she thought. If she hurried, she could make it to the late-night Zumba class at the gym.

"Feel like going to the gym?" Brianya asked Cashmere.

"It's seven-thirty!"

"I know. But if I eat this cheesecake—and don't get me wrong, I *am* going to eat it—I don't want to feel guilty about it, so I gotta put it on the gym floor!" She scooped up the remainder of pie and shoved it in her mouth. Brianya felt how she imagined a junkie felt taking that first hit after being clean for years. "Have you done Zumba before?"

Cashmere's eyes grew big. "Zumba? I don't know if I'm ready for that!"

"It's fun; you'll love it!"

Cashmere wavered a bit. "Okay, I'll hang with you," Cashmere said, stuffing the empty cake tin back into the box and throwing them both in the trash. "What gym do you belong to?"

"Mind Your Body 24/7. Not too far from where you live. We'll swing by and get your clothes. We've never worked out together; this should be fun!"

Cashmere made a face and playfully rolled her eyes at Brianya.

***

Two hours later, sweat-drenched and out of breath, Brianya felt invigorated and exhausted all at once. She wanted to stand under a hot shower and let the water wash away all the negativity of the past twenty-four hours. But if she did, it would be 12 or 1 o'clock before she'd fall asleep; her energy level was through the roof. That's why the instructor tried to persuade her not to do the class, which was meant for people who worked 3rd shift. But Brianya, hard-headed and guilt-ridden, didn't listen. And she'd pay for it tomorrow morning, at the 9 o'clock staff meeting, no doubt.

"I have never worked out that hard before in my life!" Cashmere proclaimed, wiping down the elliptical trainer. "An hour of Zumba was bad enough, but an hour on the elliptical machine? Remind me never to work out with you again!"

Brianya laughed. "You'll thank me some day. So, do you think you'll do Zumba again?"

As Cashmere was answering, the doors to the gym opened and in walked Lonnie. At 10 o'clock at night, the gym was practically empty. It didn't take him long to spot Brianya and Cashmere. He headed in their direction and Brianya groaned.

"Dang, just who I was hoping *not* to run into!"

"Who is he?" Cashmere asked.

"The owner and my trainer. Now I'm going to have to hear his mouth about me working out so late at night, blah, blah, blah."

"Ladies," Lonnie said, sizing up Cashmere. "Lonnie Parker." He extended his hand to Cashmere. "I don't believe I've seen you here before."

Cashmere shook the outstretched hand. "I'm Cashmere Masters, a friend of Bri's. I'm using her guest pass. The guy at the desk signed off on it."

"No problem. I hope you enjoyed your visit and that you'll consider making the Mind Your Body 24/7 Fitness Center your workout home. Let me show you around."

Brianya listened as Lonnie went into his spiel about what set his gym apart from all the rest and how important it was to exercise the mind as well as the body. . . . On and on he went. She had to give it to him, the brother was smooth and all about business. She could see why the owner of Cleveland's largest gym had bad-mouthed him when he cancelled his membership and told him he was going into business for himself. When he left, the gym had lost almost a third of its clients to Lonnie. Brianya knew first-hand how good Lonnie was. If he could whip her into shape and get her to change her eating habits, he had to be good.

"And you," Lonnie said retuning to where he'd left Brianya. "I'm not even gonna waste my breath fussing at you about Zumba at this hour. But I'm surprised to see you here. You drove off so fast last night."

"Yeah, well. I was upset, what did you expect? So where is Cashmere?" Brianya asked, changing the subject.

"She's filling out a membership application."

Brianya shook her head. "I have to give you props, Lonnie. You've got skills!"

"Yeah. And I even gave her the family discount, since she's a friend of yours. Plus, it was the least I could do." Lonnie looked contrite. "You know I got your back, don't you, Bri?"

Brianya remained silent.

"Look, I screwed up. I'm owning that. I can't apologize any more than that." He folded his arms across his chest and leaned on the leg press machine.

Brianya toyed with the towel wrapped around her neck and contemplated Lonnie's apology. She couldn't stay mad at him forever, nor could she dodge him every time she came to the gym. He was still her trainer, after all. She just hated empty talk, and that's what she now felt Lonnie's promise to her was. Or was she being overly-sensitive? He didn't owe her anything. When she thought about it, why should he feel any sense of duty toward her? Darnell was his friend too. That's how she had met Lonnie. Although he had sided with Brianya, he had still maintained his friendship with Darnell. She couldn't expect him to divide his loyalties. Brianya was just going to have to take off her rose-colored glasses and see things for what they really were.

"Apology accepted."

"Good." Lonnie pushed away from the machine and unfolded his arms. "Now about your friend Cashmere. Is she single?"

"Oh, no!" Brianya said. "Don't try to make me the middleman. Look, whatever you want to know about her, you ask her." On so many levels and for so many reasons, Brianya was not going to play matchmaker. "I learned my lesson the last time. Lanette still isn't speaking to me because of you."

"Come on, now. You can't blame that train wreck on me. That girl had serious mental issues before we even hooked up."

"Maybe so, but you didn't have to sic those dogs on her when she came to your door wearing nothing but a rain coat. Andre said he saw her running down Libby Road with her coat wide open. By the time the police got to her, she didn't have a stitch of clothes on!"

They were laughing so loud that everyone in the gym turned to stare at them.

"Besides," Brianya said, wiping tears of laughter from her eyes. "You go through women like a wino goes through Night Train."

"So, I guess that's a 'no' to the heads up on your girl."

"You got that right!"

"Whatever," Lonnie said, obviously through with the subject. "All jokes aside," he said seriously. "Did you take care of that courthouse business today?"

"I didn't file the restraining order. I told Andre about it; he'll take care of it."

"What was so funny that had ya'll laughing so loud?" Cashmere asked joining Lonnie and Brianya.

"We were just reminiscing about old times, that's all. So," Brianya said after a beat, "you ready to go, Cash?" She tugged at her still damp sweatshirt. "I'm ready to get out of these wet clothes."

"Nice meeting you, Lonnie."

"Nice meeting *you*, Cashmere. Looking forward to seeing you around the gym." To Brianya, he said, "Six o'clock Saturday morning, Bri. No excuses."

She waved off the comment and headed for the lockers to retrieve their purses.

CHAPTER FOURTEEN

W HEN HAD SATURDAYS gotten to be so jammed with activities that it had practically morphed into a semi workday? All she'd done was trade office work for volunteer work. Barely one o'clock in the afternoon and already Brianya had worked out at the gym for an hour and a half, volunteered on the Rape Crisis hotline for two hours, and put in two hours at Love's house, the women's shelter where she'd normally spend almost half the day on Saturdays. But not this Saturday. This Saturday she was going on a movie-and-a-dinner date with Monty.

She'd been dying to see the movie *Dream House* and today she and Monty were going to the 2:55 showing. This would be the first time she'd actually been out in public with Monty and Brianya was feeling a little self-conscious. Even though Monty was small time in the NBA, mostly a bench warmer, and he hadn't played for the Cavs in over two years, he still had a level of celebrity. There were still those few fans that recognized him and treated him like royalty, which was strange really, because Cleveland wasn't known for its warm, fuzzy treatment of their sports players, especially ones who cost them a chance of going to the NBA finals, or so the opinion was. The jury was still out on that one.

"He's just a man, Daughter. Flesh and bone just like me and you," Roger said to his eldest daughter, when she confided her feelings to him. The three of them, Brianya, her father, and Cinthia sat in the family room of her parents' home chatting while Cinthia helped Brianya beautify herself for her date with Monty.

Roger watched his younger daughter perform a painful looking procedure on her sister's face. He winced and shook his head when Cinthia plucked more hairs from Brianya's eyebrows. He'd asked all the questions before and debated with his girls about the value of inner beauty versus outer beauty, but they'd only mocked him and told him he didn't understand. So, he'd keep his comments about these unnecessary tortuous rituals to himself.

Cinthia dipped a towel in a bowl of ice water, wrung the excess water out, and pressed the towel to Brianya's eyebrows to help the swelling go down.

"I know, Daddy, but that doesn't make me feel any less nervous."

"Well, there's nothing more I can say then."

"What's wrong? Are you mad at me or something?" Brianya asked. Her father always had more to say about anything and everything all the time. That's what she loved about him—you could always count on Roger Johnson to tell you what he thought, no holds barred.

"I'm worried about you, Daughter. You behavin' like somebody me and your mama don't know. Runnin' 'round with all these different men. We raised you better than that." Roger ran his hand across the worry lines that creased his forehead and sighed.

Brianya pushed Cinthia's hand away from her eyebrows and turned to face her father. "Daddy! I'm not *running around* with anyone. Those men are people that I'm getting to know by spending time with them, Endo included. You make me sound so cheap." Brianya's lower lip quivered.

"Oh boy, not the waterworks!" Cinthia said.

Brianya glared at Cinthia.

"Come on now, Daughter. I didn't mean it like that." Roger moved to where Brianya sat and joined her on the couch. He patted her hand and kissed her on the cheek. "I just don't want people getting the wrong idea, that's all."

Cinthia, never one to pass up an opportunity for a barb, added her two cents. "I agree with Daddy, Bri, you been actin' like a hoochie!"

"Keep talkin', hear, and I'm gonna reach up and yank your tongue right out of your smart mouth and slap you with it!"

"I'm just sayin'!"

"Enough!" Roger bellowed. Like five-year-olds caught committing mischief, Brianya's and Cinthia's eyes grew big and they went silent. Rarely had their father raised his voice and whenever he did, nothing pretty followed. "Can't the two of you ever be in the same room without always threaten'n to come to blows? This ain't no jokin' matter!" He turned softened eyes on Brianya. "I thought you liked EJ. What's the problem?"

She couldn't afford to get into this conversation right this minute. It was twenty after one and she had to get back home by two or she'd be late for Monty picking her up.

"I like Endo. I think he's a nice guy. A little older than I'm used to, though."

"That's the type of man you need, someone older. Somebody who's head isn't filled with all that foolishness, like that young man whose been chasing you all over town."

Brianya gasped. "I knew it! You only pretended to like Darnell so that I would go out with Endo."

Roger, a sheepish expression on his face, remained silent.

"Suppose your plan had backfired, Daddy, then what?"

"I don't know what you're talking about."

"Pitiful!" Cinthia said as she walked out of the room, shaking her head at her father.

"Well, it was the only way I could get you to give EJ a chance," Roger admitted. "And from what he tells me, he likes you, too."

"I know," Brianya said drawing out the one syllable word.

"So tell me, Daughter, why you need to get to know those other fellas? It just don't look good," he added. "Back in my day they had a name for a young lady who spent time with more than one fella."

"That was back in your day, Daddy. This is the twenty-first century. That type of sanctimonious attitude doesn't exist anymore."

Roger pointed a shaking finger in Brianya's direction. "Times may change, but people's attitudes pretty much stay the same."

Brianya glanced down at her watch. She rose from her seat on the couch. "Look, Daddy, I know you love me and you're concerned about my reputation. But, really, you have nothing to worry about. All I'm doing is getting to know three men in very wholesome way." She bent to kiss her father on the cheek. "Trust me, there is absolutely no hanky-panky going on."

***

"Did you like the movie?" Brianya asked Monty as they exited the theater.

"It was okay. Kinda slow. But it picked up in toward the end."

"Really? I thought the pace was good. I loved the ending; I honestly was not expecting that. I'll definitely be adding this one to my collection."

Monty looked sideways at Brianya. "I'd like to be added to your collection."

"Pulled that one right out of the air, did you?" she teased.

Monty blushed. "You don't believe in cuttin' a brother any slack, do you?" He stared down at Brianya and chuckled.

She hadn't realized how tall he was; he practically towered over her. Five-feet six inches in her bare feet, Monty was a foot taller than Brianya. "I can't afford to cut anyone any slack. That's how you end up being a doormat."

They reached Monty's Escalade and he held the door open while Brianya got in. "He really did a number on you," Monty said, climbing in and buckling his seatbelt. He watched Brianya's face display a range of emotions before settling on contempt.

"Why do you always go back to that, Monty? I wish you wouldn't. You don't have to scrutinize my every word to try to find some hidden meaning behind what I say. Like I told you the other night, that chapter of my life is closed." Brianya turned completely sideways to get a better look at Monty. "You know what I think, Monty?"

Monty pulled out of the parking spot and into the flow of traffic. "No, what do you think?"

"I think you're trying to get me to reassure you that it's not an act of disloyalty, you being interested in me."

Monty was overly concentrating on the traffic. By Brianya's estimation, this was a sure sign that she'd struck a chord of truth. When Monty didn't reply, Brianya let the conversation drop. Maybe he was embarrassed that she'd exposed what he might consider a weakness. She didn't think it was weak. She thought it added weight to his character. Most men wouldn't think twice about trying to get with their friend's ex. Fair spoil for the game is what they would have thought. Your ex, my next. Although she would never date a friend's leftovers, she knew plenty of women who did. She wasn't making any judgment calls. She just couldn't do it, because if things turned intimate, it would be too creepy knowing that her friend had been there too. Besides, she valued her friendships and dating an ex would almost certainly kill it.

So far, the ride to Mitchell's Fish Market, where they had reservations for five-thirty, was void of conversation. Brianya closed her eyes and leaned back into the headrest, letting the music move through her.

"Wake up sleepyhead," Monty said several minutes later. "We're here."

"I'm not sleep. I was just enjoying the music." Brianya stretched and let out a small yawn.

"You hungry?"

"Sure. I could eat."

"Good! None of that bird food that people on diets eat. I like a woman with a good appetite."

"Oh, trust me. There is nothing wrong with my appetite! That's why I passed up the concession stand at the movie theater."

They exited the SUV and walked into the restaurant, Monty's hand accidentally brushing against Brianya's. Brianya pretended not to notice. Almost immediately, they were seated at a semi-private booth. Monty must have requested it. Brianya wondered if it was because he didn't want anyone he knew to see them and risk it getting back to Darnell or if he just preferred semi-private booths. Probably the former.

The server took their drink orders—water with lemon for Brianya and iced tea for Monty. No alcohol she noted, and was relieved. It always made her nervous riding with someone who'd been drinking.

Monty cleared his throat and toyed with the ring on his right hand before looking up at Brianya. "You know what you said back there in the movie parking lot? Well you're right. We've been boys so long; it feels like a betrayal."

Brianya pondered the statement. "It surprises me that you feel that way. I didn't think that men cared about that sort of stuff."

"I can't speak for all men, just for myself. And this brother does care about that sort of thing. But I know where you're coming from. Generally, men don't worry about that type of stuff."

"Let me stop you right there," Brianya said, holding up a single digit. "Right now, we're just friends . . ."

Monty cut her off before she could finish her thought. "Ohhh, not the f-word! You say that to a brother who's trying to get to know you and you just about shut the door on all possibility of moving ahead."

The server brought their drinks and asked if they were ready to order.

Brianya ordered an Ahi tuna dish and Monty ordered the seafood gumbo.

"Oh, puh-lease," Brianya said when the server left. "What is it with you men and your irrational fear of friendship with a woman?"

"It's not that we're afraid of being friends with females—I have a few female friends. I mean straight up friends. None of that friends with benefits stuff. What it is, is we don't wanna hear that word from the person we're spittin' game at."

Brianya reared back in her seat, glowered at Monty.

"Wait a minute, wait a minute. That came out wrong!" Monty said, rubbing his hands together as if he was about to get into a tasty treat. "How can I clean that up? Okay, what I meant was," he took a deep breath then continued. "When you're trying to get to know somebody because you think that person is beautiful inside and out and all you can do is think about her every day, all day, and pray that she'll give you a shot, the last thing you want to hear her say is 'we're just friends.'"

Brianya wore a devilish expression. "Oh, I get it. It's like that time when we all came down to the Q to watch the Cavs play against the Knicks and you kept getting fouled and sent to the free throw line. Instead of sinking the shot, you bricked every time. Is that what you meant?"

Monty's jaws strained under the pressure of trying not to laugh but he lost the battle. He roared with laughter and the other patrons in the restaurant turned to stare in their direction. Brianya sat straight-faced, as serious as she'd ever been.

"What?" she said deadpan. "That's what you meant, right?"

"Quick with the wit *and* you got jokes!" he said, traces of laughter dotting the corners of his mouth. Monty had just barely pulled himself together when a guest approached their table. The man, red splotches on his face the size of a small child's hand and looking a little disheveled, greeted Monty and introduced himself. "I apologize if we disturbed your dinner, sir," Monty said.

"No sir, not at all. I wanted to come over and meet you in the flesh." He proffered his hand. "You're Monticello Belvoir, aren't you?"

Monty stood and shook the outstretched hand. "Yes, sir. It's nice to meet you."

The man asked for an autograph and Monty obliged. They talked a bit about Monty's short stint with the Cleveland Cavaliers until the man's wife beckoned him to join her at the exit.

"*Monticello?*" Brianya asked when the man left. "Don't tell me. That was your parents' way of paying homage to Thomas Jefferson."

The astonished expression on Monty's face confirmed Brianya's guess. "How did you know that?" he asked, baffled. "Few people ever make the connection. Are you a history buff or something?"

"Nah, nothing like that. We learned about the Monticello house in American history class. I thought the name was unusual that's why the story behind it just stuck with me." All Monty could do was stare at Brianya with those indescribable eyes of his. "So, Monticello, tell me some more things that I don't know about you. Like what you do for a living now that you're not playing ball anymore."

The server brought their food and conversation temporarily halted.

As they sampled each dish, Monty told Brianya that he owned a non-profit organization called Tag You're It. The organization provided financial assistance to low-income families who have high school seniors with a GPA of 3.5 and higher that are college bound. He also coached at basketball camps during the summer months, when school was out. "Let's see," he said volunteering more information. "My parents are high school sweethearts, who're still married to each other. I have a younger sister. No kids that I know of—knock on wood." He rapped his knuckles on the table for good measure. "And I've fallen for a woman who's way out of my league."

"Very impressive!" Brianya said wide-eyed. Of all the job choices Brianya would have guessed at, philanthropy didn't even make the list. "You're full of surprises."

"Why does that surprise you?"

"Hmmm . . . I never took you for the philanthropic type."

"Don't tell me you're one of those people who think all athletes are self-serving, self-absorbed jerks."

Brianya wanted to say *not all athletes, just you* half jokingly, but the seriousness with which Monty spoke those words and the slightly injured look on his face made Brianya pull back. Thinking back on what she could remember of him, Brianya vaguely recalled Darnell mentioning that his friend was trying to set up a scholarship program. She remembered thinking how shocked she was then, too.

"I don't think that about all athletes, just the ones who are," she said and smiled. She couldn't resist the playfulness; something about Monty brought out the jokester in her. Maybe it was because she felt a sense of familiarity with him since he was someone who had known and desired her before the transformation. She asked him if his non-profit was the one he was trying to set up almost four years ago. When he told her that it was, he looked surprised that she would know that. Brianya told him how she knew and the conversation moved on, with her telling him all about her family and her volunteer work.

As the evening progressed, the occasional interruption by a star-struck fan halted their conversation. Monty didn't seem at all annoyed by the requests for autographs, though at one point he commented that he didn't get that much love when he was playing the game.

They bypassed dessert and opted for a nightcap at Brianya's house instead. Monty paid the check and they left the restaurant.

"So, Brianya, why didn't you acknowledge my statement about falling for you?" Monty asked when they reached the corner of Brianya's street.

Brianya looked thoughtful and shrugged. "I don't know. I guess I'm still trying to wrap my head around what you said the other night about liking me when I was with Darnell."

"Stop," Monty said and put a huge hand on Brianya's. "From here on out, this is about you and me. I don't want to hear you speak Darnell's name. We're gonna focus on you and me and getting to know each other. All right?"

Brianya blushed and just at that moment, she noticed a car moving slowly down the street. A lot slower than 25 miles per hour. She squinted out the window to see if she recognized the driver. It was 8:30 at night and nearly impossible to see anything without the aid of the streetlight that kept flickering on and off. When the car crept closer to her house, the motion light came on and illuminated the interior of the car.

Darnell! How had he found her, she wondered. *Probably the same way Monty had—the Internet.* There were probably lots of B. Johnson's who owned homes in Shaker Heights, but Brianya was the only one with a distinctive name, and she was sure that's how he would have searched. "Dang!" Brianya said under her breath.

"What? You don't want to get to know me?" Monty asked a quizzical expression on his face.

"It's not that," Brianya said. "Look!" She pointed in the direction of the car, which had stopped at the bottom of her driveway. Darnell was exiting the car by the time Monty turned and looked out the window.

Monty turned an angry expression on Brianya. "I thought you told me y'all were through."

"We are!" Brianya shot back.

"Then what is he doing here?"

"Stalking me," she said matter-of-factly. "Ever since he got back he's been trying to get back with me."

Monty stepped out of his SUV and before Brianya could tell him to let her handle the situation, he was halfway down the driveway, quickly approaching Darnell.

"Oh so it's like that?" Darnell said throwing up his hands.

Brianya hurried to meet them before they could exchange any more words. "Look, don't bring that ghetto mess to my home!" she said to Darnell.

Ignoring her, Darnell addressed his remarks to Monty. "You heard me, man!" he shouted to Monty when he didn't reply. "Wassup?" Darnell stepped up to Monty in a threatening manner.

"You need to pull up, man. The lady asked you not to bring that ghetto mentality to her neighborhood."

Brianya touched Monty on the forearm and whispered to him that she could handle the situation. "Wait for me in the car."

"I'm gonna let you handle your business, but I'm not going anywhere." Monty moved only a few feet away and still remained within earshot.

"What are you doing here, Darnell?"

"What you doin' with him?" Darnell countered.

"Why do you care? It didn't matter to you three years ago, when you knew how he felt." Why was she bringing that up? It was old news and it was irrelevant. Brianya mentally kicked herself. "Look!" She spat the word at him as if it were poison on her tongue. "My personal life is not your concern. Why are you here anyway?"

"I gotta talk to you." Darnell slurred his words. He leaned into Brianya's space and whispered, "I want another chance. The baby ain't mine!" he blurted.

It wasn't obvious at first that he had been drinking. In close proximity, however, the smell of alcohol and peppermint was strong on his breath. It made perfect sense, his showing up at her house even after Andre had warned him to stay away. Too much alcohol always gave Darnell a bravado that he lacked in a sober state.

"Are you serious?" she asked, feeling an odd stirring within her. Suddenly the statement struck her as funny and she bent double with laughter. "You've got me confused with Boo-Boo the fool!" she said, recovering her composure. Brianya took a deep breath and let it out slowly. "You need to leave, right now! I've heard everything you had to say to me. Trust me, there's nothing else you have to say or that I need—or want—to hear from you." When Darnell only stared at her through glassy eyes and made no attempt to move, with shaky hands, Brianya began rummaging through her purse.

Monty saw the commotion. Within seconds, he was at Brianya's side telling her she didn't need to do this.

"Do what?" Brianya asked, brandishing the cell phone she pulled from her purse. "If you don't leave here right now, I *will* call the police and let them deal with you," Brianya threatened. "Jail might be a good place for you to sleep off your drunk."

Darnell waved away Brianya's statement. Nevertheless, he headed for his car. Jail was the one place he never wanted to end up; too many of his relatives were guests of the state of Ohio.

"I'm sorry you had to go through all that," Monty said after the ordeal was over. He held Brianya's hands in his.

She felt the calluses on his palms and it was oddly comforting. The rough skin reminded her of her grandfather's hands. He'd spent forty-four years in the steel yards in Cleveland and he was proud of every callous, often telling Brianya that he'd come by them honestly. "Don't trust no man ain't got calluses" granddaddy Johnson would say. "Man with soft hands gets you nothing but a hard life."

This small act of intimacy was having a huge effect on Brianya. She found herself pulling her hands free of Monty's grasp, albeit reluctantly.

"Can you take a rain-check on the night cap, Monty?" she asked regretfully.

Monty looked disappointed. "I understand."

"I just need to be by myself right now, wrap my head around what just happened."

"I'm gonna hold you to that rain-check."

"Thank you for a great evening—except for . . . Well, you know."

Monty bent down and gave Brianya a quick peck on the cheek.

From the confines of her living room, Brianya watched Monty drive away and wished that she had let him come inside.

CHAPTER FIFTEEN

T WO WEEKS AGO, they wouldn't be having this conversation. If Hamfred Larsen hadn't signed off on this cock-eyed deal, Marlon Taylor wouldn't be sitting in her office asking about health care plans and deductibles. In a world where people were used to those in rank positions behaving badly, Brianya didn't see what the big deal was. So what that a man of sixty plus years, who ran a corporation of a thousand or so employees, married for over forty years with three grown children (all male) and eight grandchildren, found it weirdly comforting, the feel of satin and lace undergarments against his pale white skin. On second thought, who was she kidding? This was definitely her frustration talking. If a story like that got out, the press would have a field day and the stakeholders would have Hamfred Larsen's head on a spit.

If knowledge was power, then Marlon Taylor was definitely holding all the cards. If it were anyone else, Brianya wouldn't have a problem explaining that former employees in the pilot program had only one option—which wasn't an option at all—for health care. And that the plan benefits were clearly spelled out in the paperwork each participant received in their packets. Because she knew that this was a ruse to infuriate her, Brianya had asked Marcy Adamson, the benefits specialist, to sit in on the meeting. That way Brianya could direct all questions to her.

Marlon pointed a bony finger at a bullet point explaining maximum out-of-pocket costs and leveled a condescending expression at Brianya. "You expect me to pay five thousand dollars out of my pocket before this policy kicks in and starts paying 80 percent of my medical expenses?"

"Yes, Marlon, that's generally how the maximum out-of-pocket costs part of the policy works." Brianya sighed inwardly.

"When you signed the contract that is what you agreed to." Brianya bit her lower lip in an effort to quell a smart remark that threatened to burst forth.

"Mr. Taylor," Mrs. Adamson cut in, "I can understand your concern. However, there are several ways to defray the cost of out-of-pocket expenses." As Mrs. Adamson gave Marlon several suggestions, Brianya couldn't help noticing the expensive watch wrapped around his delicate wrist. He was squawking about paying thousands out-of-pocket for health care, and yet he probably thought nothing of shelling out the eight to ten grand a watch like that would cost. Not to mention the fortune he was probably spending on the Landrover she saw him driving whenever he picked up Celine from work.

"So," Marcy said getting to her feet. "I hope I've answered all your questions satisfactorily, Mr. Taylor?" Brianya heard Marcy ask as she struggled to bring her attention back to the meeting.

Marlon reluctantly nodded his satisfaction.

Relieved that the charade had finally ended, Brianya rose from her seat. "Well, all righty then. This is a wrap. Thank you, Marcy, for taking time out of your *very* busy schedule to address Marlon's concerns." Marlon didn't miss the sarcasm and the slight eye roll Brianya directed toward him.

As Marlon and Marcy exited the office, Debbie hurried in. "I'm sorry to just barge in Brianya. Your mother called twice while you were in your meeting and she wouldn't let me interrupt you. She sounded panicked and anxious. Then your brother Andre called five minutes ago."

The alarm in Debbie's voice was unsettling; and Brianya's mood went from annoyed to attack mode. Her brother and mother had phoned? It could only be bad news. Fear rose to the surface and the taste of metal filled her mouth; and now she was beginning to feel panicky. The biting reply that shot out of her mouth was tinged with stress. "You knew my mother sounded panicked and anxious and you didn't have the good sense to interrupt my meeting? A totally useless meeting that served no purpose except to tick me off? I swear, I don't know why I keep you around!" Brianya paced the length of her office.

Debbie, who was used to Brianya's stress-induced emotional outbursts, had learned not to take anything she said personally, especially when she was in this state of mind. She stood silently, watching Brianya, knowing that fear was taking over. In a calm tone, Debbie said, "Brianya, you're stalling." Debbie picked up the telephone and dialed Alice Johnson's cell number. She handed the phone to Brianya and walked out the office.

"Hey, Ma," Brianya treaded lightly. "Everything okay?" Her heart beat double-time and her breathing became labored. She braced herself.

"Your daddy had a stroke while he was driving!" Alice sobbed.

***

Traffic was light on MLK Boulevard at 2:45 in the afternoon and it had taken Brianya less than 20 minutes to get to Cleveland Clinic, find a parking spot, and make it to the ICU ward on the sixth floor. Scanning the faces in the waiting room, Brianya ran toward her family. Slumped on a vinyl couch, eyes almost swollen shut from crying, Alice Johnson looked like a woman on the verge of a nervous breakdown. Brianya sat beside her mother and stroked her cheek and asked softly, "What did the doctor say, Ma?"

"Pops had a stroke," Andre cut in. "He was on 90 going around Dead man's curve and crashed into the guardrail."

"Oh no! Did anybody get hurt?" Brianya asked.

"No, thank the Lord!" Alice said.

The tears that streaked her mother's face now wet the tips of Brianya's fingers as she brushed them away with a tissue. Always impeccably dressed and perfectly coiffed, Alice was far from that now. Her long hair was disheveled and her clothes were rumpled. Brianya went in search of a nurse to find out if there was somewhere her mother could lie down. Finding none, she resumed sitting at her mother's side.

"Where's Cin?" Brianya asked, only just now realizing her sister's absence. Andre, clearly distressed, paced the floor. He either hadn't heard the question or was ignoring it. It wouldn't be the first time Andre had mentally checked out after a tragedy had struck home. Three years ago their grandfather had suffered a heart attack and had to have triple bypass surgery. Now, just as then, Brianya was going to have to step up and be the one to hold the family together. "Did you hear me, Andre? Where's Cin?" Brianya asked again.

"She stayed back there with pops. They gon' keep him and we're waitin' on the doctor to tell us what caused the stroke."

Brianya looked at the double doors then back at her mother and brother. Although she would be just steps away, Brianya couldn't leave the two of them. They looked fragile and helpless. Torn between wanting to comfort her mother and being at her father's side, Brianya chewed the inside of her lip. "Why didn't y'all stay with Daddy, like Cinthia?" she wanted to scream. Her father could slip away any minute and his last memories wouldn't be of his loving family surrounding him; it would be of strangers poking and prodding him, only his baby daughter brave enough to stand guard at his bedside.

Brianya stroked her mother's hand and whispered that she was going to check on her father. Just as she rose to go, two of the most unlikely faces greeted her.

"Brianya, I'm so sorry. I saw the accident on the news and recognized your father's car!" Endo said, before wrapping Brianya in a consolatory hug.

Television? How bad was the accident? Brianya hadn't thought it was newsworthy. Her heart plummeted to her stomach as Endo's words settled in. The reality that she could lose her father hit her hard. He just had to be all right. Brianya broke free from Endo and headed toward the double doors.

"What you doin' here, man?" Andre asked. "I thought I told you stay away from my sister and my family."

Brianya turned to see who Andre was speaking to and got a face full of Darnell. In her desire to get to her father, Darnell's presence hadn't fully registered. She couldn't be bothered with this now. As she headed toward the nurse's station, she wondered how Darnell had known about the accident. Approaching the door of her father's room, Brianya didn't know what to expect. Would her father be some mangled replica of his former self? Would he even recognize her? She should have asked the nurse to fill her in on what to expect. *Run!* her mind told her but she wouldn't. Instead she put on a brave face and entered the room. She smiled through liquid eyes at Cinthia sitting stoically watching the monitors.

Except for the soft beeps of the machines, the room was eerily quiet. The covers were pulled up tight over her father's chest. He looked peaceful lying there, almost like he did when he'd catch a quick nap on the oversized sofa in the living room on a lazy Saturday afternoon. "What did the doctor say?" Her voice was low so that she wouldn't disturb her father.

"Nothing yet. They took a CT scan around an hour ago." Cinthia choked back tears and cast a forlorn expression her father's way. "BB," Cinthia said reverting to Brianya's childhood nickname. "Do you think Daddy'll die?"

Cinthia's childlike cadence reminded Brianya of just how fragile the human race is. The atmosphere was heavy with the clanking of metal trays and announcements over the public address system as Brianya contemplated the question. Rationally, she knew that someday we'd all die; no one lives forever. As a child, you think your parents will always be there. Death could never touch them. Other people's parents, but not yours. Even as an adult, you'd hold on to that way of thinking, although in reality you know that it's flawed. "No, Cin, Daddy is not going to die," Brianya said, taking her sisters hand. Glancing at her father lying in the hospital bed looking small and fragile, Brianya hoped she was right.

"You got that right, Daughter." Brianya jumped at the unexpected sound of her father's voice.

Roger Johnson slowly turned his head toward his daughters and gave them a weak smile. "Where's your mama?"

Brianya rained kisses on her father's cheeks and brushed away the wetness that her tears had left with the sleeve of her shirt. "She's in the waiting room with Andre." Brianya spotted a box of tissues on the nightstand, plucked out several and began wiping at her own face. "Oh, Daddy, I was so scared! It's so good to hear your voice!" The tears started afresh.

"I'll go and get Mama," Cinthia said. Her knees creaked as she rose from the chair she'd occupied for almost 3 hours.

"Wait!" Brianya touched Cinthia's arm. "I'll go." She needed to walk off some of the anxiety and get her crying under control. The last thing her father needed was a hysterical female who couldn't control her emotions. Besides, her father hated when women cried. Said it made him feel helpless.

Before she went in search of the rest of her family, Brianya walked two laps around the ICU, reining in her emotions. Approaching the waiting area, she heard loud, angry conversation from just a few feet away. Brianya rushed in, ready to do battle. But the voices didn't belong to anyone she knew. Brianya pulled out her cell phone and dialed Andre's number.

They were in another waiting room on the same floor, Andre said, when Brianya asked where they were. "Go to the ICU. Daddy's awake and he's asking for Mama."

Although the hospital allowed each patient no more than two visitors in the ICU at a time, the nurse made an exception. She and Andre went to find more chairs.

Alice squeezed her husband's hand and patted him on the cheek. "How you feeling, Sweetheart?"

Roger smiled and returned the squeeze. "I feel lucky, Alice. Real lucky."

"Has the doctor been in yet?" Alice asked.

"When they brought him back to the room, they said we could expect to hear from the doctor in about an hour or so," Cinthia answered.

Brianya let out a long sigh of relief. She'd come close to losing her father and the thought of that happening had overwhelmed her. "Where are Endo and Darnell?" Brianya whispered to Andre when he returned.

"That fool Darnell bounced and that Endo cat is still in the other waiting room. I tried to tell him that you would hit him later tonight, but he said he wasn't budging."

"He works with Daddy; he's concerned about him," Brianya volunteered.

From Andre's skeptical look, Brianya knew he wasn't buying the explanation. "Yeah, that's what he said, too. He looked like he was more concerned about *you*, though."

The doctor, expressionless, carrying what looked like an iPad, entered the room and all conversation stopped. "Evening, everyone. I'm Doctor Ramsu." He proffered his hand to each member of the family to shake. "Is this the rest of your beautiful family, Mr. Johnson?"

Roger beamed and nodded slowly.

"Well," the doctor began. "I've got good news and better news, Mr. Johnson. The good news is that you get to go home in a few days. The better news is that there doesn't appear to have been any permanent damage. The CT scan showed that you had a transient ischemic attack, which in laymen's terms is a mini stroke. You were very fortunate, Mr. Johnson. You can thank that Good Samaritan who called 911," Doctor Ramsu said, smiling at Alice, who squeezed her husband's hand. "These TIA's or warnings," the doctor continued, "generally do not leave any permanent brain damage; however, they are caused by a temporary blockage—a clot—to the blood flow to your brain. I'm going to admit you, because we need to determine why this occurred, and from there we can discuss treatment options." The doctor glanced at each face. "Are there any questions or concerns?"

Brianya swallowed the fear in her throat. "Doctor, you mentioned that this type of stroke is called a warning stroke. Does that mean that my father will eventually have a full blown stroke?"

"Sometimes, yes, but not necessarily. Once we run some more tests and determine the cause, we'll be able to decide the best form of treatment to help prevent that from happening. What I can tell you for certain," the doctor spoke directly to Roger, "is that your blood pressure concerns me. Have you been treated for high blood pressure, Mr. Johnson?"

"Well, Doc, a few years ago my doctor gave me a prescription for some pills and told me that if I watched how much salt I ate, that I probably wouldn't have to take them permanently. So, I figured that if I just cut down on the salt right then, I wouldn't have to start taking them, since I would be getting off of them anyway."

"Roger! How come you never told me that?!" Alice asked.

"Daddy!" Brianya and Cinthia scolded in unison.

"Man!" Andre said.

Roger lay in his bed, his shoulders slumped, looking small and defeated and thoroughly ashamed.

"Mr. Johnson," the doctor said and all eyes focused on him. "I'm going to write a script for bp meds and we'll take it from there. In the meantime, get plenty of fluids. I'll make a notation in your chart that you're to have only low sodium meals." He addressed his next comment to Brianya. "I'll take good care of your Dad. We want him to be around a long time so that he can play catch with his grandkids."

Brianya did a double-take in her mind. *Is he flirting with me? Lord, not another one!*

"Well, it was nice meeting you all. If you have any more questions or concerns feel free to contact me personally." The doctor reached into his smock and pulled out two business cards. He handed one to Brianya and the other to Alice. "I'll see you in the morning, Mr. Johnson," he said and touched Roger on the shoulder before leaving the room.

After Dr. Ramsu left, Brianya stayed a while longer before going to the visitor's lounge to see if Endo was still there. On her way, she glanced into the open doors of patients' rooms, many of whom seemed to be at death's door. The smell of disease and antiseptics filled her nostrils. Brianya hated hospitals; they reminded her that life was temporary. That someday, no matter how good you are, when it's your time, you've got to go. *Thank you, God, that today was not my Daddy's day!* she thought, a woozy feeling washing over her as she finally reached the visitor's room. She spotted Endo on the other side of the room staring out of the window. Brianya went to take a step in Endo's direction and the Earth seemed to have shifted beneath her. Endo must have seen her reflection in the window, because he was by her side, catching her before she hit the floor.

When Brianya came to, a woman, wearing what looked like kids pajamas, was standing over her. "What happened?" Brianya asked tenuously.

"You fainted," the woman said.

"Who are you and where am I?"

"My name is Bethea. I'm a nurse. You're in a lounge on the other side of the waiting room from where you were." The woman had a pleasant smile and mild manner. Instantly, Brianya felt safe. "If your friend hadn't caught you, you might've done serious damage to your face."

"What friend?" Brianya vaguely remembered someone standing by her side, but she couldn't remember who.

"A distinguished looking older gentleman."

Endo.

"He said you were here with your dad, who was in a car accident. So, I'm guessing the fainting may have been stress related. Just to be on the safe side, you should let someone here take a look at you to rule out more serious causes."

"No, that won't be necessary," Brianya said, rubbing her forehead. "It's probably stress, like you said. I've never fainted before."

The nurse's pager went off. "Sorry, I've got to go." The nurse looked torn. "I can't make you see a doctor. . . . Lay flat for another ten minutes," she ordered. "I'll send your friend back."

Before Brianya could protest, the nurse had disappeared through the double doors.

Brianya peeled back the blanket and started to rise. She needed to get out of there and out into the open before something bad happened. Just as Brianya stood on shaky legs, Endo came through the doors. "Dang!" she said at the sight of him. She steadied herself with the back of the chair lounger. Endo ran to her side to help her stand. "The nurse said you were supposed to lie still for ten more minutes."

It was ridiculous the way he fawned over her, as if she were a helpless invalid. If Brianya thought she could get away with not being considered certifiably crazy, she'd scream to the top of her lungs right then and there. Instead, she ran her hands across her hair—today she'd pulled it into a ponytail—and smoothed down her dress. She caught Endo ogling her rock hard calves.

"I really appreciate you coming to check on my father. The doctor says he'll have to stay a few days for them to run some tests. But all in all, things look promising. According to the CT scan, it was a mini stroke." A heaviness descended upon her. Speaking the words aloud made everything real. Brianya wanted to curl up in the chair she'd just vacated and cry like a baby, but she had to hold it together.

"Come here," Endo said. Before Brianya could protest, he was hugging her to him. He stroked Brianya's back as he reassured her that everything was going to be okay.

Her nostrils drank in the woodsy scent of his aftershave lotion and her body came alive in ways that it hadn't in years. She slowly pulled free of Endo's embrace. "I'm okay. Really, I am," she lied. Brianya was anything but okay. Her nerves were unraveling and she didn't want to admit to herself that it felt good to be held. She reminded herself of her promise when an uninvited image skittered across her mind. The awkward silence that passed between them was deafening and Brianya let her gaze rest on a coffee stain on the floor.

"Hey, look. I'm sorry, Brianya. I didn't mean to be forward. I just thought you could use a hug. You know, with everything you're dealing with." Endo made a move toward a couch nestled in a corner. "Come sit with me." When she didn't make a move to join him, Endo added, "Please, just for a second?"

Brianya felt like a schoolgirl, called into the principal's office for cutting up in class. She didn't want to sit, but she joined Endo on the couch anyway.

"I get it," Endo said, chuckling. "The whole celibacy thing." His voice was like sunshine when he spoke. "I get what you're trying to do and I respect you for that. And I'm not trying to take you anywhere you're not ready to go. But if you're serious about holding out until marriage then you'll need to figure out a way to handle something as simple as a hug."

"I don't have a problem with someone hugging me," Brianya protested. "It's the backstroking that got to me." She let out a breath. "But you're right. I need to figure some things out."

"And while you're doing that, I'll be right here. Like I told you before, I'm not going anywhere."

Brianya felt Endo's eyes boring into her face. When she turned to look at Endo, Brianya felt an odd sensation of white, hot anger tinged with sadness. The tender way in which he watched her reminded Brianya of how Darnell had gazed so lovingly into her eyes before shattering her world with the words, "You know I love you, and I need you in my life." He had stroked the side of her face with the back of his hand. Then he clasped her hands in his, gently brushing the tips of his fingers against hers before saying, "I think we need to call it quits, but let's still be friends."

Brianya jumped up off the couch and almost ran to the door.

"What's wrong?" Endo said, obviously alarmed by the hateful look he'd seen on Brianya's face.

Needing to put distance between herself and Endo, Brianya kept moving toward the door. Where were these feelings coming from? She hadn't thought about the events of that ugly day in a long time. *Why now?* All she wanted was to be free of Darnell. She had thought that she was. But these memories were relentless and they kept coming up at the most inopportune times. Brianya needed to get somewhere where she could think, just let her thoughts take her where they would so that she could understand what was happening.

At the door, Brianya turned to face Endo. "This is all too much for me to process right now," she said, her voice quavering. "What's important is that I deal with my Dad and his health issues. Anything else will just have to take a backseat." Brianya took a deep breath and let it out. "I appreciate you coming and I'll let my father know you were here. But like I said . . . Right now . . . . I just can't . . . Sorry."

"Wait, Brianya . . ."But she wasn't listening. The gentle swooshing sound the doors made as they shut behind her was the only evidence that someone other than Endo had shared the room.

***

Brianya tossed the empty Breyers Blast! Mrs. Fields Chocolate Chunk Cookie Dough ice cream container in the trash can. She reached for the half-eaten giant bag of potato chips. As she licked the last of the gooey substance off her spoon, a dull pain, that felt like her intestines were quivering, went through her. From the time she arrived home until now, it had taken her approximately 4 hours to polish off the quart and a half of ice cream that she'd picked up on the way home from the hospital.

Brianya felt as though she wanted to vomit.

Scurrying to the bathroom, she leaned over the toilet and heaved up chunks of liquefied chocolate chips, cookie dough, and potato chips. The energy it took for her body to relieve itself drained Brianya of most of her strength. She closed the lid of the toilet and sat down. Brianya reached for the facecloth that hung on a rack, ran cold water over the cloth and patted her forehead and chest with it. Her father's stroke, Darnell and Endo showing up at the hospital, Marlon's passive-aggressive behavior, Celine's betrayal, and all the other troublesome events that had taken place over the past month or so had sent Brianya crashing headlong into bad habits she'd thought she had under control.

Glancing at the clock on the bathroom wall, it read: 2:15. Much too late to go to the gym. She'd go later today after she came from visiting her father. Brianya rinsed her mouth with warm water and flipped the bathroom switch to off on her way out. All she could do now was try to get some sleep.

As she lay in bed, the day's events kept replaying themselves in her mind like an old movie. The doctor had said that her father didn't appear to have suffered permanent damage. What if he was wrong? Roger Johnson was a proud man and having to rely on anyone for assistance would wound him deeply. Would her mother be able to handle the challenges that came with being a caregiver? And how would the rest of the family view her father? She'd seen the way the family had treated her maternal grandfather when they had to put him in a nursing home after he'd had both legs amputated. Those family or friends who'd bothered to visit, treated him like a three-year-old, talking down to him, as though he'd lost his mind and not his legs. Even the nursing staff had mistreated him, refusing to change the bandages on his stumps, whenever her grandfather was belligerent after having a rough night, unable to sleep.

No, her father was not going to a nursing home if she had anything to say about it. And she would have plenty to say. The first time any of the staff even looked like her father wasn't the ideal patient, she'd come out swinging. *Get a grip, girl* she told herself. *The doctor told you what the scan showed. Now stop trippin' and go to sleep!* Brianya's head began to throb from clenching her jaws together. She wasn't even aware that she was doing that. She massaged her cheeks and tried to relax. When she closed her eyes, all she could see was Endo's forlorn expression as she raced out of the waiting room.

Endo was right, Brianya thought. She did need to figure out how to deal with simple human contact between a man and a woman. She thought about her reaction to Ed's hugging her. Even a hug minus the backrub had sent a current of excitement coursing through her. *Yeah, I definitely need to figure out some things.*

CHAPTER SIXTEEN

THE TEMPERATURE OUTSIDE had dropped at least ten degrees, making the living room feel fifteen degrees colder. Brianya nudged up the thermostat and wrapped the afghan around her shoulders. She leaned back in the recliner and resumed reading the latest murder mystery from Jonathan Kellerman. This was one of those rare Saturdays when Brianya found herself with nothing to do. She'd spent the earlier part of the day playing scrabble with her parents and losing miserably. Three weeks since her father's mini stroke and Roger Johnson still showed no signs of any lost brain functions. His health was on an upswing, as he was eating better and taking his blood pressure medicine faithfully. Her father's close call had served as a wakeup call for him, but it had the opposite effect on Brianya, unfortunately.

She hadn't been to the gym in three or four weeks and she could stand to make wiser food choices. This morning when she stepped on the bathroom scale, the number that stared back at her had to be wrong. She couldn't have gained that much in just three weeks? She'd rushed right out and bought another scale. Not only did the new scale confirm the weight gain, it added two pounds! Thank goodness Brianya wasn't at the point where she needed to buy new clothes; but if she didn't get back on track and quick, she and 200 pounds would be BFFs for life.

Try as she might, Brianya couldn't break the cookie spell. There wasn't a cookie invented that she didn't like. The cookie of the moment was an old-fashioned shortbread made with real butter and loaded with macadamia nuts and white chocolate chips. The clerk at the Gourmet Cookie shop a few streets from her house, always made sure to put a few "imperfect" cookies in the box if there were any left when Brianya came in.

As Brianya flipped through the pages of her book, she plopped cookie after cookie into her waiting mouth, enjoying every bite. Just when she'd finished dunking the cookie in a glass of orange juice and taking a bite, the door handle rattled and a burst of fear jolted through her. Brianya nervously tiptoed to the door and peeked out the small pane of glass.

"Girl!" she scolded as she swung open the door to let Dreama in. "You scared the—"

"Mess out of you," Dreama said, finishing Brianya's sentence. "Yeah, yeah, I know. When you gonna give up on that ridiculous notion that you can stop cussing?" Dreama pushed past Brianya and started toward the living room. "You need to just go ahead and let it out. You'll feel better, plus you might stop trying to eat yourself out of house and home." Dreama took off her coat and threw it across the back of the couch next to where she flopped down.

"Says the woman with no restraint," Brianya mocked.

"Say what you want, honey chile. You don't see me stuffing my face with," she picked up the box that lay on the table and examined the contents, then took a small bite, "macadamia nut cookies. Da—. Oops, sorry. I mean *dang* that's a good cookie."

Brianya rolled her eyes at Dreama. She couldn't help smiling at Dreama's attempt to be supportive. She really was a good friend. As hard as Brianya knew it was for Dreama to curtail—because there was no way she would quit cussing altogether—her swearing, it was even harder for her to keep a secret. Whatever it was must be juicy because that's the only thing that would make Dreama come to Brianya's house without first calling to make sure she was at home.

"Spit it out, Drama!" Brianya said on her way to the kitchen to get two wine glasses and the bottle of Moscato that she kept on hand.

"Bri, girl, I can't wait to tell you. Hurry up and get back in here and don't forget my lemon wedge!"

Dreama was the only person in the world that Brianya knew who squeezed lemon in Moscato wine. Gathering up everything as quickly as she could, Brianya rushed back to the living room. She handed Dreama the wine and placed everything else on the table. "So what is it? Spill it, girl!"

"Wait a minute!" Dreama placed the wine on the table unopened. "What are you doing home on a Saturday night?" Lately Brianya was hard to pin down. Now all of sudden, she wasn't? This realization smacked of suspicion.

"Never mind that, Drama. Dish the dirt!"

Dreama pursed her lips. "Umph. I'm gone let it ride for now, but we ain't done with that subject! Anyway," Dreama said as she uncorked the bottle and filled the glasses. She squeezed a small amount of lemon in her glass and took a healthy swig. "Okay, so you know Darnell and them opened up the nightclub three weeks ago. Well, mama, it was off the chain! Girl, they had all kind of folks up in there. They had to turn people away at the door! But guess who they didn't turn away?" Dreama took a dramatic pause.

Brianya sat on the edge of her chair. "No clue. Who?"

In a dead-on imitation of Maury Povich, Dreama said, "You are *not* the father!" and raised one eyebrow.

"No!"

"Yes! You shoulda seen her, Bri. She was rollin' three deep. Looking like Charlie's Angels with a plus one. Her and her little entourage was sauntering around the club like they owned the place."

"She probably does own the place, at least partially. I bet you any amount of money Darnell borrowed the start up cash from her." *Once a low-life user, always a low-life user.* Although she shouldn't care about what went on in Darnell's life, Brianya felt physically ill at hearing the news that *that woman* was still in the picture. She reached for a cookie to tamp down the nausea.

"That was my reaction too," Dreama said, misinterpreting Brianya's expression. "I can't tell you how glad I was when you woke up and left that Ni—"

"Don't say it!" Brianya demanded.

"What? That's not a cuss word."

"May as well be. It's a hateful, derogatory word. And no decent, self-respecting person would ever use it."

"Dang! Since you put it that way." Dreama laughed at Brianya's seriousness. "Lighten up, sistah-friend."

"I'm serious. I get so tired of hearing us call each other that word. Then we get all bent out of shape when white folks use it." Growing up, Brianya had heard the racially derogatory word often. Her aunts and uncles used it liberally as though it was an exclamation point at the end of a sentence.

"Okay, okay," Dreama conceded. I get it. No N word! Anyway, let me finish telling you about your boy and his girl."

Brianya pulled a face and rolled her eyes at Dreama. "No, really, you don't have to tell me anymore. I'm sick to death of thinking about him!"

"What?" Dreama's eyes flashed a look of surprise and she cocked her head to stare in amazement at Brianya.

"What?" Brianya asked dumfounded.

"You just said you were tired of *thinking* about him. What do you mean by that?"

Brianya knew good and well that those words did not come out her mouth! Dreama full of drama had heard wrong. Hadn't she?

Hearing no answer from Brianya, Dreama said, "I swear Bri, if you're thinking about getting back with that piece of trash, I'll reach across this table and slap you so hard, you'll be tasting last week's dinner!"

"Oh trust me, if those words came out of my mouth, I'll slap myself!"

"I know what I heard!" Dreama insisted.

Glancing out the window, Brianya watched a streak of lightning race across a sky made black by rain clouds. Dreama let out a small yelp. Brianya, now on edge, gulped down the remaining contents of her wine glass as she waited for the inevitable. A clap of thunder roared throughout the house and both women jumped simultaneously as a shadow passed across the window.

"Did you see that?" Brianya asked, the previous conversation forgotten.

"Yeah. What was it?" Dreama cowered on the sofa.

"How should I know? I'm sitting right here with you." Brianya got up to inspect the shadowy figure. Squinting into the darkness, she noticed someone getting into an idling vehicle with no headlights or interior lights on. "Come here, Dreama! Hurry! Do you see that?" Brianya pointed a finger in the general direction of the vehicle.

Dreama joined Brianya at the window. "See what? What am I looking at?" Dreama cupped her hands to the glass. She inhaled a sharp intake of breath. "Is that a station wagon?"

"Looks like an SUV." Brianya ran to the door and yanked it open. "Hey!" she yelled through the screen door, but the vehicle had already begun its way down the road. Brianya unlocked the screen door to get a better look. As she stepped onto the porch, she nearly tripped over a package left in front of the door. Brianya bent down and scooped up the package. "Whoever it was left this," she said shutting the door and showing the package to Dreama.

Dreama backed away. "Girl, you shouldda left that on the porch. You don't know what's in that box!"

The box was addressed to Brianya but it bore no postage or return address. It felt feather light in her hands. "Stop being so melodramatic," Brianya chided as she ripped off the plain brown wrapping paper.

Dreama's curiosity got the better of her and she inched closer to view the contents. Brianya fingered the smooth silkiness of a purple and gold scarf with an abstract design and held it up for inspection. "This is gorgeous!" The designer label and Saks Fifth Avenue box was evidence that the gift-giver thought highly of her and had good taste. *Wear this the next time I see you* the embossed card read.

"Who's it from?" Dreama asked.

"Monty."

"From the way you're cheesing, I see y'all must be getting serious."

Since her father's hospitalization, Monty had proven a real source of comfort. Every day at 8:00 A.M., Brianya's phone chirped and there was an inspirational message from Monty. The message sent today had simply read: U R priceless. "I guess he's growing on me."

"So why did he just leave it and run?" Dreama asked.

"When my dad got sick, I told him that I needed time to deal with some things and he's been giving me my space." By the look on her friend's face, Brianya knew that Dreama hadn't changed her opinion of Monty. Though she didn't know him well, Dreama had voiced her suspicions to Brianya, which didn't sit well with her. It was just like Dreama to pass judgment before having all the facts. This was one time Dreama was wrong. Brianya knew it in her gut.

"What exactly is it you don't like about him?" Brianya had asked. To which, Dreama had replied, "I just don't trust him, that's all!"

"Be more specific," Brianya had prodded.

"Okay. For one thing, why did he wait all this time to approach you? Why did Darnell just happen to show up at your house the day y'all went to the movies? It smells like a set up to me."

"A set up?" Brianya had asked, baffled by Dreama's wild imaginings. "To what purpose? Oh, wait, let me guess. Monty shows up, declares his long time attraction to me, an attraction he wasn't free to act on because he had a girlfriend at the time, and begs me to go out with him. Meanwhile, Darnell is due back in town just weeks later. At which time he starts stalking me, shows up in my office, pleading for another chance, all the while Monty is setting the stage for the ultimate showdown in my driveway, in which Darnell shows up drunk and causes a scene so that I almost call the police to haul him off to jail just days before the grand opening of his club. A club, mind you, where all the big city officials are due to make an appearance because of the connectedness of one of the partners." At this point, Brianya had scratched her head and rested her chin in the palm of her fist and looked sideways at Dreama. "Hmmm ... now that I think about it, you might have a point, Dreama. Let me call channel 19 news and see if they'll send out Scott Taylor; I think you've cracked the mystery of the century!"

Brianya had laughed so hysterically that all Dreama could do was storm off without responding. Now she was about to go down that road of outlandish speculation again and Brianya wasn't in any mood to hear it.

"Don't start that again, Dreama." Brianya placed the scarf back into the box and put the package on the top shelf of the hall closet.

"Well, I think it's creepy and childish the way he just rang the bell and ran." She watched Brianya for a reaction and not seeing one said, "You know he was at the club, don't you?"

"I know!" Brianya said and crossed her arms. If Dreama noticed the catch in Brianya's voice—a sure sign that she was lying, she didn't let on. Maybe Dreama was right and Monty was only putting on an act, but what would be the point? It's not like she was *somebody*. With his looks and money, Monty could have any woman he wanted. Yet, he chose her. And not just since the weight loss either. He wanted her even when she was twice her size. Brianya slammed the closet door and leaned against it.

Dreama took a big gulp from her wine glass and eyed Brianya. Her friend was hurting, but she was only looking out for her like any good friend would do. She had practically held her hand through the ugly breakup with Darnell. Had witnessed the pain and anguish of Brianya wanting to give up on life because of it. As hard as it was to watch, feeling helpless most of the time, Dreama could only imagine what it must feel like to actually live it. She'd never had a man step on her self-esteem and make her feel worthless. And thank God Brianya hadn't fallen into a funk for a long period of time. Dreama had confessed to her that if she'd been down any longer, she'd have been on a plane to Virginia hunting Darnell down like the dog he was. Just as then, Dreama couldn't stand idly by when she had the chance to help steer her friend away from obvious danger.

Dreama could tell that Brianya was lying about knowing that Monty was at the club. Her voice always cracked like a pubescent teenager when she was concealing the truth. "I'm just looking out for you, Bri. Ask yourself: If Monty going out with you was supposed to cause bad blood between him and Darnell, why would he be at his club opening?"

That was a good question for which Brianya had no answer. Although she knew there could be any number of reasons, she couldn't fathom even one reason why Monty would keep it a secret from her. She shrugged the uncertainty away and began straightening up the living room. "We're not dating. He doesn't have to run his whereabouts by me," Brianya said sweeping crumbs from the table into her cupped palm.

Dreama swigged the last of her wine and corked the unfinished bottle. When Brianya started to clean up, that was Dreama's cue that Brianya was done with the conversation. "So, you're okay with him not even mentioning to you that he went to the opening?" she pushed.

"What I'm saying is," Brianya said coming dangerously close to losing her temper, "I'm done with this subject."

Dreama made a sucking noise with her tongue. "Whatever!"

CHAPTER SEVENTEEN

THE CONVERSATION WITH Dreama had revealed something to Brianya about herself. She had reacted the same way toward Celine dating Marlon Taylor as Dreama had reacted to her involvement with Monty. Could I *be as a wrong about Marlon as Dreama is about Monty?* Brianya wondered. She supposed anything was possible, but in this case, she knew she was right in her assessment of Monty. After saying goodnight to Dreama last night, Brianya had tossed and turned, her sleep coming in fits and spurts. Too late then to call Celine, Brianya had promised herself that she'd call her first thing in the morning to apologize for her behavior toward her. It had been months since they'd spoken and it was time to put an end to this foolishness. Friends should be able to disagree without the friendship ending. Besides, if a friendship was going to die, let it be over something more substantial than an opinion about a boyfriend. What were they, in Junior high school?

As she dialed Celine's number, Brianya prayed they could patch things up. She missed her friend terribly and was prepared to tell her that if she answered the phone.

"Hey baby, that was quick. You must've ran to your car?" Celine's voice said on the other end.

"Celine?"

"Oops, sorry Tricia. I thought you were Darnell."

"Wrong again!" Brianya snapped. "Oh, I know you're not talking about *my* Darnell!"

The barely perceptible intake of breath was evidence of Celine's guilt. "You mean your *ex* Darnell," Celine said coolly.

White spots danced in front of Brianya's eyes and she was thankful for the miles that separated them. "How could you?" Brianya shrieked.

"How could I what?" Celine asked and didn't wait for an answer. "Grow up, Brianya. As I told you before, life is not all about you!"

Brianya didn't get a chance to respond because Celine had ended the call. Despite what had just transpired, instead of being angry, outraged, or incensed, calm washed over her and she placed the phone in its cradle. Lifting the car keys from the key rack beside the garage door, Brianya adroitly drove to Heinen's.

"Is everything okay ma'am?" the cashier asked, a look of alarm spreading across her face.

Brianya gazed curiously at the older woman, wondering why she would ask such a question. "I'm fine," Brianya said and smiled. "Why?"

"You're crying, Miss."

"Crying?" Brianya touched her cheeks with her fingers. The wetness caused her to draw back her hand in astonishment. How long had she been crying? She'd never even felt the tears, but the wetness that soaked her blouse told the whole story. The cashier bent down, fumbled around under her cash register and produced a small packet of tissues.

"Thank you," Brianya said, taking the tissue from the cashier. The woman's French manicure reminded Brianya of the first time she'd formally met Celine and had spilled her guts about the break up with Darnell. Now here she was almost three years later spilling her guts again. Only this time the perpetrator of betrayal wasn't a lover, but a friend.

The cashier named Madge, according to her nametag, gave Brianya a sympathetic smile as she listened and rang up the items Brianya had placed on the belt. "Fifty-two dollars and eighteen cents," Madge said, placing the food in four separate bags as Brianya swiped her bankcard and signed the electronic box.

Madge smiled once more at Brianya and appeared to contemplate her next words. "I'm not trying to tell you your business, but I'll tell you what I'm always telling my own daughter, who's about your age. Life is too short to waste on nonsense. Every night we lay our heads on our pillows and fall asleep, we're not guaranteed to open our eyes the next morning. So rather than worry about who this woman or that man is making time with, make sure you use every day the good Lord gives you to make yourself the best person you can be. And always look for a lesson in your pain."

Madge's words were heavy, spoken with authority. Only someone who had experienced hurt and pain could speak with such conviction. The seriousness behind the statements told Brianya that this was advice she needed to heed. A line was growing behind her and the low grumbling of the other customers was beginning to grow louder. Before it erupted into full-blown chaos, Brianya thanked the cashier for listening and for her advice and took her leave.

Standing at the isle in the center of her kitchen, Brianya emptied the bags of food and put everything in its proper place. When she had the bags folded neatly and put away, Brianya's mind drifted back to the previous night. Had Dreama seen Celine and Darnell together and that was the big secret she was trying to tell her? It had to be. Only news as big as that could bring Dreama to her door unannounced. If Brianya hadn't lit into Dreama the way she did, Celine wouldn't have had the chance to slap her in the face with the news! She really needed to stop being so hotheaded and quick tempered. Somehow, it always backfired.

Thinking back to Madge's advice, Brianya tried to put the thought of Celine and Darnell out of her mind, but found that it was a struggle. Without thinking, she grabbed the bag of Lays Garden Tomato & Basil potato chips from the cabinet. She filled a large cup with ice and poured in Pepsi Cola. Halfway through the bag of chips, Brianya decided to add a few scoops of vanilla ice cream to her second glass of Pepsi, sans ice. The relief she experienced after consuming the calorie-dense junk food, was immeasurable. Her troubles seemed to melt away in an instant. This feeling of euphoria would last only as long as the food did. At some point, she'd have to stop eating and then the guilt would take over. Yet, knowing this did nothing to prevent Brianya from shoveling in the next handful or taking the next slurp. At this moment, everything was inconsequential. All she cared about was the right here and the right now.

Overstuffed and under nourished, Brianya belched loudly and plopped her head on the kitchen table. She moaned from the gaseous bubbles churning in her belly. Feeling drained, Brianya headed for the bedroom; it was time to lie down. As soon as she awoke from her nap, but after she came from Love's House, Brianya vowed that she would go to the gym.

The ringing phone awoke Brianya ten minutes before her alarm was set to go off. Blindly, she groped for the telephone and mashed the talk button. "What?" she said heavily into the mouthpiece.

"Is that any way to greet someone who thinks the world of you?" the caller said.

Brianya tried to drag herself to a sitting position and only managed to slump half way between sitting and lying. She grunted and hauled herself up the rest of the way.

"What are you doing?" the caller asked, and Brianya caught his voice.

"Hello, Ed. I was taking a nap. I was just about to get up and go to Love's House, *in ten minutes!*" she said tight-lipped. Brianya hated being woken up before the alarm sounded. Premature awakenings always made her feel incomplete. She'd spend the rest of the day feeling on edge.

"Sorry I woke you," Ed said, though he didn't sound the least bit sorry. "I won't keep you. I just called to tell you that I'm really looking forward to cooking dinner for you at my place tonight." The smile in Ed's voice was obvious.

Through all the ugliness of this morning, dinner at Ed's had slipped Brianya's mind. After her party for one an hour ago, food was the last thing on her mind. Brianya was feeling fat and unattractive and spending an evening at Ed's place, his eyes sliding up and down her body the way they always did when they were alone, was unthinkable. Sooner or later, Ed was bound to mention the twenty extra pounds Brianya had packed on since they started spending time together almost three months ago. Since he had made it clear from the beginning that he wasn't into fat chicks, Brianya knew that it was just a matter of time before Ed lost all interest, regardless of his proclamations about her beauty and intelligence.

After hanging up with Ed, Brianya jumped in and out of the shower quickly, anxious to get her day started.

CHAPTER EIGHTEEN

"I HAD NO IDEA you could burn like that!" Brianya said, complementing Ed's culinary skills. Dinner consisted of salmon stuffed Portabella mushrooms, wild rice, broccoli, garden salad with raisins and almond slivers, topped with raspberry vinaigrette.

"Ah," Ed said, clearing the dishes from the table. "I got a lot more secrets where that came from." Ed chuckled as he rinsed the dishes before loading them into the dishwasher.

"I just bet you do." As Brianya admired the blue Bahia granite countertops, the Pergo floors, the glass and wood cabinets, and the stainless steel appliances, she began putting away the leftovers. Brianya put the lid on the bowl of leftover salad and scraped the remainder of the wild rice into a storage container. She opened the huge refrigerator, stacked with an assortment of nutritious foods, and deposited the containers inside.

Ed left off what he was doing and steered Brianya in the direction of the living room. His hand faltered when he gripped her around the waist. Brianya didn't fail to notice the hesitation. "Look, I told you, tonight it's about me doing for you."

"Okay, okay," Brianya squirmed out of Ed's grasp. She still didn't understand why he was going to so much trouble for her. When she'd questioned him about it, all she got was an unsatisfactory answer of "Why not?" Brianya could hardly remember the last time a man had cooked for her. Come to think of it, no man had *ever* cooked for her.

"Make yourself comfortable," Ed said, seating Brianya on the gigantic sofa. "I'll be back as soon as I finish putting everything away. Give me five minutes. Can I bring you anything?"

Brianya took in the sparse décor of the living room. It looked like something out of a Homes and Garden magazine. From the neatly lined pillows on the love seat to the magazines resting in the metal rack, everything was perfectly in place. Had he spruced up things for her or was this how he lived? She wondered. Brianya had dated her share of neat men before and found that it was always an indication of some sort of compulsive disorder; and it never turned out well in the end.

She asked for cranberry juice and a few minutes later Ed was placing a tall glass of juice on the table in front of Brianya, and sitting down beside her.

"I want to thank you for this evening. Everything was superb!" Brianya smiled appreciatively and cupped her chin in her hand. "So tell me, Ed, what's the deal? And this time I want a real answer."

Ed moved closer. "All right," he said. "I like you, Brianya." He leaned his elbows on his knees and rubbed his face with the palms of his hands.

Blank stare from Brianya.

"I mean *really* like you, Brianya." He paused then continued. "Ever since we've been . . . well, doing whatever it is we're doing, I can't get you out of my mind. I don't want to be with anybody else. Not that I was some sort of player before, I wasn't. But I wasn't a monk either. I can't even think of being with anybody else in that way."

"So what are you saying?" Brianya asked, confusion settling in.

A sheen of perspiration broke out across Ed's forehead. "I guess what I'm saying is I want us take this to the next level." Ed looked Brianya directly in the eye.

Brianya's eyes grew wide with surprise. She'd heard what Ed had said, but she couldn't believe it. Couldn't he see that she'd put on weight? He'd felt the extra roll on her middle, that's why he'd pulled his hand back. He had to see that her eating was out of control. Hadn't he noticed that she'd gone back for seconds twice and that she hadn't been to the gym in she couldn't remember how long? She had baggage; hadn't he heard a word she'd said in the last three months? Brianya shook her head in confusion. "The next level," she repeated. "Well, I guess that would be letting you hug me without me freaking out." Brianya laughed when she said it, although she saw nothing funny about having a potential suitor recoil in disgust when he discovered she'd put on weight.

Ed laughed, too. "You got a point," he agreed. "But, honestly, that's not a problem for me." Ed rose from the couch. "Come here," he said, holding out his arms to Brianya.

Brianya moved with skepticism into Ed's arms. It was just a hug, she told herself. What was the big deal? When Brianya had first arrived, she'd noticed the striking aroma of Ed's cologne wafting throughout the house and asked what it was. "*Black*, by Kenneth Cole," he'd responded. Now, as she snuggled close to Ed, her head resting in the crevice of his neck, she drank in the scent and tried hard to hold herself together.

"You okay?" Ed asked, obviously feeling the tension emanating from Brianya.

"I'm good," Brianya croaked out.

In an effort to put Brianya at ease, Ed began humming the melody to the song, *Two Occasions*, by The Deele. Their bodies began to move in sync as Ed went from humming to singing the lyrics to the hook. He spun Brianya around and brought her back into his embrace and they began hand dancing to the beat of a silent tune.

Brianya, giggling like a schoolgirl, collapsed onto the sofa. "I'm cured!" she declared, shaking her head at Ed. "And I thought *I* couldn't carry a tune!"

"Hey, I warned you from the beginning."

Ed, like Endo, had a good-naturedness about him that Brianya found refreshing. Most of the men she'd known before were always so hung up on trying to be hard, tough guys. At this moment, Brianya felt drawn to Ed. As much as she wanted to take it to the next level with him, she couldn't. The next level, of course, meaning a declaration of exclusivity. "You did warn me," Brianya agreed. Building on the theme of forewarnings, Brianya added, "And I warned you from the beginning, too."

Ed joined Brianya on the couch. "Yeah, but it doesn't have to be written in blood does it? I mean, I know how I feel about you." Ed took Brianya's hand in his and brought it to his lips. He held Brianya's gaze with his. "You're the kind of woman a man would kill for," he said planting a whisper of a kiss on the back of Brianya's hand.

The room went still. The heat of electricity coursed through Brianya and she found it impossible to speak. "Whew," Brianya said, finding her voice and fanning herself in a mock gesture. "You're moving a little too fast for me."

"Too fast? It's been three months. Look, I know what you said about not giving the candy away . . . but I'm not talking about a one-night stand. I'm talking about a commitment." Ed's brown eyes flashed with excitement.

"Whoa!" Brianya moved away from Ed's grasp. "We're not on the same page. Are you talking about sex?"

"Well, yeah!" Ed's voice went up an octave. "What did you think I was talking about?"

"I thought you were talking about being exclusive."

Ed looked puzzle. "We're already exclusive, aren't we?"

"How can we be exclusive when we're not even *dating*?" she wanted to add "duh!" but she didn't dare.

Ed stood and stalked to the window. "So, you're seeing other people while we're dating, or doing whatever it is we're doing?"

Although she didn't mean it to be a secret, Brianya hadn't mentioned to Ed that he was one-third of a triad. Something in his tone and the way he was staring at her, told Brianya that it was better to deny all accusations. "No, Ed, that's not what I'm saying." Brianya found that in times like these, when there was a huge misunderstanding about expectations, it was best to say the person's name. It helped to reassure the other person that all was still well.

"Then what are you saying?" Ed stuffed his hands in his pockets.

"All I'm saying is, from the beginning I told you that I was celibate until *marriage* and that we weren't dating." Brianya sucked in a her breath then slowly let it out.

With the exception of the low hum of an appliance in the distance, the room was quiet. After what felt like an eternity, Ed spoke into the silence. "You're right. You did say that. It's just that you're so much more than I imagined you would be. I never expected to fall this hard for you. I mean, just the thought of you being with somebody else. . . ." Ed's thoughts trailed off. "Listen to me," Ed said, shaking his head. "I'm a forty-three-year-old grown man acting like a school boy with a crush."

Brianya let out a sigh of relief. "I thought you were about to go all *Misery* on me!"

Ed chuckled. "Yeah. I saw that deer-in-the-headlight look you were giving me." His brows furrowed. "I would never intentionally hurt you, Miss Johnson."

"Intentionally?"

"The fact of the matter is no matter how well-intentioned we are, without meaning to, we almost always end up hurting the ones we care about." Ed crossed the room to sit, once again, at Brianya's side. "So yes, Miss Johnson, I would never *intentionally* hurt you." Ed took Brianya's face in his hands and she let him kiss her with a passion that mirrored her own feelings, as deep as the Congo River.

CHAPTER NINETEEN

SIX DAYS, TWENTY-THREE hours, six seconds, and ten milliseconds since she'd first tasted the sweet nectar of Ed's lips, Brianya stood in the middle of her kitchen about to pour cooking oil in a cast iron skillet, moving her hips and bobbing her head to the sho nuff truth of the lyrics of Mary J. Blige's *Take Me As I Am*, and smiled in triumph. Although she hadn't agreed to a one-on-one relationship with Ed, he was willing to give her more time to make up her mind. In the meantime, Endo and Monty were perfect gentlemen in not pressuring her to define what they had. So far, all three were willing to take Brianya as she was. She just hoped the she could remain as she was: Celibate and still within a safe weight range.

Of course, if she kept up with her current eating habits. . . . Well, she didn't want to think about that right now. Instead, she seasoned the pork chops and beat them with a meat tenderizer before lightly rolling them in flour. Grease sizzled and popped as she laid the chops in the pan and covered it with a lid.

A quick peek out the window confirmed that today was definitely a hat day. All week, the only thing on her mind was getting together with her girls and going to the Eric Benet concert. Any minute the bell would chime and Cashmere and Dreama would push their way in ready to scarf down Brianya's food as if they hadn't eaten in days. The clock on the microwave read 1:15. A good six hours before the concert was to start.

Like clockwork, three minutes later, Brianya pushed open the front door and admitted two scruffy looking women with dirt on their faces and hair all over their heads, shopping bags in tow.

Brianya doubled over with laughter. "Y'all are two crazy fools!"

After the exchange of greetings, Dreama and Cashmere breezed past Brianya, dropped their bags on the floor in the foyer, and marched to the kitchen.

"You got this kitchen hoppin' up in here," Dreama said. She opened containers of salad, sweet potato casserole, green beans, and macaroni and cheese and made noises of approval. "We gonna be so stuffed we might not even make it to the concert."

"Don't be touching my food with your ole dirty unwashed hands. Get in there and wash your hands." Brianya pushed Dreama and Cashmere toward the bathroom off the kitchen.

"You expecting an army?" Cashmere said, chuckling.

Dreama came out of the bathroom drying her hands on paper towels. "All kidding aside, Bri. We got something we need to talk to you about."

A shadow of worry crossed her face. "What is it?"

Dreama glanced at Cashmere and the look Cashmere shot back at her answered the question.

Cashmere cleared her throat. "First let me just say, you know we love you and care about you. And we're so proud of everything you've accomplished in your life."

"Oh for crying out loud!" Dreama cut in. "Look, Bri. It's like this. You been packing on the pounds like a Sumo wrestler and we don't wanna see you get back up to 400 pounds and hate yourself for it."

Dreama was never one to mince words. That's what Brianya both hated and loved about her. She was the hit woman, always willing to do the dirty work that nobody had the stomach for. When she had first introduced Dreama to Cashmere, years back, Brianya figured the differences in the two women's personalities would be a bone of contention, but she was wrong. They hit it off like long lost sisters. Now here they were standing in her kitchen, about to wrap their lips around her food, tag teaming her. Brianya wanted to be mad at them, but she couldn't.

Nobody had said a word to her about the obvious weight gain. People were always willing to cheer you on to your face when you were making progress, but when the scale started going in the opposite direction, no one was brave enough to step up to the plate and call you out. As Brianya glanced at the two women's expressions, Cashmere's one of terror and Dreama's one of no-nonsense, take-no-prisoners, she was overcome with feelings of love.

Brianya sat down at the kitchen table and covered her face in her hands, shoulders heaving.

In a soothing tone, Cashmere said, "She didn't mean it like that," Bri.

Chairs scraped against the floor as the two women joined her at the table.

"Yes, I did! I meant every word I said, just like I said it." Dreama was unapologetic. "The last thing you need is for us to coddle you and act like we ain't lookin' at least forty extra pounds. We fam, Bri. If we're not gonna tell you the truth, who will?" Dreama reached across the table and pulled Brianya's hands away from her face. "Now go dry them crocodile tears so we can get our grub on, 'cause after today, we taking our big behinds to the gym!"

And that was that.

Five hours later, three impeccably dressed women stepped out of Dreama's Range Rover ready to scream for Eric Benet.

CHAPTER TWENTY

I N THE BACKGROUND a shrill scream shattered the quiet and the sound of a saw cutting through something hard and unyielding added to the chorus. Eerie silence followed. A man dressed in coveralls and covered in blood emerged, holding a severed leg in his hand.

Monty frowned at the image on the TV screen as he entered the great room. "Boo!" he said, causing Brianya to jump.

Brianya put her hand on her chest. "You scared me!"

"What's that you're watching?"

"I have no idea. I was just flicking through channels." Brianya's lackluster reply was an indication that she wasn't feeling this night at all.

The other night, while standing in her living room, and then talking on the telephone, they'd had a long debate about the virtue of forgiveness. In the end, Monty had finally managed to convince Brianya to go to his company's annual benefit dinner at Club Amadeus.

***

"So you can dish out advice about forgiveness, you just can't take it," Monty had said when Brianya refused to hear a word about setting foot inside Darnell and Marlon's club.

"Don't lecture me about forgiveness," Brianya threw back. "I'm having to do business with the two of them because of *forgiveness*. I lost a good friend because of *forgiveness*. I can't pick up the phone in my office and not hear the voice of one or the other of them because of *forgiveness*. *Forgiveness* got you in my door, truth be told! So don't you dare stand there with your pompous, pious attitude trying to lay a guilt trip on me. As a matter of fact, get out of my house with that crazy talk!"

Monty had grabbed his car keys off the table and snatched his coat off the rack. He turned to Brianya. "You're a hypocrite, Brianya. You don't forgive. You file stuff away until you can use it to your advantage."

Monty's words pushed something to the surface that had lain dormant in Brianya for so long that she'd forgotten she was capable of feeling self-pity. "Get out!" she screamed.

Shaken from the confrontation, Brianya had turned to the one friend she knew would never disappoint. She had crumbled a chocolate bar with almonds into a big bowl of vanilla bean ice cream and wolfed it down. Later that night, Monty had called to apologize.

"I can't say you were totally off base," Brianya admitted. "Maybe I do need to take a deeper look at what it means to truly forgive."

"I'm sorry I said that. You're one of the most forgiving people I know."

"Don't back track now. You said what you did because you believe it and you meant it. So own it. I was angry at first, but I see your point."

"Really?" Monty asked cautiously. "You ain't trying to punk a brother are you?"

Brianya's laugh broke the tension.

Taking his cue from Brianya, Monty said, "Okay then can I just say this one thing then I'll leave it alone?"

Brianya didn't want to have this conversation again. The wound hadn't yet scabbed over. At the same time, she didn't want to discourage honest dialogue with Monty. "Tread lightly," Brianya warned.

"After my girl—ex-girl—tried to take me for my Bennies, I went through this period where every female I dated was a surrogate for my ex and that's how I treated them. I mean, there I was, Mr. Successful—ex-ballplayer—businessman, driving around in a Benz, going home to a Pepper Pike address every night, and I couldn't keep a woman." Monty cleared his throat.

"Not to be rude, but what does that have to do with me?"

Nonplussed, Monty soldiered on. "I had never admitted to myself that I was wounded; how could I? I was Monticello Belvoir. Up until the time me and her started kickin' it, I used to think: What woman wouldn't be grateful to get with me? That's how cocky I was back then. Then I met her and she turned my head all the way around. I did everything right. I never cheated on her, treated her like a princess. She didn't want for anything. All the time, while I was patting myself on the back about being this stand-up dude, she was plotting and planning how to take what was mine. I couldn't admit this back then, but I can now. What she did crushed me; knocked me off my game."

The silence that followed Monty's last statement left a gaping hole in the conversation. Neither spoke.

Finally Monty said, "I'm not proud of the way I treated those other women, but I was hurting and didn't know it. Wasn't until a good friend of mine sat me down and told me what's up. Once I owned up to the fact that I had been hurt, I was able to move forward."

Brianya let the words hang in the air. She took in as much air as her lungs could hold then breathed out. "One woman breaks your heart and all of a sudden you're an expert on forgiveness? Give me a break! Try having your heart broken in *every* relationship you've ever been in, and then come talk to me about forgiving and moving on!"

With the patience of Job, Monty said, "You're missing the point. I said all of that not to tell you about me, but to tell you about yourself. Until you own up to the fact that you have been hurt by *all* those dudes, you'll stay stuck. And every man that looks your way is gonna pay the price for what those other dudes did to you."

Out of frustration, and to stop him from saying more, Brianya had huffed into the phone and said, "Just to prove you're wrong, I'll go to this little company dinner with you!" But Monty was right, Brianya hadn't really forgiven anyone. That was one of the reasons, the shrink had said, she sought solace through food. Feeling uncomfortable with the depth of emotions they'd begun exploring, Brianya had quit going to sessions. She had learned most of what she needed to conquer her food issues, and she had a ton of lost pounds to prove it.

***

"Ready?" Monty asked, cutting into Brianya's thoughts and bringing her back to the present. He handed Brianya her coat and scarf.

"As ready as I'll ever be."

The roads looked as if someone had covered them in a thin coat of polyurethane. As dusk descended, a ferocious wind blew the tops of the naked trees, making them look menacing and ominous as they dipped and bowed, just inches from wreaking havoc on whatever lay underneath them. In a few months time, the Earth would rejuvenate. And Brianya wondered if Monty's interest in her would die, now that he had seen her personality stripped bare.

"What turns you off, Monty?" Brianya blurted as they drove along Green Road.

"Where did that come from?"

"I'm curious, that's all. I haven't been nice to you. After all the encouragement you gave me when my father got sick, I should be much nicer to you. Instead, I belittle you and throw you out of my house." Brianya turned and stared out the window of the SUV. Tears were ready to break forth and the last thing she wanted was for Monty to see her cry and feel sorry for her.

"Oh, don't worry," Monty said, remembering the conversation. "I didn't say I had mastered the art of forgiveness. I'm still working on it. So for now, I'm keeping score."

Brianya turned away from the window and playfully punched Monty's arm. "I think you're too good to be true."

Monty smiled. "Maybe."

"You didn't answer my question."

"Turn-offs?" His lips pursed as he contemplated an answer. "Are we talking appearance-wise, or attitude-wise?"

"We're talking whatever turns you off-wise."

"Physically: nasty, unwashed, unkempt females. Attitude: whiny, woe-is-me people who think the world owes them something."

"That it?"

"That's it." Monty pulled the Escalade into a VIP parking space and killed the engine.

The conversation forgotten for now, Brianya sat up straight in her seat and took in her surroundings. Before Club Amadeus moved in, the building was a DIY storage facility with inside storage units as opposed to stand-alone ones, typical of such businesses. From what she could see of the outside, they'd done a decent job of erasing the utilitarian look. Two ferocious looking concrete lions stood guard on either side of the heavy, black-lacquered doors. A black and gold awning with gold trimming covered the entryway and announced the club's moniker.

Brianya opened the glove box and took out a napkin to wipe the moisture from her palms. Rummaging in her purse, she pulled out a plum raisin lipstick and black eyeliner pencil and freshened her face.

Monty watched as Brianya deftly moved from her face to her hair. "You can't improve on perfection," he said and leaned over and kissed Brianya on the cheek.

"What was that for?"

"That's me showing my appreciation for you agreeing to do this."

"You're welcome."

***

Teenage boys of various heights and ages surrounded Monty and Brianya as soon as they stepped into the club and whisked Monty away. It happened so fast, Brianya had no time to register what had happened. Okay, so this is how it would be all night. That was fine with her. She'd find a nice little cubbyhole off to the side and try to be inconspicuous. *Maybe I won't have to deal with those two losers.* Too late, she spoke too soon. One of the losers was heading her way.

The woman hung from his arm like a cheap Brooks Brother's suit. The loud, clownish make-up she wore would look better on its intended target—Howdy Doody—and the hair that grew unnaturally from her scalp, had spent the better part of its life hanging from the rear-end of a horse long past its usefulness. She didn't speak, she purred, and by no stretch of the imagination were her words intelligible. Tricia Yancy had spotted Brianya before she could retreat to another part of the club, and mumbled a greeting that left Brianya tilting her head in confusion.

"Excuse me?" Brianya said in awe of the woman's audacity.

Marlon spoke up before Tricia could repeat herself. "Welcome to Club Amadeus, Brianya," He leaned heavily on the last syllable of her name. "I didn't think I would ever see this day."

Brianya waved off his greeting and comment with a one-finger salute and turned to walk away but not before adding, "Y'all are all kinds of nasty up in here!" It shouldn't have surprised her, what she'd just seen, but it did. First, Tricia and Darnell, Marlon and Celine; now, Tricia and Marlon, Darnell and Celine. *Straight up low class.*

Brianya spotted Monty on her way to a table in the corner and got his attention. She pointed in the general direction of where she was heading so he'd know where to find her. A server approached her table and asked if she'd like something to drink. Brianya asked to see a menu. She perused the menu and she thought her eyes had betrayed her when she lighted on the coffee selection. A slow smile of triumph lifted the corners of her mouth and Brianya thought she had died and gone to heaven. "Oh, happy day!" she said and placed her coffee order.

The rest of the night went over without a hitch.

CHAPTER TWENTY-ONE

"LET'S WRAP THIS thing up today, Mr. Larson," Harold Teamer from the legal department said. "This is a straight forward case. Mr. Taylor violated the agreement of his contract, pursuant to section four, subsection 2D, where it states—"

Hamfred waved a dismissive hand in Harold Teamer's direction. "No need to waste time reading what I already know, Harold." Hamfred swiveled in his chair so that his expression was unreadable. "What I need to know is what legal recourse I have to keep Mr. Taylor from following through on his threat to go public with what he knows about my . . .," Hamfred faltered and fidgeted with his watch, "proclivity."

Harold leaned forward in his chair, steepled his fingers. "Defamation of character, slander, maybe even libel. Take your pick. Just the threat of any one of those charges should deter Mr. Taylor from moving forward with whatever information he *thinks* he has on you. Unless he's seen you . . . uh," Harold paused and searched for the right word, "on display. Otherwise, whatever he says is hearsay and therefore slander. I can tie this thing up in court for however long it takes; and I doubt Mr. Taylor has the wherewithal or the funds to withstand a lengthy court battle." Harold leaned back in his chair and crossed his legs.

Mollified, Hamfred turned to face the lawyer. "Let's get this over with then." Hamfred pressed the speaker button on his phone and spoke into the unit. "Send them up, Sharon."

As they waited, the two men grilled Brianya, for the umpteenth time, about the menu and the coffee selections listed on it. Things couldn't have gone any better if she had planned this herself. Her only regret was tipping her hand to Marlon by confronting him about it that night at the club.

"Hey, Snake!" Brianya had bellowed at Marlon, finding him in an office at the back of the club, after seeing what she was sure was a big ole typo. "This is a typo right?" She waved the menu in Marlon's face as if it were the elixir to a deadly disease.

Like a snake, Marlon had, in one fell swoop, torn the menu from Brianya's hand and ran it through the shredder next to his desk in a matter of seconds.

"How stupid could you be? You had a sweetheart deal and you go and ruin it. All you had to do was give Mellow Beans exclusivity for one year, *one year*," she said, holding up one finger. "Not the standard three years that everyone else had to agree to, and you would clear ninety percent of the profit, not the sixty-five that all the others had to agree to. And you got the product at a seventy-percent discount, not the fifty that everyone else had to pay. Not to mention the other perks you swindled out of Hamfred Larson." A light bulb of understanding went off in her head and Brianya had to laugh out loud. "I've been giving you too much credit." She hit the heel of her hand against her forehead. "Here I thought you had this diabolical plan to ruin my career at Mellow Beans and all along it was yourself you were planning to sabotage." Brianya shook her head in disgust.

Marlon had tried to save face by downplaying the discovery, but even he knew he was beaten. Surprise of all surprises, he had begged Brianya to overlook the obvious, even appealing to her friendship with Celine. Sorry louse that he was, he didn't know that that friendship had faltered months ago and that she knew that he and Celine were no longer a couple. Then he resorted to bribery. "I can throw a little something your way, make it worthwhile. Thirty percent of the profit. Who couldn't use some extra coin?"

In the end, Brianya wound up feeling sorry for Marlon, that he was such a loser. "We'll be in touch," she said and headed out the office, feeling a lot lighter in spirit than she had before the evening began. After that conversation there was no way she could stay at the club, so she told Monty what had happened and with regret, he sent her home in a cab. In her celebratory mood, Brianya hadn't thought to grab another menu on her way out as evidence, but she had taken a picture with her phone of the one the server had handed her initially. *Thank God for camera phones.*

Armed with photographic proof in hand, Brianya had marched, unannounced, into Hamfred's office and laid it all out for him. She'd told him she knew about the history behind the deal he'd cut with Marlon and that she had every intention of going to the board members with her proof for breach of contract if he didn't act on what she'd told him. By the time she walked out of his office, Hamfred was falling all over himself promising that he'd get the matter taken care of post haste.

And so here they were—Hamfred Larson, Harold Teamer, and Brianya Johnson—sitting in Hamfred's corner office, wall to wall glass windows, a mural of an azure sky with visibility as far as the eye could see, the waves of Lake Erie lapping gently at the unfrozen shores, getting ready to meet with Marlon Taylor and his lawyer, an exercise in futility.

At every turn, Harold Teamer batted away the other lawyer's arguments as though he were an annoying Canadian soldier insect. By the time the meeting was over, Marlon was apologizing and thanking Hamfred Larson and Mellow Beans Coffee Corporation for the opportunity to do business with them.

Brianya resisted the urge for one last snipe at Marlon.

CHAPTER TWENTY-TWO

A T THE END OF the day and happy to be rid of what she considered a tumor on the backside of the Mellow Beans Coffee Corporation, Brianya was still smiling. She whistled all the way to the parking garage.

That triumphal feeling of joyous elation evaporated exponentially the closer Brianya got to her car. Wearing a scowl that rivaled only Cruella De Vil's in *Lady and the Tramp*, Tricia Yancy stood, arms at her sides, looking like she wanted to scratch Brianya's eyes out.

Fear rose to the surface. "May I help you?" Brianya asked, her tone cautious. In the self-defense classes she'd taken years ago, the instructor, an ex-FBI agent, had told the women to always have their keys at the ready and to carry them splayed between their fingers, to use as a weapon. From that day forward, Brianya made a habit of carrying her keys that way. So when Tricia spit in her face, Brianya's sole reaction was to lash out with her keys, and ask questions later, which is what she did, opening the flesh on the woman's cheek, missing her eye by mere centimeters. "Are you crazy?!" Brianya said and swiped at Tricia's face again, missing her.

Touching her face and feeling a warm, sticky liquid, Tricia let out a blood-curdling scream and lunged at Brianya, allowing Brianya the opportunity to swipe at her face a third time; this time catching her on the chin. Before Brianya could swing again, she felt herself being pulled away from Tricia and simultaneously heard someone calling her name.

She turned to see who had pulled her away. "Get your hands off me!" Brianya screamed at Marlon, shaking herself from his grasp. "What, you're not man enough to handle your business, you have to send your girl to do your work?" Breathing heavy, her words came out choppy.

"It's not even like that!" Marlon ran his hand across the front of his suit jacket and trousers, straightening the disarray. "I tried to stop her."

"I bet you did!"

"Brianya! Brianya!" Debbie kept shouting as she pushed her way through the crowd that had gathered to watch the commotion. Debbie, eyes wide in bewilderment, took in her boss's disheveled appearance. "Are you okay, Brianya? I saw what she did!" Debbie turned toward a stricken-faced Marlon and a whimpering Tricia, who tried to stop the bleeding with her coat sleeve, and screamed at them. "What is wrong with you people? You act like animals!"

Brianya took a packet of tissues from her purse and wiped the spit from her face.

Ignoring Debbie, Marlon asked, "You okay, baby?"

"Do I look okay? That crazy heifer cut me in my face!" To Brianya she said, slow and deliberate, through clenched teeth, "You better watch your back!"

Brianya narrowed her eyes at Tricia, took a step in her direction. "Correction: You'd better watch *your* back!"

"I'm calling the police," Debbie announced. She was all business now as she whipped out her cell phone and began pressing buttons. At the mention of the police, most of the crowd disbursed, including Marlon and Tricia. "Yeah, that's right, run!" Debbie screamed after them. "We got your information anyway."

As they waited for the police to come, Debbie asked, "Are you okay, Brianya? You need me to call someone?"

"No, Debbie. I'm fine." Only she wasn't. Brianya's hands shook as she reached for the car door handle and she almost lost her footing as her knees buckled slightly.

"You're not okay, Brianya." Debbie persisted; she was like a dog with a bone. "You're breathing like you're about to pass out and your hands are shaking. I'm going to call Mr. Hollister. His car is still here so he must still be in his office." Debbie fished her phone out of her purse again. She had a good head for numbers and she knew Ed's by heart. "Mr. Hollister," she said into her phone, "this is Miss. Johnson's secretary, Debbie. Some crazy woman attacked Miss Johnson in the parking garage. Could—" Debbie shook the phone. "Hello? Mr. Hollister? Hmmm . . . We must've got cut off." She frowned at the phone, puzzled, and redialed. It rang until it went to voicemail and Debbie left a message. She turned to Brianya. "Do you want me to call anybody else, Brianya?"

"No, I don't, Debbie. I didn't want you to make that last call." In that way she had of exasperating Brianya, Debbie was outdoing herself today. Secretly grateful to have her own little guardian angel watching over her, Brianya crooked a finger at Debbie and beckoned her to come closer. She whispered, "I don't want you to think I don't appreciate what you're doing for me, but I really am fine; embarrassed, and becoming more so by the minute, but fine. So if you could somehow get the rest of these people to go about their business, I'd –"

A voice from the crowd bellowed, cutting through Brianya's conversation. "Brianya!" Running like a Price is Right contestant in her direction, Ed literally skidded to a stop in front of her. "What happened? Are you all right? Your secretary said someone attacked you!"

Oh good, just what she needed, more attention. This show just kept getting better and better. All she needed now was for Endo, Monty, and Andre to come running to her rescue.

"For the love of all that is good and wholesome, I'm fine!"

The police arrived several minutes later and took their statements. Brianya told them all she could remember about Marlon, from off the top of her head, and what little she knew of Tricia. As attested to by Debbie, the few remaining looky-Lous, and even the police officers, this was clearly a case of self-defense.

Breathing out a huge sigh of relief, Brianya was thankful that she wouldn't be going to jail.

After reassuring the officers that he'd see to Brianya getting home safely, the last of the squad cars pulled off. Debbie, satisfied that Brianya was in capable hands, left too. When they were alone, and only the sound of squealing tires could be heard in the distance, Ed turned to Brianya. He took one look at her and his face became a mask of concern. He caressed each word. "I can see it in your eyes."

"What can you see?" Brianya had read corny lines like that in cheesy romance novels and she always wanted to ask the authors why they used such trite, untrue sentiments, when everyone knew that you could no more read a person's true feelings in their eyes than you could predict a person's destiny at birth. Knowing Ed, he'd say she was feeling something mushy, like hurt or sadness. How he knew she wanted to get the world in a big ole circle, hold hands, and sing Kumbayah. Honestly, had he not learned anything about her in all the time they'd spent together?

"You look like you want to snap somebody's head off!" Ed said in answer to Brianya's question.

She wasn't expecting that. Brianya laughed until she cried tears of relief, and then beat back the slight discomfort she felt as Ed dried her tears with his fingertips.

"So how did this all happen?" Ed asked.

When Brianya finished giving Ed a blow by blow rundown of the incident, commentary included, Ed locked fingers with Brianya and said, "I'm glad you made the police report. So if something else jumps off, they'll be the first people the police will look at."

"Oh no! They won't even get that chance! I got protection that's a whole lot better than a police report."

There was that look of concern again.

"Don't worry. It's nothing like that." No doubt, Ed thought she meant to use a weapon. "But it is a weapon, of sorts."

***

The cell phone chirped, signaling a new text message. Brianya lifted the phone from its charging base and read the screen: "Problem neutralized" was all it said. Andre and his cloak and dagger speech never ceased to amuse Brianya. He was like her very own Terminator.

Brianya wondered how it went down. Had Andre done his Andre thing, where he pulled no punches and came right out with it? Or had he done his Patrick Jane thing and acted totally clueless until the last moment when he came out swinging low and hitting hard, laying out all the facts? She hoped that he hadn't played a Bruce Willis or Arnold Schwarzenegger role and laid down the law with his fists. Curiosity got the better of her and she ended up texting Andre: "What did u do?" she typed. When the answer came back: "I did me," relief flooded through her. Loosely translated, that meant that Andre had talked to one or both of them and told them to back off, letting them know in no uncertain terms that if they didn't they'd have to answer to more than just him.

"Done," Brianya said to a puzzled-looking Ed.

Ed had insisted on following Brianya home and making sure she didn't get into any more altercations with crazy women. He'd already been there two hours, not that Brianya wasn't enjoying his company. Ed was easy to be around, always insightful and funny. It's just that Brianya had a routine and Ed's presence prevented her from engaging in that routine. After being caged in all day, Brianya liked to unleash the girls and let them swing free as soon as her foot hit the threshold. Besides that, she needed to wash her face. She was about to gently suggest to Ed that he could leave now, his work being done, when Ed asked, "Your brother really an ex-Panther?"

Brianya sighed inward. "Something like that." It was better to be vague, in case she had to sic Andre on Ed someday, if he got out of pocket. Brianya couldn't see that happening. She hoped it wouldn't come to that, because she was beginning to think of Ed as a serious contender. The problem, though, was that she was also starting to feel that way about Endo and Monty.

As if reading her thoughts, Ed said, "Better to keep me wondering, huh?" and chuckled. He chugged the last of the bottled water he'd been nursing and rose from the chair. "We'll, I don't want to wear out my welcome." He stood and stretched his legs, twisted from side to side. "I know you probably have things you need to take care of. Places to go, people to see." He smiled a crooked smile.

His mouth said the words, but he made no attempt to move toward the door. Ed had something on his mind; Brianya could tell by the way he stood, glued to the spot, looking conflicted. "What?" Brianya asked.

Ed shook his head. "It's nothing."

"It's not nothing, it's something!" Brianya tried to keep the irritation out of her voice, failing, she tried a calmer approach. "When, you're ready to talk about it, you know where to find me." She forced a smile.

Ed stepped into Brianya's space and she instinctively stepped back. "I know we talked about this the other night and I don't mean to keep bringing it up. But I'm really feeling you, Miss Johnson." This time when Ed moved in closer, Brianya didn't flinch. "I can't stand thinking that there's another man out there that might win my prize. I really don't see what the problem is." He pulled Brianya into his embrace and kissed her lightly on the neck. "We're right for each other."

Why is it that men always say one thing but do another? Brianya wondered. From the beginning, she had stated her stipulation: No sex before marriage. Ed had assured her that he was okay with that. The rule hadn't changed. Okay, so she'd gotten a little more affectionate with Ed than maybe she should have. Until the passionate kiss the other night, the most they'd done was hug. What was the harm in that? *Well . . . Hmmm . . .*

"Ed, I don't know what to tell you." Brianya met his gaze with determination. "I'm not going back on my promise to myself. I'd rather eat my way back up to 353 pounds than do that."

Ed eyed Brianya's curves. "I can see that!" came his clipped reply.

Brianya moved out of his embrace. "What did you say?"

"That came out wrong!"

She knew it. The other night hadn't been her imagination. He had hesitated when he put his hand around her waist. Just like a typical bully—try to destroy what they can't have. "No, it came out just right." Brianya felt hot tears of anger sting her eyes. "It's time for you to go," she said dangerously calm. The last time Brianya had a calmness of this magnitude was three years ago, when, knife in hand, Darnell was almost history. Unlike most people who believed that that sort of calm in the face of a storm was God's peace washing over them, preventing them from doing something they may later regret, Brianya had no such misconceptions. The calmer she remained, the angrier she became. So, before she did something that just might send her to jail this time, she spoke only two words, quietly, politely, and barely above a whisper. Ed had to strain to hear her. "Please, leave."

"I really don't have a problem with the extra weight," he protested. "You think if I did, I'd be standing here pleading—"

As if she hadn't heard a word Ed said, tears of anger streaming down her face, Brianya said, "God, please let this man get out of my house right now. Because the next time he opens his mouth to say another word, I won't be responsible for my actions. Amen."

Ed stared at Brianya, dumbfounded. Realizing she was serious, he gingerly lifted his jacket off the back of the kitchen chair and almost tiptoed to the door, closing it softly behind him.

Brianya sank down in the kitchen chair after Ed left. What was she doing? She had come so far in her journey, addressing her eating issues, dealing with anger triggers. The twice-weekly sessions, the countless—no, not countless—104 hours, to be exact, spent in therapy couldn't have been in vain. If Brianya didn't get out in front of the eating and the anger train wreck she was currently on, then she may as well stick a sign on her forehead that read: "World's Biggest Loser"; and not in a good way. Brianya knew what she needed to do.

She needed to go through her cupboards and refrigerator and toss out every piece of junk food. Then she needed to put one foot in front of the other and march herself right down to the Mind Your Body 24/7 Fitness Center and take her butt-whipping like a man. Need and want never made good bedfellows. At the thought of the gym, Brianya remembered that Lonnie had called, again, threatening to break down her door if he didn't see her at the gym in the next week. In spite of good intentions and willing hearts, Brianya and Dreama hadn't made it to the gym as they vowed they would after the concert.

CHAPTER TWENTY-THREE

I T ALWAYS CAME back to the number on the scale. From childhood to adulthood, if Brianya wasn't the one making an issue of her size, someone else would happily step up. Whatever victories she gained in the way of weight-loss were always short lived. Living at her goal weight had lasted only a couple of months before the pounds started coming back. *Not everyone is meant to be model-thin*, Brianya told herself. Not that 147 pounds was model thin. But given where she'd come from—353 pounds—147 pounds was darn near anorexic. She may as well face the facts: her weight would always be an issue, and there was no sense in fighting what was meant to be. Her mother seemed happy enough to see her "back to her old self," as she had put it, after Brianya had stuffed herself on the four-course Sunday meal they enjoyed in the dining room of her parents' home.

Endo sat across from Brianya and watched with pleasure as she visibly enjoyed her meal.

Brianya had been promising her parents that she would be more regular at church and today she'd made good on her word. Johnson family tradition was that if you went to church as a family on Sunday, you ate Sunday dinner at the Johnson home. There was no way Brianya was going to get out of it. So not wanting her to break her date with Endo, her father suggested that she invite him to Sunday dinner.

Now here they all sat—Roger, Alice, Cinthia, Brianya, and Endo—enjoying one of the best meals Brianya had had in a long time. Hands down, no one could cook like Alice Johnson. Her mashed potatoes and gravy was the right amount of lumpy and creamy and the pot roast was seasoned with just the right amount of rosemary, tender enough so that you had to scoop it out with a spoon. The collard greens with cabbage had just the right amount of firmness, but not so much that it was crunchy. The hot water cornbread was soft and chewy, the edges golden brown and a little crispy, the way Brianya liked it.

Endo dunked his cornbread in the middle of his plate, sopping up the juices that had pooled there. "Mrs. Johnson, you put your foot in this meal!" he said as he chewed and smacked his lips with satisfaction.

Alice blushed and accepted the compliment. "We're not done yet! Save room for dessert. We're having blueberry pie and homemade vanilla ice cream."

Brianya almost choked on the spoonful of mashed potatoes she'd just stuffed into her mouth.

"I can't eat another bite, Ma!" Cinthia said and then turned to Brianya. "And you shouldn't either, Bri. We need to just toss that dessert." Cinthia shook her head at Brianya. "All that hard work, for nothing!"

"Cinthia!" Alice scolded.

Brianya ignored Cinthia and ate the last of her collard greens and cornbread.

Endo remained silent, though Brianya could tell by the way he opened his mouth slightly then closed it, that he wanted to say something in her defense. She imagined that he would say something like, "Even a dog likes a little meat on his bone," or something equally as cliché. Whatever he would say would be inconsequential. Because no one—*absolutely no one*—was going to shame her out of sinking her teeth into her mother's famous blueberry pie and homemade vanilla ice cream.

"I'm gonna go throw it away!" Cinthia announced as she rose from her chair.

Roger knew his eldest daughter. In fact, his expression said that he knew exactly what she was thinking. That's why he turned a sorrowful eye on his youngest and said, "God help you if you do."

"You take one step toward that kitchen and I swear you'll live to regret it!"

Something in her sister's tone made Cinthia stand stock-still. Her expression said that she knew Brianya meant every word she said.

"Are you okay, Brianya? What's going on with you?" her mother asked.

Her mother's warm expression and the concern in her voice annoyed Brianya. She didn't need everyone treating her with kid gloves. She was a grown woman, capable of making her own decisions and if she wanted to eat the whole pie and scarf down the whole container of ice cream, whose business was it?

"Just get off my back! I'm sick to death of everybody policing me. I can eat what I want, when I want. Got it?" Brianya jumped up from the table, knocking over her chair in the process, and stormed out of the dining room. She flopped down on the couch in the living room and put her head in her hands. What was wrong with her anyway? Lately, it didn't take much to set her off.

As if he had read her mind, her father said, "What got into you, daughter?"

Brianya whipped her head around to see her father standing directly behind her. She hadn't heard him enter the room. "I don't know, daddy." She took a deep breath. "I feel like everybody's walking around with a magnifying glass watching everything I eat and I'm sick of it."

Her father gave her shoulder a squeeze and joined her on the couch. "You was doing so good with your weight. What happened?"

Good question. What had happened could be any number of things. Could be that her ex-friend had betrayed her by going out with her ex-boyfriend. Perhaps it could be that she was still feeling humiliated after being spat on by Tricia. Or it could be the pressure that Ed, and now Monty, was putting on her to make a decision about moving their relationship out of "friendship" mode. Or maybe it was Endo always fawning over her. Or it could be the massive amounts of sugar she was stuffing herself with lately. The reality was it was all of those things, but she wasn't going to tell her father that. What she did say was "I got a lot on my plate at work and my eating just got off track, that's all." It was partially true.

Roger looked at Brianya skeptically. "Look to me like it did more than just get off track; I think it got derailed."

In spite of herself, Brianya smiled. Her father always could bring her back around whenever life got too heavy. "Daddy, I don't want to laugh," Brianya protested.

"I know," Roger said, pinching his daughter's cheek playfully. "You just wanna sit here and be mad at the world and feel sorry for yourself." He rose to his feet. "Sorry, Daughter, not today. Today, we gon' go back into that dining room and you gon' apologize to your mama and your guest and then you gon' eat as much ice cream and pie as you want to."

Properly chastised and feeling like a small child, Brianya did as she was told.

***

Endo was unusually quiet on the ride back to her house. Brianya had noticed, too, toward the end of the meal that he kept watching her father as though he was waiting for a sign. Two streets from her house, Endo turned a serious expression in Brianya's direction. "Do you mind if I come in when we get to your place?" he asked.

They hadn't had much time alone together, going from the church directly to her parents' house. She had planned to ask him in anyway. "Sure, I don't mind."

Endo scooped up two of the care packages from off the back floor that Mrs. Johnson had packed for them and bumped the car door closed.

Brianya made a beeline for the bathroom. "Put those in the fridge for me, please," she said from behind the closed door. She heard running water and assumed that Endo was washing his hands. She liked a man who was hygienic. She emerged from the rest room, paper towel in hand, to find Endo rearranging the food in her fridge. "What are you doing?" Brianya snapped and then caught herself. Endo was just trying to be helpful. No need to bite the man's head off, she reasoned. After all, she was the one who had asked him to put the food away. "I'm sorry," Brianya apologized. "I didn't mean to speak to you in that tone."

Endo continued rearranging the items in the refrigerator. "It's no problem," he said, pushing aside a casserole dish of candied yams. "You got a roommate that I don't know about? There's enough food in here to feed a small army." He jammed the plastic containers of leftovers in the space he made and shut the refrigerator door.

"Oh that. No, I like to cook ahead of time so I don't have to think about what I'm having for dinner."

"Looks like you're set for the next month or so."

"So," Brianya said, moving away from the subject of food, "you sounded like you had something on your mind." She ushered Endo out of the kitchen and into the sitting room.

Endo made himself comfortable in the oversized chair. "I really like your family," he said and smiled. His two bottom teeth were a little crooked, but not so much that they took away from his handsomeness. Brianya hadn't noticed before how smooth and blemish-free his skin was. It was true what they said—"black don't crack"— because there wasn't a line, a wrinkle, or a crow's foot anywhere in the mahogany complexion of his facial features. "Your mother reminds me a little of my mother, the way she chooses her words carefully."

He'd told her that before, the first time he'd met her mother, at the hospital when her father had had a stroke. "Your mother's a strong woman. She has a beautiful spirit. You know the whole time we were in the waiting room, she was praying. I could see her lips moving." A sadness had come into his eyes. "My mother was like that too, prayed all the time. No matter what happened, good or bad, she was thanking God. Used to drive me crazy."

"Why?" Brianya had asked, befuddled. She had assumed that Endo was a religious man. Why else would her father go to all this trouble to set them up?

"Ah come on, don't look at me like that," he said. "I'm not an atheist. I believe in God. I just think people can get a little unbalanced."

Relief swept over her. "Okay. You get no argument from me on that." Brianya hugged the arm of the couch and leaned forward. "What's on your mind, Endo?"

"Um . . ." He cleared his throat several times. "We've been seeing each other for how long?" he asked, as if he didn't already know the answer.

"Around three months, I think." What was he getting at?

"And in that time, have I disrespected you or tried to pressure you into doing anything you didn't want to do?"

Brianya looked sideways at Endo. "Uh, no," she answered, skepticism creeping into her tone.

Endo pressed on. "When I first met you, I wasn't sure how things would pan out with us. I got the feeling that you didn't care that much for me." He rubbed the stubble growing on his chin. "But the more time we spent together, you seemed to warm up to me." He smiled nervously. "I told you from the beginning that I wasn't going anywhere and I still hold to that." Endo stood up and reached in his pants pocket, pulling out a fuzzy black box. "I've always been a man who knows what he wants, Brianya. And I've never hesitated about going after it." Brianya's eyes grew wide with shock. Endo got down on one knee and took Brianya's hand in his. "And what I want more than anything is for you to make me the happiest man in the world by agreeing to be my wife."

Brianya was speechless. "I. . . . I. . . . We. . . ."

"You don't have to answer now," he said.

The hopeful expression that slid across Endo's face made Brianya choose her words carefully. "Endo, three months isn't a long time. There's a lot you don't know about me—"

"I know all I need to know!" Endo cut in. "After our first date, I knew that you were something special."

She didn't like having to hurt his feelings, but Brianya wasn't about to say yes to a marriage proposal from someone she wasn't even dating. Well, not officially. Endo was looking at her expecting a reply, although he had said she didn't answer right then. "I'm sorry, Endo. I just can't."

Raising himself from the floor, Endo brushed off his trousers and closed the box. A little bit of happy had gone out of him. "Are you seeing someone else?" he asked, apparently too ashamed to look at Brianya. His forehead creasing with curiosity, Endo lowered himself back into the chair.

Brianya leaned back on the couch. She wondered if she should tell Endo about Monty and Ed. She hesitated. "My ex has been coming around and I'm not sure how I feel about that." *What?!* Was she insane? *Okay, girl, check your pulse. Those words did not just come out of your mouth!*

"I see," Endo said as if he didn't' believe her. "This is the person who dropped you because he said you were too heavy?" Brianya could hear the accusation in his tone. "I'm good for you, Brianya; we're good for each other. Even your father thinks so."

So, that's what the looks between Endo and her father had been about. And the invitation for Endo to join them for Sunday dinner after church. "I love my father, Endo, and I respect his opinion. But I haven't needed his approval for a date in a long time. Ideally, I would love for him to approve of the man I choose to marry, but the truth is I'm a grown woman and very much capable of making my own decision about whom I choose or don't choose to marry." She leaned forward and touched Endo on the forearm. "But thank you for thinking enough of me to ask me to marry you and for running the idea past my dad. I know his opinion means a lot to you."

Endo stared at Brianya, his expression one of disbelief and bewilderment. "What just happened here? Did you just turn me down and chastise me at the same time?"

Brianya pulled her hand from Endo's arm. "Didn't mean to chastise you; I was just speaking from my heart."

Endo nodded and looked thoughtful. "See, that's what I mean when I say you're something special." With intensity, he said, "I'm a patient man, Brianya. You're worth waiting for. Something tells me you're not the sort of person who believes in going backward." Endo breathed out heavily and hoisted himself from the chair. "Well, I'd better get going."

Brianya walked him to the door and said goodnight. This time when Endo hugged her and lingered, she didn't freak out.

CHAPTER TWENTY-FOUR

DREAMA SLAPPED THE glazed Krispy Kreme doughnut with chocolate icing out of Brianya's hand and dared her to pick it up. "That's your third doughnut; I told you I was gonna do that if you reached for another one."

Brianya glowered across the table at her friend. She knew she didn't need the doughnut, but she didn't appreciate Dreama acting like the food police either. It was only because Dreama loved her like a sister and wanted to keep her from self-destructing with her weight that Brianya didn't go commando on her. "I'll let that pass this time. But if it happens again, I'ma have to dot that eye."

Dreama laughed the comment away and held up her fist, the universal sign of power or solidarity. "Peace and love sistah, peace and love.

Rolling her eyes playfully at Dreama, Brianya glanced at her watch. "What's taking Cash so long. All she had to do was drop the car off across the street."

"What you in a hurry for? We ain't doing nothing but going back to your place to watch movies."

"That's not the point. The longer I sit here smelling these doughnuts the more tempted I am to order a dozen and take them home, *just for me.*" Brianya eyed the discarded doughnut lying on the table where Dreama had smacked it and sighed. She picked it up and balled it into a napkin.

"Yeah, well, you'll have to get them past *me* first." Dreama sucked up the last of her strawberry banana smoothie and made a slurping sound with the straw. "So, it's been a while since we had a movie marathon Saturday. What gives? I mean, you're usually out with one of your boy toys." Before Brianya could answer,

Cashmere sauntered through the door. "Saved by the bell," Dreama teased.

"Hey," Cashmere said, shaking a dusting of snowflakes from her coat.

"Hey, yourself. Now let's go." Brianya made a gesture to rise.

"Oh, so the two of you get to scarf down doughnuts and gulp down smoothies and all I get is to enjoy the aroma? I don't think so." Cashmere twisted her lips. "We're not going anywhere until I get my fill."

"Can't you get it to go?" Brianya whined.

"No, she cannot. Because if she gets some to go, you're gonna want some to go, because you're not gonna want to smell them all the way home knowing that you don't have any. So we're gonna squash all that and Cash is going to sit here and eat whatever she gets and," Dreama made a face, "you're going to answer my question."

Cashmere took off her coat and draped it over an empty chair. "What question?"

"Why she doesn't have a date with one of her men."

"Don't answer that until I get back." Cashmere hurried to the counter to place her order. "Okay, go!" she said upon returning.

Brianya didn't know why Dreama was giving her a hard time about her availability when the same could be said of her. She and Curtis were practically joined at the hip and now all of sudden she was free? Also, why wasn't she at the shop? Saturday was their busiest day. Brianya wasn't sure about Cashmere's Saturday routine; they were still at the getting reacquainted stage. "Don't put this on me, Drama," Brianya said in a huff. "Why aren't you working or spending time with Curtis?"

"One," Dreama said and held up a single digit. "Curtis went back home to Tennessee, to see about his mama and check on some things. Two," a second finger went up, "I scheduled today off, simple as that."

"Got an answer for everything, don't ya?"

Dreama shrugged a response. Cashmere looked expectantly at Brianya. "Okay, fine. I don't have a date because I'm taking a break. Everybody was getting too serious, too fast, and I'm just not ready for that. Endo's proposal last Sunday was the breaking point."

"I'm still floored by that," Cashmere said. "On the one hand, I can sort of see how you can know that a person is the *one* after only three months. But on the other hand, wouldn't you have to spend like almost every waking hour being with that person to be *that* sure?" She took a sip of her acai berry smoothie. "Y'all spent time together, but was it all like that?"

Brianya reflected on the question before answering. They hadn't gone out on many dates, but they'd spent a lot of time talking on the telephone. Plus, Endo had a built-in source of information right at his fingertips. "Um, he probably thought it was 'all like that.' He knows more about me than Monty or Ed, especially since he has his own little information source."

"Yeah, yeah," Dreama said waving away Brianya's remark. "And you probably know a whole lot about him, too. But, how do you *feel* about him?"

How did she feel about Endo? Brianya hadn't really given her feelings toward him serious thought. Confronted with the question, she contemplated her answer before saying, "For an older guy, I guess he's all right." She waited a beat before adding, "Can I see myself married with children to him? I don't know. But one thing I can say for sure is that when I'm with him, he makes me feel like I'm the center of his universe." Brianya's face alighted with dreaminess.

Cashmere fanned herself.

"Oh, give me a break! What is this, some sixties sitcom?"

"No, I'm serious," Brianya protested. "Endo has this way of swallowing up the space around you so that it feels like there's no one in the room except you and him. And when he talks to me, I can feel that he genuinely cares about me." Brianya drew imaginary doodles on the table with her finger. "I have to admit, I only went out with him to please my dad. But, I never imagined that I would end up considering him as a serious contender."

"And you're cool with him being so much older than you?" Dreama asked.

"Don't knock older men, Dreama," Cashmere added. "At least with them, you pretty much know what you're getting." Cashmere paused. "Well . . . most of the time."

Brianya noticed the pained expression that flitted across Cashmere's face. She was thinking about her ex-fiancé, no doubt, and his betrayal. His lies and cheating had altered Cashmere's life forever. What was supposed to be a happy and joyous occasion had turned out to be a daytime nightmare. Sure, by the time a person reached a certain age, you would expect that all the foolishness and childish behaviors would be in the past, but some men never grew up. Young fools became old fools. But Endo wasn't like that. His growth was evident in the way he carried himself, his conversation, and how he treated her. In every way, he was respectful and respectable. So were Monty and Ed. Endo could give her the stability she needed, but what about the fun, the zest, the excitement? He had shown that he was flexible and spontaneous, but only after she'd coaxed him. What Brianya wanted was for that spontaneity to be inbred, a part of who he was as a person. Monty had that quality. He was—

"Girl, where are you?" Cashmere said, cutting across Brianya's thoughts.

"Sorry, I was just thinking about Monty."

"What about Monty?" Cashmere and Dreama asked in unison.

"I was thinking about how much fun he is to be around, and how he likes to do things on a whim. Remember that scarf he put on my doorstep in the pouring rain?" Brianya directed the question to Dreama, who frowned in response.

"What scarf?" Cashmere asked and Brianya filled her in. "Aw, that's so romantic. Where can I get a Monty?"

"And you know what else? He told me that when he was going through a tough period with his ex that he thought about me. He said he's liked me for years, even when I was with Darnell."

Cashmere, who was hearing this for the first time, raised an eyebrow at Dreama, who was miming talking signals with her hands. "Problem?" Cashmere asked Dreama.

"Ignore her," Brianya said. "She doesn't trust Monty. Thinks he's up to no good."

"You know me, Bri. I'm a sucker for romance, but I'm gonna have to agree with Dreama on this one. It sounds a little too convenient."

"Really, Cash? *Really?* I thought you liked Monty."

"I did. I do," Cashmere wavered. "I don't know! I'm so confused," she said, doing a dead-on imitation of John Travolta's seventies character, Vinnie Barbarino. They all laughed. "All kidding aside, you're okay with him being cool with Darnell?"

"You both keep forgetting that me and Monty aren't dating. I'm simply getting to know him better. So at this point, to make a big deal about his friendships is premature. If it becomes more then we'll cross that bridge when we get to it."

"Didn't you say he wanted it to be more?" Dreama asked.

"Yep, but at this point it's not." Brianya reached across the table and swiped one of Cashmere's doughnut holes. She plopped it in her mouth and chewed, while Dreama gave her the evil eye.

"So where does that leave Ed in all of this?" Cashmere asked.

"Oh. . . My. . . . God!" Brianya said, her eyes the size of saucers. "I can, like, totally see myself with Ed. He is the total package. And his body is, like, un-be-lieve-able!"

"Lawd have mercy! Brianya done turned into a Valley Girl!" Dreama said. "Like, Really, Bri? Seriously?"

They all laughed so loud that the young girls behind the counter joined in.

Brianya replayed her comment in her mind. "Oh, my goodness. I just heard myself, girl. That was scary!" She hugged herself around the middle, trying to ease the cramp she got from laughing so hard.

"Girl, if he's got you going gaga like that then you need to just drop the other two and stick with Ed."

Brianya wiped away the residual tears of laughter with a napkin. "I don't know, Cash. I can't get past the secrecy."

Cashmere looked confused. "What secrecy?"

Brianya told her about Ed's reaction to her inquiry about his chipped tooth.

"Hmmm . . . I don't know, Bri," Cashmere said and shook her head. "I think you're making something out of nothing. A lot of guys have chipped teeth. Plus chipped teeth can add a certain air of mystery to a person." Cashmere struggled to maintain a straight face.

Dreama cosigned Cashmere's statement. "She's right, Bri. Take this guy named Troy that I used to date. He didn't have just one chipped tooth, he had three!"

Brianya rolled her eyes at Cashmere and Dreama. "Okay, point taken. Maybe I'm overreacting just a tad bit."

"No, what you're doing is procrastinating. The same way you always did when we were younger."

"No," Dreama corrected. "The same way she always *does*. She hasn't changed."

Brianya harrumphed, folded her arms, poked out her lips, and looked askance at her so-called friends. They were talking about her as if she wasn't sitting just two feet away. "I do not procrastinate! I make my decisions very carefully," she declared. Well, maybe she did procrastinate, just a little. But she wasn't about to admit that.

"So where does Ed stand?" Cashmere pressed.

"All right. Dang! Give it a rest. You're like a pit bull." A slow smile spread across Brianya's face as she thought about Ed and the night he sang to her and kissed her. "You know, I really, really, really like Ed. I mean, he's sensitive, honest, spontaneous. And I feel so comfortable when I'm around him. But, he's got this thing about fat women."

"So, you're not fat." Dreama said.

"In my mind I'll always be fat. I'll always be one cookie away from where I started."

Cashmere stared sympathetically at Brianya.

"Oh please! And you call me dramatic? Girl, get over yourself." Brianya closed her eyes and prepared for Dreama's tirade. When Dreama got this way, all anyone could do was hold on and wait for the storm to pass. "So you put back on forty pounds; big deal. Nobody held a gun to your head and told you to stuff your face with all that junk food. Or stop going to the gym, and whatever else you did to put back on the weight. If you think 187 pounds is a cookie away from being 353 pounds, then you better go back to school and take remedial math. Look at me, I'm 217 pounds, twenty pounds heavier than when Curtis and I started dating." Dreama gathered more steam and continued. "Do you see me sitting around worrying about what he thinks of my weight? Truthfully, I could care less. If he wanted to walk away today, I'd hold the door for him."

Brianya looked sideways at Dreama and pursed her lips.

"Okay, maybe I wouldn't hold the door for him, but I wouldn't stop him from leaving. 'Cause, girl, after getting to know a person, outward appearances shouldn't matter. What should really matter is what's in your head and your heart. And that's all I got to say about it." Dreama took in a mouthful of air and looked from Brianya to Cashmere.

"Amen!" Cashmere said. "But seriously, Bri, you have to stop over-thinking everything. Like I said before, just live in the moment. I only wish I had your *problem*. You got four men trying to get with you. You know how hard it is to get holla from one brother, and you got *four*? You may as well add Darnell to the list, even though there's no way you're getting back with him," Cashmere added when Brianya frowned at her.

Brianya had listened patiently to Dreama and Cashmere and while they each had some valid points, she wasn't ready to make a decision. If she made the wrong choice, she could end up right back where she was three years ago. "I hear what both of you are saying, but I'm not ready to declare a winner yet." She looked from Cashmere to Dreama. "But I'll tell you what I am ready for. I'm ready to get my scary on. So let's go watch some movies!"

CHAPTER TWENTY-FIVE

B EFORE TURNING IN for the night, Brianya set the alarm for
7:00 A.M. She wanted to get an early start for Love's House so
that she could come home and have the rest of the day to herself.
Last Saturday's girl fest had reminded Brianya of how much she
missed spending quality time with her girlfriends. But it was also
exhausting. Trying to get to know three men at one time was also
exhausting. Brianya couldn't keep this up much longer. She was
thankful that Ed was giving her time to make up her mind about
how, or if, they would move forward. The same for Endo and
Monty. If only she had disclosed to each of them in the beginning
that they weren't the only ones. She could've avoided this
awkwardness now. Telling them now would make her look bad,
as if she were trying to be sneaky, which wasn't true. It simply
hadn't occurred to her that she would end up having serious
feelings for all three of them.

A new year was only four weeks away, and Brianya didn't want
to go into it still undecided. She'd give herself three weeks to
come to a decision. She would have to tell them the truth and let
the chips fall wherever. Now all she had to do was figure out *how*
she'd tell them.

That was the last conscious thought Brianya had until the
jangling telephone, very early on a Saturday morning, pulled her
out of a sound sleep. She awoke with a start and glanced over at
the digital clock on her night table. *Who the heck is calling me at two-
thirty in the morning?* Immediately her thoughts went to her father.
This time had he had a full-blown stroke? The doctor had said
that a mini-stroke was sometimes a precursor to a full-blown
stroke. Brianya braced herself and snatched up the phone without
looking at her caller ID. "Is Daddy okay?"

"Uh, I'm not sure. But I'm fine," the voice said.

Brianya let out her breath, relieved that the phone call wasn't about her father. "You idiot!" she shouted into the receiver. "Why in the—" Brianya caught herself before the profane word left her lips. Although her eating had gotten out of control and her weight kept fluctuating, Brianya was proud that she had managed to stay on track about not using profanity. Instead, she said, "Why are you calling me at this time of morning, Darnell?"

"I apologize, but I'm just getting home from the club and I've been thinking about you all night." This was so like Darnell. He could be rash and selfish. "I needed to hear your voice."

Brianya stifled a yawn and said with sarcasm, "Needed to hear my voice? Why?" She could hear what sounded like ice dropping into a glass and the sloshing of liquid. Darnell didn't care much for hard liquor, but when he did imbibe it, he preferred bourbon. Brianya assumed the long pause was Darnell taking a sip from his glass.

"I miss you, sweetheart. I came back because I was hoping we could get back together and I could make things right." Darnell took another sip. "The club is doing well. I'm at a place in my life where I feel like I'm holding my own, but the one person I owe a debt of gratitude for helping me keep it together when I was at a dark point in my life won't give me the time of day."

As much as Brianya wanted to tell Darnell what he could do with his plea for sympathy, the note of sincerity in his voice wouldn't let her. Self preservation instincts were telling her to hang up and keep as far away from Darnell as possible, but curiosity made her sit up in bed and ask, "Why are you still trying to be with me when you're with Celine now?"

The glass made a thudding noise as Darnell sat it down on a hard surface. "That was a onetime thing. She came on to me at the grand opening." Darnell stopped abruptly, and then cautiously asked, "How did you know about that?"

"You haven't changed a bit, Darnell. You're still the same conniving, low-life you always were. How could you do that? You knew she was my friend."

"What? I didn't know she was your friend."

"Don't play dumb. I'm sure your friend Marlon bent your ear about the beef he had with me. I know he told you how I tried to talk Celine out of getting involved with him. Let's forget about the fact that Celine and I were friends and concentrate on the fact that she was your friend's ex and your ex's cousin. Is that what you're about now, Darnell?" As Brianya asked the questions, she heard her father's voice in her head saying: *Never ask a man a question if the answer really matters.* She questioned the motive behind her inquiry and couldn't come up with a valid reason. Except that it was really Celine she wanted answers from.

"She didn't mean anything to me. Like I said, it was a onetime thing. I wasn't looking to get attached to her." Darnell's voice rose slightly. "Don't you get it? It's you I want. I came back for you! I could have started up a club anywhere; this club thing was my idea, you know." He blew out a gust of air and said more softly, "I owe you, Anya. I did you wrong. I need to make it right."

He was serious, Brianya realized. Aside from calling her Anya, Brianya hadn't known this new Darnell. So, that's what this was all about. What he really wanted was for her to say she forgave him and mean it. Monty's speech about forgiveness came to mind and Brianya reflected on what he'd said. *You don't forgive. . . . Until you own up to the fact that you have been hurt . . . you'll stay stuck.*

"You and I will never get back together. I hope you understand that, Darnell."

"You still have feelings for me, Anya. I could feel it when I kissed you in your office." She could hear him moving about, that restless way he had of fidgeting when he was agitated. "All I'm asking for is a chance to make it up to you."

Brianya's words came out in a hoarse whisper. "You made a fool out of me, Darnell. You humiliated me. Do you know that when you dumped me like that, all I could think about was making the pain stop by ending it all?" She'd said too much. She had never wanted him to know what his leaving had done to her, but the more she talked, the harder it became for her to stop. "I was going to do it. If it wasn't for Dreama and Celine talking me out of it . . ." Her words trailed off.

"I know," He sounded resigned, beaten. "That's why I need you to forgive me."

In that instant, Brianya realized why she was so reluctant to give Darnell the forgiveness he was seeking. It was like a missing piece of a puzzle falling into place. He had never *asked* for forgiveness. He'd only apologized but it wasn't the same thing. An apology was only an acknowledgement that a wrong was committed; Brianya deserved more than that. Asking for forgiveness, on the other hand, was an admission of guilt; it was the wrongdoer asking for absolution in order to find peace. Only Darnell hadn't asked, he'd demanded. *I need you to forgive me.* Even if she wanted to—and she didn't—how could she grant Darnell something that she hadn't granted herself? She did, however, want to move past the hurt, which meant that at some point, preferably soon, she'd eventually have to have a real conversation with Darnell about their past.

"What do you really want from me, Darnell?" Brianya asked, testing her theory.

A pregnant pause hung in the air, then the steady, deliberate intake of breath. Brianya envisioned the left vein just below Darnell's jaw line throbbing, a clear indication that he was upset. The object of his displeasure, of course, was Brianya's insistence on making him beg. She could tell by the puffs of air Darnell exhaled that he was probably thinking about the day she'd paid him a visit in the parking lot of Target at quitting time.

***

Brianya had timed it just right. At ten past seven, the security guard unlocked the gate and let Darnell out of the store. Seeing him after a long absence, his ordinary face, arrogant swagger, and lithe body, was a welcome sight to Brianya.

Only a few feet away, Darnell stopped abruptly when he spotted Brianya kneeling by his car door. "What are you doing?" His words came out sounding smug and Brianya knew she must look ridiculous but she didn't care.

"Please don't leave me, Darnell," Brianya cried. "I can't make it in this world without you!" Brianya felt as if someone had taken a pair of pliers and ripped her chest wide open, squeezed her heart until there was no life left in it. She had nothing to lose. She'd gone from strong and determined, the night she cleaned out the condo, to this weak, groveling shell of herself in the space of a few weeks.

"Do you know how ludicrous you look down there on your knees?" Darnell surveyed the parking lot. As far as he could see, except for street traffic, they were alone. He grabbed Brianya's arm to pull her up but she yanked free, and in the process lost her balance and lay sprawled on the ground. "Get your big behind up and act like you got some sense. You're embarrassing me!"

Brianya ignored Darnell's protest, while struggling to heave herself onto her knees again. "You can see your child whenever you want. I won't stand in your way. Please, just give me another chance!" she begged.

Darnell looked down at Brianya, tears dropping heavily from her eyes, and shook his head in pity. His voice softened. "Why should I give you another chance?"

"Because I love you," Brianya whispered. "And I know you love me."

"That's where you're wrong. It's over! Like I told you before, all I can offer you is my friendship. As far as being a couple that's out. I need someone who's . . . well, not you." Darnell stepped over Brianya and opened the car door.

Brianya wiped the snot from her upper lip with the sleeve of her shirt. Out of the corner of her eye, she saw Darnell wince as if someone had pinched him. "I can lose weight, Darnell; I promise. Please, just give me time! You'll see."

Groaning, Darnell got into his car. "Look, I'm trying not to hurt your feelings but you don't get it." He put the key in the ignition and started the car. "Get this through your head: I'm not in love with you. I'm not interested in you. I'm moving to Richmond, Virginia to be with my son and his mother. Got it?" He put the car in gear and rolled forward slightly. "Now could you please move so I can leave?"

Hearing the truth put so bluntly, something in Brianya broke. She was no longer one person but two. The broken Brianya looked down at her desperate self, finally seeing for the first time what she'd become. She was despicable and pathetic. Darnell had made her that way with his lies and deceit. But she was also to blame. She had allowed him to use her, to treat her in ways no man before him would have dared.

Brianya rose unsteadily to her feet. "I hate you!" she said in a low voice between clenched teeth. "Everything in your world might be peaches and cream right now but I promise you, one day you'll reap what you sowed. And when that happens don't come looking for me, trying to make amends. I'll never forgive you or forget!" With each word, Brianya could feel her temper slowly rising.

Darnell could feel it too. His pupils shrank to the size of a period and Brianya could tell he was thinking of their last night in the condo and how he'd just barely escaped with his life when she wielded the butcher's knife against him.

Brianya barely had time to jump out of the way, as Darnell peeled rubber out of the parking lot.

***

"I don't want to do this on the telephone." Darnell's reply held a note of impatience. "I want to see you in person."

Brianya's heart and head were at polar opposites. On the one hand, she wanted to give Darnell what he needed, because freeing him meant freeing herself. But, on the other hand, she felt vindicated and his mental suffering justifiable. Finally understanding why she had felt weighed down, or stuck, despite the positive things that had happened in her life was liberating. Brianya felt more empowered than she had since before lifting the self-imposed dating moratorium. Embracing that empowerment, Brianya could choose to be small and petty and tell Darnell to kick rocks. Or she could be the person she'd transformed herself into after the parking lot incident, someone who was all about self-awareness and positivity. In an attempt to ease the dull throb emanating from her forehead down to the base of her neck, Brianya massaged her temples.

"I remember you always talking about Karma," Brianya said. "How's that working for you?"

"I came looking for you. What does that tell you?"

Brianya moved from the bed to the wingback chair in the corner of her room, suddenly self-conscious. It didn't feel right, talking to Darnell while in bed. The geography conjured images and awakened feelings she didn't want to have for him. "It tells me that you have something up your sleeve."

"Look, I understand that you're skeptical and you don't trust me. I get that. All I'm trying to do is make things good between us."

"I meant what I said in that parking lot, Darnell. I'll never forgive you or forget." It felt good to say the words on emotionally solid ground, especially having the upper hand.

"The Anya I know is bigger than that."

"Reverse psychology, so sophomoric."

Darnell remained quiet, probably staring at the telephone in that way he had of fixing his gaze on a person until he wore down their resistance.

Brianya put her feet up in the chair and hugged her knees to her chest. She chewed the inside of her bottom lip. The clock read 3:01. She had no plans for the day; what was to stop her from saying yes? Her heart raced in her chest and she was gasping for air as she thought about a sit-down dinner with Darnell.

"Anya. Anya!" Darnell shouted in a panic. Brianya didn't answer. "Are you okay? You need me to call 9-1-1?"

At the mention of 9-1-1, Brianya made a greater effort to control her breathing. She was on the verge of having a panic attack. "No," she squeaked out. "Give me a minute." Brianya put the phone down. Lowering her feet to the floor, she put her head between her legs, inhaled and exhaled slowly until the feeling subsided. Like the elephant in the room, she needed to deal with this situation. The only way to do that was to face it head on. Whether Brianya liked it or not, they were going to have this conversation and it was going to be face-to-face.

Brianya retrieved the phone. "Are you still there?"

Sounding relieved, Darnell said, "I'm right here, Anya. I'm not going anywhere."

"Yeah, that's the problem," Brianya said under her breath.

"I didn't hear you, baby. Can you repeat that?"

"Nothing. Look, Darnell, I'm not promising anything, but if I did agree to meet with you, when would you want to do that?"

"I'm off tonight," Darnell said eagerly.

I was afraid of that. "I'm not making a decision right this minute. I'll call you at a *decent* hour and let you know."

Darnell gave Brianya his contact information and they ended the call.

It was useless trying to get back to sleep so Brianya headed for the kitchen. She fried the Tilapia that had been thawing in the refrigerator—for dinner.

CHAPTER TWENTY-SIX

WITH HER ADRENAL glands pumping on high after the events of earlier this morning and after downing two huge pieces of fried fish at four o'clock in the morning, Brianya drove to the gym. Thankful that Lonnie was not on the premises, she spent two hours doing cardio. Not wanting to risk running into Ed or Lonnie, lest they suddenly show up, Brianya skipped the showers. She was drenching wet and shivering by the time she pulled into her garage.

Brianya turned the showerhead to pulsate and let the water beat against her scalp and back. Although it would never take the place of a masseur, it was a pretty good stand-in. After twenty minutes of water therapy, Brianya switched the setting back to normal, then lathered and rinsed her body and hair. She had just stepped out of the shower when her cell phone jangled and Dreama greeted her. "I was just about to call you." Brianya said.

"Oh? What's up?"

"Are you sitting down?"

"Yeah, why?"

"You'll never—and I mean *never*—guess the conversation I had last night." Brianya towel dried her hair, patted her skin down, and lotioned up as she told Dreama about her late night phone call from Darnell.

"You did what?!" Dreama screamed into the telephone. "Stay your behind right where you are. I'm on my way over there."

Fifteen minutes later Brianya opened the door to a highly agitated Dreama. "No, you did not drive over here in your robe and pajamas!" Dreama looked at her wardrobe as if seeing it for the first time. "And where the heck are your shoes?" The temperature had to be in the low twenties.

"Forget all that!" Dreama barged in, dropped an overnight bag onto the floor, and reached up and grabbed Brianya by the ear, dragging her into the living room.

"Ow! That hurts!" Brianya struggled to free herself but Dreama's grip was tight. "Let me go, girl!"

Dreama let go and glared at Brianya. "You better tell me that this is a joke," she threatened. "How could you agree to go out with that maggot?"

Brianya massaged her throbbing earlobe. "First off, I didn't agree to anything, yet."

"Why, Bri? Why? Why would you want to go down that road again? I swear to God, you'll travel that road by yourself this time. I can't do it. I *refuse* to do it. Have you forgot what we went through the last time?" Dreama pulled her thin lips into a straight line. A look Brianya knew all too well. Dreama was trying to hold her emotions in check.

If Dreama hadn't been relentless in her refusal to let Brianya out of her sight when she'd started talking about ending it all. . . . Brianya didn't want to think about that. She was a different person then, in a different place. "That was then. This is now," Brianya said softly.

"Exactly!" Dreama shot back. "Let the past stay in the past. I know I joke with you about y'all getting back together. But that's all it is, is a joke." Dreama paced back and forth. She did that whenever she was stressed. "I need coffee."

Brianya headed to the kitchen, Dreama followed. "You don't have anything to worry about. If I do agree to meet with him, it'll be strictly for closure."

"Can't you do it over the telephone?"

"I tried." Brianya filled the coffee maker with water and measured out the beans and handed them to Dreama to put through the grinder. "He said he didn't want to do it on the phone."

Dreama dumped the beans in the canister, slammed down the lid. She set the grind consistency then pressed the on button. "You know, Bri, I'm trying real hard to be patient. Because what I really want to do is cuss you out and scream in your face. But I'm not gon' do that because I know it wouldn't do a lick of good. You gon' do what you wanna do regardless."

"I don't get you, Dreama. You're always telling me that I need to get over Darnell and move on."

"Yeah, but—"

"But nothing," Brianya cut in. "Either I do it this way, which, since I thought about it, is the easy way. Or, I do it the hard way and keep going like I'm going, wondering and speculating. At least if I go, it'll be a one-time thing and I'll never have to deal with him again." The two hours of cardio had allowed Brianya to put things into perspective. Darnell's persistence had given Brianya a small semblance of the peace she could have if she forgave him. Brianya filled a filter with four heaping tablespoons of ground coffee and plugged in the coffee maker. They waited for the coffee to brew, each in their own thoughts.

Brianya let her nostrils take in the rich, chocolaty bouquet as she dropped a dollop of whipped cream into her cup and stirred.

"You know you just ruined a perfectly good cup of coffee," Dreama said. She always drank her coffee black, the way it was meant to be drunk.

Brianya ignored the comment. She blew across the top of the coffee then took a small sip. Tiny particles of liquid danced on her palate and the full-bodied richness of the dark roast sent excited tingles throughout her body. "You know if I do this, I can finally make a decision about Endo, Monty, and Ed."

Dreama didn't say anything, just kept sipping her coffee. Her facial expression and body language were loud and clear. Brianya was not going to persuade her to see any side of the coin but the one that ended in her friend's unhappiness. "Do what you wanna do; I don't care," Dreama said and banged her cup down on the table. Coffee sloshed over the edges. "I'm going to take a shower."

As Dreama stormed off, Brianya smiled to herself. Despite what Dreama had said, she wasn't about to let Brianya go through this ordeal by herself. She had come prepared to talk sense into her friend, her duffle bag full of clothes a dead giveaway. The conversation wasn't over; Brianya had enough sense to know that. Otherwise, Dreama would be at home taking a shower in her own bathroom. Brianya wet a dishrag and wiped off the countertop and table, seriously contemplating the consequences of saying no to Darnell. *What's the worst thing that could happen?* she mused.

***

As Brianya dialed Darnell's cell number, it occurred to her that she was about to make a decision that would impact the rest of her life. The phone rang several times and right when she was about to give up, an older female voice said, "Darnell's phone." Brianya's first reaction was to hang up. Why? She didn't care about his personal life. Her only connection to him was to close a chapter of her life that was left unaddressed far too long.

In a professional voice, Brianya said, "Hello. This is Brianya Johnson. I'm calling for Darnell Jones."

"Brianya!" The woman exclaimed. "This is Mrs. Jones, Darnell's mother. How are you?"

"Oh. Mrs. Jones." Brianya felt foolish. "I'm fine. How are you?"

"As a mother, I'm feeling much better. Darnell tells us you two might be getting back together." Brianya could hear the smile in her voice.

"He said what?" Brianya asked taken aback.

"His father and I have been worried about him for the last year. He's been in a funk since that girl told him that our grandbaby wasn't his."

Although she had only met Darnell's mother once at a family cookout, Brianya must have left a good impression on the woman, so much so that she felt comfortable telling her son's business. It was satisfying to hear. Gloating about it in front of Darnell's mother would be inappropriate and just plain wrong. About the funk he was in, Brianya could only imagine his parents' worry for their youngest son. Brianya knew all too well about Darnell's low moods. He'd fallen into a depression shortly after they had started dating when he lost his job. And it was only by constant attention and around-the-clock emotional care that she was able to pull him out of despair. "I'm sorry for you and your husband, Mrs. Jones." Brianya paused. "I don't want to sound rude, but may I speak to Darnell?"

"He's just out of the bathroom now."

"Been telling lies," Brianya said when Darnell came on the line. "So now we're getting back together?"

Darnell sounded surprised to hear Brianya's voice. "Oh, uh."

"You know that's not about to happen. Ever!"

"You sure about that?" Dreama's voice came from behind Brianya.

Brianya covered the mouthpiece with her hand and shushed Dreama, who wasn't about to be silenced.

"You piece of trash!" Dreama screamed in the direction of the telephone. "She ain't hardly gettin' back with you!"

Brianya mashed her hand tighter against the phone. She wanted to punch the mute button but if she lifted her hand, she was afraid Darnell might hear Dreama's rant.

"Who was that?" Darnell asked.

Brianya shot a warning glance at Dreama. "Be quiet, Dreama. Stop acting so childish." Brianya tried to escape to the living room, but Dreama was on her heels shouting into the air.

"You shoulda stayed your sorry behind in Virginia!"

"Is that Dreama?" Darnell asked. "Is she talking to me?"

"Hold on," Brianya said to Darnell. She pressed the mute button and turned her attention to Dreama. "You were supposed to be taking a shower."

"I needed to get a towel set from the linen closet." Dreama stood in the middle of the living room with her hands on her hips. "You see what he's about? Still going around telling people y'all gettin' back together. That's really what's up." Dreama pointed her finger at Brianya. "Hang up the phone, Bri!" She tried unsuccessfully to wrestle the phone away from Brianya.

With effort, Brianya held her temper in check. "Calm down, Dreama."

"You calm down!" Dreama said and kept shouting the words until she was hoarse.

Brianya stared at Dreama, not sure what to make of her behavior. She had never seen her friend behave like this. The scene was surreal, something right out of a psychological thriller. Brianya spoke softly, her fear meter on high. "Dreama, what's the matter with you?"

Spent, Dreama said, "You don't know what it was like for me, Bri." The words came out laden with sorrow. She flopped down in the wingback chair. "When you were staying with me, I couldn't go to sleep unless you went first. I used to set my alarm clock for every hour on the hour just to make sure you hadn't done anything. I would get up in the middle of the night and check on you. The last thing I prayed at night was the first thing I prayed in the morning, that I wouldn't find you dead in your bed. Even though you went to work every day, I'd come home three, four times to make sure that you didn't get off early and come home and do something to yourself." Dreama let out a huge sigh and closed her eyes. "Most of the time, I felt like I was losing my mind. That's why I can't do it no more." She looked at Brianya apologetically. "I just can't."

Brianya was overcome with a love and respect that she'd always had for Dreama, but hadn't been aware of its depth. Sitting next to Dreama, on the arm of the chair, Brianya hugged her

215

around the shoulders. "I didn't know," Brianya confessed. "But I promise you, you don't have anything to worry about. All I'm going to do is end this chapter of my life so that I can start the next one."

Dreama looked doubtful.

Brianya's disappointment sat heavy in her chest. "With or without your approval, I'm going to do this, Dreama." Running her hand slowly across the butter soft leather of the chair, Brianya masked her disappointment in a bravado that she didn't quite feel. "It would be nice to know that you've got my back. But if you can't get behind me on this, I'll understand."

Through a half-smile, Dreama gave in. She stared at the phone in Brianya's hand and Brianya suddenly remembered that she left Darnell holding on. Just as she suspected, he was still there when she un-muted the phone and agreed to go out with him.

CHAPTER TWENTY-SEVEN

A FTER THE SCENE with Dreama this morning, Brianya didn't think her day could get any more exciting, but Love's House was crazy today; Brianya had to help out all over the place. She had to organize activities for the women and children, and answer the hotline for two hours. Did two intakes and helped prepare a safety plan with a woman whose husband had once beaten her so severely that she was now permanently blinded in one eye. She wouldn't leave him, though. No, she kept insisting that this time he hadn't meant to hurt her when he rammed her head into the refrigerator. He was upset, she said, because he lost his job and it just so happened to be on the same day that she'd made a mistake and let his peas touch his mashed potatoes, and he hated for his foods to touch.

In four years of volunteering at the shelter, Brianya had heard almost every excuse women give for staying with their perpetrators. Some of the justifications were enough to turn her stomach. But reality for some women took longer than for others; for some it never set in. If she had a dollar for all the women who defended their batterers, she'd be richer than Bill Gates. Try as she might, on days like today, it was hard for Brianya to compartmentalize her feelings for the women at the shelter from her own experiences. It was shortly after starting to volunteer at the shelter that the realization smacked her square in the face. As she listened to one of the guests relate her husband's mental abuse, so much of what the woman said could easily have been Brianya's story. Like Darnell, the woman's husband derided her in the form of jokes about her weight, often soliciting comments from their children and other family members.

As Brianya listened to the woman, her thoughts had drifted to a several instances of open hostility toward her size 32 body. She was shopping at Heinen's grocery store when the bag boy had the nerve to screw his pimply face into a scornful expression as he threw Brianya's groceries—chips, Sara Lee cheesecake, cookie dough ice cream, ground beef, ham hocks, three different kinds of greens, and diet soda—into plastic bags and nastily tossed them into her cart. Then there was the woman at the movie theater, who'd snorted loudly when all but the seat next to her was occupied, and Brianya had no choice but to ask her kindly to move her purse, so that she could squeeze into the seat. Brianya had experienced enough prejudice to know that the snort was not because the woman had to sit next to a stranger; it wasn't even because she had to sit next to a Black stranger. No, it was because, sin of all sins, she had to sit next to a *fat* stranger.

As humiliating and powerless as those encounters were, they were nothing compared to the situation she'd encountered in an Urgent Care center where she had gone because she was having trouble breathing. That ugly November night, the doctor told Brianya she'd have to be x-rayed, because determining whether there was fluid in her lungs was difficult to diagnose by an aural exam.

Snippets of a conversation floated through the air as Brianya walked back from the lab. When she rounded the corner, she overheard the doctor say, "She's so big . . . I hate touching all that fat." From the way the nurse quickly nudged the doctor, and the semi muted "shush," Brianya knew that the comment was about her. The doctor had looked at Brianya defiantly, offering neither an apology nor an excuse. *The nerve of that dirty-faced freeloader, who barely speaks English, to criticize me,* Brianya had thought. Livid, hurt, and devastated, Brianya had wanted to cry. Instead, she allowed the hurt to motivate her to do something about her weight.

Just as back then, Brianya had to find a way to get control of her eating or she'd find herself right back in those ugly, humiliating weight-related situations.

Even with the extra weight, Brianya still marveled at her body as she turned the porcelain knobs on the shower and a steady stream of tepid water gushed out. Nudging the hot-water tap until the water became a little less than scolding hot, Brianya stepped in, cautiously optimistic about tonight. The smell of the watermelon body wash brought a smile to Brianya's face as she squeezed a generous portion onto her loofah sponge. Warm, soothing water traveled down her back and found lodging between her buttocks. Something it would have been hard-pressed to do almost three years ago, she mused. Nowadays whenever Brianya showered or bathed, she celebrated her new body, happy that she no longer had to squeeze into the thirty-by-sixty inch tub, the water barely rising above her navel. And when it did rise higher, it wasn't long before it sloshed over the sides of the tub and onto the floor.

Brianya washed furiously, hurrying so that she wouldn't be more than fashionably late for dinner. Butterflies danced in the pit of her stomach, and she had to admit that she was feeling a certain amount of exhilaration. Just a few moments ago, the combination of going into Love's House today and agreeing to have dinner with Darnell tonight had brought up so many memories of weight discrimination that Brianya was tempted to call and cancel. She wouldn't though. She needed this be over, done with.

Brianya stepped out of the shower, toweled off, brushed her teeth, gave herself a quick facial, lotioned her body, and then slid into a pair of cream lace panties with matching bra. Fingering the lace waistband, she smiled to herself and thought, *No more cotton bloomers for you!* and then danced a jig to her vanity table to apply her make-up.

The doorbell chimed seven times. It could only be an impatient Dreama.

Brianya hastily swung open the door. "Let's get this show on the road," she said, ushering Dreama to the basement.

Forty-five minutes later, Brianya was taking the stairs two at time to finish dressing. She sprayed *Pleasures* into the air, danced into it, dabbed a little behind each ear, shimmied into her pantyhose, then poured on the Armani dress. Brianya pulled her black leather, 4-inch platform-toe Via Spiga boots onto her slender feet and sauntered back to the basement.

"How do I look?" she asked, half-afraid that Dreama might say her make-up looked clownish. She was never any good with makeup.

"Like a trump card!"

"Are you sure? I don't have on too much make-up, do I?"

"Everything looks great, Bri. Make-up, hair and dress, which, by the way, is huggin' you *just* right. And I love those boots!"

"I don't know, Drama. I've got a funny feeling that tonight will be a disaster."

Her face set in stone, Dreama warned, "Don't forget, Bri, it's all about closure! And don't let him talk you into anything! Remember the vow you made to yourself."

***

Turning into the parking lot of Giovanni's Ristorante at exactly seven-forty, ten minutes fashionably late, Brianya had to admit that tonight was also a little bit about gloating. She knew she shouldn't, but part of her wanted to rub Darnell's nose in her weight loss success. He'd told so many jokes about her weight and laughed at her expense that she wanted to show him who had the last laugh now.

Brianya honed in on a parking spot three rows in, and raced a late-model Jaguar to the spot, graciously maneuvering a sharp turn as she pulled into the space. The driver, looking dangerously explosive, flashed angry eyes at Brianya. If Brianya didn't know any better, she'd swear that was the sister from one of the local news stations. *I guess even the nicest seeming people can be a little ugly sometimes.* As the woman exited her car, Brianya hurried into the restaurant, not wishing to create a scene.

When she stepped into the hallway, Brianya's breath caught in her throat. The highly polished brown wooden doors, flamboyantly carved, resembled something straight out of 16th century Italy.

The hostess greeted Brianya and asked if she had a reservation. On the way to the table, Brianya marveled at her surroundings. From the elegant velvet drapes that did double duty as dividers between the two sides of the restaurant, to the rows of wine racks lining the walls, and the wood beams that graced the ceiling; along with Picasso paintings and white clustered sconces that hung on the walls, the place was a collage of eclectic designs that blended effortlessly. Darnell certainly had chosen well. He always did have class when it came to picking upscale restaurants. How he managed to swing a reservation on short notice, though, was a mystery to Brianya.

Darnell stood as the hostess seated Brianya. She introduced herself as Heidi and took Brianya's drink order before rushing off.

"I was starting to think you had stood me up," Darnell said as he sat back down. "I remembered you always being on time." With effort, he tore his eyes away from Brianya's cleavage and managed to look her directly in the eye.

Brianya didn't answer, just gave Darnell a half smile. She perused the menu and did a quick calculation in her head. For what it would cost the two of them to eat here, Brianya could make almost two car payments. She felt bad for Darnell. "You didn't have to go all out, Darnell. Applebee's or Outback's would have been just fine." Then a thought occurred. "I hope you don't think that just because you brought me to this five-star restaurant, you're entitled." He hadn't actually brought her there, but he knew what she meant.

Brianya's words bit into Darnell's pride; he stiffened and looked pained. "I brought you here because I thought you deserved it. That's all that's on my mind. If you prefer Applebee's or Outback's it's no problem."

Brianya flicked her wrist. "We're here now. We may as well stay." She knew she shouldn't care about how pricey the restaurant was. It was Darnell's money and if he wanted to spend it on expensive food and fine wine, that was his prerogative. She was just along for the show. "Hmmm . . ." Brianya picked up the wine book and flipped through it until she got to the section of white wines. She was no wine expert, but she knew what she liked. "You can never go wrong with a Sauvignon blanc or a Cabernet sauvignon. Tonight, I think I'll have both." Brianya put the book down but left it open.

Darnell, trying not to appear obvious, casually scanned the room then let his gaze fall upon the open page. When his eyes lazily found their way to the right side of the wine list, a small frown formed on his lips. *At forty-two dollars a glass, I'd frown, too,* Brianya thought. "I didn't eat much today. I've been saving my appetite for tonight." With a flourish, she picked up the food menu. "Let's see. I'm in the mood for something spicy! I think I'll start with the Shrimp Fra Diavolo appetizer and a glass of Sauvignon blanc."

Darnell took a sip of water, acting cool. His brown eyes bore into Brianya—a look that defied words, but spoke volumes.

Brianya shrugged. "You brought me here to eat and that's what I plan to do."

"I didn't say a word."

"You didn't have to. The *look*," she said, pointing at Darnell's face and making small circles with her finger, "says it all."

Darnell's voice dropped to a whisper as the server approached the table. "You can have whatever you want, Anya."

Brianya shook the napkin loose and placed it on her lap. Using a knife and fork, she meticulously cut out the center of the still-warm bread and dipped it in herb-flavored olive oil. A smile spread across her face as the oil, infused with oregano, garlic, thyme, and other herbs, mingled with the saliva on her tongue and then melted.

Darnell stared, amused by Brianya's enjoyment. Watching Brianya eat had always been something of a theater experience. "I see you haven't lost that gusto for food."

Sitting across from Darnell in this fancy restaurant and making small talk like they were friends felt too familiar. Brianya was here for one reason and playing catch up wasn't it. They practically ate their meal in silence. When the dessert cart rolled around, Brianya thought about passing, but decided on cheesecake. She didn't fail to notice Darnell's raised eyebrow. When they were together, Darnell would sometimes cast looks of annoyance in Brianya's direction when he was sure she wasn't looking. Like most things, Brianya let it slide because she was a woman on a mission and she thought Darnell loved her. But when Darnell asked: "What are you doing, Anya?"his tone heavy with condemnation, Brianya was in no mood to let it slide this time and she was no longer a woman on a mission.

Brianya slowly put down her fork and wiped her mouth with her napkin. "Really? You want to have this conversation, right here, right now?"

"That's why we're here isn't it?"

What was before just ambient restaurant noise—lovers, friends, and families laughing and conversing, dishes clanking—suddenly seemed to Brianya a loud cacophony of chatter. Brianya raised her voice to be heard over the noise. "We're here because, as usual, Darnell gets what he wants. I can't believe how stupid I was to let you talk me in to having dinner with you. You're the same old arrogant, immature person."

"Calm down, Anya." Darnell's tone was soft, almost apologetic. "People are staring at us."

Brianya looked around the room. People were staring. Not a lot, but enough to make her feel uncomfortable. What would her grandmother, who was a paragon of decorum and social graces, say if she saw her eldest granddaughter behaving in public as if she didn't have any home training? She would be furious, mortified even. Ruby Morgan, who had migrated north from Lexington, Georgia at the height of World War II, and cleaned the houses of wealthy white families in the suburbs of Cleveland, had demanded only one thing from her children when they became parents. Brianya's mother and her siblings had to allow their mother to teach her grandchildren social etiquette, something Ruby's great grandmother had learned, and passed down, serving at her master's table. At the memory of Grandma Ruby, Brianya ducked her head and put her hand to her mouth.

"Why don't we get out of here and go for a ride?"

"Why would I want to do that?" Brianya whispered.

Darnell caught the attention of their server and asked for the check. "Because if I'm going to beg and grovel for your forgiveness I'd like a little privacy," he said when the server left to get the check.

Brianya turned the suggestion over in her mind. She wondered how they managed a 2-hour dinner without talking about the reason they were there in the first place. Darnell was clever; Brianya had to give him that. She saw now that he had maneuvered the conversation so that they only talked about superficial things like her work and his investment in his club. Except for the occasional mention of a shared interest, there was no mention of the past. If Brianya wanted closure, she had no choice but to go for a ride with Darnell.

Standing in the vestibule, waiting for Darnell to fetch his car, Brianya stood like a statue, hating that Darnell had tricked her into this. She stepped outside as the white Porsche pulled up to the door and shook her head. *Fraud!* she thought. He'd had another car the night he showed up in her driveway. It was just like Darnell to put on airs, living beyond his means. That's all he'd talked about over dinner; how a few investments had paid off and now he was paid. And if he played his cards right, in two years they could open a second club, blah, blah, blah. Brianya had felt guilty at first about ordering the more expensive items on the menu, but the more Darnell talked about his finances, the more she regretted getting the Long Bone Veal Chop instead of the Dover Sole, which was at market price. The three glasses of wine she had—none under $42 a glass—had more than made up for it.

CHAPTER TWENTY-EIGHT

DARNELL PULLED THE car to a stop at the Bedford Metroparks and killed the engine. "Feel like walking? I know how much you love the winter.

"Sure." Brianya unfastened her seatbelt and stepped out of the car, before Darnell made it to her side. She pulled the collar of the fur coat up around her neck and fastened the belt snugly around her waist. Reaching into her pockets, she pulled out black leather gloves and slid her slender fingers snugly inside. Unseasonably warm weather had settled upon Cleveland and left the city with only a dusting of snow.

Darnell yawned and stretched as they began their walk. He checked his watch and saw that it was close to eight o'clock. He was probably thinking about his club and wishing that he was there instead of taking a freezing cold walk in a metropark, trying to make amends with a woman who couldn't care less about his so-called Karma. Summer was Darnell's season; he couldn't tolerate any temperature below 50 degrees. So, his presence here in this weather said something. The Darnell Brianya knew wouldn't put himself out for anyone. Yet here he was doing just that. He knew that Brianya needed to close this chapter just as much as he did. He had said as much on the telephone last night.

Darnell's teeth chattered as he spoke. "Thanks for having dinner with me, Anya." He rubbed his hands together rapidly. "First, I want to say that I'm sorry for the way I treated you when we were together. You know . . . the jokes. And for the way I did you when we broke up."

"*We* didn't break up. You broke up with me." Brianya thought her emotions would be stronger than they were, but she was surprised at how calm she felt. She wanted to be angry with him, to rip into him the way she'd fantasized when the breakup was fresh.

"Okay," he breathed a small sigh, "when I broke up with you." They had only walked a short distance before Darnell changed his mind and wanted to turn back.

"I was wondering how far we would get before you gave up. Let's just go back to the restaurant."

They turned back and headed for the car. When Darnell pointed the key fob in the direction of the car and clicked it, the car's engine hummed to life. A couple, hugged up like high school sweethearts, strolled past them and shot a conspiratorial glance their way as if they all belonged to some clandestine club. Darnell caught the look and smiled at Brianya.

"Did you ever love me, Darnell?" Brianya blurted out.

The question caught Darnell by surprise. "No lead-in, huh? You just laid it right there." He unlocked the car doors remotely and slid onto the toasty seat.

Inside the car, warmth and silence surrounded them. While Darnell fidgeted with the various buttons on the dashboard, Brianya scolded herself for being so blunt. She should have been subtle about it, she knew. But this dance they were engaged in was becoming tiresome and all she wanted to do was get it over with and go on with her life. She'd felt tortured sitting across from him at dinner, listening to him go on and on about how well his life had turned out. What he should have been telling her was that his life was in ruins or that he had some horrible disease and only a few months to live. At least news like that could justify why, as he'd been talking, all she could think about was taking his face in her hands and kiss—

"I did love you," Darnell said breaking the silence and interrupting Brianya's thoughts. He momentarily took his eyes off the road to watch Brianya's expression. "I just didn't know how to be honest with you."

"What you did to me was cruel." She felt her emotions rising to the surface and pushed them back down.

"I know."

Brianya folded her arms across her chest. "Look Darnell, the only reason I agreed to this 'date' was because you said you didn't want to do this on the phone. So far, all you've said is what I already know."

"I'm just trying not to say the wrong thing." He took his eyes off the road again to glance at Brianya. "When I met you, Anya, you struck me as one of those no-nonsense women who knew what she wanted in life. Someone who wasn't afraid to check a dude when he got out of pocket. That's the person I fell in love with. But . . ." he hesitated.

"But what?" Brianya said, impatient.

"But after a while I started to think maybe I had you pegged wrong."

"Had me pegged wrong? What are you talking about?"

"When I lost my job, I had only known you for three months. You weren't that vested in the relationship; you could have walked away, but you didn't. Instead, you started paying all my bills, even moved in when I asked you to, knowing that living together went against everything you believed in. At that point, I knew that you were after a wedding ring and as long as I made it seem like I was gonna deliver, I could get you to do anything I wanted."

Brianya sat stone-faced.

Darnell pulled into a remote area in the restaurant's parking lot and put the car in park. He let the seat all the way back and stretched his legs. "At first, I thought you were this self-assured woman who knew what she wanted out of life and wasn't afraid to go after it. But, when you didn't check me when I started making jokes about your weight, I saw you as desperate. I mean, here you were—this beautiful woman, with no kids, a good job, and a good head on her shoulders and you were willing to let a man disrespect you just so you could call yourself Mrs." Darnell shifted his weight. He waited for Brianya to respond, but all she did was stare out the window as if she hadn't heard a word. "I know this is hard to hear and I'm sorry." Darnell reached for Brianya's hand; she pulled back. "You know me, Anya. If you ask, I gotta say what's on my mind."

It was true. Darnell's forthrightness was one of the traits that had attracted Brianya to him. Hearing him utter the words she'd said to herself a thousand times, was more than hard, it was devastating.

Darnell retracted his hand. "Anyway, when Tricia called and told me she was pregnant, I didn't know what to do. I knew I couldn't keep my condo *and* help her out too. I had just about run out of the money I got from selling all my furniture and other stuff and from my 401(k). I had maxed out all my credit cards. That's when I asked you to move in." He cleared his throat and looked nervous. "You know, uh, all those times I told you I was out with the fellas or stuck at the store working late?" He ran his hand across his chin. "I was out with . . . . You know—"

"Who, Tricia? All of sudden you can't say her name?" Brianya was again losing patience with Darnell and his game of charades.

He wriggled in his seat. "No. I was out with other women."

Brianya looked incredulous. "What other women?"

When he spoke, his words came out soft and filled with remorse. "Other women, that's all. You don't know them. I'm just saying that I cheated on you. I'm not proud of what I did. I felt guilty about it for a long time, still do."

Brianya flashed back to the scene in the living room almost three years ago when Darnell had finally confessed that he was in love with the woman who had accused him of sexual harassment just because she didn't get a promotion she thought she deserved. Saw the fear in his eyes when she raised the knife and pointed it left of center at his chest and told him, "You've got to the count of three to get out! And don't come back!" Heard him stammer,

"B-but this is my condo," when he saw that she was serious. And now she wondered, "How can you sit there and fix your lips to condemn me when you just admitted to being a cheater and you were stupid enough to let a woman ruin your career and then follow her like a dog in heat all the way to Virginia, where she punked you and finally came clean about the baby not being yours? Are you *serious?*"

Darnell sat up straight. The veins in his jaw and neck pulsed and he looked like he was about to lose his cool. It was obvious that he was choosing his words carefully. But he couldn't mask the underlying anger. "I wasn't condemning you, Anya. I'm doing for you what most men would never do. Think about it. In all the relationships you've ever been in, how many of those dudes came back and apologized? Not just apologized, but also came clean about what was really going on? Huh?" Darnell's tone was persistent and it grated on Brianya.

Brianya remained silent, just looked at Darnell as if he'd lost his mind.

"Yeah, that's what I thought."

"Don't kid yourself, Darnell. You're doing this for you. I know it and you know it. So you made a few dollars from investments, and life is good for you. What does that have to do with me?"

Darnell reached into his breast pocket and pulled out an envelope that contained a folded piece of paper. He took the paper out and handed it to Brianya. The words 'will I have to take you to court?' written in bold, capital letters, spanned the bottom of the paper that was divided into two columns of dollar amounts and furniture items.

Brianya jolted when she saw the note she left Darnell three years ago and tried to cover her shock with a flippant remark. "Humph. A worthless piece of paper you keep; me, you treat like garbage and throw away."

Darnell opened his mouth to say something and then changed his mind. Shaking her head, Brianya frowned at his silence.

"Why didn't you come back to pick up the furniture?"

"By the time I got to the trash room, I had decided that I didn't want anything that had even a trace of a memory of you." Brianya pulled the collar of her fur coat up around her neck. A quick glance at the controls confirmed that Darnell had turned the heat to the lowest setting. She reached over and tapped the button a few times. *That's odd,* Brianya thought. *He used to hate when I readjusted his settings. What is he up to?*

"I know you don't believe in Karma, Anya, but I do. Some people call it retribution, some people call it reaping what you sow, but whatever it is, I'm ready for whatever I got coming my way. In the last few years, things weren't always good for me. In a lot of ways, I paid for what I did to you. But that's all turned around now, and so far it's been nothing but positivity. I want that to continue. That's why I needed to put the truth out there and ask you to forgive me for taking you for granted, for cheating on you, and for treating you like you were a piece of garbage."

There it was, finally. Wrapped up nicely in an admission of guilt, tied up with an apology, and topped off with a plea for forgiveness. This was what Brianya had said she needed so that she could truly close the door on this chapter in her life. It should have been a no-brainer, yet she wavered.

Darnell looked expectantly at Brianya, his brown eyes clouding with concern.

"You know something, Darnell. I'm not even mad. A couple of years ago, I would've been mad. Would've cussed you out, cried and acted a fool. Would've even tried to cut you."

"True."

Brianya turned and faced Darnell. Her words, though somber, reflected a lightness of spirit that had come over her. "But I've done a lot of work from the inside out," she continued, "and I'm proud of what I've accomplished. I guess what I really needed was for you to admit to what I'd always suspected and to ask for forgiveness. The truth is I was so messed up back then, that if you had told me you were cheating, I would have found a way to work it into our relationship. My opinion of myself was so low; I felt I wasn't important unless I was important *to* someone; I wasn't lovable unless someone loved me. My self-worth amounted to the value that someone else placed on it." Brianya reached over and turned the heat back to low. "In answer to your question, Darnell, I forgive you." The euphoric feeling Brianya imagined would accompany those words, didn't happen. Instead, she felt a sense of finality. She could now symbolically write the words "The End" on this chapter of her life and finally allow herself to let someone else in.

Darnell's sad eyes took in the brightness emanating from Brianya and he smiled ruefully. He picked up the discarded envelope from the middle console and pulled something else out. He handed it to Brianya.

"What's this?" Brianya asked, puzzled. She turned the item over and gasped.

"I'm not gonna lie to you, Anya. When I met you, I wasn't ready for anything permanent. Relationships never worked for me so that was the last thing on my mind. But you made me a believer. When I lost my job and was almost homeless, you stepped in and stepped up and you never asked me to reimburse you for anything. When I got back on my feet, the thought of paying you back had never even crossed my mind. But when I got to Richmond and had my behind handed to me, all I could think about was making things right with you." Darnell cleared his throat but he couldn't hide the moisture that pooled in his eyes. "I love you for what you did for me, Anya. You deserve every dime that's written on that check, plus some."

Brianya looked from the cashier's check to Darnell then back to the check and backed to Darnell. "Is this a real check?"

If the question offended Darnell, he didn't show it. He laughed. "As real as the two of us sitting here."

"I can't accept this." Brianya held the check out to Darnell, who didn't make a move to accept it. "That's triple the original amount. It's too much."

"That's the least I could do."

There's no way Darnell was willing to give up that much cash and not expect something in return. Either he was playing her for a fool, or. . . . Or what? Brianya didn't know what to think anymore. One thing was for sure, though. Before she accepted the money, she would have to make it clear to Darnell that he didn't have anything coming. After tonight, they had nothing more to talk about; she wanted him to stop calling her and to stop showing up at her job. This was the end for them. He'd gotten what he came for—her forgiveness—and she'd gotten what she needed.

"I gave you what you needed, Darnell. I don't expect to see you or hear from you again. If you thought this money was some sort of gateway back into my life, then take it back right now." She was still holding the check out to him. An almost imperceptible flicker of disappointed skittered across Darnell's face telling her what she wanted to know. "Take it!" Opening the car door, Brianya wadded the paper into a ball and threw it at Darnell. When she exited the car, Brianya turned back. "When you watch me walk away, think about this: The life lesson you taught me is not for sale."

CHAPTER TWENTY-NINE

AT SIX O'CLOCK A.M. Brianya was feeling good this fine Sunday morning. After last night's eye-opening revelation with Darnell, she'd done like Lady Patti and tidied up her point of view and got a new attitude. She danced around the basement, vacuum in hand, belting the words to her new mantra. This unfamiliar feeling of overwhelming peace was new. The truth had certainly set her free. She'd broken the chains that had bound her for so long, and now there was nowhere to move but forward. On the drive home last night, Brianya had made up her mind that she would tell the men in her life about one another. Then she'd decide which one to continue seeing, exclusively. They all had good qualities, great even. But she could only date one of them. Well, she could date them all, but she wouldn't like what that said about her; and she didn't want to disrespect the memory of her maternal grandmother. Grandma Ruby would roll over in her grave if she knew that her favorite granddaughter was behaving like a loosey-goosey.

After spending nearly three hours going through and discarding boxes of old, unused, long forgotten items that she'd dragged with her from her apartment, Brianya filled the tub with hot water and tossed in the Calm Balm bath bomb from the set of twelve that Cinthia had given her as a housewarming gift months ago. Two hours after she had lowered her aching body into the tub of steaming, fruity-fragranced water, Brianya arose refreshed and reinvigorated. The bath had done wonders in clearing her head and helping her sort out the pros and cons of all three men. Four months ago, if anyone had asked Brianya where her life would be in as many months, she'd have confidently said work, work, and more work. For the last few years, work had consumed Brianya. So much so, that she hardly noticed there was a world out there where people did things like go to the movies, restaurants, plays, re-establish lifetime bonds, live. She most definitely would not have said, going through a mental list of likes and dislikes, trying to decide which of the three men she'd been keeping company with would be crowned "The One."

The doorbell peeled and Brianya jammed on her slippers and bounded down the stairs. "Not you two again!" she said when she saw it was Cashmere and Dreama.

"And hello to you, too!" Dreama barged her way into the house. "We're here for two reasons: to find out how last night went, and to eat!"

Cashmere laughed and pushed Brianya playfully on the shoulder as she scooted past her. She wiggled out of her Candies and headed for the kitchen. "Dreama dragged me over here. I told her we should call before coming."

The two women were becoming a permanent fixture in Brianya's home and Brianya loved it. Houses should be filled with families who love and care about one another. Although there was no blood between them, Dreama and Cashmere were as close to her as any sister could be, even closer. Growing up, Cinthia was her best friend. But as they got older their circle of friends widened. And although Brianya still shared secrets and confidences with Cinthia, Cinthia was still her baby sister. And there were some things that one just didn't share with one's baby sister.

"Don't you all have homes? I swear I'm tired of looking at the two of you. Every time I turn around, y'all got your hands held out begging for my food."

Cashmere looked sideways at Brianya, an unsure expression creeping across her face. A playful roll of the eyes from Brianya set Cashmere's mind at ease. Her face relaxed and she continued peeling the orange she'd swiped from the fruit bowl in the center of the island. "Okay, girl," Cashmere said when she realized Brianya was joking, "'cause I was about to put this orange down."

Dreama, who was too busy rummaging through the refrigerator for the leftovers she knew Brianya had from last night, had missed the exchange. "What?" she asked, pulling herself away from the task at hand, sounding every bit as clueless as she was.

"Nothing. Now get out of my fridge because I didn't have a doggie bag."

Dreama slammed the door, flopped down in the chair, and pouted. "Hmmm . . . I need food."

"Tell me something I don't know." Brianya reached in the bottom cabinet and pulled out a large cast iron skillet and a nonstick pan. "Dreama, get your lazy self up and hand me that bag of cut up veggies in the vegetable bin, a carton of eggs, the provolone cheese, and that package of turkey bacon. Cash, reach in that drawer and hand me the whisk."

They did as they were told and by the time Brianya finished ordering Cashmere and Dreama around the kitchen, they were sitting down to a scrumptious breakfast of Brianya's famous Western style egg white omelets. Over the sound of smacking and gulping and silverware banging against stoneware, Brianya filled them in on the details of last night's dinner date with Darnell.

Dreama licked ketchup off her fork and almost choked when Brianya told her the amount of the check she'd refused to accept. "You gave him back a check for thirty thousand dollars? Have you lost your mind, girl?"

"How could you say that, Dreama? He was trying to use the money as a way to get back with her. She did the right thing."

"No, she didn't do the right thing," Dreama demanded. "What she should've done was take the money and tell him to go crawl back under the rock he came from. After what he put her through, he owed her that!"

"I don't know too much about all of that, but I do know about living with regrets. Believe me, if Bri had taken that money knowing the expectations that came with it, there's no way she would have walked away from that date feeling like she'd gotten closure."

Brianya shot a scrutinizing glance at Cashmere. She couldn't help feeling that there was more to Cashmere's story than she had let on. What could Cashmere possibly have to regret? She wasn't the one who had been living a double life and because of it had infected her fiancé with HIV. She was the victim.

Dreama stopped arguing and turned her attention to Cashmere. "What do you have to regret, Cash?"

Brianya recognized the tenderness in Dreama's voice as the one she used only with people that she felt protective of. They waited for Cashmere to answer. As Brianya had suspected, Cashmere hadn't confided in Dreama; otherwise, the question wouldn't still be hanging in the air.

"Typical stuff. You know, like most people." Cashmere cleared her throat.

The lie tripped easily off her tongue and Brianya made a mental note to ask Cashmere about it later.

"Oh. Well, anyway—"

"Well nothing," Brianya said, cutting across Dreama's unfinished thought. "Y'all need to stop wasting your time debating a dead subject. And stop talking about me as if I'm invisible." Brianya took a sip of tepid coffee and changed the subject. "Let me run something by y'all. I've decided to tell Endo, Ed, and Monty about each other. What's the best way for me to do that?"

Cashmere and Dreama stared at one another, disapproval written all their faces. Cashmere was the first to speak. "I don't think that's a good idea, Bri."

"Yeah, me either. I mean, what would be the point?"

"The point is I would feel better if I put it out there. It's not like I deliberately set out to be sneaky. It had just never crossed my mind that I should've made it known upfront that I was also getting to know other guys." To her ears the reason sounded completely plausible. She had already made it known from the beginning that what they were doing shouldn't be considered dating. The only thing on Brianya's mind was making the guilty feeling go away.

"Hmmm . . ." Cashmere appeared to be processing Brianya's statement.

"Look, Bri. I ain't a big fan of all this transparency mess. I'm from the old school of ignorance-is-bliss way of thinking. Unless you plan to seriously date all three of them, I say leave it alone. Besides, if you were gonna tell them, you should've done it way back in the beginning."

In the beginning, Brianya was too busy trying to wrap her head around the reality of what was happening to her. Not that men weren't interested in her before; it's just that she wasn't in a place to receive their attention without being suspicious of their motives. When she finally did get her head on straight, she was flabbergasted that three good-looking men of quality wanted to go out with her— men with good jobs, their own cars, their own residences, and no children. A combination that was almost unheard of in today's world.

"I realize that now," Brianya said in response to Dreama's statement. "What do you think, Cash?"

"Well," Cashmere said and snatched a piece of crisp turkey bacon from the plate in the middle of the table and chomped on it. "I agree with Dreama. But . . . if you've decided which one you're going to date, then tell the other two that you're not interested and move on." Cashmere shrugged apologetically.

Definitely not what Brianya wanted to hear. However, it was a reasonable alternative to her initial plan. Without thinking, Brianya blurted, "I've made up my mind. I know who I'm going to date!"

CHAPTER THIRTY

B RIANYA WATCHED AS Ed expertly maneuvered his way through the throng of people blocking the aisles as they stood chatting, waiting for the sold-out Kem concert to begin. His broad shoulders heaved from the effort it took to balance the drinks he carried. Ed's brow knitted in concentration as he quickly sidestepped the uneasy gait of a woman who appeared to have already had one too many drinks.

"You should have been part of the act," Brianya joked when Ed finally reached their seats.

Ed handed Brianya the drinks and settled comfortably into his seat. He surprised Brianya by leaning over and pecking her on the cheek.

"What was that for?" Ed missed a small patch when he'd shaved and the rough stubble scratched against Brianya's chin. She loved the feel of it; it reminded her when she was a little girl and her grandfather, who had never mastered the art of being clean-shaven, would rub his cheek against hers before hugging her.

"I couldn't resist; you look gorgeous in that red dress." Ed smiled devilishly and took a swig of his gin and tonic. "I gotta tell you, Brianya, I was surprised when I got your call."

Brianya thought about how each man had responded to her decision.

***

After weighing all three men on the scale of compatibility, Ed's qualities had far outweighed Endo's and Monty's. She'd done what Dreama and Cashmere had suggested and kept the information about seeing all three of them to herself, and she was glad she had. After her last conversation with Endo, Brianya had an uneasy feeling that news like that wouldn't have sat well with him. He'd taken the news well, she thought, although he was still insisting that he was patient and would wait as long as it took. Brianya had to get firm with him—she hadn't wanted to. But she couldn't leave it with Endo thinking that all she needed was time.

"I understand you're still a little gun shy after the way your ex treated you," Endo had said. "You just need some time to deal with those feelings. I understand." His voice had gone all watery when he said, "I'm not going anywhere, Brianya. When you're ready to do relationships again, I'll be right here. Your father was right; we are made for each other."

Like a cool morning breeze on a brisk spring day, a chill ran through Brianya. "Endo," she'd said quietly. "You're not hearing me. It's not that I'm not ready for a relationship, I am. It's just that I don't think we're right for each other. You're a nice person and I think you have a lot to offer a woman, but I'm not that woman."

"Oh, I see," he'd said, light dawning. "Can I ask you something?"

"Sure."

"What is it about me that you don't like?"

The question surprised Brianya. She didn't want to hurt Endo's feelings, but the fact that he'd asked that question was part of the problem. No confident man would ask; he'd simply accept that you couldn't win them all and move on. Endo's neediness, his desperation for Brianya to want him was what gave her pause about him. That was the only thing she couldn't get past, and it was big turn-off.

"Don't take this the wrong way, Endo" Brianya said. "But I think you're a little too needy." Her heart sank as she said the words. She could imagine his warm brown eyes clouding with disappointment, and a tear spilled from her own eye.

"Oh. Okay, thanks for your honesty." There was a slight pause. "Well, you take care of yourself, Brianya. It was a pleasure to get to know you."

Before Brianya could reply, the flat monotone of the dial tone had squawked in her ear.

Monty, on the other hand, took the news in stride. In fact, he was so okay with them not becoming an item that it left Brianya questioning whether Monty had been truthful when he'd said he'd liked her ever since she was with Darnell.

"It's all good, Bri. No hard feelings. To be honest, I really wasn't down with that whole celibate thing. I mean, girl, a dude get 'round you, he wanna do thangs. Na'ah mean?"

Brianya had laughed so hard, she couldn't be mad at Monty for saying how he felt. Monty had given her a big bear hug before he left and asked if they could hang out sometime. Brianya had to admit that she liked Monty's company; he was fun. She had platonic male friends, one more wouldn't hurt. In all truthfulness, she was still having a problem with Monty reminding her of a past that was now behind her. Brianya secretly hoped that he was just giving lip service to his request to hang out.

A few days after Monty had left, Brianya had phoned Ed. He'd answered on the first ring.

"I don't think I've ever known anyone to answer on the first ring," Brianya teased.

Quick with the response, Ed had answered, "That's because I knew it was you."

Brianya had regained some of her composure. As she waited for the rest of it to return, she quickly ran through the speech she had rehearsed incessantly in her mind.

When Brianya didn't acknowledge Ed's comment, he said, "So, to what do I owe this phone call? Everything okay? I haven't seen you around the building or in the garage lately."

"Everything's good. I've been coming in later and parking on a different level." Brianya's heart thudded in her chest and she thought she would pass out. *Come on, Bri. You can do this. Make small talk to break the ice then just go all in!* "How've you been?"

"You know me. Taking it one day at a time."

"That's a good way to be; keeps down the stress level."

"Yep."

The silence grew louder. This was not going well at all. Watching paint dry would be more interesting than this excruciating conversation.

"This is nice, listening to you breathe on the telephone." Ed said cutting across the silence. "Hey, I've got an idea. Why don't I come over and we can breathe together?" Brianya could hear the smile in Ed's voice. He chuckled and some of her nervousness melted away.

"You can come over some other time. Right now I've got something I need to say." Brianya breathed in deeply. "I gave some thought to what you said about seeing each other exclusively," she swallowed hard. "And I think I'd like that."

Ed didn't respond.

Brianya felt foolish and embarrassed. This was a bad idea; she had taken too long to make up her mind and now Ed wasn't interested anymore. He was probably trying to find the words to let her down easy. "I appreciate you trying to spare my feelings, Ed; but it's not necessary. I'd rather you be honest than polite." Why shouldn't she be the one to get the boot? She'd given it to Endo and Monty; it was only right that she be on the receiving end now.

"You want honesty?" Ed's voice was thick with sentiment. "I'm glad you chose me."

"You're what?" Brianya asked, hardly able to believe her ears.

"I knew about the other guys; Celine told me a few weeks ago."

At the mention of Celine's name, Brianya felt a pang of sadness. What had Celine hoped to accomplish by telling Ed about Endo and Monty? It was clear that she was miserable since the escapade with Darnell had blown up in her face. It was hard to believe that at one time they were as close as sisters were. Funny how you think you know a person only to find out that your entire relationship was nothing but a big fat lie.

"So what did she say?" What Celine said didn't really matter at this point. Yet, Brianya wanted to know anyway.

"I don't know if I want to tell you." Ed chuckled. "It doesn't make me look good."

Brianya was confused. "Excuse me?"

"Alright," Ed said. "I'll just put it out there and risk looking foolish." He sounded badgered, as if Brianya had beaten a confession out of him. "The night we went to Starbuck's, all the way home, I kept thinking about our conversation. In particular, the not dating and being celibate until marriage part. It sounded farfetched, unbelievable. Even though I had been out of the dating scene for a while, when I was out there, I had never met anyone like you. And I wanted to know if you were for real and if I had a chance with you. So I called up Celine and she told me what was up."

Brianya felt anger rising. She made an unintelligible noise that sounded a lot like disapproval.

"Don't be upset with her, Brianya. She didn't want to tell me; it was like pulling teeth. Finally, she gave it to me straight. Said if I wanted a shot with you, I had to step up my game because I wasn't the only one trying to get to know you. That's when I knew I had to bring out the secret weapon."

"What secret weapon?" Brianya asked laughing.

"My chef hat! What," Ed said, his voice elevating an octave, "it wasn't obvious?" He feigned a hurt tone. "You wound me, Ms. Johnson."

"Let me not wound your pride, my brother. I gotta give props where they're due. You sho nuff can burn in the kitchen!" Brianya paused before saying, "You were okay with not being the only one I was seeing?" Because from the last conversation at his house, it sounded like Ed might have a problem not being number one.

"Why wouldn't I be? We hadn't made any promises."

"That's not what you were saying a couple of weeks ago."

"Ahhh . . . That. By then, I knew about the other two. That was me shaking the tree to see what would come loose."

Brianya was quiet on the other end of the phone. Finally, she asked, "Did anything shake loose?"

"Most definitely! I got to kiss you like a drunken sailor!"

They had both laughed heartily and in that moment they'd sealed the deal.

***

Smiling at the memory, Brianya said, "I was just as surprised as you were when I called," in response to Ed's statement.

"And why's that? I can't be that repulsive." Ed took another swig of his drink. The piped in music stopped and there was less chattering as the crowd anticipated the opening act.

"In case you hadn't noticed, I'm very inquisitive. In being inquisitive, I like to have my questions answered. When they're not, I tend to get a little suspicious."

"Where're you going with this?" He asked the question with a slight air of impatience in his tone.

"Tell me the story behind your chipped tooth."

The MC came to the stage and ramped up the crowd with a snippet of her version of *I Can't Stop Loving You*. The crowd went wild, with men shouting catcalls as the popular radio personality, dressed in a form fitting Maxi dress, gyrated and gesticulated around the stage. Ed looked relieved for the interruption. He leaned in close, his hot breath tickling Brianya's ear. "Let's enjoy the concert."

When the opening act had finished, Brianya spent the entire intermission waiting in line to use the restroom. She made it back to her seat just in time to see Kem take the stage and hear the deafening roar of the crowd as women shouted obscenities and proclamations of love at the soulful crooner. Ed and Brianya spent the remainder of the concert on their feet, dancing in the aisle as song after song Kem kept encouraging the crowd to "turn loose those seats and let love move your feet to the streets." Corny but effective. By the time the concert was over, there was hardly a behind left occupying a seat.

Ed was a great dancer. The way he gripped Brianya's waist, turned, and tilted her smacked of professional dance lessons. His singing, on the other hand, left a lot to be desired.

On the way home from the concert, Ed was quieter than usual. Brianya wanted to resume their earlier conversation but it probably wouldn't have been a good idea. She didn't know Ed well enough to decipher his moods. Out of the corner of her eye, she could see Ed glance periodically in her direction. He obviously wanted to say something. "Is everything okay, Ed? You're quiet. You liked the concert didn't you?"

Ed cleared his throat. "Yeah, I'm good."

A terse comment like that didn't leave much room for exploration. Brianya didn't want to come off as nagging, but not knowing what Ed was thinking or what had brought on the silent treatment was driving Brianya crazy. She wouldn't push this time. Whatever it was, if he wanted her to know he'd tell her.

It was nearly midnight when they pulled into Brianya's driveway. "Thanks for tonight, Ed. I had a good time."

Ed shut the car off. "You don't have to thank me. I'm glad my client came through with those last-minute tickets. Guess it pays to have connections."

Brianya clicked the mini garage door opener on her keychain, listened to the pulley squeak as the door rolled up. She unfastened her seatbelt and tugged at the door handle. Ed put his hand out to stop her from leaving. "Uh, look Brianya. I know you probably think I'm being evasive by not answering your question." That had crossed Brianya's mind. "It's just not something I feel comfortable talking about."

"When you're ready, I'm a good listener."

"I know you are."

It was true: Brianya was a good listener. People often remarked that talking to her was therapeutic and had probably saved them thousands of dollars in counseling. Her ability to give a person her undivided attention is what had impressed her former boss and endeared her to most of the MBCC staff. She chose wisely in making her career in Human Resources. Such high praise wasn't without its drawbacks, however. People assumed that because she was a good listener and often offered sound, solid advice, that she was as astute at handling her own problems. They couldn't be more wrong. Without even realizing it, Brianya had become this omniscient figure who effortlessly solved everyone else's problems while her own life lay in ruins because she was too afraid to ask for help, lest the world discover that she was nothing but a fraud. She was so used to living in the shadow of everyone else's opinion of who she was, that Brianya didn't recognize herself when she finally emerged from the physical and emotional cocoon that had enveloped her for far too long. She was still getting to know herself, discovering the true self from the self the world had saddled upon her.

So naturally, when Ed had tensed up at the mention of his tooth and looked relieved when he had an excuse to abandon the subject, Brianya couldn't help exploring her reasons for desperately wanting to know the story behind the mystery. She was a nurturer in every sense of the word. Now that they were officially a couple, without stepping over lines or crossing boundaries, Brianya wanted to know everything about Ed, especially the painful truths. She was sure that there was pain because she could see it in his eyes each time she'd asked.

Brianya hadn't realized that Ed had gotten out of the car until her door opened and he stood smiling at her with an air of expectation. The sudden shock of cold air smacked her in the face

245

and took her breath away. Ed led Brianya by the elbow out of the vehicle and shut the door.

They walked through the garage that led to the kitchen, Ed stopping short of entering the house. "It's late. I don't want to wear out my welcome, so I'll say goodnight here."

"You sure you don't want to come in for a nightcap? I promise, I won't ask you about the," Brianya pointed to her tooth.

Ed smiled and hung his head. "Nah, it's not that. It's just that this type of relationship is new to me. The learning curve might be steep."

"So what does that mean; you're never going to be alone with me? This is new to me too, you know."

"I didn't realize that; you've got a point." He checked his watch. "Well, then, I guess I'll take you up on that nightcap."

CHAPTER THIRTY-ONE

"I ONLY HAVE WINE. I don't stock the hard stuff." Brianya took their coats and hung them in the hall closet.

Ed tried not to stare at the body-hugging wrap-around red dress that showcased every curve and accentuated all of Brianya's positive assets. The peek-a-boo neckline allowed him to see just enough to know that he wanted more. "That's cool." He pulled his eyes away long enough to get situated on the couch. "I'll take a glass of white wine, if you have it."

Brianya smiled at Ed's difficulty and sashayed over to the wine rack, pulled out a bottle of White Zifandel. "Don't get up," Brianya said, when Ed made a move to give her a hand.

"I've be meaning to ask you, how that garage situation turned out."

"It turned out just fine. I haven't seen or heard from them. Not that I expected to."

Brianya joined Ed on the couch. She sat on the opposite end.

"I won't bite you." The corners of his mouth lifted but his eyes weren't smiling.

"You look like you've got something on your mind, Ed."

"I was thinking—

Brianya's eyebrows shot up and she resisted the urge to blurt out the one-line zinger that lay on the tip of her tongue.

"Christmas is next week and I was wondering if you had plans?"

"This might sound weird to you but in my family we don't really 'celebrate' Christmas." Ed looked surprised. "Long story short, my Dad's sister, who's like a mother to him, is married to a

Jewish man. To keep the peace, we have a big family dinner and invite a few friends over and enjoy the day."

"Hmmm . . .," Ed said, scooting closer to Brianya and putting his arm across the back of the couch. "You just keep getting more and more interesting. "Does that mean you won't accept a gift?"

"Nope. I love gifts! But how about for this year, instead of doing the gift thing, we concentrate on getting to know one another better?"

Ed contemplated the suggestion. "Guess I can take that Hope diamond back then, huh?"

Brianya cozied up to Ed. "I bet you used to spoil your wife with gifts." The minute the words left her mouth, Brianya regretted having said them. Ed's gift giving and lack of physical attention to his wife is what had contributed to the failure of his marriage. Brianya felt two-feet tall for reminding him of that fact. "I'm sorry, I shouldn't have said that."

"I'm a big boy. Don't feel you have to tiptoe around my feelings." Ed smiled, displaying the chip on his incisor. Once again, not knowing the story behind it rankled Brianya. Ed noticed Brianya tense up. He removed his arm from the back of the couch and turned to face her. "Okay, I can see this is getting to be an issue; I'll tell you what happened." He took a deep breath, sighed heavily. "My wife—ex-wife—had anger issues. We had been trying for a baby for a long time. Finally, after five years of trying, she got pregnant. We were happy, making plans for the baby, picking out names, talking about moving to a bigger house, etcetera." Ed stopped talking and looked away.

Brianya folded her hand over Ed's and stroked the back of his hand.

"Around three, four months into the pregnancy, we were in bed. . . . you know. Afterward, she got up to take a shower—she was funny like that, always had to clean up right after. Anyway, I noticed she had been in there for a long time, and I didn't hear the shower running. I went to the door and asked if everything was alright. When she didn't answer, I opened the door and went in. She was standing over the toilet bowl just staring in . . . so much bl . . ." His words broke off as he choked back emotions.

Brianya's hand flew to her mouth, she gasped in horror. "Oh my God, Ed! I'm so sorry."

Ed ran his hand across his face and closed his eyes. "Anyway, I called 9-1-1 and they rushed her to the hospital. The doctor said it was a spontaneous abortion, miscarriage. They don't know what caused it, but she kept reassuring us that it wasn't our fault."

As she listened to Ed struggle with his story, Brianya felt like an intruder. She'd practically forced him to reveal something that he hadn't wanted to, at least not yet. And now, he was divulging an event in his life that was deeply personal and hurtful, all because he wanted to allay the friction that Brianya's not knowing would inevitably cause. It was too late to tell him that he didn't have to continue, that she couldn't bear the guilt that this knowledge would cause her. As much as Brianya wanted to stop Ed, she knew that in talking about it he was facilitating his own healing, much like the women at the shelter. So she let the process play itself out.

"After that happened," Ed was saying, "we weren't the same. My wife blamed me for the miscarriage, even though the doctor had told us both that it was nobody's fault. She always had a mean streak but when our baby died, she started getting physical with her anger. She would purposely pick fights with me, knowing I wouldn't hit her back." Ed looked embarrassed. "Finally, I shut down. I didn't find her desirable anymore. I worked late so I wouldn't have to deal with her hatred toward me. When she would get in my face telling me, screaming at me, that she needed me to make her feel like a woman, I'd tune her out. The next day, I would go and buy her a piece of jewelry or clothes just to shut her up."

The words came pouring out of Ed like water from a dam that had been stopped up for too long. "I should've handled the situation better. I blame myself for my failed marriage. If I had tried to understand what she was going through, made us get counseling or something . . . . I don't know." He rubbed his neck, deep in thought. "I came home later than usual one night, from working, and she accused me of cheating on her. The more I denied it, the angrier she got. I was tired of going back and forth with her, so I walked away. Next thing I know, she had jumped on my back and started punching me all in my head and face. I was trying to shake her off, but I ended up tripping over my own feet. I went down hard and ended up cracking my chin on the marble floor."

When Ed stopped talking, Brianya remained silent, letting him process what he'd just said. She resisted the urge to speak first.

Ed smiled weakly and raised his eyebrows. "So, that's how my tooth got chipped."

Brianya said softly, "It wasn't your fault; you know that don't you? None of it."

"I know," Ed said, sotto voce, not sounding convincing.

"May I ask you something?"

"Sure."

"Are you still in love with your wife—ex-wife?"

Ed didn't answer right away. "Before the divorce, we were legally separated. A year into the separation, we decided to try to see if we could salvage our marriage. Our reconciliation attempt ended almost as violently as our legal separation began." Ed's expression was one of sadness and loss. "I'll always love my ex-wife, Brianya; but I'm not in love with her."

Ed looked so sad sitting there, his personal business hung out like the days wash, for any passerby to gawk at, and Brianya was to blame. She was thankful that he hadn't cried. She couldn't have handled that. Brianya moved in close to Ed and kissed him first on the cheek, then the forehead, and finally on the tip of his nose. When her lips found his, Ed pulled back and fixed Brianya with a forlorn expression that communicated a need so intense that

Brianya shrank under his visage. He searched her face, perhaps hoping to find in it a clue as to how far she was willing to go. *Don't do this Brianya if you're not willing to go all the way.* "I'm sorry, Ed. I shouldn't have done that." She looked away, regretful.

"Please, Brianya, don't do this to me. I need you."

She hated herself for what she'd done. Ed wasn't the only one feeling the moment. Three years was a long time and although she wanted to answer that carnal urge, Brianya was determined to honor her promise to herself. She thought about the plaque that hung on the wall of a restaurant she frequented in her early days at MBCC. The inscription read, "If you always do what you've always done, you'll always get what you always got."

"I can't. I'm sorry," Brianya said again.

Ed's tone was brusque. "Stop saying you're sorry. I don't need to hear that right now." He got up and retrieved his coat from the hall closet. "I think this was a mistake."

"Obviously," Brianya said, feeling wounded. "It's not going to work. I need to just—"

"Whoa!" Ed went back to the couch, where Brianya was sitting. "That's not what I meant. I'm talking about the concert, the conversation. Not us."

"Oh."

"Look, sweetheart."

Sweetheart. I like the sound of that.

"Until we figure out how to date while celibate, maybe we should stay away from certain things, like sensual concerts and sensual music, movies with wild sex scenes, stuff like that. And you can't be kissing me like that, no matter what the conversation is about. I'm not Superman." Ed laughed but Brianya could tell he was serious.

"I can agree to that," Brianya said. "Also, it might be a good idea that we not keep late night hours/early morning hours. There's something about those early morning hours." Brianya smiled, she was all giddy inside, happy that instead of giving up on her, Ed was willing to give it try.

"One last thing," Ed said. "Maybe you can start dressing like those Amish women, wear those sensible shoes with the thick soles, no makeup, and a hair bonnet."

CHAPTER THIRTY-TWO

S ITTING IN A booth at B & M restaurant in Maple Heights, Dreama snatched another barbecued chicken wing from the plate she shared with Brianya. "See, girl, that there, that's a good man. You wanna be holding on to that one," she said between bites, when Brianya finished telling her about her date with Ed.

Brianya licked barbecue sauce off her fingers and plucked up her third wing.

"Ease up, Bri. I thought you said you had this eating thing back under control."

"I did, I mean I do. I'm nervous about this weekend, that's all. Everybody'll be meeting Ed for the first time, and he'll be meeting everybody. I just want y'all to like him."

"You ain't gotta worry about me; I like him already! Anybody that's willing to deal with your brand of crazy is alright in my book." She polished off the last of the fries and sucked down the rest of her Pepsi. Dreama leaned back in her chair and loosened the button of her jeans. "Before we leave here, I'm going back there and slap that cook, girl! B & M know they can burn!"

"Before I forget," Brianya said as they drove away from the restaurant, "ask Curtis to make his famous sweet potato rolls."

Dreama looked out the window. "He won't be coming; we broke up."

Brianya reached over and grabbed Dreama's hand. "I'm sorry, boo."

"Yeah, well. It just wasn't meant to be. We were having problems."

"You never said anything." Brianya tried to keep the hurt out of her voice. She felt slighted. Dreama had been there for her through all of her tribulations; Brianya wanted the chance to reciprocate.

"I know. I was hoping we could work it out." Dreama sighed heavily.

"Whenever you're ready to talk about it, I'm here." She squeezed Dreama's hand tight before letting go. Tears welled up in Brianya's eyes and she fought hard to keep them from spilling over.

Brianya sniffled and Dreama turned to see the tears racing down her cheeks. "Don't be feeling sorry for me," Dreama scolded. "I'm not pressed. Man don't want to do right, he got to go."

Brianya retrieved a tissue from her console and dried her cheeks and eyes. But the two of you were inseparable. I just knew y'all would get married."

"Yeah, well . . . ."

"Tell me what happened, Dreama."

Dreama took a deep breath. "It started with him not wanting to go out anywhere, and then he stopped spending money on me. Every time I asked him what was wrong, he would say, 'Why something always gotta be wrong? Maybe I'm just tired.'" Dreama's impression of Curtis was spot on. "Okay, cool. I figured maybe it was his time of month or something, I don't know. So I left it alone. Then his mother got sick and he had to go see about her. When he got back, he did a complete 180-degree turn. He was all sweet and wanting to go here and there and buy me presents and stuff. You know that's always a dead giveaway." Dreama took a breath. "So I called down to Tennessee and talked to his sister, the one that can't stand him. She told me that he had hooked up with some girl he knew back in high school while he was there."

Brianya shook her head.

"You know me. That's the deal breaker right there. You cheat, you walk."

"I can't believe it. I never thought Curtis would do something like that."

"Humph, I don't know why not. He's a man, ain't he? The mistake he made was getting caught."

"Not all men cheat."

"What? I can't believe you're taking that position, with your history."

Some women were conditioned to believe that it was in a man's nature to stray. That as long he took care of his family and found his way home at the end of the day, his philandering was excused. Brianya never had and never would accept that. She knew many men who were faithful to their wives and girlfriends. Just because she had yet to find one was no reason to throw her lot in with the doubting Thomases and lower either her standards or opinion of men. "If I subscribed to your way of thinking, what would be the point of dating? It would be one big waste of time."

"Not a waste of time. You'd be wiser in your expectations that's all. And you would be preparing yourself for the obvious. That way, when it happened, you wouldn't be talking about ending it all, because a man would only be doing what he was supposed to do."

Dreama was known for her over-the-top opinions, but this one was way out there. Did she really believe the garbage she was spouting? "Okay, then, for the sake of argument, let's say you're right. Now let me ask you this: Why did you hope your relationship with Curtis would lead to a marriage that would only end in divorce?"

"Huh?" Dreama said, puzzled.

"Well, according to your way of thinking all men cheat, so Curtis was bound to cheat. And your motto is 'you cheat, you walk,' so once that happens, the marriage is over, right?"

Dreama sucked her tongue and rolled her eyes. "You got a answer for everything, don't you?"

"Nah, just the stuff that doesn't make a bit of sense."

They laughed.

"I really wanted it to work out, Bri. I'm almost forty and I want kids." She glanced at Brianya with a hurtful look.

"Yeah, I know. I wanted it to work too." Brianya paused, not sure if now was the right time to point out the silver lining in Dreama's situation. "Well," she began cautiously, "Andre's not seeing anyone—if it's not too soon."

At the mention of Andre's name, the hurt expression vanished, replaced by one of hope. "Too soon for what? Me and Curtis ain't getting back together. Anyway, I'm on a mission and I'm not getting any younger. You just make sure that Andre comes to dinner solo."

They were a hundred feet away from Brianya's house and she was about to mash the garage door opener when Dreama asked, "Who is that pulling out of your driveway?"

Brianya squinted through the dusk and didn't recognize the car, but the profile looked liked Celine. "That's Celine!" She could hardly believe her eyes. Why hadn't she called first to make sure Brianya was at home? Odd that she hadn't seen Celine since she'd betrayed her by going out with Darnell. Brianya thought about chasing after the car to see what Celine wanted but decided against it.

"You back on friendly terms with her?" Dreama's tone was thick with accusation.

"Nope. I haven't seen or talked to her in months."

"Really? Humph, I wonder what she wanted."

Brianya didn't know what to make of the visit. Her mind was a million miles away, turning over possibilities. "I don't know," she said still pondering the meaning of the visit. "She probably came to apologize."

Dreama fumbled with the door handle. "While you're trying to figure all that out, I need to be working on my outfit for Sunday!" Dreama sprang out of the car. She gave Brianya a quick hug before sliding into the driver seat of her SUV and speeding off.

***

Brianya pulled into the North Coast parking garage and drove to her usual space, hoping to run into Celine. If the visit to her home the previous night was any indication, it was time they stopped acting like children and put all this foolishness behind them. She grabbed her purse and satchel and did a balancing act with her coffee mug.

When she didn't see Celine in the garage or at the elevators, Brianya rode up to her office and dropped off her things, and then headed upstairs to see if Celine had arrived at work early. She pressed the elevator button for two floors up and thought about what she'd say. Expecting to see Celine sitting at her desk in the outer foyer, well-coiffed and wearing the pasted on smile she donned for visitors, Brianya was shocked to see a young girl half Celine's age occupying her desk and having an animated conversation with someone on her cell phone.

"Excuse me," Brianya said when the young woman failed to acknowledge her presence.

Without looking up, the woman held up a finger. "May I help you," she said, closing her phone.

"I'm looking for Celine Connors, but I can see she hasn't gotten here yet. I'll come back later."

"Celine doesn't work here anymore," the young woman said.

Brianya pursed her lips and stared at the woman, waiting for the punch line. None came. "What do you mean she doesn't work here anymore?"

"She quit." The statement was so matter-of-fact that Brianya had to ask the girl to repeat herself. "All I know is I got a call from the temp agency I work for telling me to show up here Monday, because their Administrative Secretary had quit Friday.

"Quit?" Brianya's head was in a fog; she shook it to gain clarity.

"Yes. I'm sorry, I can't tell you any more than that. Oh," the young girl said as an afterthought. "I know that prior to quitting, she was on a leave-of-absence. For what, I don't know."

Brianya turned and hurried out of the office. When she got back to her desk, she dialed Celine's cell number and got a message that said the callee was not accepting phone calls. Then she dialed the home number, only to hear a message saying the number was no longer in service. *What is going on?* Brianya wondered. She dialed Ed's number; maybe he could provide some insight.

"I don't know, I haven't seen or heard from Celine for a while. Stop worrying, Ms. Johnson. I'm sure she's fine. She probably found a better job."

Not likely. Celine had been with the law firm for almost twenty years and she was talking about retiring from there. "Yeah, I'm sure you're right," she said downplaying her concern. "What you got planned for lunch today?"

After lunch, Brianya tried Celine's cell again and got the same message. The thought occurred to her to call Celine's parents in North Carolina, but she didn't want to sound like an alarmist and cause them unnecessary worry. If she didn't hear from her by Friday, Brianya was definitely calling Mr. and Mrs. Connors.

CHAPTER THIRTY-THREE

F RIDAY ROLLED AROUND and Brianya still hadn't heard from Celine. When she'd phoned the Connors in North Carolina, the phone rang and rang. No voicemail or answering machine kicked in so she couldn't leave a message. Celine had said that her parents rarely left the house, so why weren't they answering the telephone? It was the holiday after all; they could be visiting family. She'd have to wait until tomorrow. Right now, Brianya needed to finish dressing for dinner; Ed would be there any minute.

"I can't believe how nervous I am," Brianya said as she and Ed approached the front door of her parent's home. "I just want everyone to like you."

"What's not to like?" Ed joked.

Brianya gripped Ed's hand. "Try not to let my brother rattle you. He means well, but he doesn't' always filter his thoughts before he speaks."

"Noted."

"And my sister has a habit of making inappropriate comments at inappropriate times. So if she says something out of the way to you, just ignore her."

"Noted, again."

"My father's not bad. He'll give you the third degree about your job and lean on you about your intentions toward me. Actually, Andre'll do that too, but you don't have to answer him. Now my mother, she'll try to feed you 'til you burst, but don't fall for that. That's her way of trying to find out what sort of upbringing you had. Don't even ask," Brianya said when Ed looked like he was about to interject a question. "Just eat what you can and take the rest home."

They arrived at the front door and Brianya turned to Ed. "You sure you want to go through with this?"

"Your family sounds like they really love you, Brianya. I wouldn't miss it for the world." Ed leaned in, kissed Brianya on the cheek. "In case I don't get a chance to say this again: You look beautiful." He pushed a loose strand of hair out of her face. "Wear your hair like this more often." Dreama had styled her hair in a loose up do and added three small twists to each side.

Cinthia opened the door, took one look at Ed and twisted her lips. "Umph, umph, umph," she said appraising Ed's appearance. "Keep this one, Bri."

Ed looked questioningly at Brianya.

Embarrassed, Brianya rolled her eyes and made introductions. Ed proffered his hand and Cinthia stared at it like it would jump up and bite her.

"You can do better than that," she said, grabbing Ed and hugging him.

"You started early, Cin. It's barely two o'clock." A faint odor of alcohol wafted past Brianya. Christmas was the one time of year Cinthia indulged in alcohol to the point of becoming inebriated.

"I'm not drunk yet; but, when you see who's in there, you'll wish you were drunk!"

"What are you talking about?" Brianya pushed past Cinthia and barged into the house.

"She's he-ere!" Cinthia shouted, making the word two syllables.

"What the—" Brianya stopped dead in her tracks when she saw Endo lounging in the living room with the men in her family. "Uh, Daddy, can I talk to you for a minute?"

"What's wrong, Daughter?" Roger looked from his daughter to the young man standing beside her. "Oh," he said on a gust of air.

"I'll be right back, Ed." Walking away, Brianya heard Ed introduce himself to the group and Andre say "Ed, my man, let's rap a taste."

"Daughter, before you get all bent out of shape, let me just say that the boy had no place to go."

"Did you have to invite him here, Daddy? You knew I was bringing a date." She couldn't believe her father could be so thoughtless. "Did you think of how awkward he might feel seeing me with someone else? Did you even tell him I was bringing a date?"

Roger scratched his head. He didn't like being bombarded with questions. "Well, I was hoping . . ."

"What, that I would change my mind?" She shook her head and sighed loudly. "I'm so mad at you right now, Daddy! I didn't know you could be so messy." She was coming dangerously close to disrespecting her father but she couldn't help it. This was supposed to be a time when family and close friends came together to break bread and spend quality time together. Thanks to her father, Brianya was dealing with a stressor that she didn't need. "I'm nervous enough with you all meeting Ed for the first time, and now I have to worry about tiptoeing around someone's feelings who shouldn't be here in the first place." The doorbell rang and before Brianya crossed over the line and ruined everyone's evening by saying something to her father that she would regret, she threw her hands up and went to answer the doorbell.

Dreama stood on the other side of the door looking like a ray of sunshine in her bright yellow wool pea coat. The color was so bright and absurd that Brianya couldn't help smiling, her anger toward her father dissipating a fraction. "You won't believe who's here," she whispered. Not waiting for an answer, Brianya blurted, "Endo! Daddy dearest invited him."

"And you call me Drama? Let the fun begin!"

"Come on, I'll introduce you to Ed."

"What about Endo?" Dreama joked.

"Not funny!"

They found Ed in the kitchen with her mother, comparing notes on how best to dress a turkey.

"Oh, that's easy," Dreama interjected. "The best way to dress a turkey is to put a suit on," she made brackets with her fingers. "Insert name here." The kitchen exploded with laughter.

"Ed, this is Dreama, our resident *non*-funny person. Dreama, Ed."

Ed and Dreama chatted away as Brianya helped her mother carve slices of ham and arrange them on a platter. "What do you think, Ma?" Brianya whispered.

Alice shrugged. 'He seems nice; a lot nicer than that last boyfriend of yours." She turned up her nose at the memory of Darnell.

"Excuse me, Mrs. Johnson," Ed said, cutting into the conversation, "can I give you hand with the food?" They had started gathering the side dishes to take into the dining room.

Brianya caught the barely perceptible wink her mother gave her and tucked away a smile. She handed Ed an extra plate of sliced ham to set on the buffet. When they finished loading the last of the foodstuffs onto the table, everyone piled into the dining room and enjoyed the meal.

As dessert plates circulated across the expanse of the table, greedy hands grabbing for Alice's famous peach cobbler, Brianya watched her family and friends interact and her heart overflowed with love. If she could, she would bottle up this moment and cherish it forever. Just as that warm fuzzy feeling settled in, her father said, "Son, I hear tell you're an investment broker; they make pretty decent money. You plan on sharing any of that with my daughter?"

"Daddy!" Brianya tapped the heel of her hand against her forehead and moaned; the rest of the group expressed similar shock. Only Endo seemed to be enjoying Ed's seeming discomfort.

Ed wiped his mouth with the corner of his napkin and without missing a beat said, "Yes, sir. I already have," and pulled out a crushed velvet jewelry box. Turning to Brianya, he said, "I know we agreed that we wouldn't give gifts this year, but I bought this before we decided that. I was going to wait until tomorrow, but I can't think of a better time than this." Ed flipped open the lid of the box and Brianya was nearly speechless looking at the sparkling diamond-encrusted dangle earrings.

Ed's display took the wind out of Roger's sails and he melted into his chair.

"How do they look?" Brianya asked everyone, lifting the earrings from the box and holding them up to her ears. It was unanimous—the earrings looked gorgeous. Never one for public displays of affection, Brianya leaned across the table and kissed Ed right smack on the lips. "Thank you, they're beautiful!"

Endo looked crestfallen. Brianya felt embarrassed for him. He was there at her father's invitation in the hopes of winning her over. However, instead of celebrating a victory, Endo was a witness to his own humiliation and the only thing he should be trying to win back was his pride, which Ed had just pulverized.

As the day progressed, Dreama eventually cornered Andre and the two of them were engaged in an intense conversation in a corner of the living room. Brianya caught Andre's eye and mouthed the words, "she's single," hoping he got the implied meaning.

Cashmere had finally joined them, after splitting her time between her parents' houses. She looked bored as Brianya's cousin tried to engage her in conversation. "Don't you see she's not interested?" Brianya asked as she approached to rescue Cashmere. Brianya pointed to the lavish earrings that hung from her lobes. "Ed gave me these. Do you think I shouldn't have accepted them?"

Cashmere, who had impeccable taste when it came to the finer things in life, appraised the earrings and smiled broadly. "He's got excellent taste." She appraised Brianya next. "Why are you second-guessing yourself; does it feel like a beholden gift?"

Brianya looked down at the floor. "Sort of."

"Bri, you have to stop over-thinking things. He obviously cares about you." She ticked off the reasons on her fingers. "One, he gave up Christmas dinner with his family to be here with you; two, even though he knows you're not giving up the candy, he bought you those *very* expensive earrings; and, three, he's still here after that crazy conversation with Andre." Brianya looked puzzled. "Dreama was eavesdropping. She told me about it as soon as I stepped in the house."

"Okay, I see your points. I'll just be in the moment. Let me introduce you to Ed." Brianya scanned the room and waved Ed over.

"So you're Ed. It's nice to finally meet you."

"Likewise," Ed said offering his hand to shake.

After a few minutes of chitchat, Cashmere excused herself to say hello to Brianya's parents. Half way across the room, she turned back and gave Brianya two thumbs up for Ed.

"Your friends are nice, but tell me something. What's the connection with that Endo character? All day I've been getting these weird vibes from him."

"Oh, well . . ." Brianya contemplated downplaying her connection to Endo. But what would that get her? It was better to be honest, just put it out there. She hated secrets in a relationship and she wasn't about to taint whatever she and Ed had with cleverly worded half-truths. "I went out with him a few times, and he asked me to marry him."

"He what?!" Ed shouted.

"Keep your voice down," Brianya whispered angrily.

"You got me sitting up here in this house—"

Andre arrived at Brianya's side a fraction of a second before their father. "What up, man? You wanna change that tone?"

"Your sister got me up in here looking like a clown. That's what's up." Although he was speaking to Andre, Ed's eyes never left Brianya's face. "I don't get you, Brianya. What were you thinking inviting me here? Did you want to do some sick side-by-side comparison?" He threw up his hands. "I'm outta here!"

Looks of confusion graced the faces of the relatives, who had no clue what Ed was talking about.

Brianya watched, bewildered, as Ed grabbed his coat off the rack and headed for the door. "So, you get to do all the talking? I don't get to explain anything?"

"Save it for some other sucker!"

She took off the beautiful new earrings that she'd already fallen in love with and flung them at Ed's back. "Take your cheap gift with you!" They made a thudding noise as they hit the floor. Ed turned around and scooped them up and Brianya saw the hint of sadness that crossed his face.

CHAPTER THIRTY-FOUR

"Have you heard from Ed?" Dreama said into the phone.

Three long days had passed since the fiasco at her parents' house and Ed was still MIA. There had been no workplace sightings, no phone calls, nothing. Brianya, who didn't believe in magic, voodoo, or any other otherworldly mumbo jumbo, was starting to feel cursed. First Celine, now Ed. *What's next?* Brianya wondered. "No, and he's not returning my phone calls."

"Give him some more time, girl. His pride is hurt and you know how men get when you hurt their little pride. . . . My next customer just walked in, I gotta go. Hang in there, sis!"

Brianya didn't know how much longer she could hang in. Now that she'd gotten a taste of the dating world again, she was fully committed to being the other half of a happy couple. She cared about Ed more than she wanted to admit, but if this was his MO when things didn't go his way, he definitely wasn't the one for her. If only he'd let her explain that she had nothing to do with Endo showing up at dinner, and that his marriage proposal meant nothing—absolutely nothing—to her.

In a last ditch effort to set things right between them, Brianya dialed Ed's number and waited with bated breath. Like all the other times, it went straight to voice mail. This time she didn't bother to leave a message. She mashed the end button hard and tossed the phone on the bed.

Brianya rummaged through the refrigerator for the last of the leftover ham, collard greens, and cornbread she'd taken out to thaw before she went to work this morning. She placed her food in the microwave and poured herself a glass of sugarless iced tea. Just as she was about to take a swallow, someone rapped on the door. She pulled the living room curtain back to find Darnell standing on the other side. "What do you want?" Brianya barked.

"I need to talk to you about something. It's important."

Darnell sounded serious. Brianya unlatched the door. "What is it?"

"I was on my way to the club and Tricia brought this envelope over and asked me to give it to you." He fumbled through the pockets of his suit jacket but came up empty-handed.

"This better not be one of your lame excuses to—"

"It's not, I promise. I must've forgot to put in my pocket. I was rushing around when she gave it to me . . . Oh, snap! I left it on the dining room table."

Brianya eyed Darnell with suspicion. "Why would Tricia have a letter for me anyway?"

Darnell glanced down at his watch. "Look, I'm sort of in a hurry. I don't know what it's all about. All I know is she showed up at my place, asked me to give you an envelope. She may have told me what it was, but I really wasn't paying attention." He ran his hand over his head. "It'll obviously be too late when I'm finished up tonight. So I'll drop it by tomorrow night on my way to the club."

"Just drop it through the mail chute," Brianya called after Darnell as he bounded down the steps.

The *Two Occasions* ring tone Brianya assigned to Ed's number sounded from a distance. She raced up the stairs to answer the call before Ed hung up. "Hello!"

"Did I catch you at a bad time?" Ed asked.

"No, I had to run upstairs to the get the phone."

There was a pregnant pause.

"Oh. Well, I wanted to tell you that I got the messages you left me. I think we need to talk."

When Ed said, "I think we need to talk," flashbacks to the breakup with Darnell clouded Brianya's mind and she fought the urge to retreat. "Okay. I was just eating dinner, but otherwise I'm free."

"I can't today. I need to run some errands with my mom. I was thinking tomorrow after work. I can be at your place at seven-thirty."

CHAPTER THIRTY-FIVE

B RIANYA WAS SO nervous that she was peeing like a racehorse. This was the third time she'd gone to the restroom. Seven twenty-eight, Ed would be here in two minutes. She unlocked the front door and ran to the restroom. Like clockwork, the bell rang. "It's unlocked!" Brianya shouted. She washed her hands and hurried out to greet Ed.

Brianya froze in her tracks.

"Bet you weren't expecting to see me were you?" the man said. When Brianya didn't respond, he pointed the gun he'd been holding at his side straight at her face. "Were you?!" he shouted.

"N-n-no," Brianya stammered, tears streaming down her cheeks. "W-w-what do you want?"

Brianya had never seen him look the way he looked now. He was unkempt and his clothes disheveled. His hair looked matted, like he hadn't combed it in days.

"What I want," the man said calmly, "is for you to tell me what makes him a better choice than me."

"I don't know what you're talking about."

"Don't lie to me! I saw you with him!" He closed the distance between them and waved the gun at Brianya's head.

Brianya screamed in fear. "Please, please, please! Don't hurt me, please. I'm s-s-s-sorry for whatever I did!" She sobbed uncontrollably.

The man snatched Brianya by the hair and pulled her head back. "For *whatever* you did?" he mocked. "You know exactly what you did! You let me spend my money on you all along knowing that you couldn't care less about me!" The man was breathing heavy and erratic as he spat the words at Brianya.

"You're just like my ex!" he said as he dragged her by the hair into the living room. "I should kill you right here and now!"

"No! Please!"

He let her hair go and pushed her violently to the floor. Brianya fell hard, making a loud thudding sound as she did. Her insides felt as if they had exploded. "Get on your knees! I'm gonna make you beg for my forgiveness."

Brianya did as she was told. Maybe if she gave the man what he wanted, he'd let her live.

"Beg me to forgive your slutty ways!" the man ordered.

Fear had taken hold of Brianya and the words wouldn't come out. She tried desperately to push the words out but nothing came. Impatient, the man raised the gun and slammed it hard against Brianya's mouth. She let out a loud wail as she felt something break loose and fly across the room. The blow had opened a gash in Brianya's lip and left a coppery metallic taste.

The chirping of her cell phone further enraged the intruder. He followed Brianya's gaze to the hall table where the phone sat charging in its base. In one fell swoop, he grabbed up the phone and hurled it. Seconds later, the landline rang. Familiar with the layout of the house, the man pulled Brianya to her feet and marched her into the kitchen, where he tore the apparatus off the wall and smashed it to the floor. He stalked to the kitchen door and removed the key from the deadbolt. Brianya felt trapped. From the kitchen, she could see the front door. The man had left it ajar and Brianya detected movement on the porch. Before she could yell for help, the man knocked her violently to the floor again. She fell, hard, wind expelling from her lungs.

"Get on your knees!" the man ordered once again. Brianya whimpered as she tried to raise herself. "Now, where were we? Oh, yeah, you were about to beg for my forgiveness."

Brianya said the words the man wanted to hear, only it didn't appease him, he became even more furious. He started overturning furniture, emptying the contents from the cabinets.

Brianya was relieved when the intruder left the kitchen. He went from one part of the house to another, ransacking everything in his path. In the distance, she heard the man destroying her precious items as he slammed and shoved them to the floor, against the wall. Fear had put Brianya's senses on heightened alert and she could make out distinct sounds in the distance, such as the soft muffled sound of a closing door. The front door? Oh, God! The man's accomplice had joined him! Where was Andre when she needed him?

She listened. Still, no sounds. The man must have left, just like that. She breathed a huge sigh of relief.

Brianya lay flat on her back, her breath coming in spurts as she forced her mind to focus. *How did she get here?* she wondered through a haze. She was in full panic mode. If only she could pull herself up. She must have broken two or three ribs when she crashed to the floor. Her lip felt at least twice its normal size. She ran her tongue around the inside of her mouth, over her teeth, and felt an opening where there used to be a tooth. She couldn't worry about that now; she had to get to her telephone, call someone. But the man had pulled the phone cord out of the wall and she didn't know where he had hurled her cell phone.

Brianya's life seemed to have spiraled out of control. She'd had no idea what she was getting into when she agreed to go out with this man whom she'd seen as an ally, a kindred spirit in pain and failed relationships. Crawling to the bathroom, she leaned her back against the wall and put her head into her hands, then scooted to the claw-footed tub and braced herself against it. She tried to get a solid hold on the cold porcelain to pull herself up, but just as she was about to steady herself, a blow to the back of her head sent a jarring pain through her entire body, reverberating to the soles of her feet. She'd thought she was alone, had heard the front door shut when the man walked out. Or had it been some other door?

Just as she was losing consciousness, she felt something cold and hard, like steel pressing against her neck, and smelled the faint odor of sulfur only inches from her nostrils. She heard what sounded like the hammer of a gun as it was being cocked. So this is how it would all end, in the bathroom of her new home in Shaker Heights, her life only half-lived. Brianya fought unsuccessfully to stave off the blackness that was coming in ripples, and felt the man lift the gun from its resting place on her neck. Her eyelids fluttered. Her heart quickened in anticipation of the reprieve she'd been granted. She was going to live after all. She felt a sliver of joy.

Brianya heard the faint sound of what sounded like footsteps coming from the front of the house. Relief washed over her as she realized the man had spared her life. She didn't dare turn around, fearing his departure might be just a hallucination. As she knelt frozen in position, Brianya heard a movement behind her and her heart felt as if it had exploded in her chest.

There was a loud boom, and then blackness slowly overtook her as she stared, uncomprehendingly, at the trail of blood snaking its way across the mosaic tile.

CHAPTER THIRTY-SIX

W HEN BRIANYA CAME to, she was lying on a stretcher and the police were taking Darnell out in handcuffs. She tried to turn her head but a huge C4 collar around her neck prevented her. Straight ahead, she saw Andre speaking in hushed tones to a lady cop, who Brianya recognized as Curtis' cousin, Serena.

"Lay still, Miss." the paramedic said when Brianya tried to raise her head to signal to Andre.

"What going on?" Her head felt fuzzy and she was woozy.

"Miss, can you tell me your name?"

"Brianya."

"Where are you, Brianya?"

"Home."

"What happened to you, Brianya?"

"A gun hit me in the head."

The paramedic shone a bright light into Brianya's eyes. "How many fingers do you see, Brianya?" He held up two fingers.

"Four," Brianya answered.

"And what's today's date?"

Brianya thought a moment. "I don't know."

The paramedic whispered something to his partner. "Brianya, looks like you might have a concussion. We're going to transport you to Ahuja."

As they wheeled Brianya out of the house, she saw more paramedics loading the intruder, Monticello Belvoir, into an ambulance.

Andre made his way to Brianya before they put her in the ambulance. "Don't worry, li'l sis. I got this. Soon as I finish up here, I'll meet you at the hospital. I called Mama and Daddy; they'll be waitin' for you at the Emergency entrance."

"What happened, Andre? Why do the police have Darnell?"

"I told you not to worry about that, right now. All you need to concern yourself with is getting better." He kissed his sister on the forehead. "We'll talk later."

When the paramedics pushed Brianya through the doors of the Emergency entrance, a small army greeted her—her parents, her sister, Dreama, Cashmere, Ed, and Endo. No Andre; he was the one she really wanted to see. She needed to find out what had happened just before she blacked out, and why Darnell was in handcuffs.

Darnell must have been the shadowy figure she saw on the porch. That pretense the day before about a letter from Tricia was just a ruse to set her up. But for what? It didn't make sense. And yet, it did. Dreama had said all along that it was strange that Monty and Darnell could still be cool even after she and Monty started keeping company. They had probably bet who would be the first to break down her resistance. May the best man win. Only neither of them had won. When she broke it off with Monty and then refused to give Darnell the satisfaction of buying her goodwill, she stung both of them right in the pride! And what had happened tonight was their way of teaching her a lesson. Something had gone wrong and Monty ended up getting shot. Maybe the bullet had ricocheted off something and shot him. Right up until she lost consciousness, Brianya thought the blood she saw was hers. She was relieved to know that it wasn't.

"Look at what that son-of-gun did to my daughter's face! Don't worry none, Daughter; me and your brother gon' take care of this!" Brianya could feel the rage coming from her father as if it were a living, breathing being.

"No, daddy! Please, just leave it alone! Let the police handle it."

"Careful, now, Roger. Your blood pressure! All we need is for you to have another stroke."

Roger batted away the concern. "Don't worry about me, Alice. Ain't no man gon' put his hands on a daughter of mine and get away with it!"

Alice caressed her daughter's forehead and kissed her gently on the cheek. "The Lord told me that you're gonna be just fine, baby."

At the sound of her mother's lilting tone, tears spilled from Brianya's eyes.

"Shhh. Hush now." Alice pulled a package of tissues from her purse and wiped the wetness from her daughter's eyes and face. "You're safe now, baby," she said stroking Brianya's hand.

The ER nurse came over and said they had a space for Brianya now.

"We'll be out here waiting for you," Dreama said as the nurse wheeled Brianya away. They all looked like scared rabbits.

***

It was six o'clock the next day when Andre finally made it to the hospital, just as Brianya was released. She'd been admitted so the doctors could monitor her overnight; make sure she didn't suffer any more concussion related symptoms. The injuries she had sustained when Monty knocked her to the floor were less life threatening than she'd thought. Although no ribs were broken and there was no internal bleeding, there was a significant amount of bruising and the pain was off the chart. The left side of her torso was a deep purplish blue, the same color as her lip.

"You're by yourself?"

"Yeah. I wanted to talk to you. Plus, Mama wouldn't let Daddy come. Said he might get too worked up."

As the orderly pushed Brianya toward the bank of elevators, Andre followed behind them. He was unusually quiet. Brianya could tell that he was working things out in his head.

No More Expectations

"Thanks, man," Andre said when they reached his car in the parking garage. Even though the orderly had secured the wheels of the chair before helping Brianya into the passenger seat, Andre, nonetheless, held tight onto the back of the chair.

"Talk to me, Andre," Brianya said when the orderly had left.

Andre fastened Brianya's seat belt and closed the door. His face was naked with unchecked anger. Pulling out of the parking lot, he nodded as if he were reassuring himself about something. His voice was gruff and full of emotion when he spoke. "That cat, Monty, he ain't wrapped too tight. He was lookin' to do some serious harm last night. He told the detectives who questioned him that he wanted to kill you. Said he saw you out to dinner with Darnell right before you broke it off with him. The night before all this jumped off, he saw Darnell leaving your house. Plus he said he saw some other guys coming and going even before that."

"How did you find out what he told the detectives?" Brianya asked, surprised.

"Me and Serena—the lady cop—we go way back. She's the one who slipped the call to me last night; that's why I got to your house so fast. Anyway, she's kickin' it with one of the detectives. So after they questioned Monty at the hospital this afternoon, she called me with the heads up."

"He was stalking me?" Brianya said hardly able to believe it. Nothing in Monty's make-up had suggested that he was of that mentality. She shook her head, confused. He had totally fooled her.

"Seems so. But don't worry, his stalking days are over. And when I get finished with him, he's gon' be wishing for a bullet."

Andre spoke from anger; Brianya understood that, because if he were going to seek retaliation, he never would have admitted that to her, for fear she might be implicated. Besides, she knew her brother would never hit a man who couldn't hit back.

"I know you're speaking out of anger, Andre, but please don't do anything stupid!" She wanted to say more, but fat tears spilled from Brianya's eyes. "All I was doing was getting to know those guys; I wasn't doing anything wrong."

"Come on, li'l sis. Don't cry. You know I hate when you cry," Andre said, rubbing Brianya's back in a circular motion. "Some dudes can't handle not being number one. And anyway, he's screwed up in the head." The last words, he had to force through his teeth, "I promise I won't touch him as long as he's in that chair." Of course, Brianya knew the unspoken meaning that lay behind those words: God help Monty if he ever walked again.

Brianya dried her eyes. "I'm just gonna forget about dating. No matter what I do, I end up paying for it."

"Don't talk like that. You can't let what one lunatic did dictate how you gon' live your life."

"All this time, I was thinking Darnell was the bad guy." Brianya stared into the expanse. "So what happened, Andre; why was Darnell in handcuffs?"

Andre talked while he drove.

According to Serena, Darnell was about to drop a letter through the mail chute when he noticed the door was slightly open and the screen door unlocked. He heard the indistinct raised voices of two people having what he assumed was a lover's quarrel. Then Brianya started begging her attacker not to hurt her and that's when Darnell knew she was in trouble. He heard the male voice calling Brianya all kinds of names and telling her she was just like his ex. At that point, he recognized the voice as Monty's. When Monty told Brianya that he ought to just kill her now, and to get down on her knees and beg for his forgiveness, he then came into Darnell's line of vision. When he dragged Brianya by the hair into the living room, Darnell saw the gun in Monty's hand and that's when he knew he had to do something quick. So he called Brianya's cell phone, hoping Monty would let her answer it. He was going to tell her that he was outside and for her to try to make it to the door. However, the ringing phone only made Monty angrier and he threw it across the room. Darnell was about to tiptoe into the house when the landline rang and Monty yanked Brianya up and pushed her to another part of the house.

He dialed 9-1-1 as he ran to his car, but he kept getting a busy signal. After he got his gun from the glove box, he sneaked back onto the porch. That's when he saw Monty tearing up the house and Brianya crawl to the bathroom. Monty saw her too. When he turned to go into the bathroom, Darnell waited a beat, making sure he wouldn't be detected and sneaked into the house. He hid in the alcove to the side of the bathroom where he could see everything that was happening. He had his gun pointed straight at Monty. Then Monty lowered his gun and Darnell was about to lower his, but Monty raised the gun and hit Brianya in the head.

"Darnell shot him on reflex. The bullet caught Monty in the spine. They say he might be a quadriplegic."

Brianya inhaled sharply. "What about Darnell?" Brianya asked. "What was he doing with a gun anyway?"

"I don't know. They still holding him, but they haven't charged him with anything yet. It's been all over the news; they calling Darnell a 'modern-day knight in shining armor.'" Andre licked his lips and smiled ruefully. His sister had come close to losing her life; he should've been the one to save her.

"I know what you're thinking, Andre. Don't beat yourself up. It could've been anybody that showed up at my door."

"Yeah, but it wasn't me." He ran his hand over his head and grunted.

Brianya sighed deeply and said, "I can't go back there, Andre," her heart heavy with grief. The turn of events left more questions than answers. Answers that Brianya felt emotionally unable to handle. All she could think was if Tricia hadn't given Darnell a letter for her, and Darnell hadn't left it at home and come back the next night when he did, her family and friends . . . Brianya whimpered in pain, she didn't want to imagine what could have happened. She cradled her jaw and moaned. Wherever they were going, she hoped they would get there quickly; it was definitely time for another pain pill.

The light turned red and Andre looked over at Brianya and winced. His brow creased with worry. "Where do you want to go?"

She felt foolish admitting helplessness but under the circumstances, her brother would understand. "I want to stay with you for a little while."

As he'd done since Brianya's childhood, Andre gave it to her straight. "You need to go home and face this thing head-on."

Brianya looked at him with sorrowful eyes. "I can't do it, Dre." Tears slid down her face as she choked back a sob.

"I'll be right there with you, li'l sis." He patted Brianya lovingly on the shoulder. "We'll all take shifts if we have to. That's your house and ain't nobody gon' run you out of it."

CHAPTER THIRTY-SEVEN

O VER THE PAST six weeks, the days and nights melted into one another, each week bringing with it a new challenge. This week, the sleepless nights were back. Four days since Brianya had slept for more than an hour a night and it was beginning to show in her slurred speech and lack of mental cognition. She couldn't go on like this. Yet she didn't know what to do to move beyond this current state. Brianya had spent the last four nights battling the recurring image of Monty standing over her, waving his gun in her face, ordering her to beg him for forgiveness. The images were so real that whenever Brianya closed her eyes, she could feel Monty strike her on the mouth with the barrel of the gun, at which point her eyes would fly open and, drenched in sweat, she'd scream until she was hoarse, and Andre would come to her room with a bowl of cold water and a washcloth. No words passed between them, only the gentle caress of sibling love as he dabbed the cloth against her forehead.

At first, Brianya hated that Andre had talked her into coming back home to recover instead of going to his own or their parents' house. The first couple of days it was as if the vile offense had never happened. The rooms Monty had destroyed in his rampage were cleaned up with no trace of vandalism. To her surprise, with Andre's approval, Endo had hired a cleaning company to spare the family from having to face the violence that had been done. Andre should never have agreed to let Endo do what he did. Now on top of dealing with everything else, she had to worry about Endo trying to insinuate himself back into her life, reminding her of what had happened.

Unable and unmotivated to handle the routine chores of life, Brianya hadn't kept up with her personal hygiene; save for the few times she'd used a toilette to clean her private areas. Except for family members, she couldn't face anyone and she didn't want to talk about what had happened. Giving up on getting Brianya to let them come see her, Dreama and Cashmere phoned several times a day to reassure her of their love and to tell her that they were there for her if she needed them; always leaving messages with whoever answered the phone or on voicemail. She did need them more than they knew, but she wasn't ready to face them. Endo and Ed had phoned daily also; seeing either of them was out of the question. How could she face them, feeling indirectly halfway responsible for what had happened to her? Looking at them would only serve as a reminder that she had trifled with the emotions of three innocent people, bringing one to the breaking point.

Brianya buried her face in her pillow. She wanted to cry, release the built-up pressure squeezing the air out of her lungs. Nothing came. Her well was dry. Where hope should have resided, there was nothing but a vast hollowness. She lifted the pillow off her face and turned over onto her opposite side, and looked into the face of her mother, who was taking the daytime shift of watching over her while Andre went to work. This morning, like the mornings before it, was drab and felt endless. At 9 o'clock A.M., it seemed a lot earlier. Listless from another sleepless night, Brianya pushed herself to a sitting position.

"You look like I feel, Ma," Brianya said on a yawn.

"Nothing a good cup of Columbian coffee can't cure. You want a cup?"

"That's exactly what I *don't* need."

"Suit yourself." Alice went to the kitchen to pour herself another cup of coffee.

Brianya sat on the side of the bed and sighed. She pushed unwashed feet into cotton slippers and went to peer at her reflection in the mirror on her vanity table. The whites of her eyes were a pinkish color and they burned from lack of sleep. The swelling in her jaw was completely gone and the cut on her lip had healed nicely with the ointment she'd used. Even the hole where her tooth used to be was no longer raw. The three-times-a-day warm salt-water rinse had proven very effective. Eventually, she'd get an implant.

Alice walked back into the bedroom in time to see Brianya cover her face with her hands and sigh mournfully. "Brianya, baby, it's good to throw your burdens on the Lord; there's nothing that he can't do. But sometimes God will lead you to someone he can use to help you with your problems," Alice said, placing the coffee of cup on the nightstand and settling in the chair next to the bay window.

"I know, Ma," Brianya replied, uninterested. She wasn't ready to leave the house, much less talk to anyone professionally, as her mother seemed to be hinting at.

Alice ignored Brianya's tone. "I think you need to go back to that doctor who helped you lose the weight."

"Dr. Tobias? I can't go back to him; I never finished my first sessions."

"Well, then, we'll find someone else." Alice stirred her coffee absently. "It breaks my heart to see you this way, Bri. I wish you would let your friends visit with you; it'll do your spirit good."

Brianya wanted to scream for her mother to give it a rest. For the past two days, she wouldn't let up about counseling or getting out of bed, or washing, or whatever else she could think of that would do Brianya's "spirit good." How was it that suddenly everyone knew what was best for her? They couldn't possibly know; she didn't even know. What Brianya wanted was for everyone to get off her back. Let her come to terms with what had happened in her own way.

"I want you to call whoever you need to, to get a referral for a doctor. It's after nine, somebody's office is open." Alice picked up the telephone and thrust it at Brianya.

"I wish y'all would leave me alone! Stop trying to get me to heal on your schedule. This happened to me, not you! Not Andre, not Daddy, not Cinthia not anybody but me! Can you understand that, Ma?!"

Alice looked stricken. "I understand what you're going through, baby. I . . ."

The frustration and lack of control that had overtaken Brianya for the past weeks came bubbling to the surface. Before she knew it, she was spitting a barrage of questions at her mother. "How could you understand, Ma? Have you ever had someone wave a gun in your face and tell you he was going to kill you, huh? Have you ever not slept in four days because every time you close your eyes you feel the butt of a gun slam against your face and knock your tooth out? And did you think you were dead on the spot because just before you blacked out from being whacked on the head with a gun you saw blood and knew it was yours? Do you obsess over the fact that you deserved to have what happened happen because you didn't stop to think that maybe going out with three men at the same time wasn't such a good idea? Which part of *my* tragedy do you understand, Ma?" The well that Brianya thought was dry suddenly overflowed and drenched her nightgown. She grabbed a wad of tissues from the vanity and mopped at her face and neck.

Alice bit back a reply and squared her shoulders against Brianya's accusing tone. Brianya seethed with anger but Alice knew it wasn't directed at her. She took Brianya by the shoulders and lifted her from the vanity. "Come on, baby," she said, leading her back to bed.

Brianya took one look at her mother's eyes, cloudy with hurt. "Oh God, Ma, I'm so sorry!" Fresh tears spilled.

"It's the fear talking, baby. I know that," Alice cooed. She held Brianya and rocked her until she was spent, then she got a cool cloth and cleaned her daughter's face. When she finished, Alice held Brianya's face in her hands. "Listen to me, baby."

Brianya turned away. She couldn't bring herself to look at her mother.

"Look at me, Bri." Alice turned Brianya's face toward her. "I don't ever want to hear you say you are responsible in any way, form, or fashion for what that man did to you. Or that you deserved what he did. That is a disturbed young man and God done dealt with him."

Alice, like everyone else, watched the news every night to keep up-to-date on what was going on with Monty. Because of his once semi-celebrity status, the news stations had followed the story from the beginning, reporting daily on Monty's medical condition. So far, the prognosis wasn't good. He had a c4 spinal injury that might put him in a chair for the rest of his life. It was a wait-and-see game. Not much of the initial swelling had gone down.

"I don't believe that God would let you survive that sort of tragedy so that that boy could get off with just a slap on the wrist," Alice said. "I believe that whatever judge gets his case is gonna do right by this family!"

"That doesn't make me feel better, Ma." Sadness tugged at the corners of Brianya's mouth. "Because of me, Monty might never walk again. Whether he does one day in prison or fifty years doesn't matter because every day that he doesn't walk, I'll be doing time with him." When Alice started to protest, Brianya slid under the covers and turned her back to her mother.

Alice sighed heavily. "No sense in me trying to convince you otherwise; you won't hear a word I say anyway. I'll let you come to terms with all this in your own good time." The doorbell rang and Alice went to answer it.

"Brianya, baby," Alice said, standing in the doorway sounding winded, "Darnell is downstairs and he wants to see you."

At the mention of Darnell's name, Brianya shot up in bed. She'd forgotten all about Darnell's going before the judge for sentencing today. Thinking back over the last 24 hours, Brianya had a vague recollection of Andre mentioning that he and their father wanted to be present when Darnell was sentenced, to show him some brotherly support.

284

Although Darnell had been cleared of Monty in Brianya's defense, he still had to answer for a having a weapon while under disability charge. It had come out in the news reports that Darnell had gotten into a situation involving an ex-girlfriend and domestic violence—long before he and Brianya started going out. That was only half of the reason why he was going to court today. The other half, of course, was obvious. Had Brianya not been in the situation she was in, Darnell wouldn't have had to use his gun. A new wave of guilt washed over Brianya.

"I can't see him, now, Ma. Look at me!" It had been six weeks since the event and Brianya had refused all of Darnell's attempts to communicate with her. She had told Andre to thank him for what he did, but that was weak and cowardly. He had saved her life; she owed him more respect than that. Brianya wanted to talk to him personally, tell him how grateful she was. Not now, though. Not looking like this. Yet, she had to find the strength and the will to face him. This might be her last chance before—if—he went to prison. Brianya threw her legs over the side of her bed and took a deep breath, sighed heavily. She rose and headed for the bathroom.

Alice brightened at the sight of her daughter making an effort to receive a visitor. She opened the closet and snatched a pair of jeans off a hanger along with a powder blue sweater. "Put these on," she said, tossing the clothes onto the bed. "He's only got ten minutes; he's on his way to court."

"Ten minutes? It'll take me at least twenty to clean myself up!" Brianya raced into the bathroom and slammed the door. "See if you can get him to wait, Ma."

Ten minutes later, when Alice returned to the bedroom, she was carrying an envelope. "He couldn't wait. He said to give you this."

Brianya stopped combing her hair and took the envelope, disappointment etched in the lines of her forehead. She placed the envelope unopened on the nightstand and crept back under the covers.

CHAPTER THIRTY-EIGHT

A KEY TURNING IN the lock startled Brianya and she let out a
shriek as the door swung open. Andre bustled inside. He
punched in the code to disarm the alarm and put his keys in his
pocket. "Sorry, li'l sis, I forgot to call ahead." They had worked
out a system to ease Brianya's fear of being home alone. Andre
would phone ahead so that he wouldn't frighten Brianya when he
unlocked the door.

"I'm okay," Brianya said, clutching her chest.

He looked around the room. "Mama gone?"

"Half an hour ago."

"Daddy tell you what happened in court today?" Andre
marched to the kitchen and grabbed a beer from the fridge.

"Yeah." Sadness enveloped Brianya. "Thanks for being there
for Darnell. Daddy said the judge commented that she wished she
didn't have to give Darnell any time. But she had to because of
the gun." Brianya thought about Darnell sitting behind prison
bars for a year all because he'd come to her defense. She owed
him so much for being in the right place at the right time. If she
lived to be 100, Brianya could think of nothing that would equal
the debt of gratitude she felt she owed Darnell.

Andre peered at Brianya. Something was different about her.
He screwed up his face in concentration then a slow smile found
its way to his lips. "Why you lookin' brand new?" he asked
referring to her fresh attire and swanky hairstyle. It was a welcome
change from the bathrobe and do-rag she normally wore around
the house.

It took some effort, but after she'd missed seeing Darnell, her
mother had managed to convince her to put on some clothes,
wash her hair, and come out of her bedroom. She'd even talked

Brianya into phoning Dr. Tobias' office and scheduling an appointment. In an attempt to make Brianya feel better, Alice had fixed her a grilled cheese sandwich, with a side of potato chips and pickles. Brianya had taken only a few bites of the sandwich and nibbled on the pickle. The chips, however, she devoured. Her appetite was spotty and she didn't want to force herself to eat when she really wasn't hungry. The upside to having a sporadic appetite was that she'd lost nine pounds.

"Didn't want to waste a good shower," Brianya said in answer to Andre's question.

"So I guess that means you feelin' up to company."

A sheen of perspiration suddenly dotted Brianya's forehead.

"Calm down, sis. I'm only talkin' about Dreama."

"Oh." When had he answered a call from Dreama? She hardly ever called on the landline. Now that she thought of it, Dreama was calling the landline more often since Brianya had turned off her cell phone. But that was usually during the day when her mother was there. She'd bet anything that her mother had put Andre up to this. So much for letting her come to terms in her own way. "Did Mama tell you to say that?"

"What? Naw!" Andre chuckled. "Dreama told me to say that."

"When did you talk to Dreama?"

"That's my business."

"You're talking nonsense. My friend called my house to—"

"Hold up. She didn't call your house."

"What are you talking about?" her eyes grew big. "Wait! You and Dreama?" For the first time in a long time, Brianya smiled.

"Maybe." Andre's tone was noncommittal but he couldn't hide the glint in his eyes.

***

Dreama had arrived in twenty minutes flat. When Brianya called her, she was in the middle of conditioning her hair. From the looks of it, Dreama had dropped everything and, knowing her, broke every traffic law to finally be able to visit with her friend. In all honesty, Brianya didn't feel up to it, but she put on a brave face and kept repeating, like a mantra, the Serenity Prayer:

God grant me the serenity to accept the things I cannot change,
Courage to change the things I can,
And wisdom to know the difference.

Dreama wrapped Brianya in a bear hug as soon as the door swung open and didn't let go until Brianya protested. "Sorry," Dreama said. "I'm just really, really happy to finally see you! Oh, God, look at you! You lost weight."

Brianya held her breath; she knew what was coming next. Like one of those spinning tops that gather speed as they go, Dreama was working her way up to the question Brianya didn't want to hear—*how are you really doing, Bri?"* She would say. And Brianya would be forced to lie, tell her she was making progress every day, getting back to normal. When the truth was, she was at an impasse. The nightmares came more often, and now she'd started having headaches. Rather than make herself easy prey—standing by waiting for the inevitable—Brianya cut her off at the pass and changed the subject. "So, you and Andre, huh?"

At the mention of Andre's name, Dreama blushed. "Looks like."

"I'm happy for you."

Dreama searched Brianya's face. "Are you, really, Bri? Because you just went through a traumatic event and I would think it would be hard for you to be happy about anything. If it was me, I know that's how I would feel."

Dreama's words rankled. The nerve above Brianya's right eye jumped and her mouth set in a thin line. "Don't you dare come in here questioning my feelings and telling me how I should feel. And for the record, it wasn't you that it happened to, it was me."

Dreama flinched from the verbal assault. "Geesh! I'm sorry. I was only saying—"

"How can you ask me a stupid question like that," Brianya said, cutting her off, "when I'm the one who's been trying to get the two of you together for the longest?" Brianya shook her head. "I think this was a big mistake, you coming over here."

Wild horses couldn't budge Dreama. She stood her ground, refusing to let Brianya's behavior send her scampering away like a dog with its tail tucked between its legs. "Look, I said I was sorry. What do you want from me?"

"I want you and everybody else to leave me alone. Stop telling me how I should I feel, what I should do, how much I should eat, when to get up, when to wash up. Just leave me alone!" She could feel herself coming unraveled and felt powerless to stop it. The visage of Dreama standing stock still, undeterred and battle-ready turned Brianya's blood to ice. The nerve of Dreama acting as if she was the affronted one. "Just go! Go!" Her hands shook violently and she became frightened. What was happening to her? *Am I having a nervous breakdown?* Brianya wondered. She dropped like a boulder onto the couch, sobbing uncontrollably.

Dreama watched, her face contorted with grief for her friend, as Brianya tried to gain control of her flailing limbs. She'd seen Brianya in a low state before, but by the look on Dreama's face, this was different. She ran to the kitchen and came back with a roll of paper towels. She handed Brianya a wad. "It's gon' be alright, Bri." Dreama sat beside Brianya and hugged her. Her own body trembled and she hugged Brianya even tighter.

"I'm sick of crying and I'm sick of not crying. I just want to be normal again," Brianya said, her voice barely a whisper. With a clumsy hand, she mopped at her face with the wad of paper towels then blew her nose. "I'm sorry for yelling at you."

Dreama rubbed Brianya's shoulder. "Don't worry about it."

They sat in silence a long while, until the shaking in Brianya's hands subsided and Dreama grew still. Brianya felt somewhat calm now. She prayed that this would be the last of the crying spells and weird physical responses to the trauma. If not forever, then at least long enough so she could come to grips with what had happened to her. The sooner she dealt with it, the sooner she could get on with her life. She hadn't been to work in almost two months, and, if she was being totally honest, she wasn't in any hurry to get back. Here at home, she didn't have to think about running into Ed or dealing with prying eyes trying to assess her every move, or well-meant but awkward expressions of sympathy.

All of this isolation wasn't good. In the earlier sessions with Dr. Tobias, they'd discussed the subject. It was an eye opener, learning that her way of dealing with the breakup with Darnell was to isolate herself, though not in a physical way. No, her way was to keep people at bay mentally and emotionally. Even after the revelation, she continued to do it because it was so ingrained in her arsenal of self-preservation. She found herself headed back in that direction now, only the isolation was physical as well as mental.

The difference between then and now is that she had Dreama and Celine to lean on when she needed to release the emotional baggage that was wearing her down. So it wasn't total isolation. Plus, this event was more traumatic and life altering, scary. She wondered if she would bounce back from this; it didn't feel like it. Brianya couldn't deny it any longer; she needed professional help. That was why she'd given in to her mother and phoned the doctor's office. Her timing was perfect. Minutes before, a cancellation had freed up a 10:30 morning spot for this Friday.

"I called Dr. Tobias," Brianya whispered.

"That's good. I think it's about time you talked to someone." Dreama appeared to weigh her next words carefully. "Isn't all this legal stuff with Monty supposed to start soon?"

Darkness washed over Brianya and she absently stuck her tongue in the hole where her tooth used to be. "Yeah. I want to be ready when his sentencing comes up."

Dreama gasped. "Really? Maybe that's not a good idea. You might have a setback."

"You don't understand. I have to be there. I want that judge to know how Monty ruined my life. He needs to pay for what he did!" Brianya took a deep breath. "I can't close my eyes without seeing him. I'm afraid to go outside, because even though I know he's paralyzed my mind keeps telling me that he's coming back." Tears threatened to spill forth again but she flicked them away with her fingers.

"I'm there for you, Bri. What do you need me to do?"

"Will you come with me to my appointment Friday?" Brianya braced herself for the no she was sure was coming. Friday was Dreama's biggest hair day. The day, she'd said, that paid all the bills. Brianya was asking a lot, she knew, but she hadn't been outside in almost two months and she couldn't face this journey on her own. Cinthia had started a new job and couldn't take off. Her dad was having a colonoscopy and needed her mother to drive him home because of the mild sedative. Cashmere was out of town; and Andre had used up all of his personal and vacation days caring for her. There was no one else.

Without hesitation Dreama said, "I'm there!"

Brianya breathed out a sigh of relief. "One more thing. Can you fix me one of your delicious cherry cobblers?"

Dreama roared with laughter. "I can do you better than that! I'll fix you *two* cherry cobblers!" Her old friend was on her way back. Hallelujah.

CHAPTER THIRTY-NINE

*B*ABY STEPS, BRIANYA. *Baby steps. You can do this. Just let go of the doorframe and put one foot in front of the other. This ain't rocket science!* With each failed attempt, Brianya's frustration grew. It was now the size of Mt. Everest. Much more of this and she'd need to call to cancel the appointment.

Dreama looked up at the clock on her rearview mirror for the tenth time then smiled encouragement at Brianya from behind the wheel of her SUV. Her thumbs drummed the beat of the theme song from the movie Rocky, the way they always did whenever she came close to blowing her top. Brianya sympathized with Dreama; she was ready to blow her top, too.

"I can't do it, Dreama!" Brianya let go of the frame and slumped against the door.

"Can't is not a word; it's an excuse!" Dreama exited the car and went to stand in the doorway with Brianya. "You're over-thinking this, like you always do. Just close your eyes and push yourself through the door." There was a slight edge in Dreama's command.

Brianya's patience with herself was wearing thin also. The appointment was for 10:00 and it was now 9:27. It would take 20 minutes to get to the Ahuja Medical facility and six minutes to get from the parking lot to Dr Tobias' office. If they didn't leave in the next five minutes then she would definitely have to reschedule.

"Okay, I got this!" Brianya gave it all she had. She straightened her spine, put one foot in front of the other and. . . . Nothing. She tried a second time. Still nothing. There was no use. They weren't going anywhere today.

Dreama gave her a look of understanding and put an arm across Brianya's shoulder. "It's okay, sis. Next time."

Brianya nodded, but inside she was screaming. She felt defeated, weak. *You're a big fat, stupid loser! How are you going to court Monday if you can't leave the house today? Loser!* Her face crumpled and her shoulders slumped from the weight of the burden she carried.

"Hey, come on now. Raise that head up and square those shoulders, and dry them tears. This ain't nothing but a chicken wing. Next time you gon' kick that door's butt!"

Despite her heavy heart, Brianya gave a chuckle as they went back into the house. She yanked a paper towel from the roll and dabbed at the wetness beneath her eyes. "Well at least now you won't have to miss all that money. You can go to work."

"Enh, wrong! We gon' dig into this here cherry cobbler and I'm gon' whip you right quick in Bid Whist!

When Dreama finally left, it was late afternoon and they had polished off three-quarters of a 9-by-12 inch pan of one of the cherry cobblers. Brianya was so stuffed and sick feeling that she told Dreama to take the other pan to the shop with her.

When Endo had hired the cleaning crew to put Brianya's house back in order, he also had the old cord-style wall phone in the kitchen replaced with a cordless countertop unit, similar to the one Brianya had in her bedroom. She didn't like people rearranging her things, especially at home. That's why when, out of habit, she reached for the telephone where it used to be, she frowned when she realized it wasn't there. Two more rings and the answering machine, with no outgoing message, would come on. She had had all the frills removed from her landline, keeping only the bare-minimum services, which only included line repair and pay-as-you-go long distance service. Brianya was expecting a phone call from Doctor Tobias' office about early morning cancellations. If it was the doctor's office and the answering machine came on, they wouldn't know to leave a message.

Right as the machine clicked on, Brianya located the telephone and snatched it up. "Hello! Hello!" An automated recording announced itself as Global Tel Link and that an inmate in the Grafton Correctional Institution, Darnell Jones, wished to add her phone number to the inmates call allow list. Would she give her permission to be added to his list? "Say yes or no."

Brianya didn't know how she felt about the prospect of finally speaking to Darnell; but she did know that she couldn't keep avoiding him. "Yes," she said. After further automated conversation, a series of clicks followed and then Darnell came on the line.

"Anya?" The timid voice on the other end of the line didn't sound anything like the self-assured man she knew.

Her voice caught in her throat and she managed to squeeze out a "Hey," in response.

"How you doing?"

She didn't want to tell him what a basket case she was; he had enough to deal with. "I'm doing good. How are you?"

"Scared," he said softly.

Brianya wasn't expecting that admission. It was like salt in an open wound. Darnell was in prison now. If he fell into one of his depressions, no one would be there to help him see that the darkness would eventually turn to light, the way she had when they were together. Brianya's heart felt as if it had literally broken in two. "Oh, God! I'm so sorry that you're in there, Darnell. If I could take your place, I would. Hang in there!"

"That's the plan." He didn't sound convincing.

"I don't know if what I'm about to say is the right thing, but I think it might help you to keep focused. Define your goal and commit to it, whether it's to get through the day without getting into trouble, or whatever. Determine right now that everyday you'll do something positive to move you closer to that goal. And remember, no matter what ugliness is going on around you, it's all temporary." The silence was loud and she could tell by the steady intake of breath on his end, that Darnell was processing her words.

She pushed on. "You don't have to be a product of your surroundings, Darnell. You're in there because the rules of justice dictated it, not because you're a bad person. You committed an act of heroism and for that, I owe you a debt of gratitude that, no matter how long I live, I can never repay. I'm so grateful that you showed up when you did." Emotions threatened to overtake her and she had to stop to take a breath. Brianya hoped that Darnell felt every word she said.

Part of her speech—the part about the rules of justice and the act of heroism—was what the judge had said to Darnell when she sentenced him. He needed to hear it again and to know that he was so much more than a number, an inmate. Brianya had known men, strong men, who got caught up in one foolish thing or another and landed behind bars, only to fall victim to a system that was designed to break their wills. She didn't want Darnell to join those ranks. He didn't belong there; he wasn't a criminal. "Do you hear me, Darnell?"

His response was slow. "Yeah."

"Listen, they got your body for 365 days, don't let them have your mind. You hear me?"

"I hear you." He sounded better. Maybe she was getting through to him after all.

"Thank you for saving my life!"

"It's not necessary to thank me. I would do it again in a heartbeat!" Darnell waited a beat. "I needed to hear your voice." His own voice was heavy with unexpressed emotion. "And I wanted to ask you something; that's why I came to your house the other day. That and to drop off that envelope that I forgot to leave before."

"Sure, what is it?"

"Well . . . . S-s-see, w-w-we—"

She had to stop him before he went into a stuttering fit the way he did whenever he was under extreme duress. The way he had done the time he couldn't find a job. And when she'd pulled the butcher's knife on him and told him that he had until the count of three to get out.

"Take your time, baby." No, no, no! Had she just called him baby? The word had flowed out so naturally, like it was just waiting on the tip of her tongue. The last thing Brianya wanted was to give Darnell false hope. "Take a deep breath and say your words slowly, Darnell."

If Darnell had read anything into Brianya calling him baby, he gave no indication. He took a deep breath and began again. "I p-put you on my list of v-visitors. W-will you come see me? Y-you have to go on the Web site and fill out a visitor's application." He took another deep breath and gave Brianya the URL when she said yes.

"I just got a 2-minute warning," Darnell announced. "Thanks for the pep talk, Anya. I needed to hear that."

Brianya glanced at the clock. "It needed to be said and I meant every word of it."

"Visiting hours and rules and stuff are on t-that Web site, too.

"Do you need anything? Can I send you something to read?"

"I guess I'll have a lot of time for reading now." Darnell chuckled. "I just got a one-minute warning."

"What do you have to do, put some more money in or something?"

"No. We only get fifteen minutes at a time, I think."

"Oh."

"I love you, Anya."

"Darnell—"

"Relax. I just meant that I love you as a per—"

No more minutes.

Brianya stared at the phone in her hand before placing it back on the base. She felt emotionally spent. The conversation had allowed her to take the focus off her own problems. The words of encouragement for Darnell had tripped so easily off her tongue. However, when it came to her own well-being there were no kind words, only self-incrimination. How quickly she had reverted to comfortable h when tragedy struck. It was as if the journey of self-discovery had never happened.

Brianya closed her eyes and listened to the noises around her. She could hear the rapid click, click, click, click of the pilot light on the furnace catch and the whir, then whine, of the motor before first the cold, then warm air was expelled through the vents. The second-hand on the Grandfather clock in the hallway moved in a steady, forward motion as it tick-tick-ticked its way around the faceplate. Bong! Five times—five o'clock. No one had called from the doctor's office. She nestled her head in her folded arms on the table. Outside, car doors opened and slammed shut. Brianya's eyelids grew heavy and she yawned noisily. *I'm so tired. I just want to sleep.*

Two hours later Brianya awoke with a crick in her neck and a sharp pain in the lower right side. She hauled herself up the stairs to go to bed in the hopes of falling back to sleep. Half way up, she started to disrobe. All she wanted to do was flop down on her bed, shut her eyes, and keep them shut, until the morning. After making sure the ringers on both phones—land line and cell— were off, Brianya dove under the soft down comforter and covered her face with a pillow.

Unaware of how much time had passed, after thrashing about and tossing and turning, Brianya finally threw off the covers and sat up. It was no use; she'd never sleep again, ever. Frustrated, she yanked the light switch to the lamp on the nightstand next to her bed, bathing the room in light. A heavy sigh escaped her. 7:45. She was a long way from morning. What was she going to do until then? There was always reading. Debbie had sent her the latest Diane Mott Davidson mystery along with a book by an independent author she'd never heard of. The title looked interesting and the synopsis had piqued her curiosity. As Brianya reached for the book and plucked it from the pile, the discarded letter from Tricia fell to the floor. She leaned over and snatched it up. Brianya had intended to open it once she'd gotten off the phone with Darnell, but just that quick, she'd forgotten.

Brianya tore open the envelope, irritated that the silly woman, Tricia, had chosen to write a letter instead of saying what she needed to say to her face. Unfolding the missive, Brianya rolled her eyes. *If anything, this should be good for a laugh,* she thought.

CHAPTER FORTY

*D*EAR BRIANYA,

I hope this letter finds you in good spirits and enjoying your holidays. I know how much you like getting mail (and I love writing), so I decided to write you a letter. I tried calling you several times, but you never took my calls. I wanted to get this out of my system while it was fresh in my mind.

First, let me apologize for sending this letter through Tricia. When she told me she wanted to apologize for what happened in the parking garage but didn't know how to approach you, I asked her to deliver this to you personally, to help break the ice.

I guess by now you know that I no longer work for Jelinksi and Frierson. I had a good run with them but circumstances dictated that it was time to leave.

The day you called me, I was upset because I had gotten some bad news. I felt like lashing out at somebody. You just happened to be within reach. I never meant to hurt you, Brianya and I'm sorry that I did. What happened between me and Darnell wasn't planned, it just happened one night when I went to the club with a group of old college friends. Marlon had just broken up with me and I wanted to show him what he was missing. Darnell and I got to talking, and, well one thing led to another.

Also, you were right about Marlon. He had it in for you. I don't know how he got hold of them, but he had several blank expense forms with MBCC's logo and watermark with your and Mr. Larson's signature already on them. He was going to rack up a lot of bogus charges and submit them to your finance department. The only reason he went out with me was because he wanted to use me to give him the heads up if you ever discovered what he was doing. I should have listened when you told me he hadn't changed. As soon as I gave him the green light, he took what he needed and moved on.

I know it might seem like I'm beating around the bush. I'll get to the point. A few months ago, I had a follow-up appointment with the doctor because I had been feeling tired and achy all the time. Anyway, turns out I have stage-four bone cancer. The prognosis isn't good. I don't really want to go into any details. I'm not giving up. Doctors aren't God, although some of them think they are. Nobody leaves this world until He says so. And I've got a feeling that it's not my time!

I moved back home to North Carolina last month to have surgery. I'm going through a heavy regimen of chemo treatments. I can tell that it's emotionally draining on my parents. But I'm grateful to God that I have them around to help me. There are days when it takes all my strength just to take a sip of water and then there are days when I feel like my old self. It's on days like the latter that I think of you and wish we could talk like old times.

I miss you, Bri. You were always a good friend to me, looking out for me, encouraging me. I admit, when you started getting all that attention, I was jealous. Don't get me wrong, I was genuinely happy and proud of what you had accomplished, inside and outside; but when men overlooked me to get to you, it made me feel undesirable all over again. I wanted men to beat a path to my door the way Ed, Darnell, and the rest were doing to you. You always had a confidence that I could never pull off. I came to accept that that's okay, because I have qualities that you didn't have. For example, I love my spontaneity. You always had difficulty with that, even though you'd never admit it (smile). And that's okay. You're you and I'm me (how's that for stating the obvious?) That's another thing I like about myself: my ability to just let people be. You, on the other hand, always try to sway people to your way of thinking.

Something else you do that you really need to stop doing. Stop acting like you don't need anyone. You're human just like the rest of us. Ask for help when you need it. Everyone has problems, including you. You might think no one sees you, but I do. Let us be there for you sometimes.

I feel like I'm rambling, afraid that if I end this letter I'd be ending our friendship too. I'm not ready to give up reaching out to you.

While I was recovering from surgery, I had a lot of time to do some deep thinking. I thought about myself, how growing up all I could think about was how much better my life would be if I had a sister. Then I met you. You were so easy to talk to; so patient and understanding. And I thought about how I'd always be Celine Connors, never having experienced marriage. The closest I came was me and Terry playing house. That's how I know it's not my time to go. I've been praying so hard to God to let me have that joy; I know he hears me because a week after I got back home, I met someone. We were both at the hospital having pre-tests for surgery. I really want you to meet him, Bri. I know you'll like him.

I want you to know that you deserve all the happiness you can snatch from life; it's too short to second-guess your every move. Sure, it's one thing to have goals and try to accomplish them, Bri, but not to the exclusion of joy. No matter what you do in this world, Bri, whether you stockpile a lot of money, buy the latest gadgets, the fanciest house or car, or have a closet full of designer clothes, when you die, you can't take it with you. Use me as example if you need to. I drove around in a 15 year-old car, paid cash for everything, lived in the cheapest places I could find. Scrimped and saved almost every dime I ever made and for what? So I could leave it all to my elderly parents, who can't even spend their own money? So be balanced, Brianya and enjoy the fruits of your hard work.

I know you're upset with me; I wouldn't blame you if you hated me. But I'd much rather you forgave me and let me back into your life. I know it'll take a while to repair the rift, but I'm willing to do the work. I could use a sister-friend right now. Please, call me.

Celine

Brianya picked up the envelope, looking for date or some clue that would tell her when Celine had written the letter. Only her name scrawled with a shaky hand across the middle donned the envelope. From what she could gather from the contents, it had to have been written after Thanksgiving, since that would be the official start of the holiday season that Celine referred to. Thinking back to the night when someone had pulled out of her driveway as she and Dreama approached the house, there was no way that was Celine. It was more likely Tricia. The family resemblance was uncanny. The beginning of a smile lifted the corners of Brianya's mouth. All the time she was trying to contact Celine, Celine was also trying to contact her.

Brianya couldn't fathom the thought of Celine going through chemo and radiation treatments alone; going home was the right decision. Although she would miss Celine, North Carolina was only an eight or eight-and-a-half hour drive down I-77. It would give Brianya an excuse to take quick well-needed getaways. What was it that Celine had said about enjoying the fruits of her labor? Brianya couldn't remember the last time she'd taken a trip or done anything even remotely resembling a vacation. Celine was right; when you die, everything you've worked hard for, all of your material possessions, your money, stays right here for the next person to use and do with as they see fit. Maybe they won't cherish your possessions the way you did; they could squander your hard-earned money or mistreat your pets, or destroy your house. *So why put undue emphasis on those things now?* Brianya thought. It's better to work on loving and cherishing people—family and friends, even strangers—while everyone's living and can appreciate one another.

With those thoughts dancing around in her head, Brianya snatched up the receiver, excited, for the first time in a long while. As she dialed the familiar number, she wondered if Celine had heard about what had happened to her. She wouldn't bring it up unless Celine did; it was better to keep the conversation upbeat. Celine was a fighter; just as she'd beat the breast cancer, she would beat this cancer also. Besides, by her own admission, Celine was too ornery to die. They had once joked about when and if that time came. Celine, wiped out from a round of chemo but with an ironclad will to survive, had told Brianya that she wasn't ready to meet her maker. Brianya had looked at her, deadpan, and said, "And God ain't ready to meet you, either! What makes you think he's ready for you to come up there, stirring up trouble?" And Celine had smiled because it hurt too much to laugh. Brianya didn't know where she stood on the heaven and hell thing, too many contradicting stories floating around. But Celine believed and that was all that mattered.

One ring shy of ten and a voice Brianya hadn't heard in a long time greeted her. "Hi Mrs. Connors, this is Brianya from Cleveland." She hoped she hadn't awoken her. "I'm sorry if I've disturbed your sleep," Brianya said, looking at the clock on the table. It was 8:15. Still early by her standards.

"No, baby, we weren't sleep."

"How are you and Mr. Connors doing?" Brianya made it a habit to always include the spouse in the inquiry. It was proper etiquette, according to Grandma Ruby.

"We're holding up okay. Considering."

Having experienced being a caregiver on numerous occasions with her own family members, Brianya could empathize with Mrs. Connors, to a degree. Of course, none of the family members she had cared for was her own child. Brianya had always enjoyed talking with Mrs. Connors. She was one of those rare women who could speak, with knowledge, on just about every subject imaginable. But stimulating conversation would have to take a backseat today, because Brianya was anxious to talk to Celine.

"Mrs. Connors, I don't want to keep you from what you were doing. But, may I please speak to Celine?" There was a long pause on the other end, and then it registered. "No! Oh, please, no, no, no!" Brianya sobbed. Saliva trickled down her chin

"I'm sorry, baby. Celine passed away three days ago. We were just sitting here with the minister going over her services. With everything that's going on, I forgot to call you. I'm very sorry."

Brianya sniffed loudly and dragged the sleeve of her sweater across her eyes and nose. "You don't have to apologize to me,

Mrs. Connors. I'm so sorry about Celine." Brianya choked on the words as fresh tears spilled. "When are the services?"

"Eleven o'clock tomorrow at Mt. Calvary." She gave Brianya the address. "I hope you can make it, Brianya. I know Celine would want you to be here. She told me about your falling out. All she talked about was patching things up with you." Mrs. Connors sighed. "She was hurt when you didn't answer her letter, but you're calling now and that's what's important."

"Yes, Mrs. Connors." She heard herself say the words and felt like a small child, properly chastised. Brianya should have known that Celine would tell her mother everything; they were close like sisters. No point in explaining why she'd just now read the letter and that she'd been calling their home but was unable to leave a message because they had no answering machine. All of that didn't matter now. What did matter was that the Connors had lost their only child and Brianya had lost a friend, forever. A wave of new tears coursed down her cheeks and a loud sob escaped her. She needed to cry with abandon to release the pent up frustration, and there was no chance of that happening as long as she stayed on the telephone.

"Whatever I can do to lighten your load, just let me know, Mrs. Connors."

"Thank you, baby, but we've got everything all taken care of; you just get here safely."

Brianya rattled off her home and cell numbers and told Mrs. Connors to call if she thought of anything. She sat the phone on her bed, not bothering to press the end button, and blew her nose.

Celine dead? Her letter had sounded so optimistic. This wasn't how it was to suppose to be. They were supposed to make up, work their way back to a place where they could look back and shake their heads at the stupidity of letting men come between a friendship as tight as theirs. Celine couldn't be dead; it was unreal. Brianya's mind couldn't wrap itself around the truth. One bad event after another had her questioning whether she could go on.

All she wanted to do was close her eyes and click her heels, erase the last few months.

She had to hold it together. If not for herself then for the people who were depending on her. Her earlier attempts to leave the house worried Brianya and she wondered if tomorrow would be a repeat performance of failure also. She wouldn't let it be. Nothing was going to stop her from being in North Carolina tomorrow morning. Her body racked with sobs, Brianya curled up in the fetal position and wept bitterly for her friend. Two hours later, Andre and Dreama found her in that position, when, worried that she hadn't answered either of her phones, they bounded up the stairs to her bedroom.

***

"Don't worry about nothing, li'l sis; you gon' be there tomorrow." Andre sat on the side of the bed, hugged Brianya to him, the way he used to when she was a toddler, and rubbed her back. "Dreama will help you pack so we can get on the road tonight."

Brianya cleaned herself up and tied a scarf around her head. She threw on sweats and sneakers and then shut off the bedroom light before joining Dreama and Andre in the kitchen.

"Let's go," she said throwing her coat across her shoulders.

The two watched as Brianya approached the doorway. Dreama sucked in her breath and stared with open curiosity.

Brianya took a deep breath, closed her eyes, and walked straight out the door into Andre's Jeep. Nobody said a word, but she saw Dreama and Andre fist bump on the down low.

They pulled into the Residence Inn on S. Mint Street at 5:32 a.m. Saturday morning, exhausted from having driven all night. What should have been an 8.5-hour drive became a seven-hour drive. Andre was like a road warrior, refusing to stop for bathroom or food breaks. Brianya had been quiet most of the ride, catnapping between states.

Andre checked them in and handed Dreama the keys to her and Brianya's room.

Dreama snatched the keys. "Remind me never to take a road trip with you again."

Andre chuckled. "Yeah, I apologize for that. But I was on a mission."

They headed to the elevators and their rooms.

"We'll see you at 9 in the lobby," Dreama said to Andre, opening the door to her and Brianya's room.

Brianya kicked off her shoes and fell across the bed. "Thanks for coming, Dreama."

Before Dreama could reply, Brianya had dropped off to sleep.

CHAPTER FORTY-ONE

MOURNERS SHOWED UP and showed out for Celine, packing the small church to a standing-room-only capacity. As Brianya looked around at the faces in the crowd, she wondered how many had truly known Celine. Indeed, who really knew anyone? Much of what makes us unique, that which defines us, is rarely known in life. Sometimes we hide our talents from the world for fear we may be ridiculed. We live our entire lives as the person we think others want us to be, afraid that if we revealed our true selves we'd be destined to live life unloved.

Few people knew that Celine played the ukulele, or that she loved Tiny Tim songs, or that when she was sad she'd go out and buy bottles of bubbles and blow them until she felt better. Or that one of her biggest fears was that she would be maimed in some way and have to depend on the kindness of strangers because she had no brothers or sisters and her parents were too old, and she wasn't close to any of her other family members.

Or that when she was in the third grade, she used to wish she was white because the white kids in her class thought that all the kids who looked like her were ugly apes. But the most unacceptable thing Celine believed she would never be forgiven for, was at age eight, hating God and saying she didn't believe He existed because he'd let her grandma die from a heart attack. Although she had since changed her view when she became an adult, a small part of her still believed that she would have to answer for losing faith; and cancer was God's chosen punishment.

In the end, Brianya hoped that Celine had reconciled her feelings about the God her parents had always preached was love. If her letter was any indication, then Brianya knew that her friend had died in peace.

Willing her legs to propel her forward, Brianya made her way to the front of the church to view Celine and greet the family. As she inched closer to the casket, her legs felt like rubber.

Celine was beautiful, her face serene; she looked like she was sleeping and that if Brianya touched her shoulder she'd open her eyes and smile, happy that they were friends again. Tears threatened at the corners of her eyes, but she fought them back, unsuccessfully. She didn't want strangers to see her cry. Brianya leaned into the casket and placed a soft kiss on Celine's forehead—it was clammy and hard to the touch—and whispered, "goodbye, Ce Ce."

Approaching the first rows of pews where the family sat, Mrs. Connors grabbed Brianya and hugged her tight. When she spoke, however, it was as if she had no strength left. "Brianya, baby, I'm so glad you could make it."

Brianya squeezed and hugged Mrs. Connors. "How are you holding up?"

The old woman smiled weakly. "I have my good and bad moments. But, the Lord is going to get us through this." She caressed Brianya's face. Recognizing that this was a loss for Brianya as well, Mrs. Connors asked, "How are you doing?"

"It's still registering."

Mr. Connors moved in and patted Brianya on the shoulder. "I don't think death ever fully registers."

Brianya gave the old man's arthritic hand a pat and then hugged him tightly. "I'll be praying for your family."

As the choir approached the stage, Brianya spotted a familiar face in the group. Tricia Yancy stepped up to the microphone as the pianist played *Precious Lord, Take My Hand*. Brianya's forehead creased with curiosity before remembering that Tricia was Celine's cousin. Noticing Brianya staring at her, Tricia gave a nod of recognition and a sympathetic smile. When she opened her mouth to sing, she belted out the lyrics of the song with such force that the notes floated all the way up to the rafters and broke through the beams before dancing their way to Heaven. It seemed a shame that such a divine gift should be wasted on someone as trashy as Tricia.

When Brianya tried to move on to allow other mourners to wish the family peace before the minister came to the pulpit, Mrs. Connors caught Brianya by the hand. "We have a seat for you up here with the family."

The church grew quiet as the minister approached the podium.

Brianya sat on the pew next to Mrs. Connors, taking to heart the minister's words as he preached from the book of Ecclesiastes.

"We are gathered here, brothers and sisters, to reflect on life. Ecclesiastes, seven and two says, 'It is better to go to the house of mourning, than to go to the house of feasting.' Say Amen! 'For,' said Solomon, 'that is the end of all men; and the living will lay it to his heart.' Let the church say Amen!" The Minister raised his voice and brought his hand down, hard, on the podium. "I say to you today, congregation, we are here to mourn and to rejoice!"

***

When the service was over, Brianya found Andre and Dreama standing in the hallway talking to a familiar figure.

Brianya was speechless as she made her way to her party. The shock at seeing Ed must have been evident in her face from the quizzical expression that Dreama wore. "We'll let y'all talk," Dreama said, motioning for Andre to follow her.

Ed stood with his hands stuffed in his pockets. "Hello, Brianya. You look stunning."

"Hello yourself. Thank you for the compliment." He was even more handsome than Brianya remembered. Her eyes lingered on his face then traveled the length of his body, taking him all in. He was beautiful.

They made small talk then Ed asked, "May I?" as he reached for Brianya. She nodded and he embraced her gently, the pressure growing more insistent as the seconds ticked by. He slowly released her and searched her face. "I've missed you," he choked out. "And I'm so sorry!"

"I know," was all Brianya could manage.

"Are you going to the cemetery?"

"I'm riding with my brother and Dreama."

"Mind riding with me?"

They rode together and Dreama and Andre went back to the hotel.

As they waited to be directed out of the parking lot, Brianya reflected on the number of young people that had come to pay their respects. Celine was considered somewhat a celebrity in the church circles in North Carolina. She'd sung in a choir before moving to Cleveland to claim her independence. Whenever she came home to visit, she was always in demand. A fact that Brianya hadn't known until today.

Looking out the window, watching the procession of vehicles that stretched at least 50 car lengths long, Brianya asked, "Did you know that she was as popular as all of this?"

Ed nodded.

"There was so much I didn't know about her; and it's too late now." Brianya sighed. "She wrote me a letter, wanting to patch things up. Too late for that, too."

Ed covered Brianya's hand with his. "Don't beat yourself up."

***

On the way back to the hotel from the repast, Ed briefly took his eyes off the road to glance at Brianya. "So how are you really doing, Brianya? In all this time, you've hardly said more than a sentence about yourself."

The last time Brianya was in Charlotte, the city was undergoing major building projects. As they drove down South Mint Street, Brianya noticed buildings that weren't there the last time she had visited. Even the hotel where she was staying had undergone a major reconstruction. Much like her own life. She couldn't keep avoiding the subject of what had happened. Although she didn't want to talk about that night, she should confide in Ed. They had been dating. She assumed they still were.

Brianya pulled her eyes off the road. "I'm doing much better."

Ed waited for her to elaborate. When she didn't, he asked gently, "What does that mean?"

"I don't want to talk about it."

They pulled into the hotel parking lot and Ed cut the engine. He took the keys out of the ignition and put them in his pocket, then he turned abruptly toward Brianya and she flinched. "Oh, wow, I'm sorry. I didn't mean to scare you." His shoulders drooped. "Look, Brianya, this is difficult for me too. It's like I have to re-learn how to deal with you. I'm a patient man, but I can't do it by myself. So, I'm asking you to help me."

Help *him*? She couldn't even help herself. What was she supposed to do, tell him how to talk to her, what to do and what not to do? It was foolish and didn't make any sense. She was learning too. "I don't know how to help you, Ed. What do you want from me?"

"What I want is for you to talk me, let me heal with you. I understand that you lost your sense of security. I lost something too; I lost you, an opportunity to patch things up with you and move forward in our relationship. Did you forget that I was coming over that night to work things out with you?"

The hairs on the back of Brianya's neck bristled and she felt white, hot anger rising to the surface. Her teeth clenched, hands balled into fists. She could sense her pupils becoming pinpricks. Ed had definitely hit a nerve. This was a new anger. Brianya had no idea these feelings were hiding just below the surface. Until today, she had assumed that her reluctance to see Ed was borne out of shame at the way she'd handled going out with each of them.

She tried to swallow the anger but, like the sun, it kept rising. "You! All of you!" Brianya spat. She wrung her hands in her lap, and tried to rein in her emotions. "My protectors! Not my father, my brother, or my man, but my ex. The man who treated me like I was nothing, ridiculed me, walked all over me, and humiliated me, that's who saved me! Now he's sitting in jail paying for being in the right place at the right time. And instead of moving on with my life, forgetting all about him, I'm indebted to him forever. Do you understand that?" She took a shuddering breath. "You were supposed to be there! Why were you late?" The words were finally out. The release brought with it a cleansing, a freedom.

Ed sank into his seat, head bowed low. He moved away from Brianya. In a tone laden with contrition, he said, "I've been punishing myself for weeks because I wasn't there for you. Going over and over in my mind what I could've done differently that would have got me to you on time. No matter how many ways I swing it, the answer comes back the same. There is nothing I could've done." Ed's head came up a fraction and he sat a little taller. "I ran by the drugstore to pick up a prescription for my mom. I gave myself plenty of time, but the pharmacist was backed up and the line was almost out the door. She needed the medicine for the next morning and I knew that you and I wouldn't be done before 9, when the pharmacy closed."

She thought the answer might bring her some satisfaction but it didn't. It only served to make her feel more shame. Brianya hadn't thought that Ed blamed himself or that he was feeling responsible. As unfair as it was to heap a heavy burden such as that on his shoulders, Brianya felt a sense of kinship knowing that he shared the blame. She felt closer to Ed than she ever had, but she couldn't be with him anymore. They were both damaged and two damaged people were no good together, she'd learned that from Monty.

"I can't do anything about who showed up at your door," Ed continued. "I'm just glad someone did. As for feeling indebted to him for life, that's not realistic. Any debt of gratitude you owe him is paid when you say thank you." Ed held his head up and faced Brianya. "Look at me, Brianya."

Brianya slowly turned toward Ed and looked into an expression that brimmed with compassion and desperation.

"There's no room in our relationship for a third person."

"We're broken, Ed; that's not a good thing."

"Broken? What are you talking about?"

"I've got a lot of work ahead me, trying to put the pieces of my life back together. Last night was the first time I've been outside my house since I was attacked. And the day before that was the first day that I actually took a shower and washed my hair. I haven't had a full night's sleep in almost two weeks. And I'm afraid to stay home alone."

"But you're here. You took that first step out the door. You got under that shower and cleaned your body and your hair. I call that progress, not broken. You can only move forward from here."

Ed was right. Brianya was so busy looking for all the reasons why she couldn't that she forgot to look at what she'd done. One more thing she had done, she had finally allowed a friend to visit, and the day of Darnell's sentencing, she had talked herself into seeing him, which is what got her into the shower in the first place. And she was making plans to go out again, when the sentencing date for Monty was announced. She'd also made another appointment to see Dr. Tobias. And finally, she *had* thanked Darnell. And he'd accepted, even telling her that she didn't owe him a thing.

"Thank you, Ed for reminding me that progress consists of all the little steps we take. I was so busy focusing on what I wasn't doing that I missed the baby steps."

They exited the car and Ed walked Brianya into the hotel. "So does this mean that when we get back to Cleveland, we can pick up where we left off?"

"Let me put it like this, when you call, I'll be the one answering the phone from now on." Brianya left Ed staring after her as she stepped into the elevator.

CHAPTER FORTY-TWO

THE SUNDAY BEFORE Monty's sentencing, he'd taken a turn for the worse. As it was touch and go for a while, the sentencing had been pushed back three weeks. Now, today he would learn his fate. Meanwhile, Brianya was making progress in therapy and had decided to forego attending the sentencing. At this stage of her healing, she wanted to put the ordeal behind her. Whatever punishment the judge meted out to Monty couldn't be worse than what he was already living with. For Brianya, the most important part was over once Darnell learned his fate. Though not ideal, it was better than anything Monty would get.

In North Carolina, Ed had helped Brianya realize that she needed to celebrate every accomplishment, no matter how small. Right now, she was celebrating sending Andre home and calling off the 'round the clock care. She relished the silence. Tonight would be night four of what Brianya had dubbed Operation Restoration. She was on a mission to restore the peace Monty had robbed her of. One more issue needed settling and then she'd be right on track.

Dialing the familiar phone number, Brianya couldn't remember the last time she'd spoken to Endo. He sounded surprised when he heard her voice.

"Good to hear from you, Brianya."

She raised the blinds to let in the afternoon sun. "Likewise. I hope I didn't get you at a bad time."

"It's good. I'm just heading out for lunch." She could hear the unasked question in his tone.

"I wanted to thank you for hiring that cleaning company; that was so thoughtful of you. I can't tell you how much I appreciated it." Brianya hesitated before continuing. "But it was a little too much and I don't feel comfortable accepting it. Let me know how much it cost, because I want to reimburse you."

"You don't have to thank me. I was glad to do it. As a matter of fact, I never got the chance to pay because your brother took care of the bill."

It was Brianya's turn to be surprised. "Oh. He didn't mention that."

"He asked me not to say anything to you about it."

A car horn blared in the background and the pounding of a jackhammer sounded loud through the phone. "I won't say anything," Brianya said, raising her voice so he could hear her over the street noises. "I'll let you go; I know you're on lunch. I just wanted to call and thank you. Take care."

Brianya ended the call and went back to straightening up the downstairs. Ed was coming for dinner tonight and she wanted the house to be tip-top. She hadn't seen Ed much since the funeral, but they'd talked on the phone every day. Tonight would be the start of a new beginning for them.

As she rolled the plush towels lengthwise and placed them in the wicker basket on the wall shelf behind the toilet, Brianya smiled to herself. She had achieved what she considered her biggest victory yet the day she stepped over the threshold of the bathroom where her world had changed. It had happened so quickly that she barely had time to process it.

"Can't you drive any faster, Cash? Any slower and I'm gonna pee all over your seat."

"You'd better not pee on my seat!" Cashmere had said and pressed the gas pedal a little closer to the floor.

"You should have used the bathroom before you left the gym," Dreama had chimed in from the backseat.

"You be quiet back there." Brianya crossed and uncrossed her legs, dancing in her seat. When Cashmere rounded the corner of Brianya's street, Brianya had pushed the garage door opener on her keychain so that she wouldn't have to wait. The door squealed open and she dashed out the car before Cashmere could come to a complete stop. She jammed the key in the lock, quickly unarmed the alarm, and made a beeline for the bathroom off the kitchen.

When she emerged from the bathroom, Cashmere and Dreama had stared at her, their mouths hanging open.

"What?" Brianya had said, puzzled.

"Bri, do you realize what just happened?" Cashmere asked.

Brianya's brows had furrowed and she pulled a face. "Duh! I had to pee so I peed."

They watched Brianya's face contort as realization dawned. *So . . . I . . . peed.* "Oh, my god! I can't believe I just did that." Brianya had smiled, triumphant. "I finally went into *that* bathroom, where it happened."

Two days had gone by until she crossed the threshold again, but she'd been crossing it ever since. When she shared her achievement with Dr. Tobias, he was pleased and told her that if she continued to make progress at this rate, he would clear her for work soon. Contrary to what everyone kept telling her, Brianya was anxious to get back to work. The sooner she resumed her normal routine, the sooner people could stop treating her like a charity.

Brianya checked her face in the mirror; lipstick unsmudged, not a hair out of place. Perfect. She looked as good as she felt. She grabbed her keys and purse from the table and armed the alarm. A quick stopover at Love's House to say hello to the director, on her way to Walmart for a few last-minute items, and she could finish dinner preparations.

In the car, Brianya turned the dial and came in on the middle of one of her favorite radio talk shows.

"So here's what we already knew, the host was saying. He went from a hospital bed to a jail cell because bail was denied. They found his passport along with a duffle bag full of clothes in his car. They charged him with burglary, kidnapping, and attempted manslaughter. He took a plea bargain and pleaded guilty to all those charges. So, today, we learned his fate. Listeners, tell us what you think about Monticello Belvoir's sentence. Too harsh, too soft, or does the punishment fit the crime? Waiting on your thoughts at . . ." The radio host rattled off the phone number and the station's jingle played. Brianya chewed the nail on her index finger, waiting to hear the callers' opinions.

"Kammy, from Euclid Heights, you're on the air."

"I think that judge was too soft. Yeah, so, this was his first offense. That shouldn'ta even mattered. He went to that lady's house with a gun in his hand. He was there for one reason only. If her boyfriend or whoever hadn'ta showed up, he woulda kilt her."

"I hear what you're saying, Kammy. But come on! The guy's in a wheelchair for the rest of his life; what difference does it make if he spends five days or five years locked up in prison? I mean, here's a guy who's an ex-basketball player, teaches kids how to play the sport. Was active right up until he landed in that chair. You don't think he's already paying for his crime? And let's not forget that he *didn't* kill her."

"That's only because that other guy shot him," the caller interjected.

"Let's talk about the other guy for a minute. What's this guy doing skulking around her house at nighttime anyway? If you ask me, I think he was stalking her or something. I know everybody's all like, 'this guy's a hero,' but it was just a little too convenient, him showing up the way he did. He shoots Monty and he only gets a slap on the wrist? Come on! We've got Barry from Rocky River on the line. What do you make of this whole mess, Barry?"

"The way I see is this: Monty got what was coming to him. Just 'cause he's a celebrity, people think he's above the law. Well, in my book, if you do the crime, you do the time. And and and, that fella that shot him, he shouldn't've gotten one day in prison. Irregardless of why he was there, he was at the right place at the right time.

"So I take it from your statement, that you've jumped on the hero bandwagon too. Come on people, get real! Word has it that the two of them used to be friends. After this Darnell guy dumps the girl, she and Monty start going out. Then she breaks up with Monty to go back with Darnell. I'm not saying it's ever right to do violence to anyone; don't misunderstand me. But when you hear about situations like this one, it kinda makes you understand how a person could be driven to do something like that. I mean I've been in a couple of situations like that myself. Obviously, I didn't go as far as this guy, but I gotta tell you, I can understand. You still with us, Dee from Erie, PA? You've been waiting a while to weigh in on this. What say you?"

"Oh, wow! Am I on the air?"

"Yep! You're on the air, Dee. What's your opinion about this love triangle slant?"

"The way I see it, Mike, is that even if she did break up with one guy to get back with the other one, he had no right to put his hands on her. It's never okay to hit a woman! He shoulda just sucked it up like a man and kept it moving. See that's what's wrong with y'all men. Y'all can't take no for an answer. I bet you one thing! He won't be hitting nobody else!"

"And on that note folks, we end this segment. Until we meet in the air—"

Brianya shut the radio off. *Five years.* Would Monty even live that long in his condition? The radio commentator was right about one thing: five years or five days, what difference did it make? As far as Brianya was concerned, the punishment fit the crime.

EPILOGUE

THE DEATH OF a child, a financial crisis, infidelity, a tragedy, to name just a few things that can kill a relationship. Fourteen months ago, her world was rocked at its foundation. Where there should have been gray skies and gloom, a rainbow had peeked through the clouds and brought with it the sun's rays of hope.

Dinner with Ed, all those months ago, was perfect. Conversation had flowed easily, as if they were of one mind. Brianya couldn't have asked for a more understanding, patient man. As much as their schedules allowed, they spent almost every free moment making up for lost time. As the months went by however, the connection, the spark she had initially felt for Ed, had dimmed and she realized that she was only going through the motions. Ed knew it, too.

He had taken Brianya by the shoulders one night after they had finished watching a movie and peered into her eyes, a lingering sadness in his own. "So, Miss Johnson, how long are we going to keep up this charade?"

No use in denying his meaning, Brianya looked away. "I kept hoping the spark would reignite."

Ed had frowned. "I understand you're still working through some issues, and I didn't want to push."

"Thank you for not pushing. I am getting better—I'm going back to work Monday. I'm a little nervous about that." She was procrastinating, reluctant to say what was obvious. The last time she'd ended a relationship it had nearly cost her her life.

As if he had read her mind, Ed said, "Let me say it for you. It's not working." Disappointment was evident in his voice.

Brianya had turned away at that point; she couldn't stand to watch reality play out in Ed's face. But he was right, albeit not totally.

"It's not working, *yet*," Brianya corrected. "I'm not giving up on us, Ed, and I hope that you aren't either." But something in his face, his expressive face, where he wore all of his emotions, told her that he had given up.

He sat up on the sofa and folded his arms. "I care about you, Brianya. A lot. But I can't put my feelings on hold while you try to decide which way you want this relationship to go. It's difficult enough that I can't be with you physically the way I want to. Now you want me to hang around until whatever sparks you once felt for me *reignite*?" He shook his head. "That's crazy."

When they got back from North Carolina, Brianya thought she was ready to pick up where they'd left off, but the guilt was too palpable, and the voice in her head kept shouting condemnations at Ed for not being there when she needed him. She could get past it; she knew she could. Lately, the voice was only a whisper.

"I know it sounds crazy."

Ed had thrown his hands up. "Is that it? That's all you got?" He stared at her expecting more than what she'd offered. "Okay, look, why don't we do this; you keep working through your issues with me then call me when you settle them." He stood up then and headed for the door. "And if I'm unattached, we'll see what's what."

She never made that phone call.

"Not the water works again!" Cinthia said misreading Brianya's expression, pulling her back to the present.

"She'd better not be over there crying!" Dreama stalked over and stared at Brianya. "You shed one tear and you gon' have to answer to Cash! She didn't spend all day applying that makeup so you could end up looking like something out of a Rocky Horror Show." She reached up and smoothed down a stray strand of hair. "And you better not mess up your hair."

"Hold still, Brianya! Now suck in your breath and hold your stomach," Mrs. Johnson ordered. She smoothed down the back of the wedding gown before stringing the corset and tying the bow.

"Ma, are you trying to suffocate me? Loosen it up some." Brianya blew out a gust of air. Although she had never gotten back to her lowest weight of 147 pounds, she could live happily at 177 as long as she was healthy.

As the small army of women poked, prodded, and fawned all over her, Brianya reflected on what she wanted from life from this moment forward. Mostly, she wanted to be happy. Sure, life could be unpredictable, often taking us to places we never imagined. Some good, some bad, and some totally unexpected. Like the night Ed had walked out of her house, leaving her sitting on the sofa, angry and confused, telling her to call him when she got herself together.

She had never made that phone call because an hour later Ed was at her doorstep on his knees asking her to marry him in song. As he crooned the words to *Share My Life* by Kem, Brianya's mouth hung open in shock, speechless.

"I love you, Miss Johnson; and I'm yours for life, if you'll have me. Will you marry me?"

Brianya had stared at Ed and, when she found her voice, said, "Is that it? That's all you got?" and Ed had watched her try to hold back a grin.

"Is that a—"

"Yes! Yes, I'll marry you, Mr. Hollister!" Then Ed had stood up and wrapped his arms so tightly around Brianya that she thought she'd pass out from lack of oxygen. The way she was feeling now, actually, as her mother again tightened the corset around her middle. The ring came the next day when Ed had taken her to Orr's Jewelers in Pittsburgh, Pennsylvania, Brianya's favorite jewelry store.

"Ma, you're too heavy-handed. Let somebody else fasten the dress, please. I'm about to fall out!"

"Fine, then," her mother said and called Cinthia.

"Come on y'all, chop, chop! Time is moving. We got ten minutes to get this show on the road!" Dreama, bossy as usual. With great care, so as not to ruin her master coiffing, she placed the veil on Brianya's head and stood back to see what adjustments she needed to make.

"Umph, umph, umph. You look gorgeous!" a male voice from the doorway said.

Dreama swung around to scold the intruder. "Hey, you can't be in . . ."

Five pair of eyes stared in the direction of the voice and five mouths hung open when they saw who had spoken. Darnell, dressed in an expensive, tailor-made two-button, double-breasted chocolate-colored suit, his lace-up shoes spit-shined, stood in the doorway looking as fresh as he did the day Brianya had first laid eyes on him. Her heart swelled at the sight.

"I heard you were getting married today; I just wanted to come and give you my good wishes for a happy life," he said, not attempting to move any further into the room.

Brianya searched his face, trying to read malice in his words, but she saw only genuine happiness. "Thank you, Darnell. I'm glad you came."

As stealthily as he had appeared, Darnell stepped away from the door and headed toward the nave of the church.

The room remained quiet as they all looked at Brianya, who tried to play down the visit in her mind, but Darnell's appearance had shaken her. The last time she saw him, he was sitting at a table opposite her in a room full of people, looking forlorn and bewildered, wearing blue pants and a shirt with a number where a name should have been. She had forgotten that he would be a free man by the time the wedding date rolled around.

"Whoa, Bri, I hate to say this, but he looks good!" Cinthia said.

322

Dreama and Cashmere nodded their agreement and Alice pretended not to hear.

"He does; I gotta give him that. But I'm with the man I love. So don't try to put doubts in my head."

"Who said anything about all that?" Dreama asked.

"Whatever! Let's just hurry up and get me down that aisle." Brianya laughed.

"So, Bri, how you gonna handle tonight?"

"Cinthia!" Alice scolded. "That's none of your business!"

"Maybe so, but I'm curious. You've been on this celibacy kick for so long; are you sure you remember what to do?"

Everybody, Alice included, eagerly waited for the answer.

Oh, she remembered what to do all right. From the candy-red bustier to the red patent leather 4-inch Jimmy Choo pumps, tucked away in her suitcase, she had it all planned. Brianya smiled slyly at the group, "I hear it's like riding a bike."

THE END

ABOUT THE AUTHOR

CATHY JO HAS been writing since the age of eleven. She lives in a little house in a suburb of Cleveland, Ohio with her dust bunnies. She is a graduate of the Cleveland Public School system.

Among Cathy Jo's most cherished childhood memories are frequent visits to the old Treasure House library on Crawford Road, where her mother encouraged her to spend time reading. In 1980 when she was hired as a Page at the Cleveland Public library, her love for reading and writing was further fostered when she began working in the Literature department, where she discovered such authors as Daphne du Maurier, Jane Austen, Toni Morrison, Erma Bombeck, and Nikki Giovanni.

Cathy Jo is currently working on completing several of her unfinished manuscripts. Up next is a novel, featuring Cashmere Masters and Lonnie Parker. Stay tuned.

If you have taken the time to read this book, the author would love to hear from you. Kindly leave a review on Amazon, Barnes and Noble, Goodreads, or wherever else reader reviews are encouraged. You may also post your comments/thoughts on the publisher's Web site at http://www.twistedwordpublishing.com. Be sure to like our page on Facebook: http://www.facebook.com/twistedwordpublishing.com, for current contests and to keep up with Cathy Jo and her latest writing projects.